MW01613838

THAD TUCKER
Wyoming Rancher

A Safe Haven Series Book

By

Karen Carr

Published in 2019
All Rights Reserved

Cover Design by Karen Carr

ISBN- 13:9781798657096

I hope you enjoy the continuing saga of the Tucker family.

Karen Carr

"WHEN MY HEART
IS OVERWHELMED
LEAD ME
TO
THE ROCK
THAT IS HIGHER
THAN I"
PSALM 61:2B (KING JAMES)

Many, many thanks to those who have had such a big part in getting *Thad Tucker, Wyoming Rancher #2 in the Safe Haven Series* into the hands of the readers. Most of all, I thank my Heavenly Father for giving me the words to write.

My beta readers have helped me in a tremendous way: Rhea Bender, Chrystal Birche, Sue Daugherty, Leigh Drzycimski, Colleen Hovinga, Jed Magee, Kayla Schmidt, Carol Schmidt, Margaret Smolik, Carol Swartz, Kathy Stauffer, Janet Thompson, and Cady Windish.

My two writers' groups, Alpha Writers and River City Wordsmiths have been invaluable to my writing.

GLOSSARY

Bed Ground: Where cattle are held at night.

Box: Another term for where the stage coach driver sits.

Bronco: A horse that is not broken to ride and bucks whenever anyone attempts to ride him

Callin': Courting.

Coulee: A Deep ravine.

Cowpuncher: Cowboy, cowpoke.

Crimany: Exclamation of surprise.

Cutting Horse: Cutting horses were special horses that could separate cattle from the herd.

Dead As A Door Nail: Utterly, completely dead.

Eatin' Irons: Silverware.

Filling Station: a special pump for filling autos with gasoline.

Gully Washer: A hard rain.

Horse Fiddle: two old disk blades fitted with a spring and a crank to a toothed gear. The teeth of the gear pull the disks apart and when the crank is turned, it creates an awful noise.

Madder than an Old Wet Hen: Very angry.

Model T Ford: 1908 auto invented by Henry Ford.

Pemmican: Easily carried food substance on the frontier. Formed by pounding the choice parts of the meat very thin, dried over a slow fire and melted fat is added.

Persuader: A gun.

Picket line: A horizontal rope, along which horses are tied at intervals

Pig Sticker: Knife or bayonet.

Sakes Alive: The equivalent of "Good heavens!"

Shecoonery: A whimsical corruption of the word chicanery. "This town's got a monstrous bad name for meanery and shecoonery of all sorts."

Shivaree: A custom of serenading the newly married with noise, including tin horns, bells, pans, kettles, etc.

Shootin' Iron: Six-gun or a rifle.

Slower than molasses in January: Really slow.

Skeersome: Frightful.

'Taint: A corrupt abbreviation for it is not.

Tear Squeezer: A sad story.

Tuckered Out: Tired out, fatigued.

Whistle Berries: Beans.

Worse Than a Cat in a Roomful of Rockers: Someone who is really nervous.

THAD TUCKER: WYOMING RANCHER

PROLOGUE - 1898

Thad Tucker, age thirty-nine, snuggled on the sofa in front of the fireplace with Lucinda, his ten-year-old daughter. Thad volunteered to stay home with the feverish Lucy--as she was called--while the rest of the family rode into Mustang Ridge for church. He pushed back her dark hair hanging loose on her shoulders, before kissing her warm forehead. Fresh from having a bath, her hair smelled like lavender. Just like his wife used when she washed her hair.

"Papa, tell me the story of us," Lucinda asked of him.

"You've heard it all before, child."

"But you always tell it like it was new."

"Funny girl. Okay. It all started with my parents, Jackson and..."

"Is that where you got the name for my big brother?" she interrupted his story.

"Yes, it is. Now, do you want to hear the story or not?"

"Yes, Papa. Go ahead."

"As I was saying, my parents, Jackson and Elizabeth Caruthers owned a horse ranch in Texas. There were three children and I was the oldest, Becca and Nate came next. When I was almost fifteen, Pa was killed when his horse threw him and he hit his head on a rock.

Ma, Grandma Beth to you, had a hard time with the ranch. Most of the hands didn't want to have a woman for a boss and the ones who stayed or joined up later couldn't be trusted. So she felt led to sell the ranch, especially when a buyer was provided. We moved to town where she took a job at a bank.

Pa's father lived in Boston and a meaner man you never met. He ran away because of his meanness. Anyway, Pa's father came to the bank, recognized our last name, and took us all to Boston before we knew what happened. He mistreated us children and told Ma that he'd have her declared an unfit mother if she interfered.

When Ma found out he'd been whipping me, she planned an escape for us. We traveled in secret to St. Jo where we joined up with a wagon train. Eastman became our last name and we shortened our first names so Mr. Caruthers could not track us. We went as far as Fort Laramie in our covered wagon. I met your Mama on the wagon train. She and her family settled in Mustang Ridge when we did.

"When we got there, Ma..."

1

"That's Grandma Beth, right?"

"Right. Anyway, Grandma Beth became operator for the Deer Creek Stage line. I was the hostler, changing the teams of horses for the stages. Sheriff Tucker became our friend and he and Ma were later married. Tuck adopted us and that is how our name became Tucker."

"Papa, tell me about when you asked Mama to marry you." Lucinda snuggled under the blanket.

"Ahh," Thad sighed. *"Now there's a story dear to my heart. One I'll never tire of telling."*

CHAPTER ONE

Sharing with his daughter about "the story of us," as Lucy called it, made Thad once again contemplate the previous years of his life. He decided Lucy had a pretty good idea. God had led them through many ups and downs, but always through them. It was good to recall all that had happened to their family.

The year was 1883...

Thad Tucker rode his horse, Rowdy, along the Mustang Mountain valley road. His horse was a descendant of Buck, the one he owned when they came out on the wagon train in '76. He had been a good horse and Thad had been saddened when his life came to an end. But now Buck's offspring followed in his sire's "hoof-steps." Rowdy reminded Thad of Buck as he also had a buckskin coat, but in looks only. Rowdy had his own disposition.

This day in April found Thad, now twenty-three, on his way to his parent's ranch where he also lived. Thad stopped on the ridge outside of the town of Mustang Ridge and surveyed the bucolic scene around him. How he loved this land. Removing his hat, he brushed his fingers through his sandy, shoulder-length hair. *Getting kind of long, guess I should talk to Ma about getting it cut.*

Tufts of dried sagebrush were carried on the breeze across the expanse of the Deer Creek Ranch land. Thad looked to the blue sky as the winds seemed to propel him along on his way home. Spring had arrived in the Mustang Mountain Valley and Thad greeted its advent eagerly.

As he cantered Rowdy into the yard, he saw his brother repairing a broken fence in the corral. Thirteen-year-old Nate was the younger of his two siblings and had Thad's hair coloring and blue eyes. Other than that, he didn't resemble his older brother. To Thad's way of thinking, Nate was a bit of a rascal. Because of what the three siblings and their mother went through, they were a very close family.

Thad and his father, Tuck, owned Deer Creek Ranch together. The two of them raised cattle and horses, the latter being Thad's portion of the business. A bunkhouse was added to the buildings after they became partners. He always surveyed the yard with pride when he entered. His eyes were drawn to the ranch-house and its wide veranda. Ma sat in a wicker rocker sorting out the seeds for planting in her garden. She greeted him as he tied Rowdy to the hitching rail.

"Morning, Thad," she said. "You must've taken off pretty early this morning. I didn't see you leave."

3

"I went into Mustang Ridge. I... uh... was at Doc's office," he explained. It was his hope she'd leave it at that. He didn't want to go into further details with her. His mother knew he'd explain further if he felt the need. But he didn't feel the need just yet.

Thad came up onto the veranda and bent down to give his mother a kiss on her cheek. "Any coffee on the stove?" he asked.

"Yes. I made a fresh pot," she answered. "Do you need any breakfast?"

"No, thanks, Ma. I ate at Sally's Café. Just coffee will do fine. Where's Tuck?" he inquired. He sensed her eyeing him; probably wondering if he were sick or ailing, but respecting his privacy.

"He went out on the south slope to check on the ranch hands," she responded. "Curly rode in early this morning with news that there was a wolf problem around the cattle."

"Do you think he needs more help?"

"Wouldn't hurt to ride out there," Beth advised.

"Okay, I'll get a cup of coffee and head south."

"Be sure to take your rifle and ammunition. Tuck packed his."

Thad nodded. He was forced to admit to himself that he was about to leave with only his Colt in his gun-belt. It had only been the last few years he'd begun wearing one since their ranch covered so many miles. Yes, this morning Thad was distracted. Distracted by the beauty of Isabelle Wells, Doc Phillips' nurse. Known to her friends as Izzy, Thad had taken to calling her Belle. She was the reason he went to town so early. In truth, he'd "seen" Doc but only when he walked Belle to his office after sharing breakfast with her. He wasn't quite ready to share his infatuation with his mother just yet.

The women of Mustang Ridge were always trying to set Thad up with their daughters and nieces. They most likely were talking about his lack of a commitment to any girl these last four years. They just didn't know he was committed. Committed to waiting for Belle to grow up.

Belle and his little sister, Becca, were best friends and the same age. Her mother, Sarah Wells, was Beth's good friend. The two families met on the wagon train, and they all left the train at Fort Laramie to come to Mustang Ridge and settle. Over time, Thad became smitten with Belle. Now that she was nineteen-years-old, Thad believed he could start seeing her socially. Five years her senior, he didn't think that was too big a difference. He supposed that soon someone in Mustang Ridge would mention to his mother about seeing the two of them at Sally's Café.

Ma had been praying for him from his childhood that the Lord would lead him to a godly woman. He learned as a teenager how her prayer life revealed her strength of character and he learned how prayer was important for him too. He trusted in Jesus as his Savior when they were still living on their Texas ranch. Belle was saved and Thad was thankful for that, believing that God desired that in a marriage. And marriage is what Thad had in mind for their future. So, this morning, he asked Belle if he could court her.

Belle had taken his hand and looked into his eyes. "Yes, Thad. I would like that very much." The beat of his heart quickened with joy.

Well, enough woolgathering. Time to get to work. After downing his cup of coffee, Thad retrieved his rifle from its place over the mantle. He stocked his saddlebags with extra shells and a supply of pemmican, and filled his canteen with water. Thad usually took pemmican in his saddlebags when he was going to be away from home for an undetermined amount of time. The Indians at Fort Laramie had taught him how to make it and he had been doing it ever since. His long legs carried him out the door to his horse. As he placed the rifle in the scabbard and the saddlebags behind his saddle, he spoke again to his mother.

"What do you plan to do today, Ma?"

"Probably finish with the seeds for the garden and prepare the stakes. You take care out there. Tell Tuck too," she admonished him, "and come back safely."

Thad knew she would be praying for their safety before he was out of the yard. "Sure thing, Ma. You take care too. See you tonight."

CHAPTER TWO
Belle's Dream Comes True

What a special day this turned out to be! Thad took Belle to breakfast before she needed to go to work at Doc Phillips'. She knew there was something on his mind since this wasn't a usual occurrence on his part. Belle didn't know for sure what it was all about, but she certainly hoped. Sure enough, Thad asked if he could court her. No question as to what the answer had been.

Belle told Thad she would like that and he held her hand. Belle's heart was light and happy, as she'd waited a long time for this day. She recalled their first meeting on the wagon train after her family joined up at Fort Kearny. She was twelve-years-old, and was surprised that Thad was only sixteen because he was so tall and mature. Not to mention, good-looking too. Her heart skipped a beat as she remembered how he looked into her eyes at Sally's Café this morning, his hand over hers when he asked her.

"So, what took you so long?" Belle inquired now. "I've waited a long time for you to ask me."

Through the years she had believed she and Thad would one day be together, more than just good friends. Tonight, when she went home, Belle told Mama and Papa about Thad asking for permission to court her. She could tell they were pleased. They thought a lot of Thad, his whole family. She was so glad Papa decided to leave the wagon train and head north to Mustang Ridge. Sadness had filled her at the thought that they could be parting ways at Fort Laramie. *Thank you, Father, for keeping our families together.*

Thad wanted to ask Papa's permission to court her, but when Elva Watson popped her head into Doc's, Belle just knew she had to tell Papa right away, or he'd hear it on the street. Elva has a reputation as a wee bit of a gossip.

"Saw you and the Tucker boy on the street," she rebuked Belle at Doc's door. "Lookin' mighty friendly, you was."

"Well, we are friends," Belle insisted. "Our families have been for a long time."

"Just the same, walkin' down the street arm-in-arm in front of God and everyone. 'Taint seemly." Elva clicked her tongue.

Doc Phillips poked his head around the corner. "Elva, don't you be stirring up any trouble for these young people. Best you remember that gossip is a sin according to God's Word. Besides, the Good Book doesn't say anything about arm-in-arm being a sin. You best be going on your way now. Isabelle has work to do."

Elva huffed and left the office.

6

Belle was thankful Doc had come to her rescue. Elva reminded her of the Grimm's Fairy Tales of Snow White and Hansel and Gretel. Not of the beautiful princess and the two children in the latter, but of the witches in both stories. Mama never allowed Belle and her brother Ben to read such books, saying they were not healthy for their spirits. But as children often will do, she looked at those books belonging to her friends back in Ohio and was plagued by unpleasant dreams for many nights. Elva was tall and decidedly skinny, quite the opposite of how one would have thought a gossip would look. Yes, more like one of the witches. Belle tried not to judge Elva by her outward appearance, but it was hard when she looked the part of how Belle perceived a witch to look. That's why she told Mama and Papa that night. She figured Doc's reprimand wouldn't deter Elva or still her vicious tongue.

Belle could see Mama's thought process when she told them. *Knowing her, she was probably planning the wedding right down to my dress.* Since she's an accomplished seamstress, Belle hoped that one day Mama would create the perfect wedding dress for her.

CHAPTER THREE
Wolves Eliminated

When Adam Tucker adopted Thad and his siblings, Becca and Nate began addressing him as "Papa and Pa," but Thad at age seventeen didn't feel quite right about that, although he dearly loved his new father. He discussed it with Tuck, explaining the reasoning behind his decision. Tuck verbalized his understanding even though Thad wasn't sure even he understood. He noted though that when on occasion he introduced Tuck as "my Pa," Tuck looked pleased about it. When Thad agreed about the wording on the ranch sign to read: "Deer Creek Ranch, Adam and Thad Tucker, Proprietors," he saw the pride on Tuck's face. *I need to change what I call him. I love him like a Pa and have his last name, why not call him Pa?*

As Thad neared the herd of cattle on the south slope, he heard the sound of rifle shots. *They must've found a pack of wolves by the sound of it.* Making sure he wasn't in the line of fire; he approached the camp. Cookie was there at the chuck wagon working on the noon meal.

"Howdy, Mr. Thad," he called. "Comin' to git in on the action?"

"Thought I might be able to help," Thad answered. "How are they doing?"

"Crimany, reckon they ran into a whole pack o' wolves afore sun-up. Curly rode up to the ranch to git your Pa and they all been out there since he came. It was shore 'nuff a fearsome morning. Been hearin' a lot a shootin' but don't know if they're gittin' any or not."

Cookie was from down Texas way, so his accent was evident when he talked, primarily when he was as excited as he was now. No one seemed to know his real name; he was just "Cookie" - always had been.

Thad mounted Rowdy and headed in the general direction of the shooting. He arrived too late. As he came upon the men and Tuck, he noted that they were engaged in skinning the wolves they'd killed. There was a bounty on wolf pelts because of such a wide-spread problem with them in the area.

"Need any help?" Thad asked, dismounting.

"Howdy," Wade said. "Got your pig sticker?"

"Sure do," he replied, pulling his knife from his boot. "Glad to give you boys a hand. Did you get them all?"

"Think so. In this pack anyway," Hank assured him.

Once the dead wolves were skinned and disposed of and the pelts bundled onto a packhorse, Tuck gave the men orders to take them to the barn and hang them on the outside to dry. Then the ranch hands could take them to town and collect the bounty for themselves.

8

Thad rode alongside Tuck as they both went back to the ranch-house. Beth was there on the porch still working with the garden supplies. This time she was winding the cord around sticks to use as a planting guide for the rows. She'd not been idle while they were gone.

They waved to her as they rode their horses into the barn and dismounted. They brushed the horses and put them in their stalls. Thad tossed hay into their mangers, and Tuck filled their water buckets.

"Well, imagine that! You boys are just in time for supper," Beth laughed. "Come on inside. It's ready to dish up." Tuck kissed his wife as they came inside the house to wash up. Tuck asked, "Where's Nate?"

"He's coming. Just finished milking the goats and went to gather the eggs."

"Why's he doing the milking?" Thad asked his mother. Becca had grown her goat herd through the years from the original nanny goat. He recalled Tuck bringing a nanny goat and her two kids that he obtained from Grey Wolf's Shoshone family. The Shoshone family had been good friends of his folks, visiting the church when the weather was good since they lived far up in the mountains. One year they even came to the ranch for a huge Christmas celebration and spent the night because of a snow storm.

"Becca isn't home from the schoolhouse yet," Beth said while the Tucker menfolk took their seats around the table.

"She sure spends long days at that school. She must like it." He was proud of his sister and knew she must be a good teacher.

"Yes, Sarah has given her more responsibility as she gets closer to retiring herself. Becca has applied for her teaching certificate," explained his mother.

"What will happen with that now?" Tuck asked.

"The Superintendent of Education for the territory will interview her. She is waiting to hear from him as to when he will come."

Nate burst into the ranch-house with the basket of eggs. *He never seems to change. Always enters a room like that.* "How come you aren't still at the school with Becca?" Thad asked his brother.

"Becca sent me on home because she wasn't done getting ready for her interview. She also asked if I would do the milking for her." Nate always rode his horse to school rather than riding with Becca in the buggy.

"That's nice of you," Beth commented, then added. "I wonder if I should take over the milking. Becca has a full-time commitment now to the school."

"Probably a good idea and I can help you now and then," Tuck responded. "How many is she milking now, Nate?"

"Four. It'd be good to share the milking now that I'm working more on the ranch," Nate replied. "The chickens don't take a lot of time. I'm okay still

9

doing that." Thad remembered how Nate had been when they first got the chickens, back when he was six-years-old. Nate never wanted to relinquish control of those chickens to anyone. That still held.

"What does she do with all that milk?" Thad asked.

"She takes milk and butter to Sam, and he sells them in the mercantile. Also, Becca takes milk for some of the poorer families whose children she teaches," Beth explained.

"That's wonderful. I'm proud of Becca!" exclaimed Tuck.

Thad noticed Nate eyeing him rather strangely. *I wonder what he's been up to. He almost looks guilty.* He needn't have wondered any longer. Nate's next words made it clear.

"So, Thad. On my way to school this morning, I saw you coming out of Sally's Café," Nate declared. "I also saw who you were with."

Uh-oh. Guess the cat's out of the bag now. Thad felt more than saw as both his parent's heads swung toward him. He noted the hopeful look on his mother's face.

"So?" Nate pried again.

"Okay, okay. I took Belle… uh...Izzy to breakfast at the café and walked her to the doctor's office when we were done."

"And?" questioned his pesky brother.

"And what?"

"And what were you talking about? You looked pretty friendly."

"Well, we are friends, Nate. Have been for a long time."

This time his mother got into the conversation, apparently frustrated with the banter back and forth between the brothers. "Thad, is there more?"

"All right, I'll tell you. I asked Belle for permission to court her."

Beth jumped up from her seat and ran around the table, hugging Thad. Tuck rose from his chair and came and thumped him on the back. "That's wonderful news, son. I assume Belle said yes, didn't she?"

"She sure did!"

"Wait! Wait! Wait just a minute! Who is Belle? I thought we were talking about Izzy," Nate interjected.

"Yes, I call her Belle. After all, her name is Isabelle, and Izzy seems so, so...uh… well, just not right for a beautiful young woman and …" Thad's words slowed to a stop since he realized his family stared at him, while Nate snickered. He hadn't realized he was going on so - his thoughts becoming actual words.

Beth brought the dish of green beans to the table and went to Thad, hugging him again and planting a kiss on his cheek. "I'm so happy for you, dear. She is a wonderful girl."

10

"Thanks, Ma. And thanks Nate for telling everyone."

"I wasn't the only one who saw you. Everyone on the sidewalks and the street saw you — even Elva Watson. You can't get out of it now that Elva knows," Nate said, verbally digging at his brother playfully by using the town's notorious gossip.

"I don't want to get out of it," replied Thad. *I want to get more into it. I have loved Belle for a long time.*

"Becca will be thrilled to find out that Izzy…uh…, Belle may be a member of our family one day," Tuck said.

"And here comes Becca now, just in time for supper," announced Beth.

"I'll go put up her horse and buggy." Tuck rose from his chair.

Becca entered the ranch-house and hung her shawl and bonnet on the wooden peg next to the front door.

"Hello, dear. Did you have a good day?" Beth inquired.

"It was busy, but I love the work. And a telegram came today from the Superintendent of Education for the Wyoming Territory. Mr. Rhodes will be coming next week to interview me and administer the testing. I'm getting nervous already," Becca shared.

"You'll do fine," her mother encouraged.

"Nate, thanks for milking and feeding my goats," Becca said.

"How do you know I did it?" Nate asked.

"Because you said you would," Becca stated matter-of-factly.

Nate wiped the smirk off his face at that; his eyes following his sister as she went to wash her hands. Then he shrugged and began eating. The display between his two younger siblings warmed Thad's heart. Sometimes Nate could be a trial, but Thad saw that Becca's expression of her trust in Nate to do what he said, had quieted any sarcastic remarks from him.

"Your brother just shared the exciting news with us, Becca," Beth informed her.

"What's that?" she turned to look at Thad.

"Belle and I are courting," he replied. Becca already knew that Thad called her Belle.

Becca squealed with joy. "Oh, that's wonderful news, Thad. I'm so happy to hear it. I was hoping for just that."

11

CHAPTER FOUR
Courting

On Sunday the wildflowers were blooming in abundance along the foothills of the Mustang Mountains. The reds of the Indian Paintbrush and blues of the Bluebells looked like a carpet that they could see all the way from the ranch. Thad took the buggy to church, choosing to go separate from his family. He asked Ma to pack him a picnic lunch in hopes that he and Belle could go on a drive and a picnic after the service was over.

It was early, but Thad wanted to stop at the Wells, mainly to pick up Belle, but also to ask Jacob for his permission to court his daughter. Jacob answered his knock at the door and invited him inside, patting him on the back. It was evident Belle had shared their news with her father, but Thad still wanted to show his respect by asking.

"Isabelle will be out shortly. I think she's finishing with her hair," Jacob informed him. "I understand the two of you have exciting news."

"Yes, Mr. Wells. I wanted to ask your permission as well. My family already knows. Nate saw us and spilled the beans," he grinned wryly. "According to Nate the whole town pretty much knows. I'm sorry I couldn't get to you before it spread."

"Not to worry, young man. I've been expecting this for a few years now."

"You have?" Thad was astonished.

"Always thought you two would get together. I'm thankful that you didn't make your move until Belle was older."

"I followed the Lord's leading, sir. I respect your daughter too much to rush ahead without God's will."

Thad looked up as Belle entered the living room. Her long dark hair was pulled back into a chignon. "Good morning, Belle. I was just asking your father for permission to court you."

"Good morning to you too, Thad," Belle said, her cheeks turning a rosy color, a shade that conflicted with the red in her frock.

"And I also wanted to ask the both of you if Belle and I might be able to take a drive in my buggy after church. Ma packed a picnic lunch for us."

"If Isabelle wants to do that, you have my blessing."

Belle went to her father and kissed him on the cheek. "Thank you, Papa." Putting her hand in Thad's hand, she said, "Shall we go now?"

Thad held the door open for Belle, taking her arm, he led her to his buggy and helped her up to the seat. He flicked the reins, and they drove to the church.

"Are you ready for this?" he asked as they neared the church.

12

"Ready for what?" she asked.

"Nate said everyone on the street saw us the other day, so I assume tongues are wagging."

"I know, but I don't mind. I'm glad that we're courting, Thad, and if our friends know about it, then I'm happy. I want to share our joy with others."

"Belle, you have a heart of pure gold," he said with emotion. He squeezed her arm closer to him.

Upon arriving at the church, Thad tied Rowdy to a nearby tree and helped Belle out of the buggy. He made sure the tarp covered the picnic basket and led her up to the steps of the church. They shook hands with Reverend Prescott. His wife Esther and their son stood with him at the door. Daniel was a six-year-old now and reminded Thad of Nate when they first arrived in Mustang Ridge. Nate was six then also.

Thad unbuckled his gun belt and hung it on one of the two rows of wooden pegs where the men kept their guns while in church. Thad felt like all eyes were upon him and Belle as he escorted her to where his family was seated. He knew his face must be red because it felt hot. He'd probably get teased about blushing like a girl from the fellas, especially Nate. Belle must be nervous too; he thought as he retrieved her dropped bonnet for her. *Father, help me to stay focused on your Word and not let my feelings for Belle keep me from hearing the message.*

Following the service, many of their friends stopped them, which slowed their progress to the door. Thad led Belle to his buggy and helped her up. With a flick of the reins, Rowdy began the trek to the lake. At last, they were driving toward the lower expanse of the mountain range where all the wildflowers were blooming in a patchwork of color.

"Oh, the flowers are gorgeous," Belle exclaimed. "How far are we going?"

"Just to the edge of the foothills by Whitehorse Lake," he answered.

"I wonder why it is called Whitehorse Lake," Belle said thoughtfully.

"It's Shoshone for Wee-A-Wah Lake, which means Whitehorse. There's a legend about them seeing a white horse here. As the story goes, a young Shoshone boy was out riding his pony when he saw a cloud of dust. Suddenly the cloud stopped and as the dust settled, he saw a horse drinking from the lake. He saw that the horse was white in color. So, he called the lake Wee-A-Wah Lake, which means Whitehorse Lake."

"Thad, that's a lovely story."

"Belle, I don't mean to alarm you, but there have been several wolves spotted lately. We need to be vigilant."

"I heard about the wolves. A couple of Deer Creek ranch hands came into town the other day, and they were talking about the wolf pelts they have out at the ranch, so there was quite a bit of talk about it then. Do you think they got them all?"

"I hope so," Thad answered. "I know they got all of them that were in the pack on our land. I don't know if there might be other packs or not. Best be alert, and I have my rifle with me with plenty of ammunition."

Thad took a quilt out of the buggy and placed it on a grassy area under a shade tree. Taking Belle's hand, he led her to the quilt while carrying the picnic basket in the other.

"This is so nice, Thad, and what a beautiful day. I'm glad you asked me on a picnic," Belle said shyly.

"I'm glad too, Belle. And I'm so happy that you agreed to let me court you."

"Thad Tucker! Let you! I've waited for you to ask me for two years now. I don't know what you were waiting for," Belle laughed. "Of course, I would agree to us courting."

Thad laughed as well. As the two of them finished eating their picnic dinner, Belle began putting things back in the basket.

As Thad folded up the quilt, he noticed Belle shiver, "Are you cold, Belle? Let me get your shawl from the buggy."

"No, Thad. I was thinking about those awful wolves. They are such scary creatures. When they howl, it sends chills down my back."

"Well, maybe the men got all the wolves."

"I hope so too. I think it's getting late, Thad," Belle said looking at the sun. "I need to get back home."

Thad assisted her into the buggy, and they drove back to town. On the way back to town, Thad stopped and picked a bouquet of wildflowers for Belle. With a flourish, he handed her the bouquet.

"Thank you." Her smile twinkled through her eyes.

As he helped her down at her parent's house, he held her hand, not wanting to let go. "I've enjoyed spending this time with you, Belle."

"Me too, Thad. When will I see you again?"

"I'll try to get to town this week. Then maybe we can have dinner at the café."

"That would be wonderful, Thad. Be sure to tell your ma thanks for the picnic."

CHAPTER FIVE
Sick Cattle

After he left Belle at her home, Thad drove his buggy back to Deer Creek Ranch. He saw a rider headed his way as he drove down the valley road. He recognized Pete, one of the ranch hands, as he came closer. *Wonder what's wrong. He sure is riding fast.*

Thad halted the buggy by the side of the road. He figured Pete would stop to tell him what had him going so fast. As it turned out, Pete was actually on his way to find Thad.

"Boss, I'm so glad I found you." Pete was as breathless as if he'd been running instead of his horse.

"What's going on, Pete?"

"Cookie found about five dead wolves around the chuck wagon this morning. He said they was dead as a doornail. He shot three shots in the air with his shootin' iron, you know, our signal for trouble, and refused to get out of the wagon until the ranch-hands came."

"Oh, no. Do the men know why they died?"

"They said maybe it's Texas fever or Anthrax."

"Oh no! "

"What do you want me to do, boss?"

"Okay, Pete. While I go up to the ranch-house and get out of my church clothes, you load up a jug of kerosene into the wagon and take it out there. We need to burn the wolves and the chuck wagon with everything in it. Oh, and take the wolf pelts in the wagon too. Wrap them in that old tarp in the barn. We will have to burn these too. I'll meet you out there."

As he hurried into the ranch-house to change, he saw Tuck sitting in his chair. He looked up at Thad's hurried entrance.

"What's going on, son?"

"Pa, can you help Pete load up the wagon? There was a bunch of dead wolves out by the chuck wagon this morning. We need to burn everything. Pete can explain it to you. I've got to change," he said as he ran into his bedroom and slammed shut the door. Even in his hurry, he had not failed to observe both his parent's reaction at his calling Tuck *Pa*. He didn't say it intentionally, it just slipped out, but he was glad he'd said it.

Rushing back out and tucking his shirt tails into his jeans, he said to his mother, "Pray, Ma. There were dead wolves near the chuck wagon. It may be Texas fever or even Anthrax." He ran out to the barn and mounted the fresh horse from the remuda, which Tuck had saddled for him, as well as unhitching Rowdy from the buggy. Tuck also saddled a fresh horse for

15

himself, and the two of them headed out to the south pasture where the men were.

"Pete told me a little of what happened before he left with the wagon. We need to move the cattle to the west meadow to get them away from the site," Tuck said.

"Is the grass long enough at the west meadow?" Thad asked.

"It'll have to be," Tuck responded. "I want the herd away from this site."

When they neared the south slope, they saw the black smoke curling into the air. "Guess Pete didn't waste any time getting everything burning," Thad observed.

"Imagine he had lots of help," remarked Tuck.

"Men, are the horses you're riding now the ones you rode the day you shot the wolves?" Thad asked of them. They all nodded.

"We need to move the cattle over to the west meadow, but before you do that, go back to the ranch and change out your horses. Let's keep them in a separate corral from the other horses just in case they have been in contact with the disease," Tuck instructed. "When you have done that, take a fresh horse from the remuda and come back to move the cattle. Don't know if that may be a problem, but hopefully, we will be able to keep it out of our herds."

The men headed back to the ranch to comply while Thad and Tuck stayed to keep an eye on the roaring blaze. "I hope we've seen the last of whatever killed the wolves," Tuck stated.

"If it moves through our cattle and horse herds…" Thad's statement trailed off.

"It could be devastating," Tuck finished.

"Here come the hands now. The fire is dying down enough so we can leave it. Men, let's get this herd moved," Tuck directed.

The cattle moved willingly as the men herded them to the west meadow. They were pretty frisky, kicking up their heels and dancing around.

"They sure don't act like they are getting sick," Nash commented. "Those wolves didn't have any open sores like you would see in Anthrax. But it sure could be Texas fever."

"What's Texas fever, Nash?" young Curly asked. He was relatively new to ranch work so wasn't aware of the terrible scare of Texas fever when cattle from Texas were introduced to the northern areas in previous years.

"It originated in Texas, and is spread by a tick. The tick will jump from cow to cow. In this case, the tick might have been on the wolves, and the packs carried it north." Nash stroked his beard. "I know that wolves can be carriers. But I wonder if it could be rabies."

Tuck entered the conversation at this point. "Did you notice any aggressiveness or foaming around the mouth in the wolves when you shot them the other day?"

"Yeah," Wade answered. "They were snarling and attacking. Foaming too. Downright skeersome."

"What about the wolves that were found dead by the chuck wagon? Was there any foaming around their mouths?" Tuck continued to question the ranch hands.

"Yeah, there was," Hank responded.

"Well, boys. I think we have rabies then, not Texas fever or Anthrax," said Tuck.

"So, we didn't have to burn everything then?" Curly asked.

"It's always good to err on the side of caution. We certainly don't want to take any chances on spreading rabies," Tuck responded. "If you boys can finish moving the cattle, I'm going to ride into Mustang Ridge and let the sheriff know about this problem. In the meantime, keep your rifles with you at all times. I'm glad we don't have any dogs on the ranch right now."

"Why, can the dogs get it too?" Curly asked.

"Yes, the wolves can make contact with dogs by fighting with them," Tuck answered.

Thad wondered about his horses as Tuck left for town. They were all the way up on the north end of the ranch.

As they moved the cows to the meadow, he said, "I want to go up north and check on my horses in the morning. A couple of you hands meet me after you've eaten breakfast so you can go with me. I'll head back to the ranch now and tell Cookie to load up another chuck wagon to bring out here. The rest of you camp out with the cattle for a couple of days until they settle down. Keep an eye out for more wolves. Curly, you come with me."

As Thad and Curly approached the bunkhouse, Curly called out, "Hey Cookie, where are you hiding?" Cookie came from the back of the bunkhouse.

"What's goin' on?" he inquired.

"Cookie, we just moved the cattle to the west meadow. You need to get another chuck wagon out there. Ma can give you any food supplies you need. When you and Curly get the wagon ready, stop up at the house, and we'll get you loaded with supplies," Thad instructed. "Oh, and Cookie, make sure you always have a rifle. It may not be Texas fever or Anthrax; we think it's rabies."

"Rabies! It's a good thing I sleep hard. If I'da stepped out of the wagon, I mighta been a goner. I coulda ended up in the marble orchard!"

17

"No, Cookie. They probably smelt your awful cooking, and it was just too much for them, and they just dropped dead!" teased Curly.

"Curly, give Cookie a hand getting another wagon hitched up," Thad said, chuckling. "Bring the wagon up to the house so we can get fresh supplies for it. I'll be up there talking with my mother for a bit." Thad rode his horse up to the ranch-house and dismounted, tying the reins to the rail. Seeing her opening the door, he stood back and held it as she exited the house with a bowl of beans for planting.

"Not more beans?" he groaned.

"Those you saw before were for green beans. These are for soups and stews. You'll be glad when winter comes, and the warm soups and stews have beans in them. So, what are you up to? Did you get the cattle moved?" she asked him.

"Yes, Pa went into town to tell them we think it could be rabies, but we still burned everything to prevent the spread. A few of the hands are out at the west meadow with the cattle. I'm sending Cookie out with a new chuck wagon. He'll be up here shortly to replenish supplies since we burned everything." Thad saw that Cookie had the wagon hitched up and was driving up to the ranch-house. "Here he comes now."

"I'll take him down to the root cellar where he can pick out what he needs," Beth said putting down the bowl of beans on the porch bench.

As Cookie climbed the steps to the veranda, he saw the bowl of seeds that Beth would plant in her garden. "Whistle berries," he commented for Thad's ears only. Thad nodded.

"We'll help so it will go faster." Thad motioned to Curly to get off his horse to help load the wagon. Many hands made light work, and he was pleased that with Curly's help, his mother didn't have to go up and down the steps to the root cellar. She works too hard.

After Curly and Cookie left with the chuck wagon, Thad went to the barn to do the chores. Tuck rode up to the barn and took his horse inside.

"What did the sheriff say, Pa?" Thad asked as he entered the barn.

Tuck heaved the saddle off his horse and answered, "Said he'd keep an eye open and let the area ranchers know. He hadn't heard anything about it around. Did the boys get the cattle moved to the west meadow?"

"Yes, and Cookie took a new chuck wagon with fresh supplies out there," Thad answered.

"That's good. It's been a busy day, and I'm hungry. Suppose your mother held supper for us?"

"I wouldn't doubt it."

When they entered the ranch-house, they could tell that she did have it ready by the delicious smell filling the living room. *Ma not only feeds us with food but with the aroma as well.*

Pa walked up behind Ma and hugged her, planting a kiss on her neck. Thad knew that his parents loved each other very much just from the way they acted when they saw each other. *There will come a day when Belle and I will have that.*

Tuck's hair showed graying at the temples, but the dark brown strands were still thick and wavy. Thad thought the gray made him even more distinguished. Tuck wore the same leather vest he wore when they first met him. It just didn't have the sheriff's star pinned to it anymore.

Becca came in with two pails of milk followed by Nate with the basket of eggs. Thad hadn't seen either one of his siblings since this morning at church. *Was that just this morning?*

"Supper's ready, everybody take a seat," Beth called. She didn't have to say it twice. When she turned around with the meat platter, they all were in their seats.

"How was the picnic?" Beth asked Thad. "Did you and Izzy have a good time?"

"Belle and I had a great time," he said smiling.

"Sorry, Belle, I mean."

"Everyone needs to be careful about going out too far from the house without a gun. If there are more infected wolves around, they may get bold and come near the ranches. Keep an eye out for dogs too. The wolves may have infected local ranch dogs," Tuck warned his family. "Even if you are on a horse, they may spook the horse and cause it to rear and throw you. Just be careful."

"Okay, Tuck. I'm glad we haven't replaced poor old Bandit yet," Beth replied.

Thad nodded, looking at his brother. Nate was devastated when his beloved dog died. Bandit was a gift from Tuck when they first moved here. *I guess he's not in a hurry to get another dog.*

"I'd like to go up and check on my horses tomorrow morning," Thad explained. "Wade and Nash are coming in after breakfast to give me a hand."

"Sounds good. I'll ride along too," Tuck said.

19

CHAPTER SIX

Thad's Horses

"So long, Ma. See you later," Thad called to her. He and Tuck and the two ranch-hands rode out of the yard. He bred his horses now that he had good breeding stock to work with and his herd had grown over the years. Although fences in Wyoming weren't always a popular choice with ranchers, the cattle drives didn't usually come up through their land. Therefore, he opted to fence off some of the meadow areas, allowing the herd to roam within the confines of a large fence- off area of the meadow. When that grass supply diminished, they would move them to another.

"Your herd's the biggest you've ever had," commented Wade. "When do you plan to sell your horses off?"

"The Army at Fort Laramie has contracted for fifty head. Soon I'll have to drive them down there, probably within a week," Thad answered. "After that, I will probably sell to Deadwood. I'm waiting to hear back from them."

"Well, here's the herd now," Tuck commented.

"You sure do have some fine-looking horses," Nash commented. "They look to be doing okay. No sign of any wolves."

Thad looked around. "The grass is starting to get short though. Since there are four of us, let's move them to the other pasture. Then we can cut fifty head from the herd to move to the corrals by the barn for Fort Laramie."

After they had moved the horses to the corrals, Wade and Nash rode on to where the cattle were while Thad and Tuck went back to the ranch-house. Once he was in the ranch office, Thad got out his record book. After doing a little figuring, he told Tuck, "I'll have to make a drive with fifty horses down to Fort Laramie. Do you think the cattle will be okay to let the hands leave them next Wednesday?"

"Should be no problem," Tuck answered. "You'll need the chuck wagon too I suppose?"

"Yes. I'll go into town tomorrow and send a telegram to Fort Laramie that we will arrive with their horses."

"I'll make the trip with you, and we'll take Pete, Hank, Lefty, and Wade to herd the horses, and Cookie, of course, with the chuck wagon. The rest can stay at the ranch. We'll leave Nash in charge."

"How long will you be gone?" his mother asked him.

"We will probably average about twelve miles a day, more or less. It's about fifty miles to Fort Laramie, so about four or five days to get the herd to the Fort. And maybe less to come back as we won't be driving a herd."

20

#

The rest of the week Thad and the hands spent working the fifty horses in the corrals getting them ready for travel. When Sunday came, he spent it with Belle. When they entered the church, he noted the smiles they received from friends. By now, Thad figured everyone must know the two of them were courting.

Thad told Belle about his plans to go to Fort Laramie on Wednesday.

"I'll miss you when you are gone," Belle whispered as they took their seat in the church and waited for the service to begin.

"I'll miss you too." He squeezed her hand.

"How long will you be?"

"Maybe eight to ten days. Depends on how smoothly the drive goes. Horses can be more difficult to drive than cattle."

"Be careful, won't you?" she cautioned him.

Thad nodded. He wanted a smooth drive so he could get back to Belle.

CHAPTER SEVEN
Driving the Horses to Fort Laramie

It was Saturday, and they were two days out from Fort Laramie with the herd of horses when Wade rode up to the chuck wagon. Instead of going to get his meal, he went to Thad first.

"Boss, three riders have been following the herd. They're hanging back, probably thinking they won't be spotted. But my keen eyesight is too good for that."

"Tell the rest of the men about it. Keep an eye on them but don't make it obvious."

Tuck entered the conversation at that point. "They might be planning to see where we go. Maybe to rob us after we leave the fort."

"You don't think they plan to steal the horses?" Thad asked.

"No, I think they would've done it by now, and there're only three of them," Tuck responded.

"Well, make sure your side arms and your rifles are ready," Thad instructed Wade. "With plenty of ammunition too."

"Sure thing, boss. We'll be ready for them when they make their move. Cookie, I'll send one of the hands in to eat as soon as I'm done," Wade said.

Sunday was uneventful, but the riders still followed the herd. They arrived at Fort. Laramie without further incident on Monday afternoon. Thad went to Colonel Watson's office with the bill of sale and received payment. When he exited the fort office with the payment, he headed to the corral where his ranch hands and Pa were waiting. He was glad Watson had used a bank draft. It might be easier to protect than cash. Thad placed the draft inside his boot, hoping it would be safer there. Since the riders hadn't attacked before they reached the fort, he believed they meant to steal the payment he received from Watson.

"I've changed my mind, men. Let's spend the night here at the fort and leave early in the morning," Thad declared when he reached the corral. "Maybe those men will be gone. If not, we will have a whole day of travel in daylight before stopping for the night."

"Good plan," Tuck observed. "Cookie, drive the chuck wagon down by the river. We'll camp there tonight."

They set up camp outside the fort gates by the river. Cookie starting to do what he did best – cooking their supper. The men had brought their horses and tied them to a picket line they had set up between two small trees. Bedrolls were laid out in preparation for an early night following their supper.

"Cookie, I want to leave before sunup in the morning. Can you have something prepared for us to eat on our horses as we ride?" Thad asked.

"Sure thing, Boss."

The next morning, Cookie prepared a sandwich of sorts by wrapping biscuits around bacon for the men to eat. They checked their side arms and rifles before mounting their horses. They stuffed more ammunition into their vest and jeans pockets. It would not do to run out in the middle of a gunfight.

"Ready?" Thad questioned the men.

They all nodded and headed out of Fort Laramie. *Father, guide us safely back to Deer Creek Ranch. And if there must be a confrontation, make it a quiet one.* He knew that Pa probably asked the same.

They were able to go at a little faster pace without the horses, though the chuck wagon did slow them down. Thad wished there would've been a way to make the trip to Fort Laramie without the chuck wagon. But then they didn't know they would run into a potential for robbery.

At the end of the day on Tuesday, Thad asked if they noticed the three riders.

Wade replied, "Yeah, they're still out there. Guess we know what they have in mind now for sure."

"Cookie, make cold meals from now on. We won't stop to eat. Men, ride up alongside the chuck wagon and grab your food. Maybe this way we can cut the journey short."

"Okay, Boss."

Thad found it hard to get any decent rest Tuesday night. Every sound roused him to wakefulness, and it continued like that all night. He felt safer when they were out in the open than when they camped at night. But Wednesday morning came, and nothing happened, so they set out on the trail once more. Thad surmised that the riders wanted them to get further away from Fort Laramie before they made their move.

They got up earlier than usual and though they missed a warm breakfast; they were on the trail again just as the bright sun began to peek over the horizon. At least they ate a warm meal at night, though it was after a long day of travel. And it was later than when they usually stopped. Thad was glad for his supply of pemmican which he shared with the men.

The next day, Thursday, brought no confrontation from the three riders, although they were still observed following Thad and his men. Nerves were tense since the ranch hands tried not to let the riders know that they were observed. The travel seemed long, but they were relieved to finally stop and camp that night.

23

Cookie provided a warm meal for them, but they stayed out of the firelight, mindful of the need to remain undetected. Tuck and Thad conversed in low tones, making plans for the night. They shared their ideas with the men and Cookie.

As the campfire was dying down, the men, including Cookie, used their bedrolls as decoys. Then they bedded down away from camp as two of the hands remained hidden to keep watch. Close to sunrise on Friday, they heard sounds and realized the riders were advancing upon the camp. By the light of the remaining campfire, Thad could see three men in western garb. They fired shots into the decoys and were surprised to find they were tricked.

"WHAT DO YOU MEN WANT?" Thad's deep voice rang out loud and accusing in the night.

They whirled around, aiming their guns at the sound of Thad's voice. Tuck fired a shot into the air to show that they were covered,

"Wal now," the leader drawled. "Guess you got the drop on us, Mr. Rancher."

"Throw down your guns, now!" Tuck demanded. "We've got you surrounded."

"They got us outnumbered, boys. Best do as he says." The leader of the would-be bandits turned around, then nodded to the members of his gang and they tossed their guns down. Wade went around the group, picking up their weapons and patting them down to see if they had more. He removed knives from each of them.

"Tie them up," Thad directed his men.

Wade and Nash took ropes and tied their hands behind their backs. Then they tied them to the wheels of the chuck wagon.

"Cookie, get us breakfast, and we'll head out," Thad said.

"What about them?" Wade asked.

"Feed them too. We'll tie them to their horses and take them to the Mustang Ridge jail," Tuck informed him.

There were no further problems with the bandits. Thad directed Hank to accompany Cookie and the chuckwagon back to Deer Creek Ranch while the rest of them took the bandits into Mustang Ridge and turned them over to Sheriff Charlie Yates at the jail.

"What's the charge, fellas?" asked the sheriff.

"Attempted murder and attempted armed robbery," Tuck replied. He took the keys from the wall peg and herded them into their cells. He knew his way around the jail since he had been the sheriff until he went into ranching full-time. Thad explained what had transpired with the bandits.

"Okay. I'll get word to the circuit judge."

After Thad went to the bank and deposited the money from the sale of the horses, the weary men headed for Deer Creek Ranch. They put up their horses in the barn, and the hands went to the bunkhouse while Tuck and Thad headed to the ranch-house.

Tuck patted Thad on the back. "Good job, son. You handled it well."

Thad grinned. "Thanks, Pa. It made me a little nervous though. Glad to be home."

"Me too, son. Me too."

"Afternoon, Ma," Thad hugged his mother upon entering the ranch-house and planted a kiss on her cheek. "How did it go while we were gone?"

"Well, the boys reported no more wolf sightings, so that's good, I guess. But I missed you both," she said reaching her arms around her husband's neck. "It's good to have you back. How was your trip? Without trouble, I hope."

Tuck and Thad looked at each other. They had not talked about whether to tell her or not. But that may have been a moot point since she could always see when any of them were hiding information from her.

"What? You might as well tell me now. I will find out."

"We were followed by three bandits. They attempted to steal the money Thad got from the fort commander." Tuck took the initiative to explain to his wife.

"Oh, no! Did they hurt you?" she asked, her eyes growing big.

"They came up in the night and fired into our bedrolls," Thad explained, holding his arm as though in pain. But after seeing the horrified expression on his mother's face, he was a bit ashamed of himself. "But we weren't in them."

"What? Oh, you! Stop that!" Beth said, exasperated.

"Sorry, Ma. We're okay. We set a trap for them. No one was hurt," he answered. "The three of them are now in the Mustang Ridge jail."

"You didn't get hurt then?"

"No. We're fine."

"Praise the Lord for watching over you. He answered my prayers."

"Yes, He sure did."

25

CHAPTER EIGHT

Holy Spirit Prompting

When Thad told her, he was driving his horses to Fort Laramie; she had mixed emotions. She'd miss him and yet knew he needed to sell his horses. After all, he was a horse rancher.

During the time he was gone, Belle kept busy at Doc Phillips' office and helped Mama plant the garden. Mama still worked a few hours a day at the school, helping Becca to be ready for the testing she would receive from the Education Department in Cheyenne. Things must have changed a bit. As Belle recalled Mama telling about what she had to do to get her teaching certificate. The only requirement was to be a graduate of secondary school. Of course, that was in Ohio, so maybe it was different here.

Mama and Belle spent a lot of time in the garden, planting vegetables with the hope that it would be a good year and it would flourish. She always canned a lot of the produce and stored the jars of canned items in her pantry. It was satisfying to look at the shelves filled with different colors: green beans and peas, yellow corn, and red tomatoes. Belle hoped to one day have a garden and to also put up a harvest. In the back of her mind, Belle saw herself preparing meals from canned goods for her husband.

One day while Thad was gone, Belle had the strangest feeling that he was in danger. So sure was she of this that she felt compelled to immediately fall on her knees in prayer. She didn't know where the thought came from, but just knew Thad was in trouble. The Holy Spirit had put it upon her heart to pray for not only Thad but also Tuck and the Deer Creek Ranch hands. She felt better after praying. Whatever *it* was, now it was in God's hands now.

When Thad returned after the drive and told Belle what had happened, she was indeed glad the Holy Spirit had directed her to pray for their safety. She knew then God had answered her prayer, but more so when Thad explained what had happened on the trail. *Thank you, Holy Spirit, for directing me to pray.*

CHAPTER NINE
Plans for the Railroad Begin

"Sam, what's all the excitement about?" Thad inquired upon entering the mercantile. Sam Garrison was also the mayor of Mustang Ridge. It was in that capacity that he was presiding over a meeting with two well-dressed men in the back of his store.

"Thad, just the man we need here," Sam called to him. "Come on over. Let me introduce you. Gentlemen, this is Thad Tucker, a prominent rancher in the area. Thad, these men are representatives of the Grand Island and Wyoming Central Railroad."

Thad could see that Sam was eager for him to make the acquaintances of the men present. "Gentlemen," he said shaking their hands. He stepped back and waited for Sam to tell him what was going on.

"Thad, the railroad is making plans to start laying track from Cheyenne to Edgewood just south of Deadwood. Well, I'll let them tell you."

Daniel Jarvis spoke then, "We're searching out sites for the rail stations in the towns along the line, Mr. Tucker."

"So, it's finally going to happen," Thad responded.

"Yes, and your mayor is working with us on that subject. He says he knows of a chunk of land where we can build the station here in Mustang Ridge," explained Jarvis.

Sam pointed to the map at which the men had been looking. "This is what I have in mind. What do you think?"

Thad leaned over the table thoughtfully stroking his chin and viewed the site where Sam pointed. "Well, I think it's pretty close to the mountain. There're occasional rock slides along there, and they'd all go on the rail. Maybe even hit the station and the train cars themselves."

"You bring up an important point, Mr. Tucker. Do you have any other suggestions?" Jarvis asked.

Thad thoughtfully searched the map. "I think that general area would work. Just not so close to the mountain. See here, pull it out to here, and the train station can stand right here, away from any damage from falling rock. And it won't interfere with the town's buildings."

As Thad walked away, he heard them discussing the price for the land on which the proposed station would stand. These were significant changes for Wyoming Territory. Maybe statehood wouldn't be far behind. Residents of Wyoming Territory were trying to get statehood granted, but they didn't have enough people yet in the territory for the United States Congress to approve statehood.

27

Thad handed George the list that his mother sent with him. "I'll be back after dinner to pick up Ma's order," he said. "No need to hurry."

"Sure thing, Thad." He noticed a bigger than usual smile on George's face. *Guess he knows where I'll be having my dinner. And with who.*

Thad went out of the mercantile and headed down the board sidewalk, the sound of his boots announcing to those around that he had a particular destination in mind. He was greeted by several of the town residents as he walked. A few people stopped to thank him for the help in ridding the area of wolves and rabies.

When he finally made it to the end of the walk and arrived at Doc Phillips' office, he met Belle coming through the door. Thad removed his hat. "Morning, Belle. Going somewhere?"

"Yes, Thad. To dinner with you," Belle responded with a smile. "I heard you were in town so was hoping you'd come to take me to dinner."

Thad laughed and closed the office door for her. Placing his hat back on his head, he offered Belle his arm, and they walked down to Sally's Café. "Sure a good thing I was hungry then. I might've just gone back to the ranch and not eaten in town."

"No, you wouldn't," Belle said, playfully punching his arm.

Thad smiled down at her beautiful upturned face. "No, you're right. I wouldn't have."

When they reached the café, he held the door for Belle, and they entered. It was busy, and the delicious smells coming from the kitchen only proved to Thad he was indeed hungry. But he would have gone without eating if it had come down to a choice of that or spending time with Belle.

"There's my favorite couple," Sally declared when she came to take them to their table.

"I'll bet you say that to all your customers, Sally," he said.

"Only to the sweetest ones," Sally said. "I'm serving roast beef today. Would you like coffee with your meals?"

"Yes, please," he said after looking to Belle for confirmation. "I'll take a piece of pie too, Sally. Belle, how about you?"

"Yes, I'll take a small slice too." Sally hurried off to prepare their food.

"What are you doing in town today, Thad? Other than seeing me, of course."

"Ma sent me with a list for Sam. That reminds me. Sam was talking to railroad men. Sounds like they are moving ahead with the laying of railroad tracks, at least buying the land anyway."

"Oh, that's so exciting. Just think, Thad. We are part of history in the making."

"Yes, Wyoming Territory is taking its rightful place in history all right."

"How soon do you think it'll be before the train comes through?"

"They're still doing the paperwork. I don't imagine we'll see a train here for another three years or so, Belle."

"Oh," she said, obviously disappointed, but she brightened, "but we will have other exciting things to think of before then."

Thad felt his heart pound in his chest when he saw her eyes twinkle. Was it possible that Belle was thinking of marriage as he had been? Dare he ask her this early in their courtship?

"Yes," she said.

Thad started. "Yes, what?"

"Yes, you can ask me."

"Did I say something out loud?"

"No, Thad. You didn't," she said taking his hand across the table, "but I know your heart, so you can ask me. It's not too soon."

"Isabelle Wells, I love you," he whispered.

"And I you," she returned, quietly.

"So?"

"So what?" Belle asked innocently.

"So, will you?"

"Thad Tucker! Is that your idea of a romantic proposal?" she asked coyly.

"No," Thad stated. "No. I have something else planned. Can you get off any time this week so we can take a drive?"

"Yes. Doc Phillips closes the office on Thursdays, so I could go then. Do you want to have another picnic? I can bring the food this time."

"That sounds great. I'll pick you up about 11:30 Thursday unless it's raining. Then we'll have to make other plans."

"Okay," she agreed. Since they had finished eating, she added, "But right now, I have to get back to the office."

Thad walked Belle back to Doc Phillips' office where they said their goodbyes. He went to the mercantile where George helped him to load the items from Ma's list into his wagon. Once loaded, Thad headed back to the ranch. He was excited for Thursday to come because he had a surprise for Belle over and above appropriately proposing to her. Before going home, Thad dropped in at Jacob Wells' blacksmith. There he respectfully asked Jacob for his daughter's hand in marriage. Of course, Jacob was happy to give it. Thad asked him not to say anything to Belle yet.

29

CHAPTER TEN
Romance at Whitehorse Lake

Thad took Belle to Whitehorse Lake on Thursday for another picnic. It wasn't raining, and in fact, they had perfect weather though it did become pretty warm as the day wore on. Thad had ulterior motives for this day. He wanted to propose, and he wanted to share with Belle his vision for their home. This time Belle provided the picnic of roast beef sandwiches and a pie for their feast.

As they finished cleaning up the remains of their meal, Belle said she wanted to dangle her feet in the lake. She unfastened and pulled off her shoes and black stockings. Thad, shocked at her bold actions, turned his back so he would not see her bare ankles. She chose one of the large boulders along the lakeshore and sitting on it; she lowered her bare feet into the cool water.

"Come on, Thad. Take your boots off and join me," she invited him.

"Belle, you are a tease. Belle, I have something important to talk to you about."

"Okay, Thad. What is it?"

"Belle, would you do me the honor of becoming my wife?" Thad removed a ring from his vest pocket, and Belle squealed with delight and put her hand out for him to put it on her finger.

"Oh yes, Thad! I will!"

"This was my mother's engagement ring that my father, Jackson Caruthers, gave to her. I hope that's okay?"

"It's a beautiful ring. Of course, it's okay. Thad, I love you."

"I love you too."

Later, he carried Belle to the quilt so she wouldn't get her feet dirty. They sat together, leaning against the broad trunk of the shade tree. "Belle, I have another surprise for you. This land we're sitting on is my land. I filed for it under the Homestead Act last year. Its 160 acres along Whitehorse Lake. I have five years to build us a home."

"Then our spot will always be our spot?" she asked.

When he nodded in the affirmative, Belle said, "This is a beautiful site for our future home. Will you have windows opening to the lake?"

"Yes, we'll take full advantage of the sunrise across the lake."

"When will you start building?"

"I need to complete the sale of my horses to the rodeo in Deadwood," he responded. "I will send a wire that I have fifty broncos for them. They aren't broken."

"What is that?"

"Participating cowboys come to see who can stay on a wild horse the longest. So, you see, if they were saddle broke it wouldn't work very well."

"Yes, I can see that," Belle said. "Then you will start building once you have made that sale?"

"Yes, but there's a lot of planning we need to do first. You and I will have decisions to make. Like how many rooms, how big, where the windows will be? Things like that."

"Will you build a barn too?"

"Yes, a big barn with adjoining stables and a bunkhouse for the ranch hands. And corrals like the ones at Deer Creek Ranch."

"Can we name it Whitehorse Ranch maybe? Since the lake is nearby, you know."

"That's not a bad idea."

"Thad, what about Deer Creek Ranch? You and Tuck are partners in that ranch."

"Good question. Pa and I have already talked about it. Nate will eventually join our partnership. But at thirteen years of age, he's too young."

"I've got another question. When shall we plan to have the wedding?"

Thad looked at Belle's bright blue eyes in a beautiful face framed in a mass of dark curls. How he wanted to say they could be married tomorrow. But wisdom prevailed, and he answered, "It'll have to be once we finish the house so we'll have a place to live."

"Of course. I'm disappointed, but I understand," Belle responded. "I wish I could help you build it, but I know I wouldn't have the remotest idea how to go about it. Have you ever constructed a building?"

"Not a house. I helped with the additions on the Deer Creek ranch-house. Pa and I built the bunkhouse and the additions for the barn and stables. I'm far from an expert though."

They sat for a while longer enjoying each other's company. The weather was beautiful and the time passed more quickly than they liked. But then, good things must eventually come to an end. Thad knew he needed to get back to the ranch.

"Belle, Pa will be wondering where I am. I need to get back, and I have to take you into town first."

"I know, Thad. I probably need to get home myself and help Mama get supper ready. You're right; we need to head back."

CHAPTER ELEVEN
Nate is Irritated

"It's about time you got back!" Nate was put out with Thad. "I need help with the chores."

"Where is everyone?" Why do you need help with the chores?"

"Okay, here's what's going on. I don't have time to stand around talking. Ma's sick and in bed. Becca's at the school taking the tests. Pa's out with the cattle."

"What do you want me to do?" Thad asked.

"Do the barn chores. I've got the chicken chores about done, and I'm going to take care of the goats. If you get done before me, come and help with the milking."

"Okay, Nate. Sorry I was away. Will Ma be okay?"

"She says she will be. Says she has the stomach sickness." Nate was starting to back down from his anger.

"Okay, I'll run into the ranch-house and change into my chore clothes and look in on Ma." Seeing Nate's response before he said anything, Thad added. "Don't worry, Nate. Leave the milking to me."

Thad entered the ranch-house and went to his room and changed his clothes. He then went to his parent's room and peered into the door which was ajar. "It's okay, Thad. I only have an upset stomach."

"Is there anything I can get you before I go help Nate?"

"No, I'll be okay until everyone gets home."

"Okay, see you later."

Once the barn chores were done, which included feeding and watering the horses in their stalls, Thad took the empty pails to the goat pen and settled down to begin milking one of Becca's four goats. He felt chagrined that while he was off having a good time with Belle, his family needed him. *I wonder how long Ma had been sick.* He hadn't seen her that morning. He'd done his chores early before going to check on his horses, and when he finished, he went in to meet Belle for dinner.

Nate came in and took one of the full pails of milk. "I'll take this up to the house and put it in the cooler. Then I'll see what I can do about getting supper ready."

"You!" remarked Thad.

"Pa should be home any time now. He'll be hungry, and I'm getting there myself."

"Make eggs and bacon. That'll be easy and will taste good," Thad suggested.

"Good idea." Nate stopped and looked at his brother. "Thanks for doing the milking, Thad. Sorry I was so grumpy about it."

"That's okay, Nate. I left you holding the bag. See you later."

After Nate left with the milk, Thad heard a horse entering the yard. He looked up from his milking when Tuck came into the barn with his horse. They talked about their day while Tuck rubbed down his horse and gave it hay and water.

"What needs doing?" his pa asked.

"Everything's done except for the milking, and I'm just about done with that. Nate went up to start supper. You could check in on Ma. Did you know she was sick?"

"No, I didn't. What's wrong?" Tuck asked, looking worried.

"She told Nate it was the stomach sickness."

"Okay, I'll get up there and see what I can do. Do you want me to take that pail up with me?" Tuck asked, seeing that Thad's pail was almost full.

"Sure," Thad said, reaching for an empty pail.

Becca rode into the yard in her buggy as Thad was coming out of the goat pen with the second pail of milk. She started to unhitch her horse when Thad stopped her. "I'll do that, Becca, if you can take this pail of milk."

"Okay, thanks. How come you're doing the milking? Where's Nate?"

"He's getting supper. Pa just got back, and Nate was stuck with all the chores, so I told him I'd do the milking. Ma is sick."

"Oh no. I would have to be stuck doing that testing when Mama is sick. What's wrong, do you know?"

"She said stomach sickness." Thad handed her the pail of milk. "I'll be up as soon as I put your horse up."

"Thanks, Thad. Don't forget to turn the kids in with their mothers," she reminded him as she looked at her goats.

When he came into the ranch-house after taking care of Becca's horse, he saw that his two siblings were busy with supper preparation. Becca was putting a pan of biscuits into the oven while Nate was frying bacon in the big cast iron skillet. Tuck helped Beth out to the living room.

"Ma, are you sure you should be up?" Thad asked her, concern lining his face.

"I've been in bed all day. I need a change of scenery, and anyway, I'm feeling better now. The smell of that bacon cooking is making me so hungry. Do you suppose I could have bacon?" she asked.

"If you think so," said Tuck, warily.

"How do you feel, Ma?' Thad asked.

33

"Pretty good. My stomach was just upset that one time this morning, then the fever came. But it's passed now. I think I'm just hungry."

Beth didn't get sick again after that and Thad watched her eat the delicious bacon with zeal. "Thanks for cooking, Nate, and Becca," he said. "Sorry you were forced to do most of the chores, Nate."

"That's okay. You did the milking, and that helped," Nate answered.

"I'm sorry too," Beth stated. "I don't know what was wrong, but I seem to be better now."

"I'm glad you're feeling better, Beth," Tuck said, as he hugged his wife. To Becca, he said, "How did the testing go? Did you finish?"

"Yes, for today, I guess," she replied. "Mr. Rhodes took the papers back with him. He will contact me once he has graded them. Next will be the oral testing, which I'm even more nervous about."

Thad was thinking that it seemed to be taking a long time for his sister to go through the testing. He wondered if he ought to look in on them one day to make sure things were on the up and up. But having other things on his mind, he let the thought slide, and it was probably just as well.

"Well, I know you and that you've done your best. That's all you can do," Beth encouraged her. "How soon before you can do the oral testing?"

"Well, he said he'd contact me, so I guess I just have to wait."

"Yes, waiting. That is always the hard part."

CHAPTER TWELVE
Belle

Another date to go for a drive with Thad, and Belle was so excited when he asked her, she barely could contain herself. This time, she made their picnic dinner. Since Thursday was her day off, she spent the morning preparing the perfect picnic basket. She made fresh sourdough bread that morning and roast beef, using them to make sandwiches. Because Belle knew how much Thad enjoyed eating pie, she also baked an apple pie. As long as she was making one, she might as well make another one for her family. She went to the pantry and got two jars of canned apples

Belle packed the picnic dinner in a wicker basket and waited for Thad to pick her up. From their conversation at Sally's, Belle believed that Thad was ready to propose. And she was ready to say, "yes!" Her belief was that God put them in each other's lives, beginning with meeting on the wagon train. Thad loved God as she did – an essential step in following His leading for their lives. *How I love this man and want to spend the rest of my life with him.*

It was a beautiful day, and Belle decided to remove her shoes and stockings so she could dangle her feet in the water. She teased Thad to do the same, but the wiser of the two prevailed. He laid a quilt under a big shade tree and carried her to it so she wouldn't get her wet feet dirty. *He is so gallant.*

Afterward, Belle's thoughts were about Whitehorse Lake and what it would mean to their future. They would build their home there on the shores of that beautiful lake. *Our own home. How happy that makes me just to speak of it. And how wonderful that Thad wanted to build a home for us.* Belle knew Thad needed to sell more of his horses to pay for the building materials. *I guess it will be a while yet.*

The following Sunday, Reverend Prescott preached from Matthew 7:21-29.

> *Not every one that saith unto me, Lord, Lord, shall enter unto the Kingdom of Heaven; but he that doeth the will of my Father which is in heaven.*
>
> *Many will say to me in that day, Lord, Lord, have we not prophesied in thy name? and in thy name have cast out devils? and in thy name done many wonderful works?*
>
> *And then will I profess unto them, I never knew you: depart from me, ye that work iniquity.*

Therefore whosoever heareth these sayings of mine, and doeth them, I will liken him unto a wise man, which built his house upon a rock:
And the rain descended, and the floods came, and the winds blew, and beat upon that house; and it fell not: for it was founded upon a rock.
And every one that heareth these sayings of mine, and doeth them not, shall be likened unto a foolish man, which built his house upon the sand:
And the rain descended, and the floods came, and the winds blew, and beat upon that house; and it fell: and great was the fall of it.
And it came to pass, when Jesus had ended these sayings, the people were astonished at his doctrine:
For he taught them as one having authority, and not as the scribes.

In John 14:13, Jesus said to His disciples Whatever you ask in My name, that I will do, that the Father may be glorified in the Son.

And in John 16:24: Until now, you have asked nothing in my name. Ask and you will receive that your joy may be full.

Belle's thoughts wandered as she heard Reverend Prescott read about building a house founded on the rock. She knew that for their home to be blessed by God, Jesus Christ would need to be at its foundation. Her thoughts returned to the present as Reverend Prescott said,

"In summary, we are to approach God in prayer through the name of Jesus Christ, His Son. Let us pray. Our Father in Heaven, we come before You with praise for Your Word. Thank You for providing Your Son to die for our sins on the cross that we might have a relationship with You. Show us Your will. You know what we hold in our hearts. Cleanse us of any sinful thoughts and deeds. We ask these things in the powerful name of Jesus, Amen.

Let's close with the hymn, All Hail the Power of Jesus' Name."

CHAPTER THIRTEEN
Matt in Crisis

After breakfast one day, Thad and Tuck, and their foreman Wade, were working with their horses in the corral when they were surprised by a buggy racing into the yard. They could see that a woman drove with two small children in the seat beside her.

"It's Mattie Cutter!" Tuck exclaimed. "I wonder what's wrong."

Tuck moved to help Mattie bring her buggy to a halt on one side while Wade did the same on the opposite side. Mattie had a wild look about her. Her bonnet hung loose and tendrils of her hair pulled free from her chignon. It was apparent her team of horses was winded from the ride. Tuck took Mattie up to the ranch-house where Beth waited at the door. Wade unhitched the horses and put them in the corral where they had access to hay and water.

Thad stepped forward to take care of her children. "Hi there, Little Tuck, Louisa. How about a drink of water? You look thirsty." I'm just about to go see Becca's goats. Would you like to help me feed them?"

Seven-year-old Little Tuck was all for it, and six-year-old Louisa forgot her fear from riding so fast. They took Thad's hands as he led them to the goat pen. Matt and Mattie Cutter were good friends of the Tuckers and lived on a ranch thirty miles southwest of Mustang Ridge, the Double M Ranch.

After a while, Thad asked the children if they would like to go up to the ranch-house and see if they could find cookies. He knew for a fact that Ma had baked them the first thing that morning.

As they entered the house, Beth rose from her chair next to Mattie. "Would you children like a cookie?" *It's like she can tell what I'm thinking!* The children sat down and ate the cookies accompanied by a glass of milk.

Tuck came out of their bedroom with his saddlebags filled. "Two Army soldiers just came to take Matt to Fort Laramie to stand trial."

"Matt! Why?" asked Thad, astounded.

"I think it's a case of mistaken identity. That's why I want to go there pronto," Tuck said.

"I'll go with you," Thad offered.

"I was hoping you'd say that. I think we should take Wade with us too. Nash can run things in our absence. We need to leave right away since they've already got a good head start on us. It took Mattie three hours to get here in the buggy. I've got my bedroll and saddlebags packed. I'll go to the stable and get our horses saddled and tell Wade. You come out when you have your saddlebags packed."

37

"Mattie and the children will stay here with me," Beth spoke up. "Nash can check with Nate or me if anything comes up." They had confidence in Nash to keep the ranch safe. And Wade would be a good hand to take along.

Thad took his saddlebags and filled one side with clothes and the other side with extra ammunition, pemmican, and a few of his mother's cookies. Filling their canteens, he headed to the stables just as Tuck was bringing the horses out. He had a pack horse also with a tent and camping supplies. Wade joined them, eager to go too since he was acquainted with Matt.

As Thad and his pa said their goodbyes, Thad asked, "Ma, could you get word to Belle, so she won't wonder where I am?"

"Sure, Thad. I'll take care of it."

"I'll keep the home fires burning and watch over the womenfolk and children," Nate informed them. "So, you don't need to worry about things at home. Between Nash and me, we'll keep things running smoothly."

"Thanks, Nate."

Hugs and kisses all around, a moment of prayer for safety on the trail, and a good outcome for Matt, and they were mounted and ready to ride by noon.

"It'll be hard on the horses, but we better ride straight through. Fast by day, slow by night," Tuck advised. "Fifty miles to the fort should put us there in a day and a half."

"What do you think this is all about?" Wade asked once they were on the trail.

"I sure don't know," Tuck responded. "I don't like that the Army can come into a home and take a man away from his family with no explanation except to tell him he's to stand trial. Mattie said before they carted him off, Matt said, 'Tell Tuck I need his help.' There are no lawyers around and my being a former lawman is why he wants me."

"So, Mattie had no idea what the trial was about?" Thad inquired.

"No, she never heard them explain although they may have told Matt when she wasn't there. She's just glad they let him come up to the house to say goodbye to her and the children."

"That's terrible," said Wade. "That man has never done anything to require a military trial. He really does need our help. He's a good man. I'm glad you let me come along, Tuck."

Thad pondered Wade's response concerning Matt. He knew Ma and Pa had been praying that Wade would turn to Jesus. They prayed for all the ranch hands as if they were part of the family, which in a sense, they were.

On the 2nd day, the men arrived at Fort Laramie. Wade took their horses to the fort livery while Thad accompanied Tuck to the commander's office.

38

Tuck carried his saddlebag with him. Colonel Watson recognized Thad immediately from doing business for providing horses to the fort. He rose to shake his hand.

"Thad Tucker, good to see you again." He looked to Tuck.

"Colonel, this is my Pa, Adam Tucker," Thad explained. The two men also shook hands.

"Adam Tucker, I've heard of you," Colonel Watson said. "You have a fine reputation as a lawman."

"Thank you," Tuck said. "I appreciate it, but I gave up the badge when I got married back in '76. I'm a full-time rancher now."

The colonel looked puzzled. "So, what can I do for you gentlemen?"

"Sir, two of your men brought in a man named Matt Cutter for trial. I'm here to represent him," Tuck explained.

"Cutter? What's this about? I don't know of anyone by that name."

Tuck and Thad looked at one another. *This is not good. Doesn't bode well for Matt if the commander doesn't even know about it.*

Colonel Watson was looking through the papers on his desk. "Oh, here it is. Mr. Cutter was brought in for treason."

"There must be a mistake, Colonel," Tuck said. "Treason, how?"

"Well, for desertion actually," Watson answered. "During the war, the War Between the States."

"What?" Tuck was astounded. "That was over eighteen years ago. Why wait so long?"

"The Federal government sent a list of all deserters and implored they be found and tried," Watson replied. "I'm sorry, but the men were following orders."

"Your orders?" Tuck asked.

"Well, no, but Lieutenant Birch, who will be prosecuting, followed the directive from the Federal government. I concur with his decision to bring Cutter in to stand for trial."

"This is ridiculous!" Thad could see that Tuck was starting to get angry. He put his hand on Tuck's shoulder.

"May we see Mr. Cutter now?" Thad asked.

"Certainly. I'll show you to the guardhouse," Watson said, rising from his desk. He put his hat on at the door and stood aside for Thad and Tuck to exit first.

As they walked with Colonel Watson toward the guardhouse, Thad whispered to his pa, "There's something wrong here. Matt would've only been a boy when the war ended."

"I know," Tuck agreed, also whispering. "We'll get to the bottom of it. They must have gotten the wrong man."

"Here we are," said Watson, stopping at the guarded building. He saluted the soldier in front who was armed with his rifle.

"Private Black, allow these men to see prisoner Cutter," he said. The private turned to unlock the door and allowed Thad and Tuck to enter."

"How long do we have?" Tuck asked Watson.

"As long as you need, seeing as how you're his legal representatives."

"Tuck, Thad! I knew you'd come. Am I ever glad to see you! You've got to help me." Matt Cutter nearly wept when he took in the sight of his friends from Mustang Ridge. Bars separated Matt from his two visitors.

Tuck pulled a stool up close to the bars and said, "Tell us all you know about this. Why would they think you deserted the Army during the war? You were just a boy."

"I never shared this with you before, but my parents and two siblings died when I was eight, almost nine."

"Matt, I'm so sorry. Did you have no one to take you in?" Tuck asked.

Matt snorted. "You could say that. I had no relatives, but I was taken in by a widow woman in town."

"That was nice of her," said Thad.

"No. It wasn't nice of her at all! She heard of the Union Army paying up to $200 for boys to be drummers in the Army, so she got the money from the Army, and I never heard a word from her again. She got what she wanted out of me. Took the money and ran."

"How old were you when this happened?" Thad commented.

"On my ninth birthday, she took me to the nearest Army camp and turned me over to them. They gave me a uniform, which was too big, and a drum that was almost as big as me. They told me to play the different drum plays."

"What time during the war was this?" Tuck asked.

"February before the war ended in April. If I'd known that, I maybe could have stayed. But probably not. I was devastated having just lost my whole family. The bloody carnage of the battle was more than I could handle. Not a day went by that I didn't throw up my food."

"You didn't stay then?" Tuck asked.

"No! I ran away one night. I went back to the widow's home, but she'd just packed up and left. Fortunately, some of my things were still there. I packed what little I could carry and headed west. I heard that the West beckoned to young men, so I set my mind to go there. I eventually ended up where I am today."

40

"Well, I think they are going to require a little knowledge of what you did in-between that time," Tuck responded.

"Yes," Thad said. "What could a nine-year-old boy do to survive?"

"I managed to get as far as St. Louis on foot. I loved to fish and spent a good deal of time along the Mississippi River fishing. I'd sell the catfish I caught to a lady who ran an eating establishment called Mary's Cafe. She never asked questions; I think she assumed I lived up the River with my parents. Mary paid me by feeding me one good meal a day and a few coins. I also sold catfish to a man who sold them in his store. He allowed me to sleep on a cot in the back. I stayed on like that for a few years.

"I saved my money and was soon able to buy a horse. Daisy was an old nag, but I took care of her, and she enabled me to head west. I hired onto a wagon train at Independence going on the Santa Fe Trail as a livestock boy."

"That's an amazing story, Matt. I never knew that about you," Thad said.

"Then what?" asked Tuck.

"By that time, I was fifteen-years-old. I was tall for my age, so I probably looked older than that. When we got to the Oklahoma Territory, I was offered a job as a wrangler by a rancher there."

"When I was nineteen, I married a young lady named Betsy Lang from a neighboring ranch. Betsy and I were able to build a cabin on the ranch where I worked as I had a good relationship with the ranch owner. We were starting to build a herd of our own horses and to have our own ranch. One day, my home was struck by a tornado, killing Betsy while I was working for the rancher."

"I'm so sorry, Matt," Thad consoled him.

"After that, I just wanted to leave there," Matt continued. "Oklahoma Territory no longer had a hold on me. So, I sold my horses and hit the trail for Texas. I found a rancher from the Territory of Montana, and I signed up as a cowpuncher with him. He was herding cattle he had purchased in Texas to his ranch back there. I stayed there working on his ranch until the Overland Trail advertised for a stagecoach driver, which is how I met you folks."

"That's quite a life you've had, Matt," Tuck remarked.

"Do you think you can help me?"

"I'll certainly do my best," Tuck replied. "I think that'll be all for now. I want to have a talk with this Lieutenant Birch and get a few facts written down. But before I do, I want to read a verse from Psalm 27:1 for you."

Matt nodded when Tuck pulled his Bible from his saddlebags.

The LORD is my light and my salvation; whom shall I fear? The LORD is the strength of my life; of whom shall I be afraid?"

He only is my rock and my salvation; He is my defense; I shall not be greatly moved.

41

"Matt, while you are in this cell and overwhelmed, these verses can be a help to you." Tuck closed his Bible and rose. "I'll see you later."

"Thanks, Tuck. I appreciate your help."

The men ended their time together with prayer and then Tuck said he needed to send a wire and he would meet Thad and Wade at the supply store. The telegraph operator slid a pencil and paper across the counter to Tuck and waited for him to write his message. Tuck wrote:

> *Urgent!*
> *President Chester A. Arthur*
> *A friend is on trial at Fort Laramie for desertion from the Union Army in the War Between the States. He was only nine and ran away. Are we going back that far to prosecute one who was just a lad? He was an orphan and was sold by a widow lady for the $200. Matt Cutter is now a respected rancher in Wyoming. Request your immediate attention to this matter since his trial is to be tomorrow.*
> *Please reply to me in care of Fort Laramie.*
> *Sheriff Adam Tucker, Retired*
> *Mustang Ridge, Wyoming Territory*

Tuck doled out the payment, thankful he'd brought enough money with him to see them through this time. "Please keep this quiet and bring me the reply as soon as you can."

The operator agreed, and Tuck left to join Thad and Wade at the supply store, where they began questioning the clerk. They learned that Lieutenant Birch was having dinner at the company mess hall which was also open to visitors.

"I'm hungry," Tuck announced. "How about you gents?"

They both nodded, and the three men made their way to the mess hall.

"So, what's it all about?" Wade asked. "Did you find out what they're charging him with?"

"Desertion. From the War between the States."

"What? That was a long time ago. Do you think you can help him?"

"Sure gonna try," answered Tuck.

"What'll they do to him if he is found guilty?" Wade asked.

"During the war, the penalty for desertion was hanging, but that was for adults. I don't know what they would do for a child, and now eighteen years later."

"Who did you send the wire to?" Thad queried.

"To Washington. To President Arthur." Tuck explained to them in a low voice what he said in the wire.

"There's the Lieutenant now," Thad pointed out a dark-haired officer who wore a drooping mustache.

Tuck approached Lieutenant Birch and asked if he might have a word with him. As Thad observed his pa seat himself at the Lieutenant's table, they watched the face of the man before him. Thad didn't like what he saw. Birch appeared to Thad to be cold and hard-nosed. Wade saw what Thad did since he remarked, "I don't like this."

Thad nodded and watched while Tuck rose and returned to their table. "Well?" he asked.

"Not good," Tuck replied. "He said he possessed a list of deserters which was sent to the fort for the Army to bring to trial. He's not giving an inch. Looks like it'll be up to my glib tongue and President Arthur."

"When is the trial?" asked Wade.

"Tomorrow. Not much time. We need to find a place to pitch our tent and settle in," Tuck said. "I've got a lot of work to do to prepare for his trial."

The men prepared the site for their tent. They found a spot just outside the fort wall along the Laramie River. The river would provide drinking water for them and their horses, as well as a place to bathe.

"How can we help now Boss?" Wade asked.

"Be my eyes and ears. You may have to question the soldiers, but be subtle about it," Tuck answered him. "We don't want to give them a reason to deny us access to Matt. That would only serve to hurry a guilty verdict."

The men built a fire and proceeded to prepare their evening meal from the supplies procured from the fort supply store. None of the three were anything great when it came to cooking, but they were all used to fending for themselves on the trail. Therefore, a hearty meal would be the reward for their experiences.

Tuck sat by the fire with paper and pencil, outlining what his procedure would be, but first, he needed to work on an appealing opening statement. While he worked on that, Thad and Wade took care of their camp and meal. Thad took one of the cast iron pots and sliced off ham which they had purchased at the fort supply store. He set it on the hot coals, and while that was frying, he sliced potatoes and added them to the ham. He then put the coffee pot which he had filled with water, ground coffee beans, and an egg.

While he was doing all of this, Wade mixed up a batch of biscuits using their flour, bacon grease, and an egg. He greased the bottom of the second cast iron pot with bacon grease and placed large dollops of the sticky dough in the bottom. Next, Wade set the pan on the coals and put the lid on it. He took some of the red-hot coals, placed them on top of the cover, and created an oven.

Thad saw Pa in front of the fire with his head bowed. He knew Pa was seeking God's wisdom and guidance. Thad offered up his own prayer that God would help his father and that his friend would be freed. By the time Wade and Thad had the meal completed, Tuck was ready to eat.

"Chow's ready," Wade announced. "Here's your eatin' irons."

After supper was over, Tuck asked, "Have you been able to learn anything useful from the soldiers?"

"I don't think the soldiers respect Lieutenant Birch very much, although they don't come right out and say so," replied Thad. "I heard some saying that the War Between the States was over eighteen years ago. It's like beating a dead horse to try someone who was a boy of nine then."

"That's good to know. However, it will be before the colonel, not a jury trial," Tuck said. "This is so ridiculous; I feel like it's a dream, or more likely a nightmare. Poor Matt. This must be so hard for him." Tuck rubbed his eyes.

CHAPTER FOURTEEN

Building on Hold Again

Beth came to the office to give Belle Thad's message. She told her about the soldiers coming to take Matt Cutter away. So now Thad was off doing other things instead of building their new home. Though she tried not to have such an attitude, she couldn't help it. She wanted to be married to Thad, and it seemed there was always something going on to prevent it. It's all she could do to keep a calm attitude. Of course, it wasn't Thad's fault. Could it be she was really angry at God for this because He is the One in control? And then she was angry with herself for being angry with God? *When will we finally be able to marry? Father God, still my soul and give me Your peace about this.*

Belle prayed for them, knowing that the sooner this whole mess was resolved, the sooner Thad would be back and ready to start building their home. She asked that God would help her to pray for them instead of selfishly thinking of herself. Her prayers were for Tuck, that he'd be given God's wisdom to know how to help Matt. She prayed for Matt because he must be just devastated, having been taken away from his family by force, and she prayed for his wife and children too. They must be so worried. Belle's outlook changed once God turned her thoughts outward. *Thank you, Father.*

Belle knew that Tuck and Thad would move heaven and earth to help Matt through this tight spot in which he found himself because he was important to the whole Tucker family. She didn't know the particulars of why the soldiers came and took him away, but she did know that Tuck and Thad would help to straighten things out if they possibly could.

Sunday was a sad day without Thad at church and Belle certainly did miss him. Oh, how she missed him. Not getting to see him made each day that much emptier. But Reverend Prescott brought comfort from God's Word and in song.

"God commands us to seek and ask. Tell God all that's in your heart," Reverend Prescott advised. "James 1:5 says;

> *If any of you lack wisdom, let him ask of God, that giveth to all men liberally, and upbraideth not; and it shall be given him."*

"Let us sing together *Come My Soul.*"

Two verses stood out to Belle. She could feel the Holy Spirit speaking to her through the words of this song:

Come My Soul
Come, my soul, thy suit prepare,
Jesus loves to answer pray'r.
He Himself has bid thee pray,
rise and ask without delay

With my burden I begin,
Lord, remove this load of sin!
Let Thy blood, for sinners spilt,
set my conscience free from guilt.

CHAPTER FIFTEEN
Matt's Trial Begins

The three men from Deer Creek Ranch rose early the morning of the trial. Thad could tell Pa was nervous. In the two days previous, Tuck made several trips to the telegraph office to inquire if there was an answer to his wire. Tuck didn't feel adequate to represent Matt, so he spent more time in prayer.

The trial was being held in the mess hall after the first meal of the day had been cleared away. The men didn't go there for breakfast, choosing instead to make their own at the camp. When they'd eaten, Tuck rose and said, "I want to check one more time for a wire. I'll meet you at the mess hall."

When Tuck joined them at the mess hall, he held a telegram in his hand, but his face showed Thad that it was not what he wanted to hear. "What does it say?"

Tuck handed the wire to Thad.

> *Proceed with defense while I look into the situation.*
> *President Arthur*

"Well. At least he responded and is not shutting the door entirely," Thad said and passed the wire to Wade for him to read.

"I sure had hoped I wouldn't have to go ahead with this. I don't feel like I have what it takes to make a defense for Matt. I don't want him to be found guilty because of me."

Thad saw the look of apprehension in his pa. He put his hand on Tuck's shoulder and bowing his head; he quietly prayed over Tuck. "Lord, please give Pa the words to say and give him the confidence to continue with this. Amen."

Tuck patted Thad's hand. "Thanks, son. I sometimes forget that this isn't too big for God to handle."

Thad noticed that Wade looked curious over this exchange between the two of them, so he silently added, *Bring Wade into your fold, Lord. Amen.* He hoped that one day his friend would trust in Jesus.

"Looks like they're getting ready," Wade said as they saw the tables pushed back and chairs lined up in a row.

They watched while their friend was brought into the mess hall, now serving as the courtroom. His hands were cuffed in front of him, and he was led to the defense table. Thad and Wade sat behind them. Lieutenant Birch sat opposite them at the prosecution's table. Tuck patted his "client" on the back and smiled, telling Matt this first day of the trial would address the charges and his identity. Matt nodded. Tuck showed no outward sign of nervousness.

47

Colonel Watson approached the front and addressed the room. "I will not be conducting the trial since there is a conflict with my acquaintance with those involved in defending Mr. Cutter. Therefore, pursuant to current military protocol and since the area circuit judge is passing through, I have appointed him to take over. All rise for the honorable Judge Horace Carmody presiding."

Thad and Tuck quickly looked at one another. They both recognized the name, even though the judge's hair was now almost all gray. Thad possessed an important document signed by Judge Carmody back in his desk at Deer Creek Ranch. A document which stated that Adam Tucker adopted Thad Eastman and his name subsequently changed to Tucker. He didn't realize he held his breath and now let it ease out slowly. *God, is this a sign?*

The judge said, "Be seated." He looked down at his papers and said, "I see this is a trial for desertion in the case of Matt Cutter. The prosecution is led by Lieutenant Birch and the defense by..." Judge Carmody looked to the defense table, having recognized Tuck's name, "Sheriff Adam Tucker, Retired."

Tuck nodded ever so slightly. Thad knew the judge recognized Pa's name, but he didn't know if that was good or not. He did note that Tuck's shoulders seemed to straighten at that point. Perhaps he felt more confident now, knowing who was presiding.

"Lieutenant Birch, state your case please," Judge Carmody directed the officer.

"Thank you, Your Honor. On March 3rd, 1865, Matt Cutter, being conscripted into the service of the Union Army, deserted his post ten days later. He's charged with desertion. He was..."

"Just a moment, Lieutenant," Judge Carmody interrupted him. "That was eighteen years ago. Is the United States Army still seeking retribution after all this time?" There was a chittering of low laughter throughout the hall.

"Order," the judge said.

"Yes, Your Honor," replied Birch. "We received this list of deserters that the Army wanted us to locate and charge. Cutter's name was on the list."

"May I see this list?"

Birch approached the judge and handed him a paper. The judge frowned. "This is a page from the Army in Washington?" he asked.

"Yes, sir...well... no, sir," the Lieutenant stammered.

"Well, which is it, Lieutenant Birch? Yes or no?"

"It's a copy of the original in my handwriting, sir," he responded.

"Most unusual. Tomorrow, I want to see the original order with an explanation as to why you copied it in your handwriting, Lieutenant," the

48

judge directed. "In the meantime, let's establish the identity of Mr. Cutter. Sir, would you please stand?"

Matt rose to his feet and waited for the judge.

"Please state your first and last name for the record," Carmody said.

"Matt Cutter."

The judge looked for a moment at the prisoner and asked, "Mr. Cutter, how old were you in April of 1865?"

"Nine-years-old, sir."

"Did you enlist?"

"No, sir, I did not! I was sold. My parents died, and a woman took me into her home, claiming she was my aunt. She wasn't. Three days later, she sold me to the Union Army." A gasp was heard throughout the room.

"Lieutenant Birch, I will need to see that list tomorrow before we can continue. Do not fail to bring it," the judge stated. "Gentlemen, we have heard the charges and have positively identified the defendant as Matt Cutter. Tomorrow we will continue. This court is adjourned," he said banging his gavel.

Lieutenant Birch stuffed his papers into his case and hurried from the hall, red-faced. Thad had the impression he was quite unhappy with how things transpired in the courtroom.

"Matt, I feel confident about this," Tuck was saying. "When I adopted the children, Judge Carmody was the circuit judge. Plus, I've had dealings with him in my work as sheriff."

Matt's eyes brightened at this. Thad knew that Pa felt more confident now that he saw Carmody was the presiding judge. *Lord, I pray this is a good sign and that we'll be taking Matt with us when we return to Deer Creek Ranch.*

"Are you going to talk to the judge?" Matt asked Tuck.

"No, I don't think that would be a smart thing to do," Tuck replied. "We don't want to give anyone cause to claim prejudice."

"Makes sense," Thad said. They said goodbye to Matt, and a private then took him back to the guardhouse. The ranchers and their ranch hand returned to their camp where they spent the rest of the day.

CHAPTER SIXTEEN
Tuck for the Defense

"All rise for the Honorable Judge Carmody. This military court of Fort Laramie is now in session."

"Be seated," the judge said. He looked over to the prosecution's table. "Lieutenant Birch, did you bring the original Federal order today?"

"Yes, Your Honor." Birch rose and took the document in question to the Judge's table.

"May I approach, Your Honor?" Tuck inquired.

Carmody waved him forward while he looked over the document, then handed it to Tuck. Tuck looked at it and gave it back to the judge who set it aside.

"Why did you bring a copy and not the original?"

"I wanted to make sure the original stayed in good shape."

Carmody shook his head. "Is the prosecution ready to give the opening statement?"

"I am Your Honor," Birch replied eagerly – too eagerly.

"Very well. Proceed."

"Your Honor, this deserter was inducted into the Union Army March 3, 1865. Ten days later he left his post and ran away. The defense will no doubt try to persuade you of his fine reputation now as a rancher. He'll provide those who will testify to his character in another move to gain your respect for him. But I'll show that this man is a deserter and ask that he be made to pay." Birch took his seat after delivering his statement with an angry punch on the last sentence.

"Is the defense ready to give its opening statement?"

"I am Your Honor," Tuck replied.

"Proceed."

"Thank you, Your Honor, I don't think Lieutenant Birch has any idea how I'll go about defending Matt Cutter. For one thing, Mr. Cutter was not inducted into the Union Army; he was sold! I'll reveal the atrocious behavior of his supposed guardian as well as the Union Army's part in it. He was a nine-year-old boy who just days before, lost both his parents and two siblings. While still reeling from his loss, he was sold to the Army by a woman he didn't even know. This woman falsely claimed that she was his aunt. Indeed, I'll speak of his fine reputation and how he is well-liked in his church and community. I intend to show that Mr. Cutter isn't a deserter. Thank you, Your Honor." Tuck sat down and waited.

"Lieutenant Birch, you may call your first witness."

Birch rose and called Sergeant Collins to the stand where he was sworn in. The lieutenant asked, "State your name and rank."

"Sergeant Daniel Collins, sir."

"Sergeant, did you arrest Matt Cutter?"

"Yes, sir. Per your orders, Corporal Simpson and I approached Mr. Cutter at his ranch two days ago. I asked him if he had been in the Union Army during the war."

"What did he say to that, Sergeant?"

"He said that he was for a short time when he was nine years old. We told him we were taking him back to Fort Laramie to stand trial for desertion."

"What did the defendant say then? Did he attempt to run?"

"No, sir. He came willingly. We allowed him to say goodbye to his wife and two children. sir, in my opinion, he didn't seem like…"

"That will be all, Sergeant," Birch interrupted him. "I didn't ask your opinion. No further questions, Your Honor."

"Sheriff Tucker, you may cross-examine the witness."

"Thank you, Your Honor." Tuck rose and approached the witness. "Sergeant Collins, when you told the defendant that you were arresting him for treason, was he angry?"

"No, sir. He just said that there must be some mistake. He wasn't a soldier. He was only a drummer boy."

"I see. Earlier you started to give your opinion when Lieutenant Birch cut you off. I would like to hear your opinion."

Birch rose from his chair. "Your Honor…"

Carmody raised his hand. "I'll allow it. I would also like to hear his opinion. Go ahead, Sergeant."

"Well, I've arrested men before, and they have acted like criminals, but Cutter didn't behave like one. I just thought we were wasting time on someone who wasn't that bad. After all, he was a boy at the time."

Thad observed Lieutenant Birch turn red at the collar. The man was pretty angry. He didn't envy Sergeant Collins after the trial was over. He believed that Birch could make difficulties for the sergeant.

"Your Honor," Tuck said. "I am done with the cross-examination of this witness."

"Lieutenant Birch, call your next witness."

"Your Honor, I call Corporal Simpson to the stand." Simpson approached the stand and was sworn in.

"Please state your name and rank," Birch directed him.

"Corporal Mark Simpson," he responded.

51

"Corporal, did you accompany Sergeant Collins to apprehend the defendant?"

"Yes, sir."

"Did you have the opportunity to converse with the defendant on the return trip?" Birch asked.

"Yes, I did, Sir. He told me he didn't even know how to play the drum. He couldn't understand why the Army did that to him. He also told me how his family had all died just the week before."

"So, he was not happy that he had been arrested?"

"Well, no sir. But he wasn't belligerent about it."

"That will do, Corporal! Your Honor," Birch said, turning to Judge Carmody. "I am finished with this witness."

"Does the defense wish to cross-examine this witness?"

"No, Your Honor," Tuck answered.

"Lieutenant Birch, do you have any further witnesses?"

"No, Your Honor. The prosecution rests."

"Would the defense call your first witness."

"I call Thad Tucker."

Thad rose and went to the witness chair and was sworn in.

"Tell us how you know Mr. Cutter," Tuck questioned his son.

"Well, he was the Overland stage driver for the Deadwood to Cheyenne route. My mother, my siblings, and I became operators of the Deer Creek Stagecoach Station. I was the hostler, and that's how I made his acquaintance."

"How old were you at this time?"

"I was sixteen when I first met Matt."

"And you found him to be of good character?" Tuck asked.

"Objection your Honor. The witness was only sixteen-years-old," Birch said, jumping to his feet. "What could he possibly know about a man's character?"

"Lieutenant Birch, Mr. Cutter was only nine when he entered the Army, and Mr. Tucker was sixteen. I find your objection ironic. Sit down. Proceed with your questioning, Sheriff Tucker."

"I'll repeat my question. Did you find Mr. Cutter to be of good character?"

"I certainly did," Thad replied.

"Thank you. I have no further questions."

"Lieutenant Birch, do you wish to question the witness?" Judge Carmody asked.

"Yes, Your Honor, I do," Birch said jumping to his feet and approaching the witness. "Mr. Tucker, if you only saw Mr. Cutter when the stage came in, how can you testify as to his good character in such small blocks of time?"

"Mr. Cutter was shot with an arrow by the Sioux Indians on one of his trips. The stage brought him into the stage station in pretty bad shape. He had lost a lot of blood by the time the stage came in. My mother nursed him back to health because there wasn't a doctor in the area. He stayed at our ranch for five weeks while his shoulder mended. My family counts him as one of our family now. We bought our cows from his ranch and found him to be fair and a good cattle rancher. He and his wife attend the same church my family does. The Cutters are always invited to our home for Christmas celebrations. Matt Cutter is an asset to the community of…"

"That's enough, Mr. Tucker," said Birch, seemingly irritated by Thad's response. "I have no more questions for this witness, Your Honor."

"Sheriff Tucker, call your next witness."

"Your Honor, I call Colonel Watson to the stand," Tuck said. There was a collective gasp throughout the makeshift courtroom.

Watson approached and took the stand, apparently unsure of why he was doing so. As Tuck neared the witness box, Thad thought he detected more of a confidence in his pa. He didn't know why Pa called Watson to the stand, but it wasn't long before he found out.

"Colonel Watson, I just have a couple of quick questions for you," Tuck opened. "Were you aware of the plan to arrest Matt Cutter and bring him in for trial?"

"No, not until he had returned with the prisoner."

"Colonel, would you look at this document and tell me who signed the order to have Matt Cutter arrested," Tuck directed him, handing over the document.

Watson took the document in question and looked at it. He raised his head and said, "No one. There is no signature."

"Since there is no signature, would you agree that this is not an order to arrest, but merely a list of deserters?"

"Yes, it's not an order," Watson agreed.

"Take another look at it, Colonel. What is the date at the top of the page?"

Watson did so, and as he read it, he looked over at Lieutenant Birch, frowning. "It says 1865."

"Thank you. Your Honor, I have no more questions for this witness."

"Lieutenant Birch, do you wish to question the witness?" Carmody asked.

"No, Your Honor. No questions."

"Your Honor, I call Matt Cutter to the stand."

53

Matt confidently approached the witness chair and was sworn in. Thad was pleased to see that he didn't appear apprehensive.

"Mr. Cutter, please tell us your age now."

"I'm twenty-seven."

"And how old were you when you entered the Army?"

"Nine-years-old!"

"Tell the court how you came to "be sold" into the Army."

"Objection, Your Honor," Lieutenant Birch rose from the table.

"Overruled, Lieutenant. We've already established that he didn't enlist," Carmody said. "Proceed, Sheriff Tucker."

"My parents and siblings died from drinking poisoned water. Since I had no relatives, a widow in town said she would take me in. Three days later, on my ninth birthday, she took me to the Union Army headquarters and sold me for the $200 induction fee."

"So, you never signed any papers when you entered the Army?"

"No."

"What was your position in the Army? Were you a Private?"

"No, I was a drummer boy."

"I see. So, you knew how to play a drum?"

"No. I had no idea how. Mrs. Lewis lied and said I did so she could get the money."

"I understand that you left your post a few days later. Tell the court how you came to leave and what you did after that."

"I was devastated by the deaths of my family. And the fact that one of the reasons the war was being waged was to fight against slavery wasn't lost upon me. I felt as though Mrs. Lewis had treated me like a slave by selling me to the Army. But most of all, the bloody carnage was more than I could handle at my young age. Every day, I threw up what little food I was given. I ran away one night and went back to the widow's home, but she'd already left. She'd taken her things, but fortunately, I found some of my belongings and some dried food that had been left. I packed that with some of my clothes that I could easily carry and headed west on foot."

"Traveling as far as St. Louis, I found a way to live by catching fish along the Mississippi River. I sold the catfish I caught to a lady named Mary who ran a cafe. I think she assumed I lived up the River with my parents. Mary fed me one good meal a day, and she paid me a few coins for the fish. A shopkeeper also paid me for catfish for his market. He let me sleep on a cot in his back room. I bought a horse with the money I saved. Daisy was an old nag that nobody else wanted, so I was able to get her real cheap. I took care of

Daisy, and I finally headed west after a few years. I hired on as the livestock boy for a wagon train heading out on the Santa Fe Trail."

"Your Honor, as interesting as this all may be, I don't think we need to hear it in this court," Birch objected, with a sneer.

"Lieutenant Birch, I will be the judge of what is heard in this courtroom. I'd like to hear about it. Continue, Mr. Cutter."

"By that time, I was fifteen-years-old and tall for my age. When we got to the Oklahoma Territory, I managed to get a job as a wrangler for a rancher. When I was nineteen, I married a young lady from a neighboring ranch. The rancher I worked for became a good friend, and he gave us a small tract of land on which to build a cabin. We started to develop our horse herd, but one day, a storm went through, and our cabin was hit by a tornado, killing my wife while I was working for the rancher.

"After losing my wife, I told the rancher I couldn't stay on in Oklahoma Territory because it was too painful, so I signed the land back over to him, sold my horses, and headed for Texas. There I signed up as a cowpuncher with a ranch owner driving his cattle to the Territory of Montana. I stayed there with him until the Overland Trail advertised for a stagecoach driver.

"While driving the stage, we were attacked by the Sioux up by Deadwood, and after five weeks, I returned to driving the stage. But even though my shoulder healed, the motion of handling the teams gave me plenty of problems. When it became too painful to drive the stage, I decided to resign, and Mattie and I got married. We started our ranch south of Mustang Ridge, the Double M Ranch. We have two children now."

"Thank you, Mr. Cutter," Tuck said. "I have no more questions for this witness, Your Honor," Tuck said.

"Lieutenant Birch, your witness," said the Judge.

Thad watched Birch as he stood and approached Matt. *I wonder what Birch will do now. Seems to me, Tuck is shooting down everything for the prosecution.*

Birch cleared his throat. "Mr. Cutter," Birch finally spoke. "Do you expect the court to believe that you are innocent of desertion, of treason against the very Army you joined?"

"I didn't "join" and I'm not a traitor!"

"So, you say, but this paper from the Army says differently," Birch said waving the list of deserters at Matt. Matt didn't blink an eye although the paper came close to his face.

"Lieutenant Birch!" Carmody banged his gavel. "Step away from the defendant!"

55

Birch stepped back as though burned. "I apologize to the court, Your Honor."

"You may continue, but I will tolerate no more of your harassment of the defendant in this court."

"Yes, Your Honor," Birch said, his face red. "Mr. Cutter, why do you think you had the right to leave the Army when your fellow soldiers could not?"

"They were soldiers, yes. But I wasn't. I was just a little boy who was treated wrongly by an evil woman."

"But you were not the only boy who served as a drummer boy, is that correct?"

"That's correct, but most were between twelve and sixteen years old. The Army had no business putting children into such service."

"How do you answer for the money that was paid by the Army for your service?"

"Lieutenant Birch, I was not paid that money. If I had, I would have paid it back long ago," Matt responded, growing tired of Birch's line of questioning.

"Mr. Cutter, this is..." Birch trailed off as the telegraph operator entered the room and went to Tuck, handing him the wire.

Tuck took a moment to read it, then standing he said, "Permission to approach, Your Honor." Carmody nodded and beckoned Tuck forward with his hand.

Handing the wire to the judge, Tuck said, "I just received this wire which has a bearing on this case."

Thad watched while the judge read through the contents of the wire and noticed a slight quirk at the corner of his mouth. Carmody looked up and smiled at Tuck and Matt. He started to say something while Tuck returned to his seat, then noticed that Birch was still standing. "Sit down, Lieutenant."

"But, sir. I have more questions for the defendant," Birch protested.

"No, you are done. Sit down," Carmody said firmly. Birch sat down.

The judge shuffled his papers before him on the table and cleared his throat. "First of all, Lieutenant Birch, the list you gave me was only a list. It was not an order for arrest and apprehension of those on it and was lacking a signature. Second, it was dated May 1, 1865, which fact I guess you failed to notice. I suggest in the future; you make sure of your facts before upsetting the lives of civilians. This wire which Sheriff Tucker brought to my attention is from President Arthur. The President says they do not wish to prosecute boys. He, therefore, has issued his pardon for Matt Cutter."

Rising to his feet, Lieutenant Birch said, "Your Honor, given this new information, I move to dismiss this case against Matt Cutter."

"How prudent of you, Lieutenant Birch, that you do not want to disagree with the President of the United States," said Judge Carmody. The Judge was almost smirking but not quite. He turned to Matt and said, "Will the defendant please stand."

Matt rose to his feet, ready for the verdict.

"Matt Cutter, you have had a hard childhood what with the loss of your family and the way you were "inducted" into the Union Army, but I believe it made you the man you are today. I apologize that the United States treated you so abominably. But I admire how you made a good life for yourself and your family and didn't allow it to affect how you lived. I suggest you keep this wire in a safe place in case an Army officer comes across an outdated list again." Carmody looked pointedly at Lieutenant Birch. "Mr. Cutter, you are free to go. This court is no longer in session." The Judge banged the gavel one last time.

Thad and Tuck vigorously shook hands with Matt and clasped him on the back. Tuck stepped back and watched as the judge prepared to leave the room. Carmody gave a slight nod to Tuck, and he returned it. They spoke no words, no acknowledgment of the fact that they knew each other.

Colonel Watson approached their group and spoke. "Gentlemen, I sincerely apologize for my lieutenant's behavior. He will not be enjoying that rank for long." He shook hands with Matt. "God speed, young man."

"Thank you, sir," Matt said.

When they left the mess hall, Tuck said, "As it says in the Bible, 'Let's shake the dust from our feet and leave this place.' It's time for us to hit the road." Wade went to the stables and retrieved Matt's horse. They began to break camp, taking down the tent and packing it along with the cooking utensils on the pack horse. They were saddling their horses when Judge Carmody rode into their camp area and dismounted.

The men shook hands with him. Matt said, "Judge, thank you."

"Matt, don't thank me. Sheriff...uh... Mr. Tucker did it all. I was just along for the ride, but I see you're getting ready to leave. Might I ask to accompany you? I find that I need to go to Mustang Ridge to hold court over three would-be horse thieves." The Judge smiled when he said this. "It seems that you Tuckers have been busy."

"Certainly, Judge. Good to have you along," Tuck happily agreed.

Thad marveled at how the arrest of the horse thieves had led to the assignment of Matt's case to Judge Carmody. God works in mysterious ways, His wonders to perform.

# # #

The ride back to Deer Creek Ranch was uneventful. They made camp along the way for two nights. The ranchers enjoyed their time with Carmody and he seemed pleased for the company. Thad supposed his was a lonely life, traveling from one place to another by himself.

They stopped off in Mustang Ridge before saying their goodbyes. Thad asked the judge, "Will you need us to testify at the trial?"

"Yes. I'll hold court tomorrow morning," the judge answered him.

"We'll be here," he promised, and they left town to head back to the ranch.

Thad laughed as Little Tuck ran out onto the ranch-house veranda and jumped up and down with excitement when he saw his father. Matt couldn't get off his horse fast enough to get down on one knee and hug his boy. Then came little Louisa running into him so hard, he nearly fell over backward. He rose, then turned to his wife, Mattie and swung her around in a circle. Matt Cutter was one happy man. His family was glad to see him.

"Tuck, I knew you'd be able to help him," Mattie said. "You're a great friend."

"Glad I was able to help," Tuck replied. "But President Arthur had a part in it too."

"I hate to run off right away, but I'd like to get my family back home," Matt said. "Make sure my ranch is still in one piece."

"Oh, Matt. Our ranch hands are perfectly capable of taking care of the ranch in our absence," Mattie said. "But I'm anxious to get back home too now that we're all together again."

"I know, Mattie. I'm just anxious to be home with my family. I was starting to think I may never see you again." Matt's voice broke while he hugged her again. Turning to Tuck, he said, "Tuck, my friend, I owe you my life. Thank you. I'll never forget this."

Goodbyes and thanks were said along with congratulations on the victory. The Cutter family left and life returned to normal for the Tuckers at Deer Creek Ranch.

CHAPTER SEVENTEEN
Emergency for Nate

A few days later when Tuck rode out to check on his cattle in the southwest meadow, Beth decided to accompany him. Becca had left early for school and Nate would go in later. After feeding the livestock, Thad headed to the ranch-house. He planned to go to the mill and order lumber for the home he was to build. However, upon entering the house, he found his brother doubled over in pain, his face a pasty kind of white.

"Nate, what's wrong?"

"Take me into the doctor," he gasped while holding his lower right-hand side.

Thad helped him to sit down, saying he would get the buggy hitched up and be back to get him. As they traveled the 30-minute trip into Mustang Ridge, Thad kept an eye on his brother. From the look on Nate's face, he felt every bump. Thad didn't know whether to slow down and take longer or speed up and risk more pain.

Nate answered his unspoken thought, "Go faster, Thad. I need to get to the doctor as soon as you can get me there."

"Okay, Nate," he said, flicking the reins above the back of Rowdy.

Thad thought they'd never get to town. Most likely his brother felt the same way. *Please, God. Help Nate and please let Doc Phillips be there.*

As the doctor's office appeared on his right, Thad swung the buggy around, halted the horse and jumped down, tying Rowdy to the hitching rail. He came around to Nate's side of the buggy and helped him down. It was hard getting him up to the sidewalk because Nate was now as tall as Thad and he had become dead weight for Thad to maneuver him. He wondered how he was going to open the door when Belle opened it for him.

One look at Nate's face and Belle knew something was seriously wrong. Not to mention the fear on Thad's face. "Bring him to the back room and lay him on the table," she instructed him.

Doc Phillips heard his nurse's voice and hurried out of his office. "What seems to be wrong?"

"Nate's in a lot of pain," Thad said after laying him on the table.

"Nate, can you hear me?" The only answer was a moan. "Does it hurt when I press here?" He pressed where Nate had been holding his lower abdomen earlier. Nate cried out.

Doc Phillips motioned for Thad to step out of the office. "Thad, he has a lot of swelling where the appendix is located."

"Appendix? "Thad asked. "What's that?"

"Doctors are just learning about ways to deal with it. I'm afraid if the inflammation is allowed to build, it may burst. But I need to operate to keep it from bursting."

"Have you done this kind of operation before?" Thad asked. He was mindful of Doc's words regarding doctors just learning about it.

"No Thad, I haven't. Nor have I seen it performed. Doctor Lawson Tait successfully performed this surgery in London three years ago. He's detailed it in a medical journal, and I believe I can do it also."

No one spoke for a while. Doc asked, "Where are Tuck and your mother?"

"They're out on the range."

"So, they don't know about this?"

"No, Will I have time to go get them?"

"No, Thad. I need to start right away. Can you send someone after them? And what about Becca? I think Nate's family needs to be here."

Belle spoke up at this point, "Thad, hurry down to the blacksmith shop. Papa can go out and find Tuck and your mother. Then you go get Becca."

Thad nodded and hurried out to his buggy. Thad raced the horse to the smithy and explained to him the problem. Jacob nodded and was mounting his horse as Thad sped toward the schoolhouse as fast as Rowdy could go. When he pulled up to the building, he saw his sister standing at the door while the students filed in, ready to begin the school day. He saw her send a questioning look his way when he leaped from the buggy.

"What's wrong, Thad?" She knew by his speed with the buggy and from the look on his face that something serious was afoot.

"It's Nate. I brought him into the office. Doc Phillips says it's something called the appendix. He may need to operate. Doc said we all should be there."

"Oh, no!" Becca exclaimed, tears beginning to form.

Sarah Wells was standing by Becca and spoke up at that point. "Becca, go with your brother now. I'll take care of the school for the rest of the day."

"Thank you, Sarah," Becca said.

"Thanks, Sarah. I sent Jacob out to get Ma and Pa," Thad said, and Sarah nodded.

"Go! Now!" Sarah directed

The siblings sat in the doctor's office while he and his nurse were with Nate. The outer door swung open, and they looked up to see Tuck and Beth hurrying in.

"How is he?" Tuck asked them. Becca went to her mother and they hugged each other.

"I don't know, Pa. I went to get Becca and when I got back, they were in there. Doc said he was concerned about his appendix bursting. Jacob must have found you right away?"

"Yes, he didn't have to look far. We were riding in from the range when he rode in," Beth stated.

Tuck pulled his chair up to his family and reaching for their hands he said, "We need to seek the Lord on Nate's behalf."

No sooner was the last prayer finished, than Doc Phillips opened the surgery door and came out. Four voices demanded of him, "Doc, how is he?"

"I'm glad everyone made it. Nate is in a lot of pain. I'm afraid I have no choice now. I need to operate to save his life. Tuck, Beth, did Thad tell you I've never done or seen this done before?"

"Yes," Tuck answered. "What happens if it does burst and you don't operate?"

"He will probably die. I'm sorry to be so blunt, but time is a factor here."

Tuck nodded, "Tell me Doc, if this was your child, would you say to operate given what you just told me?"

"Yes, I would. Immediately."

Tuck looked to his wife who nodded. "Do it, Doc, operate and save his life."

CHAPTER EIGHTEEN
Nate's Surgery

Following the surgery, Doc came to talk to Nate's family. "As I suspected, it had started to burst. However, I think I was able to drain all the infection out while I had him opened. He's still under the effects of the ether, so I can't tell you how he'll recover. I do know that he did well during the surgery."

Thad breathed a sigh of relief. Thank you, God, for this news. Please help Nate to heal.

"Will we be able to take him home when he wakes up?" Beth asked.

"Oh, no!" Doc exclaimed. "I'll need to keep him here for a few days. Complete recovery will be about six weeks. I don't think we should risk a ride to the ranch. He will need to be on bed rest so I will keep him here at the office for one week. If at least one of you can stay with him, it will help us out."

Nate's family opted to stay until he woke up. Thad talked with his parents and Becca about going home to do chores. They knew Tuck would not leave Nate's side and neither would their mother. Now, they would wait for him to waken.

Belle opened the door and called, "Doctor, could I see you for a moment?"

Thad's heart dropped when the doctor hurried through the door, closing it behind him. *Something is wrong. I can feel it.* He could see in his family's faces they were fearful of the same thing. After what seemed like an eternity, Belle entered the waiting area with the news.

"Doc sent me out to let you know that Nate was waking up, but the pain was so intense for him he was forced to put him under again. He won't be waking up for a while now."

"Can his mother and I be with him? Just to sit by him and hold his hand?" Tuck implored Belle.

"I'll ask Doc Phillips," she replied.

When she returned, she said, "Doc said it would be okay for you to sit with him."

Tuck and Beth rose to enter the room; then Tuck turned to Thad and Becca. "Maybe you can go down to Sally's Café and get dinner," he said. "I'm sure you're probably hungry since its well past meal time."

Thad looked to his sister who nodded. "Can we bring you something?"

Tuck nodded. "Maybe a sandwich or something like that." He knew they wouldn't be any good to Nate if they were weak from hunger.

When they entered the café, Thad saw Sam Garrison having a cup of coffee. He came over to their table and asked if everything was okay. Sam thought it unusual that Thad and Becca were in town in the middle of the afternoon, especially when Becca was the school teacher.

"It's Nate," Thad explained. "It was his appendix. Doc just finished operating. Nate was in so much pain; Doc was forced to put him under again."

"I'm so sorry," Sam said. "Are your folks with him?"

"Yes, they sent us to get food," Thad explained

"Doc said he'd need to be confined to bed for six weeks," Becca said. "The ride to the ranch would be too bumpy."

"Folks, I'm going to go tell Martha and I'll stop by Reverend Prescott's to tell him too."

"I hadn't even thought of him. Of course, we'll want him there. Thank you, Sam."

They returned to the doctor's office and Thad gave Beth her food. Tuck came out of the surgery room to stretch while Doc examined Nate.

"Is there any change, Pa?" Thad asked giving his pa a sandwich.

"No, he's still out."

"We saw Sam at the café, Pa, and he said he was..." Thad stopped when the outer door opened and in walked the Garrisons with Reverend Prescott in tow. "And here they are now."

Martha Garrison hugged a teary-eyed Beth as well as Becca while the menfolk shook hands. Sam patted Tuck on his shoulders. The newcomers were apprised of Nate's condition, and they joined hands and bowed in prayer with Reverend Prescott leading.

Martha sat down next to Beth and said, "My friend, I understand that Nate has to be confined to bed for six weeks, that the bumpy drive to the ranch is out of the question. I want to offer our home for him to recuperate in as soon as the doctor thinks he can be moved there. We have those two guest bedrooms you know, so there would be plenty of room for you and Tuck to stay there too. That way, he would be in town and close by if the doctor were needed."

Beth nodded. "Thank you, Martha. You're so kind."

Tuck said, "Yes, Martha. We appreciate your offer. We'll see what the doctor says after Nate is awake."

Belle came out to the waiting area. There had been no change, but she still wanted to offer comfort to the family. She took Thad's hand.

I guess this will put a hold on my plans to build for a while. I can't leave the ranch now that Nate isn't there. He looked to Belle while that thought settled in his head. Belle returned his look. Was she thinking the same thing? Still, Thad didn't want his parents to be left short-handed so that he could build his and Belle's future home.

After a week went by following Nate's surgery, Doc Phillips talked to Tuck and Thad about moving him to the Garrison's home to recuperate. They brought a wagon to the office and made a bed in it for Nate to lie down. Thad and his pa carried him to the wagon bed using a canvas stretcher. They slowly drove the wagon to the Garrison's home and moved him into their house in the same manner.

The guest room where Nate was to stay was on the first floor, which was fortunate because the men didn't have to carry him up any more steps than necessary. The five steps up to the porch were enough for them. It was a large room, and next door was a room where Beth and Tuck could spend the night without being far from him.

Nate had not spoken since coming out of the ether-induced sleep a week ago. Thad was worried about his brother. No one in his family wanted to voice this fear to each other, or Doc Phillips. Doesn't anyone notice this except for me? He vowed to ask Doc about it the first chance they were alone.

The opportunity arose when Thad drove the doctor in his wagon back to the office.

"Just drive the wagon around to the back," Doc directed him.

As Doc prepared to leave the wagon, Thad said, "Wait, Doc. I need to talk to you."

"Sure, Thad. What is it?"

"Doc, surely you've noticed that Nate hasn't said one word since the day of the surgery. There is something wrong that you aren't telling us." He stated this rather than questioned.

"No, Thad. I don't believe there is. This surgery proved to be life-saving for your brother, but it was quite traumatic as well. I've had other surgical patients react in similar ways following the trauma of invasive surgery, though not for this long a time. And he is still in pain. The fact that I had to introduce the ether a second time may have a bearing on it also. I will be reducing the amount of Laudanum. It can be quite addicting, so I don't want to use it any longer than necessary. It's my opinion that now he is with the Garrison's and your ma and pa are staying with him, that he will revive as the love of family and friends surrounds him. Discontinuing the Laudanum should help too."

"Thanks for putting my mind at ease, Doc," Thad said, and they shook hands.

"Thad. I'm not abandoning him. I will visit him every day until I am satisfied that he is improving. And Belle will be there daily to change his surgical dressing too."

Thad's sigh of relief at what Doc told him was nearly audible. He was glad he had spoken to him about his concerns.

In the following weeks, when Thad visited Nate, he made sure to time his visit to when Belle came to change his dressing. When she was done, they would go to Sally's Café for a cup of coffee before she returned to work. He was pleased with the improvement he witnessed in his brother. Nate was now talking and enjoying his visits from family and friends from church. However, the ordeal of the dressing change and the bath in bed was exhausting for him. The Laudanum was now given only at that time, so when Belle left his bedside, he fell into a deep slumber.

Tuck returned to the ranch to take care of ranch business. Though he was thankful to the Garrisons for the use of their home for Nate, Tuck was looking forward to having his family back home with him. Thad understood how Tuck felt. When they first met, seven years ago, a special friendship developed between six-year-old Nate and then-Sheriff Tucker. Tuck was drawn to Nate because he was the same age as his own son would have been. *Father, please let Nate continue to improve and help us to be patient with his healing.*

CHAPTER NINETEEN
Belle

Poor Nate was in so much pain. Belle was nervous, wondering if everything would work out okay. She could see that Doc Phillips was concerned too. Having worked with him for as long as she had, she'd learned to read him pretty well. And it scared her to see his concern. Or maybe it wasn't concern. Perhaps it was his fear. Fear that he didn't know what to do.

The fact that he had never performed this surgery he needed to do now on Nate was equally scary. *Father in Heaven, please guide the doctor's hands and bring Nate through this safely.*

Belle tried to be as helpful as she could to the family, but Doc kept her busy assisting him. She knew it was touch and go for Nate. When Tuck and Beth agreed for Doc to do the surgery even though it had not been done here before, Belle knew it was Nate's only chance of survival. That and the hope they all had from God.

After the surgery, Doc went out to talk to the family, and Belle applied Nate's dressing while he was still unconscious. Nate began moaning and thrashing around. She couldn't settle him down, and knew he would be in trouble if he didn't. She went to the door and as calmly as she could, asked Doc if he could come back in. Belle realized her calmness didn't fool Thad for one minute when she saw the fear wash over his face.

One member of Nate's family stayed with him in Doc's office for the first week. Usually, it was Beth who stayed, but sometimes Tuck or Thad did. It was a help to Doc and even Belle to have someone care for Nate while she and Doc dealt with other patients' needs.

Then the day came when Doc said they could move Nate to the Garrisons home for the remaining time. It wasn't far and the men were careful in moving Nate. Belle went ahead of them to prepare the room, so she was at the Garrisons when they brought him. Both she and Doc checked to make sure he was okay after the move.

Belle was glad that she could do her part in giving Nate's family a sense of peace with his recovery. Seeing Thad every day was a plus for her, but she knew that the whole Tucker family was still worried about Nate. Hopefully, by being there, she could offer them a small amount of comfort.

Belle realized this proved to be a setback in the building of their home. She understood it, but it was still disappointing. *Father, heal Nate and help me with my impatience.*

#

As time went on and the warmer weather arrived, Mustang Ridge began to plan for the big Independence Day celebration. The town women had many activities planned, and Thad was planning to race his new horse, Tops, in the town's horse race. They were all invited to sit on the Garrison's veranda to watch the race. Nate would be able to come out to watch, and as his nurse, Belle would be there to supervise.

Belle had sewn a special red, white, and blue scarf for Thad to wear while he raced his horse. Just before the race began, she tied it around his neck and wished him a good race. She probably should have done it before he was at the starting line because he seemed to forget why he was there. She could see the love in his eyes. She was so thankful to God for bringing Thad into her life, even when she was only twelve-years-old. *God plans things in our lives before we're even able to consider them. And I'm so thankful that Thad waited for me to grow up.*

67

CHAPTER TWENTY
Independence Day Celebration

It was Independence Day and the town made ready for a big celebration. Tuck obtained permission from Doc Phillips for Nate to sit on the Garrison's front veranda to enjoy the festivities. The town planned a horse race, and when they neared the finish line, they would run past the Garrison's house. Thad knew that Nate had planned to ride in the race and hoped he could enjoy it without being too disappointed. He planned to race Tops, one of his thoroughbred horses. The horse was all black except for a white face.

The whole family was seated on the veranda with the Garrisons, along with Belle and her family. Following the race, the group would have a picnic in that spot. When it came time for the race, Thad excused himself to go with Tops to the starting line. There, Belle tied a red, white, and blue scarf around his neck, wishing him a good race.

The course began in front of the mercantile, headed north away from the ridge, west across the flats, and came in on the south side of Mustang Ridge. The riders passed the Garrison home on the way to the finish line which was in front of the mercantile.

As Thad sat on Tops at the start, he held Belle's scarf to his face, breathing in the scent of her rose water. It was almost intoxicating to him. *I'd better get my head back into the race.*

The riders gathered at the starting line while Sheriff Charlie Yates stood ready to fire his revolver to start them on their way. A couple of horses were giving their riders problems because they wouldn't stay in one place. *I guess the horses are as excited to get going as we riders are.*

Bang! And they were off.

"Atta boy," Thad called to his horse. "Go, Tops, go!"

He and his horse raced as one, intent on the trail ahead. All thought of Belle was relegated to the back of his mind, making room for the task at hand, that of finishing this race. Aware that Tops was not the only good racing horse, he paced him, not wanting to tire his horse like the other riders seemed to be doing. It was a five-mile course, and he didn't want his horse to be used up before the finish. When they neared the town, Thad didn't have to urge Tops on. His horse moved ahead on his own.

"You can do it, boy. I know you have it in you. Let's go, Tops. Go!"

As the riders came around through town, Thad and Tops had moved up to third place. He was vaguely aware of his friends and family cheering him on when he sped past the Garrisons. By the time they approached the finish line, Thad and another rider were neck and neck. However, crossing the finish line, the other rider's horse sped ahead at the last minute, and Thad came in second. Thad was happy with second place. After all, it was a day of celebration. He congratulated the winner wholeheartedly.

"Tops, you ran a good race. Good boy." Thad dismounted and led Tops around in a slow walk. After his horse seemed to catch his wind, he let him drink from the trough, and then he took the horse into the livery to rub him down. The sweat glistened on the horse's coat, and Thad wanted to make sure he was dry.

"Thad!" Belle called his name when she entered the livery. "Congratulations. You and Tops ran a good race. I am so proud of you."

"Thanks, Belle. It was a good race. Tops did a good job considering there hasn't been much time to train with him."

Becca patted the horse's neck and whispered, "I have a treat for you, Tops, since you ran such a good race." She slipped a fat carrot from her skirt pocket and gave it to him. The horse snapped it up greedily.

"Tops, if you are that hungry, you'd better eat these oats," Thad said laughing.

"Now that he is dry, fed and watered, we can go back to the Garrisons and feed and water us as well," Thad said. "The smells at the ranch early this morning made my mouth water."

"Okay, then. Let's go have a picnic! My family is there too, so it will be a good time." Belle placed her hand on his arm and practically skipped along the sidewalk.

When they mounted the steps to the Garrison's veranda, Tuck came and slapped Thad fondly on the back. "Well done, son. Well done."

"Thanks, Pa. It was a thrill. And to think – I just about didn't race what with everything going on."

"Good job, Thad," Nate called from his seat. "What is the prize for second place?"

Thad laughed. "My practical brother. Second place prize is $5 and first is $10. I think Tops and I will have to work to train for next year. He's a good racer. Good advertisement for my horses."

"Hopefully, I can take part in the race next year too," Nate said.

"The Tucker brothers riding again," Tuck remarked. "That would be great!"

"I've got just the horse for you too," Thad said.

The large group filled up the veranda. They had a great time visiting and eating. The food table was inside the house, and when they wanted more, they just went inside to help themselves. Thad was pleased to note that Nate's voracious appetite returned.

69

When evening settled on Mustang Ridge, the town wound up the celebration with fireworks. Thad was sure that Sam took on the cost, having sent away for them himself. The group enjoyed the fireworks from Sam's veranda, and Thad enjoyed spending the evening with Belle watching. Another Independence Day had come and gone.

CHAPTER TWENTY-ONE
Nate's Homecoming

Nearly six weeks had passed since Nate's surgery and now they were bringing him back to the ranch for good. Becca was at home because it was Saturday, so of course there was no school. Thad took the buggy into town to pick up Nate and Tuck. Beth returned to the ranch the day before so she could get things ready for Nate, leaving Tuck to stay the night with Nate.

Nate was a chatterbox while Thad drove them to the ranch. *And to think, six weeks ago I was concerned that he never spoke.* His glance at Tuck revealed his pa's full grin. Evidently, he was thinking the same.

When they pulled up to the ranch-house Beth and Becca rushed to greet Nate. Even though they visited him the day before, it was as if they hadn't seen him for days. Thad knew his ma was happy to have everyone back home again. He watched while his parents shared a warm hug and kiss when they thought no one saw. Once again, he thought, *there will come a time when Belle and I will share our love in the same way.*

"Nate, are you hungry?" Becca asked. "I made your favorite meal for dinner."

"You mean, you made a beef roast with potatoes and carrots?" Nate almost drooled.

"I did. Are you ready to eat or has your convalescence decreased your appetite?"

"Ha! That would be the day," Tuck laughed. "Poor Martha probably never cooked so much food in one day before."

They laughed while they each took their seats at the table and Tuck offered the blessing over the food.

"It's good to be home," Nate shared. "Becca, thanks for the welcome-home dinner." He began shoveling the food into his mouth, as if he hadn't already eaten a huge breakfast prepared by Martha.

"So, how's everything on the ranch?" Nate asked around a mouthful of food.

"Nate, don't talk with your mouth full," his mother protested.

"Sorry."

Tuck laughed. "Welcome home, Nate. Just like you never left."

"So, did the doctor say you could get right back to ranch work?" Thad inquired. "Because if he said it was okay, one of us needs to ride our north fence-line." Thad laughed at the horrified expressions on both Nate's and his mother's faces.

"I don't care if the doctor said he could or not! He's not getting up on a horse for quite a while," Beth declared. "Tuck, what did the doctor say?"

"Just what you said," Tuck replied with a grin directed towards his wife. "No lifting anything heavy and no horseback riding until after he goes back for Doc Phillips to see him. Just walking for exercise."

"When will he need to see Doc Phillips again?" Beth asked.

"In two weeks."

"Well, I guess no line riding then, unless you could do it in a buggy." Thad laughed, but seeing the look on his mother's face, he said, "But I guess that won't work either. Don't fret; we'll find a chore for you to do."

"Well, I think I will just him continue his convalescence here in the ranch-house where I can keep an eye on him. At least until he goes back to see Doc Phillips," Beth stated. "I'll continue to do his chicken chores."

"How are my chickens doing?" Nate asked, apparently anxious to turn the conversation away from what he could and couldn't do.

"Growing," his mother shared. "The younger hens are laying very well indeed. And I think the older hens are ready to be butchered. When we butcher them, I will can the meat. You've got quite a few nice-sized roosters too, which'll make some good Sunday dinners." Nate nodded. Thad knew he was proud of his chickens and the fact that they did their share to supply food for his family's table. They weren't pets; they were an investment.

After cleaning two plates of food, Nate asked, "What's for dessert?"

"Gooseberry pie," Becca said. "I made it just for you."

"Well, bring it here then," he invited. "I always like to have your gooseberry pie, Becca."

After the trip out to the ranch and all that food, Beth decided that Nate needed to go lie down and rest and she sent a perfectly willing Nate off to his room. He was apparently more worn out than they knew for he slept the entire afternoon away, only waking at chore time. He came out of his room with a yawn and stretched as he asked, "Ma, is it okay if I walk out to the barn with you while you take care of the chickens?"

Beth looked to Tuck, who said, "Yes, Doc said for him to do lots of walking. That will help to keep things working inside."

"Pa!" Nate protested, embarrassed that these things were being talked about openly.

"It's family, Nate," his mother replied matter-of-factly. "Yes, come along. I'm going out now."

Thad and Tuck went to the barn to take care of the livestock. Becca was taking care of her goats in their shed. A couple of years ago, Tuck erected a shed just for her goats with their own little corral. Nate's chickens also had an addition added to the side of the barn since they had outgrown the original area.

Nate used the hand scoop to put chicken feed into their pans. He even gathered the eggs, but his mother held the pail. When the eggs had been gathered, he walked over to the goat shed where Becca was milking her goats. "Wish I could help you, Becca."

"Maybe you can. Matilda likes to be milked up here on her platform. Do you think you could do that?"

"Sure," Nate said eagerly. "That oughta be okay with Ma."

"What should be okay with Ma?" Beth asked from the doorway."

"Do you think he could milk Matilda from her platform?" Becca asked.

"As long as he's not bending too much, I think so. And maybe just for a little while."

Becca herded Matilda up on to her platform and Nate began milking her. Thad and Tuck stood outside the goat shed watching as they were finished with their livestock chores in the barn. *It's good to have everyone home again. Father, thank you for my family and please continue to heal Nate.*

They all helped carry the eggs and milk to the ranch-house, except for Nate, that is. Becca set the milk in the cooler in the root cellar. Later she would skim the cream from the top so she could churn butter. Beth took the eggs to the cooler also then went back upstairs to put supper on the table. There was left-over beef roast even though Nate had eaten quite a bit at noon. She'd made sourdough bread that morning and she used that to make delicious sandwiches.

Thad thought his mother and sister were wonderful cooks. Their meals were always so delicious. He recalled how the stagecoach passengers would praise Ma's cooking when they were operating the station. *I wonder if Belle is a good cook. I've had delicious things she has made, so that is a good sign. But I'd love her regardless.*

CHAPTER TWENTY-TWO
Nate Receives Clean Bill of Health

The day arrived when Nate was to see Doc Phillips, so Beth drove him in the buggy while Thad and Tuck rode their horses into Mustang Ridge. They all went to the doctor's office with Nate to see what Doc said.

"Nate, you are healing nicely," Doc said after examining him. "I'm releasing you to light lifting only, but it's too soon for you to ride a horse. You need to wait another five weeks before I can okay that. Simple chores and like I said, light lifting. Go at it slow and easy."

"Thanks, Doc. That's good to hear. It was getting hard not to do anything in the way of chores."

"Just don't go out and lift a boulder. Slow and…"

"I know. Slow and easy."

Thad looked at Belle and asked, "Would you like to have dinner after a bit?"

"Yes," she replied. "In about thirty minutes."

Later, as they sat eating in Sally's Café, Belle asked Thad, "Why are you all in town?"

"We're all interested in Nate's outcome," Thad responded. "Ma and Pa, of course, wanted to be with Nate. Me? I wanted to see his nurse."

Belle smiled at him slyly. "You're such a rascal!"

"Yes, I admit it. I did have an ulterior motive."

"When are you going to start on our ranch-house?" Belle asked him.

"Well, now that Nate is better, I can start getting ready," Thad answered her. "I'll wait a few weeks to make sure he can handle things and be sure he can ride a horse. I don't want to buy the lumber and have it just set out there in the weather because I can't get to it. And I still need to sell my horses."

"I understand."

"Thanks, Belle. I'm getting rather anxious about getting started myself. I think I'll stop at the telegraph office after I walk you back to Doc's office. I'll send another wire to the buyer up north."

"I'd wait forever for you, Thad. I just hope I don't have to."

"Look who just came into the Café," Belle said, looking toward the door.

Thad turned to look and was surprised to see his sister with a well-dressed young man. He had short brown hair and was clean-shaven.

"I wonder who that is with her," she said. "I haven't seen him around here before. Should we acknowledge them?"

74

Thad could tell that Belle really wanted to. He knew she wanted to know the identity of the man with Becca. "Maybe it's that education superintendent. Let's wait for them to notice us."

As Becca and her companion made their way to an empty table, she glanced their way. Thad saw her mouth form an "O" and she turned to the fellow with her. He looked toward Thad and Belle and his eyes lit up. However, Thad knew from her expression that his sister was reluctant to talk to them.

As they started to wind their way towards Thad and Belle's table, Belle asked him, "Should we ask them to join us?"

"No," he answered. "Pretty sure Becca doesn't want that. This guy is special to her, but she isn't ready to share him with us over dinner."

"Yes, I saw that expression too. My dinner time is about over anyway, so we can just excuse ourselves once we meet."

"Thad, Belle. What are you doing here?" Becca questioned them.

"Came in for Nate's return doctor appointment. I took the opportunity to have dinner with my favorite nurse."

"This is Peter Rhodes, Superintendent of Education," Becca said. "Peter, this is my brother, Thad and his fiancée, Isabelle Wells."

Peter stepped forward to shake Thad's hand. "Pleased to meet you, Thad, Miss Wells. Becca has told me so much about the two of you."

Ain't that funny? She hasn't said a thing about you, Thad thought. But he kept his peace. "So, more testing?" he asked instead.

"Yes, Peter…uh… Mr. Rhodes is doing the oral testing today," Becca explained. "We just took a break for dinner."

"Thad, I really should get back to the office," Belle said.

"Right," he said getting up from the table. "Enjoy your dinner. Sally serves good food. "How long will you be in town, Mr. Rhodes?"

"A couple of days," he replied. "I have a room at the boarding house."

Suddenly Thad had a great idea and there was no stopping him. "Becca, why don't you bring Mr. Rhodes out to the ranch for supper tonight so he can meet Ma and Pa?"

Thad saw his sister turn so red that she looked feverish. "Well. I don't know…"

"I'd love to do that," Rhodes answered for her.

"Okay, tonight then. Becca can show you how to get to the ranch," Thad said as he and Belle left.

"You're going to be in so much trouble with Becca! Did you see her face?"

"Ha, ha, sure did. Looking forward to tonight. Want to come?"

"I would but I'm pretty sure I'll have something else to do. Be sure and let me know what all happens though."

Thad thought that might have been a lame excuse, but he didn't pursue it. Once he left Belle at the doctor's office, he high-tailed it to Deer Creek Ranch to let his mother know what he had done.

#

"Ma, I invited a gentleman-friend of Becca's to supper tonight," Thad told his mother upon entering their home.

"You what?" Beth demanded. "Wait, who is the friend?"

"Peter Rhodes, the guy who has been testing Becca. Belle and I saw them in Sally's Café. Since he's staying at the boarding house for a couple of days, I thought it would be nice to invite him to supper tonight."

Thad watched his mother as she went from shock to pleasure. He knew she would enjoy meeting this young fellow who might be someone important to Becca.

"That won't be a problem, will it Ma?" he asked, knowing full well she wouldn't feel put upon. He was sure the repercussions from his bold move would be felt for a while, even if it was so worth it! But it would be from Becca not his mother.

"No, dear. It will be fine. I will get a large ham out of the root cellar and add more potatoes. I'll start making a cake."

"I'll get the ham up for you," Thad offered.

"Thanks, dear. Bring up potatoes too."

CHAPTER TWENTY-THREE
Becca and Peter

Poor Becca. Thad almost felt sorry for his sister. At the supper table, Peter answered questions with ease concerning his position as Educational Superintendent. Thad found that he was genuinely impressed with Peter. He believed his sister had found an engaging young man. Becca, on the other hand, barely said a word. When Tuck asked about the testing that he was conducting with Becca, Thad saw his sister turn bright red. Peter began to stutter. This had gone too far, farther than he intended. He'd better fix it.

"Becca has always excelled in teaching," he said. "Even when we were younger, she helped Ma with teaching Nate. She helped teach the children on the wagon train too. Nate, remember what happened the time Becca was helping you and your friends to understand your studies on the wagon train?"

"Huh?" Nate raised his head as he looked squarely at his brother.

"Remember, about the dye that the Indians used?"

Nate choked on his food, but Thad appeared not to notice.

"Mmm-mmm," Nate mumbled. "I'd just as soon forget."

"What happened?" Peter asked Nate.

"Nothing, I…Thad was …well some boys and I got sick eating too many berries and Becca was showing us how the Indians used those berries for dye. That's all," Nate declared, glaring at his older brother.

Thad noticed during the laughter at the table, Becca also laughed and her embarrassment seemed to flee. Crisis averted, Thad went on to talk ranch-related subjects with Peter and Tuck. Becca relaxed and continued eating without further embarrassment. However, he kept an eye on his family during the rest of the meal, particularly Becca and Peter. Although he was no longer head of his family once Ma married Tuck, he still had a protective spirit where any of them were concerned. However, that didn't prevent him from engaging in the occasional teasing as evidenced earlier in the evening.

As Becca helped her mother to clear the table and put the food away, Thad noticed that Nate excused himself to go lie down in his room. He also saw his mother's concerned look follow Nate. Thad touched her arm, "Nate's okay, Ma. He's just a little tired. Doc said he would be."

She nodded and patted his hand on her arm. "Yes, dear. I know."

Thad saw that Tuck was taking Peter into their ranch office. "Coming, Thad?" Tuck inquired.

"Sure, be right there." He wasn't sure why he needed to join them. Maybe Tuck was being considerate of him. He soon found out that it was Peter who wanted him to come into the office.

"I wanted to talk to the both of you," he stated. "Becca has explained to me that while you are her adopted father, Mr. Tucker, that you, Thad, were the head of the family for several years. Because of that, I wanted to direct this question to both of you."

Thad chose that moment to sit in one of the leather chairs since he saw that this might take a while given how Peter had trouble getting to the point. He thought he knew what was coming and glanced at Tuck who also took a seat. "Have a seat, Peter," Tuck invited. Peter did so and continued with his speech.

"I would like to ask both of you for permission to court Becca." *Well, I guess he can come to the point*, Thad thought.

Thad again looked to his pa and nodded, indicating for him to go ahead. "Well, Peter. You seem like a nice young man. Is Becca agreeable to a courtship?"

"Thank you, sir," Peter replied. "Yes, she is."

"How do you plan to court her when you live in Cheyenne? That's quite a way away."

"I know it won't be easy, especially for Becca. Most of our courtship will have to be by letter, I'm afraid."

"Well, I guess you've thought it through. In that case, I am okay with a courtship. Thad?" Tuck's glance swung over to Thad.

"Huh?"

"Do you have anything to add?"

In his opinion, although Thad liked what he saw of Peter, he didn't think Becca could continue a long-distance relationship with Peter for very long. She would tire of being tied to someone who was never there and end it. In any case, he was saved from making a decision that would alienate his sister. So, he said, "No, nothing to add. I say go ahead."

The evening came to a close and Peter made ready to head back to his room in Mustang Ridge. Becca said she would walk with him to his horse.

"Mrs. Tucker, thank you for the splendid meal. Mr. Tucker, Thad, you won't be disappointed. Thank you."

After Peter and Becca went outside, Beth asked, "What was that about?"

"Peter asked Thad and me for permission to court Becca," Tuck explained.

"Oh my! I figured it would be coming, just not this soon," Beth said. "May I ask what you told him?"

"We agreed," Tuck said. "Peter explained how their courtship would be mostly through letters."

"I don't envy them any in a courtship with that many miles separating them," Thad commented. "Thirty minutes from Belle seems a long way to me at times."

78

"There's a difference though," Beth said. "You're engaged to be married. Becca and Peter will only be courting."

"You don't think they will eventually marry?" Tuck questioned her.

"Oh, I don't even want to think about it anymore tonight," Beth said, turning to brush invisible crumbs from the table. Tuck walked up behind her and put his arms around her, nuzzling her neck with his whiskers.

"Beth, sweetheart, God has given us our children and it has been our duty to raise them in His ways so they will be ready to go out into the world. We need to be ready to let them go."

Beth's tears came and she turned and wept into her husband's chest. Her words were inaudible. Tuck took her by the shoulders and gently pushed her from him. "What did you say?"

"Why does it seem that it happens so soon?" she sobbed. "I'm just not ready."

"You're not ready for what, Mama?" Becca said as she entered the ranch-house and overheard Beth's last statement. Seeing her mother's tears, she became concerned and asked, "Mama, what's wrong?"

"Nothing of importance, dear," Beth said wiping her tears with a corner of her apron. "Just thinking about how you have grown up so fast."

"Oh, Mama." Becca hugged her mother.

Thad had been feeling like an intruder for a while now and he silently backed out of the living area and into the ranch office. He supposed it was hard for his mother to think of both him and Becca leaving home. Speaking of that, he wondered if the buyer from Deadwood had responded yet about buying his horses. *I'll go into town tomorrow and see if there's an answer to my telegram. Maybe I can have coffee with Belle again.*

# # #

Two weeks later, Chet Banks came to Deer Creek Ranch with several men to collect the horses which he bought from Thad. Once Banks left to begin the horse drive to Deadwood and Thad possessed the money from the sale in his pocket, he left to go to the Mustang Ridge bank to deposit it. He stopped at the mill to order the lumber he would need to build his and Belle's home.

CHAPTER TWENTY-FOUR
Belle

Thad came to take Belle to dinner at Sally's. She so enjoyed those days when they spent time together even for short periods at a time. It was good to see Nate's improvement too. *He's really coming along.* Will Thad move ahead now with his building plans? She hoped so.

They finally met the elusive Mr. Rhodes. Belle had thought he was just a man who came to do the testing with Becca. She even pictured him as slightly balding and a rather heavy-set little man. He was anything but that. *Becca, Becca, you have been keeping a secret.*

As Thad said goodbye to her at the door of Doc Phillips' office, Belle had to chuckle to herself. *Thad, Becca is going to be sooo mad at you!* She didn't think Becca was ready to let the relationship be known. Becca was always a shy girl, especially around boys. She appeared to be rather smitten with Peter Rhodes, and he with her. *Perhaps... but I'll leave that to God and pray for His will to be done. Still, I continue to hope for the best for my friend.*

Belle would like to have been a mouse in the corner at Deer Creek Ranch that night though. *I'm sure it was quite interesting. Thad occasionally has been too impulsive.* Oh, she knew Beth would not mind the last-minute guests. After all, she used to operate the stagecoach stop there until she married Tuck. So, she knows how to provide for unexpected guests at her table. *Maybe I should've taken Thad up on his offer to supper after all.*

Poor Becca. Belle knew how she must have felt, that her brother placed her in these embarrassing situations. She is so timid, but maybe this little shove of Thad's was just what she needed. Belle continued to pray for her.

#

Sunday they were all at church again. Belle was anxious to hear what Thad said about Becca and her young man. Thad explained about Peter asking to court Becca. Admittedly, Belle was surprised they were moving ahead this quickly. She also could see how it pleased Thad that Peter included him in asking permission. *My fella is quite easy to read at times - or is it just that I've grown to know him so well?*

The Sunday sermon dealt with being called to repent and believe. Reverend Prescott preached from Hebrews 4:11-13

> *Let us labour therefore to enter into that rest, lest any man fall after the same example of unbelief.*
> *For the word of God is quick, and powerful, and sharper than any two-edged sword, piercing even to the dividing asunder*

of soul and spirit, and of the joints and marrow, and is *a discerner of the thoughts and intents of the heart.*
Neither is there any creature that is not manifest in his sight: but all things are *naked and opened unto the eyes of him with whom we have to do.*

"Hebrews 4:12 describes the word of God as quick, powerful, sharper than any two-edged sword," Reverend Prescott shared. "It is a is a discerner of the thoughts and intents of the heart."

Reverend Prescott closed with these words, "We are held accountable. It is our responsibility to believe and trust in Him joyfully. The words in the Bible are given to us so that at times, it will reveal our hidden thoughts."

CHAPTER TWENTY-FIVE
Thad's Discovery

Thad went out to Whitehorse Lake to plot where he would build the house, barn and stable, and bunk-house. As he walked off the measurements, he glanced up at the gray and salmon colored mountain ridge above him. He thought he detected movement. No doubt it was either an antelope or a deer. It'd been a while since he had shot one and Ma would be able to use the meat. So, he grabbed his gun and canteen from his horse and hiked up the side of the mountain slope.

Nearly an hour later, the sun was suddenly blocked out by an ominous black cloud. A downpour began immediately and Thad quickly sought shelter in a small cleft within the mountain wall. After the storm passed, he rose and left his shelter. It was then he noticed his hands were black. He returned to the crevice and lit a match to see what it was. *Sure enough, that's what I thought it was – coal.*

Thad never did find the deer or antelope. No doubt the animal had found shelter from the storm too. He finished plotting his home site and returned to Deer Creek Ranch. Upon arriving, he went into the ranch office where he found Tuck.

"Got it all measured?" he asked.

"Yeah, decided to go hunting while I was out there. Then I got caught in a downpour and made quite the discovery." Thad showed Tuck the piece of black substance he had chipped off from inside his shelter.

"Coal! Where did you find it?"

"On the other side of the ridge above Whitehorse Lake."

"Still on our land?"

Thad nodded.

"Take me out there to see it," Tuck said, rising from his chair.

After Thad and his pa arrived at Whitehorse Lake, they tied their horses to the same tree as Thad had done earlier. Already the rain from that morning was drying. He led Tuck up to the place where he sought shelter from the sudden downpour.

"Here it is, Pa."

"Well, I'll be. Sure enough, this is coal alright. Guess we'd better get enough samples to send to the geologist in Cheyenne. See what he has to say," Tuck observed.

They brought several small chunks of the coal back to the ranch and packaged it up ready to send the next day. A letter went along with it explaining where he found it and they signed their names at the bottom.

#

The following week, Tuck and Thad arrived at the telegraph office. When they entered the building, Walt Grimes raised his head from his telegraph key.

"Just got a wire for you men," Walt informed the rancher and his son. He handed the wire to Tuck who shared it with Thad.

> *Excited to see your site.*
> *Will arrive by stage your town next week.*
> *Douglas Prouty, Geologist.*

"Well, I guess that answers that," Tuck said after reading it.

As they left the telegraph office, Tuck said, "I hate to ask this of you, but do you suppose you could hold off on building out there until after we meet with Prouty?"

"I was just thinking that very thing," Thad responded. "Though you can't see it from my building site, still it's best to wait and see. Any activity at the coal site would be seen by riders coming from town."

Tuck patted him on the back. "We'll get you going yet, Thad."

"I suppose I'd better go see Belle and tell her we're on hold again."

"Yes, I think that's my cue to head back to the ranch," Tuck laughed. "See you later, Thad."

CHAPTER TWENTY-SIX
Thad Breaks the News to Belle

"What is it, Thad? You look so serious."

"Well, I guess I am." He hung his head, not wanting to disappoint Belle again when in fact, he was disappointed himself. Thad explained to her the problem, about the need to keep it quiet, and the fact that Tuck believed they should at least wait until the geologist came.

"I hope it won't be too long, Belle."

Disappointment showed on her face as he'd expected. But then she surprised him by smiling. Leaning toward him, she kissed him softly on the cheek. "Thad, like I told you before: I'd wait for you forever because I love you and want to be your wife."

"I sure don't deserve you," he said, putting his hand to his cheek where she'd kissed him. He felt a little light headed. "Oh, how I wish we could be married even though we don't have a home."

A thought suddenly occurred to him. "Belle, do you think we could be married even though we don't have our home built yet?"

"But where would we live?" Belle's excitement was building.

"At Deer Creek Ranch—in my room. It's not ideal, especially when we have wanted to start our married life in our own home."

"Yes, although I do know that many couples start out that way until they can get their own home," Belle said thoughtfully.

"Let's take a few days to think and pray about it," he encouraged her. "Then we can make our decision with God's leading.

"I agree, Thad. We need His blessing before you make any decisions. Let's talk about it Sunday. That'll give us a couple of days."

When Thad returned to the ranch, he found Pa in the stable starting the feeding of the horses. "Sorry I left you to start the chores, Pa."

"I figured you were busy. Did you tell her?"

"Yes, she was disappointed, of course. But she's wonderful. We did think of another idea though," Thad paused. "Actually, it was my idea, but Belle agreed."

"What's that?"

"We're thinking about setting a date for our wedding soon and staying here at the ranch-house until the building on our house is done. Do you think you and Ma would be okay with that?"

Tuck grinned, "I would, and I'd bet your ma would too."

"We decided to pray about it, and then we'll make the decision Sunday."

84

"Sounds like a good plan to me. Never make a big decision like that without asking the Lord's leading first. Let's finish the chores and go tell your ma."

Beth was all for it just like Tuck said she would be. With her arm around her husband, she said, "I know it's hard to keep putting off your plans. If it's God's will, then you also have our blessing."

"Thanks. There are times I can really relate to Jacob when he was trying to win Rachel for his wife," Thad said.

"Hopefully, you won't have to wait as long as he did," his mother said hugging him.

That night after Thad retired to his room, he sat reading his Bible by the light of his kerosene lamp. When he finished, he closed his Bible and bowed his head. "Father in Heaven, I ask Your leading on this matter of our wedding. If this is Your will, make it clear to us so we'll know how best to proceed. Thank You for Belle and her love, but most of all I thank You for sending Your Son for us. Amen."

Thad turned down the lamp and crawled into bed, confident that his future rested in the Hands of a loving and wise God.

#

Belle wanted more than anything in the world to become Mrs. Thad Tucker. But she also wanted to follow the Lord's leading. If this was not her Father's will at this time, she knew He would make it known to the two of them. God often makes known to us things that we wouldn't think of on our own.

She knew Thad felt the same way that she did about getting married before they had their home built. She tried to be patient with all of the things that had been interfering with his work on it. First, Thad needed to sell his horses to have the money to pay for the materials, so he made that harrowing trip to Fort Laramie. Then the Army arrested Matt Cutter and Thad and his father went to his aide. Next, Nate was recovering from a serious surgery, so Thad deemed it was necessary to hold off. And now, just when Belle thought Thad would at last be able to start building, coal was discovered on their ranch. She wondered why all these things happened that prevented Thad from beginning construction. She felt confident that their plans to marry were in God's plans, but maybe He had a different idea for when that would take place.

That night Belle sat with her Bible opened, searching God's Word for enlightenment. Perhaps He wanted them to be patient in hearing His Word. She would wait and talk with Thad the next day at church.

85

Father, I place my life in Your hands, knowing full well that You have my best interests at heart. You're all-knowing and You know our future even when we don't. Help me to be at peace with the leading You provide.

When Belle met Thad out in front of the church Sunday, she felt that same little thrill that started in her chest and landed in her stomach that she always felt when she saw him. She hoped that feeling never went away.

Later as the service neared an end, Belle was amazed at how God worked, He cleared things up for her through the minister, reading from Jeremiah and Proverbs and even the lyrics to the hymn they sang. God had used Reverend Prescott's message to speak clearly to her. She knew they had His blessing and she squeezed Thad's hand.

Thad and Belle Make a Decision

Thad met Belle at the church on Sunday when she arrived with her family. As they walked down the aisle to a seat, Thad looked at her with a question. She whispered, "After church we can talk with our families."

Thad felt disheartened. He hadn't received a real clear message from God and if Belle's response was any guide, she didn't either.

Reverend Prescott began the morning's sermon with Scripture.

> *For I know the plans I have for you," declares the Lord, "plans to prosper you and not to harm you, plans to give you hope and a future. Jeremiah 29:11*

> *To humans belong the plans of the heart, but from the Lord comes the proper answer of the tongue. All a person's ways seem pure to them, but motives are weighed by the Lord. Commit to the Lord whatever you do, and He will establish your plans. Proverbs 16:1-3*

"Let us sing together "When We Get Home," Reverend Prescott said.

> *We are bound for the mansions of glory,*
> *In that beautiful city of gold,*
> *Where, beholding the face of our Savior,*
> *It will fill us with rapture untold.*
> *Refrain:*
> *When we get home we'll shout and sing*
> *The praises of our Redeemer and King,*
> *And make the heavenly arches ring*

86

With the songs of home, sweet home.

Reverend Prescott's closing words were, "You know it is God speaking if a thought comes to you and He won't let you rest until you move forward."

Thad felt as if his head was spinning. Was this God's answer for them? Was it even an answer to their situation or a solution for another? Yes, maybe the Lord was speaking to him and Belle through Jeremiah and Proverbs, that God's plan was to give them hope for their future. Perhaps that meant to go ahead with the wedding and trust the building of their home to God. The song even spoke of home, though of a heavenly home. He felt a peace come over him once he believed he had God's answer. At the same time, he felt Belle's hand clasp his hand. He looked at her and she nodded. They were of one mind.

CHAPTER TWENTY-SEVEN
Wedding Arrangements Are Made

Belle and Thad were busy with plans for their wedding since the day was fast approaching. The couple set Saturday, September 29 for the date of the happy occasion. This meant that the mothers of the couple were busy. Beth Tucker and her good friend, Sarah Wells, were spending every spare moment strategizing to bring about the perfect wedding for their two offspring. It was a big undertaking given that the wedding would be so soon, but what mother is not pleased in doing so for her child?

The mother of the bride had a lot of work to do in sewing Belle's wedding dress, but Sarah had been keeping a secret which she shared with Belle, who then shared with her betrothed.

The couple took a break to sit on the porch swing at the ranch-house while their mothers were inside working on the invitations which would be handed out Sunday in church. Belle spoke, "Thad, you'll never believe what my mother admitted to doing?"

"What?" He was startled at her words. Had her mother been engaged in some nefarious action?

"When we first started courting, my mother made a pattern for my wedding dress and sent for the material and embellishments to make it. She has held onto these things ever since."

"What's an embellishment?" Thad asked, entirely missing the fact that Sarah had started the wedding dress long ago.

"It's a decorative detail added to the dress to make it more attractive."

"Just putting you in the dress will make it more attractive," Thad declared.

"Oh, Thad you are so sweet."

"Belle, could you and Thad come in here for a minute," her mother called from inside the ranch-house.

"Be right there, Mama." Thad held the door for Belle as they entered. Piles of material, bows, and other adornments lay on the big table.

"What are you two up to?" Belle inquired of her mother. "Looks like you brought all your sewing materials here."

"No, just the materials we need to decorate the church and the ends of the pews," Sarah responded and added. "We need input from the two of you about colors and which style you would like.

Belle looked at Thad, who said, "You decide for us, Belle. With you in the room, all I see is your beauty."

Belle blushed a deep red. She was used to Thad saying such things to her when they were alone, but in front of their mothers was a different thing. Beth and Sarah merely laughed.

As time marched forward for Belle and Thad, they became more vocal about their love and admiration for each other. Mushy was the word Thad thought about himself later that night alone in his bedroom with his Bible in hand. *Lord, I pray You'll help my mind to be steady, especially when I'm working with ranch-related things.* For he'd noticed the reactions of the ranch hands; the rolling of eyes and snickering. Even the whispering between them that immediately stopped when he came near.

It was with these things in mind that he made his way to The Mountain Hideaway at the northern edge of Mustang Ridge run by Mabel Patton. Mabel was a kindly woman and somewhat stout, which was evidence of the mouth-watering food she provided to her guests. There Thad reserved Mabel's best room for the night of their wedding, but not until she had plied him with one of her delicious cinnamon rolls. No sense in allowing that kind of loud noise and celebration to be at his folk's home on his and Belle's wedding night. His and Belle's wedding night! Oh, how he liked the sound of that. In his considered opinion, a cowboy shivaree at Deer Creek Ranch would be quite disruptive for everyone involved, especially the newlyweds.

Mabel Patton and her husband, Howard, built a beautiful home tucked back in the piney woods. But as fate would have it, Howard passed away before they lived there a year. To make ends meet, Mabel then turned it into an inn. It was on the north edge of town, set back into a nook of the Ridge for which Mustang Ridge was named. There was a barn to care for the horses and it would keep them and the buggy out of sight as well. He hoped they'd be able to keep it secret from those who wished to disrupt their wedding night. He extracted from Mabel a promise not to say a word about his plan to anyone.

CHAPTER TWENTY-EIGHT
Belle

Belle felt so blessed to have both their mothers working on their wedding decorations. Mama had been working hard on her wedding dress and Belle was so anxious for the day to come when she could put on that beautiful dress, walk down the aisle on Papa's arm, and be joined in marriage to the love of her life. Mama was doing her most wonderful work on her dress and Belle felt honored.

Beth was wonderful in helping with the decorations. The two mothers were best of friends and it warmed Belle's heart to see the joy they displayed while they brought these wedding plans to fulfilment.

Belle loved that Thad felt free to express his love for her not only with his words, but with his eyes and actions. At times though he seemed to forget that they were not alone, it was a little embarrassing. But Mama and Beth just smiled.

Will two weeks be enough time to get everything done for the wedding? She hoped so. They asked Becca to sing at their wedding. Belle could tell she was honored. Together they chose the song she would sing and she began practicing with Grace Norby who was the church organist. They met at the church after school let out so they could work on the song.

Papa was busting his buttons. All he talked about to his friends was how his daughter was getting married and that he had to walk her down the aisle. He made it sound like he was being forced to do an unpleasant task, but Belle knew better. Her Papa loved her and was proud of her. She knew he also loved Thad. They got along really well. What more could a bride ask for?

Another Sunday and another moving sermon. Reading from 1 Corinthians 13:4-6,

> *Charity suffereth long, and is kind; charity envieth not; charity vaunteth not itself, is not puffed up,*
> *Doth not behave itself unseemly, seeketh not her own, is not easily provoked, thinketh no evil;*
> *Rejoiceth not in iniquity, but rejoiceth in the truth*

"Many believe that 1 Corinthians 13 is a marriage chapter since it speaks of love. But it's meant for the Church, as an expression of giving to others," Reverend Prescott said. "In closing, what motivates your life? This week, be sure to seek opportunities to show love."

"Let us sing What Wondrous Love is This."

90

What wondrous love is this!
O my soul!
What wondrous love is this!
That caused the Lord of bliss!
To send this precious peace,
To my soul, to my soul!
To send this precious peace
To my soul!

When I was sinking down,
Sinking down, sinking down;
When I was sinking down
Sinking down
When I was sinking down,
Beneath God's righteous frown,
Christ laid aside his crown
For my soul, for my soul!
Christ laid aside his crown
For my soul!

CHAPTER TWENTY-NINE
The Geologist Arrives

Tuck and Thad greeted the stagecoach as it rumbled down Main Street of Mustang Ridge. They were waiting for the arrival of Douglas Prouty, the geologist, who was to be on the noon stage from Cheyenne. They had reserved a room for him at the new Mustang Hotel on main-street.

Will Barrett called to his teams as he brought the stage to a halt in front of Sally's Café. When Matt Cutter resigned as driver of the stage, Will took over full-time. Now, he hopped down from the box and greeted the two ranchers.

"Howdy, Tuck, Thad. What brings you Deer Creek men to meet the stage?"

"You have a passenger name of Prouty?" Tuck asked him.

Will nodded and opened the door to the stagecoach and placed a wooden step in front for the passengers to alight from the stage. The first passenger to step off was a lady who accepted Will's hand to help her. Next was a man who waited beside her for the man riding shotgun to get the luggage down from the top of the stage.

"Tuck, Thad. This here's Douglas Prouty and his wife." Will introduced them to each other.

"Gentlemen. I hope it won't be a problem that I brought my wife with me," Prouty explained. "I've been gone so much recently. She needed to get out for a while."

"No problem at all," Tuck replied, taking their baggage in hand. "Let me show you to your hotel. You and Mrs. Prouty can get the trail dust off of you." He led them across the street to the hotel while Thad brought up the rear with the last of the bags.

"How soon will you want to go to the site?" Thad asked Prouty while they waited for the hotel clerk to check them in.

"As soon as we change out of these dusty clothes and get a bite to eat," Prouty replied. "We're a mite hungry, aren't we, dear?"

"Famished. I noticed an aroma of delicious food coming from Sally's Cafe when we unloaded from the stage."

"We're planning to eat there," Thad explained. "Why don't we go get a table for all four of us and you can come over when you are ready?"

"Good idea. We'll see you shortly," said Prouty before they were escorted up to their room by the clerk.

"Seems like an okay fella," Tuck remarked later as they were seated at Sally's.

92

"Yes, he did. I thought they…" Thad stopped. "Well, lookie here who came to eat with us!"

"Beth! I didn't know you were coming to town," Tuck exclaimed, rising to help her to be seated. "But I'm glad you did."

"Ma, I didn't see the buggy outside." he said peering through the window.

"No, I rode my horse. Sarah wasn't able to work on your wedding things with me, so I thought it would be a good time to get out and go for a ride." Beth gave her husband a peck on his cheek. "I knew you'd probably eat here so I thought I'd join you. Where's Mr. Prouty?"

"Here he comes now," Tuck replied waving his hand to Prouty who just came in the door with his wife. "He brought his wife with him, so could you spend a little time with her while we're out at the site."

"Glad to," Beth replied.

As the Proutys were getting settled at the table, Tuck introduced them to Beth. "Mrs. Prouty, my wife would be happy to spend time with you while we men are gone,"

"I'd like that very much," she said, "but please, call me Ruth."

"So how far is this site we're going to visit?" Prouty asked before he forked a bite of chicken and dumplings into his mouth.

"We can take the trail heading north out of town," Thad explained. "My building site is near the ridge, about thirty minutes. I found it when I went up into the rocks hunting."

"So, you have your ranch in that area?" Prouty asked.

"Yes and no. Pa and I own all of Deer Creek Ranch. I added 160 acres to homestead. I'll be getting married in a couple of weeks, so I went there to start building my home. That's when I discovered…uh…the site," Thad explained dropping his voice. "We decided to wait until we saw you before I let people come out to help me build."

"Probably not a bad idea," Prouty agreed thoughtfully. "The sample you sent is good grade. Just hard to tell how much of it there is until I can assess the site."

"Well, if you're done eating, I'll pay for our meals and we can get on the road," Tuck spoke to Prouty and Thad.

Tuck leaned over and kissed his wife on her cheek. "You ladies don't have to leave just because we're leaving."

"You men don't worry about us," Beth articulated. "We'll be just fine while you are gone."

With that, the menfolk left the café and proceeded to their horses. The Tuckers had brought a saddled horse from their ranch for Prouty. He tied his bag of surveying equipment behind his saddle and they mounted up, heading north out of town.

"Sure is pretty up here," said Prouty as he surveyed the green of the valley and the salmon and gray of the Mustang Mountains rising upward. "I think I'll rent a buggy and take Ruth out here on a ride. She'll love this scenery."

The men dismounted and Prouty retrieved his surveying tools from the back of his horse. Thad helped him carry them to the site where he'd discovered the crevice in the wall of the mountain. He wondered what the outcome would be. Would Prouty pronounce it a large find of good quality coal? Or would it merely be a small amount of poor-quality?

After several hours of testing and surveying the site, Prouty announced, "Mr. Tucker, I believe this is good quality coal. I'm prepared to buy this in the name of the Union Pacific Coal Company."

"No," Thad responded immediately. "This is on our land; we don't want to sell. We may make arrangements with the company to buy our coal, but the land stays under our control."

"I see. May I ask why?"

"I've heard of problems at other mines where Chinese and Greek workers were abused and paid very little. I'm not against hiring the Chinese and Greek workers. What I'm against is the abuse of them," Thad stated firmly. "This way we'll have control over the workers and can treat them humanely, paying them a fair wage." Thad saw his pa nod his agreement. "I believe that God values all people and we'll be obeying Him by caring for our labor force in a fair manner."

"I certainly understand, believe me," Prouty replied. "That's been the hardest part of this business for me. Unfortunately, I don't have any say in how they handle the workers. But I do understand that the railroad is going to be coming through Mustang Ridge. That should prove to be a good market for your coal. You might be able to sell directly to the railroad once it comes through."

"Yes," Thad agreed. "We had considered that fact. We also want to sell it for heating homes in this area."

Back in Mustang Ridge, Prouty gave the two ranchers information on who to contact regarding hiring and obtaining the necessary mining machinery. Thad immediately sent telegrams to the individuals to follow up. He wanted to get this going so he and Belle could build their new home without being concerned about interference from the coal mine.

94

CHAPTER THIRTY
Wedding Day

"Mama, I can't find my strand of pearls!" Becca called from her room. "Do you have them.?"

Beth came out of her bedroom and went to the doorway of her daughter's room. "Did you look in the drawer of your side table?"

"Well, no. But I don't know why they would be...," Becca's voice trailed off as she opened the drawer and found the elusive pearls.

"I surely don't know why you're so flighty. One would think you were getting married today instead of your brother."

"I know, but Izzy is my best friend and now she'll become my sister. I'm so happy for them."

"Are you nervous about your solo?" her mother inquired.

"Not really. I just want to look nice while I'm singing."

"When you are done there, can you come help me with my hair? It won't go where I want it to. My braid is so crooked."

"Yes, Mama. I'll be right in as soon as I finish my own hair," Becca replied. "Is that bacon I smell? Are you cooking breakfast in addition to getting dressed?"

"No, not me." Beth looked out toward the kitchen and discovered Thad with her apron around his neck, cooking bacon and flipping flapjacks. "Thad! What on earth are you doing?"

"Cooking breakfast," he replied nonchalantly. "I was hungry and you were busy getting ready."

"Well, you should be getting ready too," his mother said.

"Ma, it's only 8:00 and the wedding isn't until 1:00. I have plenty of time to get ready."

"Men!" his mother mumbled as she went back into her room with Becca at her heels.

"What about us?" asked Tuck when he came through the door carrying the pails of milk. But his wife didn't answer as she was already in her room with Becca. He saw Thad and asked, "What's going on, son? Am I missing something?"

"Ma and Becca are excited about the wedding. They think I should be getting ready too instead of fixing breakfast."

"Well, I'm glad you're doing what you are because I'm hungry. I'll wash my hands and take care of this milk, and then I can help you."

"It'll be ready to eat by then," Thad replied.

"I can help with that too." Tuck grinned.

"Tuck, come in here," Beth called from their bedroom.

"What is it?" he asked going to her and giving her a kiss on the back of her neck.

"I've brushed your suit and it's ..." She turned, scrunching up her nose. "Oh, Tuck, you smell like goats!"

"Yup, and for good reason. I was milking them and now I'm going to take care of the milk and go eat breakfast. Which is something you and Becca should do."

"I couldn't possibly eat now," Becca called from her room next door. "I've got to finish getting ready."

"You two have plenty of time to eat a good breakfast. Besides, Thad's made bacon and flapjacks for us. I think you should stop and eat."

As the four of them sat around the table, they bowed their heads for the prayer that Tuck offered. "Lord God, we thank Thee for Your faithfulness to us. We're also thankful for Your provision of food and sustenance for our bodies, for family, and for soon-to-be new family members. I pray Your blessing on Thad and Belle as they become one today. Grant all of us a peace as we make ready for this momentous occasion in our son's life. Amen"

Becca looked at the plate of flapjacks and sorghum that Thad passed and said, "I shouldn't be eating this in my good dress. I'll get it all sticky."

Thad looked at his sister. "I think your days of getting sorghum all over you are long past, but if you're so concerned, here," he said handing her an apron from the peg on the wall. He took off the one he was wearing and handed it to his mother. "Now you ladies can eat breakfast without worrying."

"Thank you, Thad. And thank you for making breakfast," his mother said. "Does Belle know what a good cook you are?"

"Probably not," he grinned at his mother. "Anyway, this is about all I can cook."

When they were done eating and both Thad and Tuck sat enjoying a second cup of coffee, Beth became exasperated with the men in her family. She dipped hot water into the dishpan and began to wash the dirty dishes. Thad saw that she kept peering sideways at him and Tuck. He drained his cup, then rose and put it into her dishwater. "Thanks, Ma. I'll go get ready now."

"Is your suit ready?"

"Yes, Ma. I brushed it earlier this morning and it's hanging on the hook on the back of my door." Thad filled the pitcher with warm water from the reservoir and went to his room. He was finally ready to get washed up and dressed in his wedding attire. He'd already placed the small box with Belle's wedding ring in the pocket of his suit so he wouldn't forget it.

96

Thad stood at the altar of the church with Nate, his best man, at his side. Becca stood opposite as Belle's bridesmaid. As the organ began playing, he saw movement at the door of the church and focusing on it, he saw his lovely bride begin her walk down the aisle on the arm of her father, Jacob Wells. Her mother had indeed worked a miracle with her wedding dress. The white satin was set off by the lace on the neck and at the end of the long sleeves. The embellishments, which consisted of tiny roses, separated the lace from the dress material. But Thad barely noticed. His eyes were glued to his Belle. Her beauty alone demanded his focus. His heart beat increased as he watched her walk towards him. At last this day was here.

As they reached the altar, Jacob handed her over to the man who would take over his job of caring and providing for her. Thad saw an expression in Jacob's eyes of both sadness and joy.

Reverend Prescott's words brought Thad's attention back to him. "Let us pray. Almighty God and Father of our Lord Jesus Christ, today we come into Your house to witness the joining of these two young people in Holy marriage. We pray that You'll be their Guide throughout their lives together. Bless this union. In Jesus' Name we pray, Amen"

It was time for Becca's solo. The song chosen for the occasion was "Oh Perfect Love." Becca's lovely voice presented this song with her usual grace.

> *O perfect Love, all human thought transcending,*
> *lowly we kneel in prayer before thy throne,*
> *that theirs may be the love which knows no ending,*
> *whom though in sacred vow dost join in one.*
> *O perfect Life, be thou their full assurance*
> *of tender charity and steadfast faith,*
> *of patient hope and quiet, brave endurance,*
> *with childlike trust that fears no pain or death.*
> *Grant them the joy which brightens earthly sorrow;*
> *grant them the peace which calms all earthly strife;*
> *grant them the vision of the glorious morrow*

Before Thad knew it, he and Belle were at long last married. He wanted to leap about and shout for joy. *I've waited so long to take this beautiful woman to be my wife.*

Following the ceremony, everyone was treated to refreshments provided by the women of the church, while friends and family wished the couple well and gave them gifts. As they finally opened the last of the wedding presents, Thad felt a sigh of relief. He was anxious to leave and be alone with Belle.

"Thad, we'll take the gifts in our buggy. There'll be more room for them." Tuck winked at his son. Thad had told his parents about his plans for the wedding night. "Take your time getting there."

"Thanks, Pa."

CHAPTER THIRTY-ONE
After the Wedding

Belle and Thad left town in his buggy following the wedding. He'd taken Ma and Pa into his confidence about his plans for the evening. No one else knew, including Belle, that they weren't going to Deer Creek Ranch. They were in the buggy and headed south out of town towards the ranch, followed by stragglers from the wedding whooping and hollering. After a ways, Thad stopped the buggy and stood up to talk with the young men on horseback.

"Okay, you fellers can head back to town now. We thank you for your well-wishes, but my bride and I would like to stop and do a little sight-seeing since it is nice weather. So, go on back to town now."

Thad and Belle were well-respected by their friends in Mustang Ridge, so after a few shouts of good wishes, the revelers turned back toward town. He waited until they were out of sight before moving the buggy ahead.

"Would you like to ride out to Whitehorse Ranch and see what I've done?" Thad asked Belle.

"Oh, yes, but what have you done?"

"I've plotted off where the house and out buildings will be, and even the rooms in the house. Of course, I want you to have input into it too." She squeezed his arm in anticipation of seeing the plans for their home.

When they arrived at the site, Thad helped Belle down from the buggy. "Over here will be the barn. It'll be a big one and will connect to the stables on the south side. The other side will open up to protect the horses in the corral from the cold of winter. Over there will be the bunkhouse," he pointed to the area. "Then back here by the trees will be the house. We'll have a wide veranda across the front of the house."

"It will be so nice to have the house close to the lake," Belle said.

Thad made a motion as though opening the front door of their home. Belle laughed as he picked her up and carried her across the imaginary threshold.

"Where will the kitchen be?" she inquired after he sat her down. He led the way, showing her the size of it.

"Do you think it will be big enough?" he asked her.

"Where will we eat?"

"The kitchen will open onto a large eating area here." He pointed to the spot. "Then over here, we'll have a living room off of the dining room."

She nodded. "And how many bedrooms will we have?"

"Four," he answered, pointing the way. "Well, what do you think?"

"I love it," she answered, as she danced through the make-believe rooms. "Oh, you've done a wonderful job and I like that we have four bedrooms.

There will be room for guests as well as a growing family. But I would like to have another room off the kitchen in which to keep food and supplies, if possible."

"I didn't think about that. That's actually a great idea. I planned to build a root cellar to keep things cool. We can have the entrance to the cellar in that room."

"Thad, I can hardly wait to have the house built so we can move in."

"Me too."

CHAPTER THIRTY-TWO
The Wedding Night

"Do you want to tell me now what you're up to, Thad?"

"Sure do," he grinned. "We're going to spend our wedding night at The Mountain Hideaway."

Belle laughed and hugged his arm. "What a wonderful idea, Thad. But I don't have my clothes. I took everything out to your ranch."

"Yes, you have your clothes. Ma packed a bag for you," he said, nodding toward the two carpet bags behind their seat. "I hope you don't mind."

"It'll be wonderful. However, I think our brothers are planning a gathering. I overheard part of a conversation about a midnight plan at the ranch."

"Ha ha! That's what I thought. Well, we'll have a quiet time by ourselves. I didn't want Ma and Pa to have to deal with a midnight celebration."

"But, Thad. Your folks will still have to deal with those who come out."

"Probably not. Pa knows about my plans and he was going to tell Nate before they left town that we won't be staying at home, so he could stop his plans and let others know."

The sun was hanging low in the sky when Thad pulled the buggy up to The Mountain Hideaway. As he helped his beautiful bride out of the buggy, Mabel opened the door and stepped out onto the veranda.

"Welcome, Mr. and Mrs. Tucker!" she greeted them. "And congratulations on your marriage."

"Thank you, Mrs. Patton," the happy bride said. "This is such a beautiful place."

"And thank you for keeping this a secret," Thad added.

"Oh, say no more. I fully understand. And you can call me Mabel. Come on in and I'll show you up to your room." As Mabel led the way up the ornate stairway, Belle gathered the skirts of her wedding dress and followed her while Thad carried their bags.

Mabel stopped in front of a door with a sign which read, "Newlywed Suite."

Once the newlyweds were inside, Belle saw the beauty of the workmanship in the wood. Hand-sewn quilts adorned the four-poster bed and the loveseat. A veranda was accessible through glass doors and provided a breath-taking view of the mountain dotted with beautiful green pine trees.

"I'll go take care of the horse and buggy," Thad announced.

"While you're doing that, I'll finish preparing your wedding supper and bring it up to your room," Mabel informed them.

"I'm going to get out of my wedding dress and put on another dress. I don't want to spill on it."

"Would you like me to help you out of it, dear? It's such a beautiful dress. Did your mother make it?"

"Yes, she did, which is why I don't want to damage it in any way. And thank you, Mabel. I'd like help."

Thad returned to the Inn just as Mabel was coming through the swinging door from her kitchen laden with a tray of food. "Would you like me to take that tray, Mabel?"

"Yes, young man, and I'll go back and bring the coffee."

They set the two trays on the table and Mabel left the room, wishing them a good night. Thad held Belle in his arms. At last, she was his wife and they would be able to look forward to a lifetime of these moments. "I love you, Belle."

Belle almost purred in his arms. He was a lucky man indeed.

CHAPTER THIRTY-THREE
Belle

Belle could hardly believe that they were finally wed. And what a handsome man she married. As she glanced sideways at Thad while he directed Rowdy to move their buggy forward, her love for him bubbled over. For a while, they would be staying at the Deer Creek ranch-house and their bedroom would be smack dab in between his parent's and Nate's rooms, but it wouldn't be forever. For now, they were man and wife. *Oh, I do love the sound of that. Thank you, Father, for this day.*

The newlyweds were accompanied out of town by a few young men who were making a lot of racket, but Thad stopped the buggy after a while and kindly asked them to leave them be since he planned a little sight-seeing. Belle wondered about that. What sights could they see that couldn't be seen every time they traveled this road? She soon learned he wished to take her to Whitehorse Lake, to their future home. *Can you believe it? Our future home! He'd plotted out where everything would be and even asked my opinion.*

As the two of them returned to their buggy and were once again on the road, Belle was puzzled when Thad turned to go around the town and come in on the north end.

"Where are you going, Thad?" she asked.

"Just wait, it's my wedding gift to you."

When they pulled up to the Mountain Hideaway, Belle thought, *what a beautiful place to spend our wedding night.* Belle was touched that her new husband surprised her with this gift. Mabel was a dear, helping the bride to get out of her wedding dress. They enjoyed a delicious wedding supper in their room prepared by Mabel. Afterwards, Thad gave Belle her wrap and led the way out to their own tiny veranda where they sat together and enjoyed the view for a time. It was starting to feel chilly as the sun began to disappear, so Thad put his arm around his bride and asked if she was cold. She nodded, so they went inside. *My new husband has many romantic qualities I didn't know he possessed. Ah, such bliss.*

CHAPTER THIRTY-FOUR
Back to Deer Creek Ranch

Thad and Belle returned to the ranch later the next day and moved into Thad's bedroom. By the time she transferred her clothes and personal belongings to the crowded room, he was of a mind to start building their new home right away. But he knew they needed to wait until the coal mine was up and going first. At least the double bed now in Thad's room was welcoming on their first night there.

They had just fallen into a deep slumber when Thad was wakened by scratching at their bedroom window. He rose to see what it was, puzzled because there was no tree close to the window. Belle heard and rose too, saying, "Thad, what is it? What's going on?"

Just then the most annoying ruckus broke out. There was whooping and shouting, clanging of pans, ringing of cow bells, and all kinds of other loud noises. As Thad looked out the window, he was able to identify several of the revelers; Nate Tucker seemed to be the ringleader. *I should have known Nate had plans for our first night back here. Rascal!* Thad also saw Ben Wells and others from town.

"Oh, no!" Thad declared. "I thought we would get out of this."

"What?" Belle demanded once more. "What is that awful noise?"

"I believe that's what is referred to as the horse-fiddle. It's made out of two old disk blades and fitted with a spring and a crank to a toothed gear. The teeth of the gear pull the disks apart and when the crank is turned, it creates the most awful noise. Don't ask me where the name came from. It is used at shivarees."

"Oh, that's what's going on! A shivaree!"

"Yup."

"At least there appear to be adults with them to supervise," he commented.

"What time is it?" Belle inquired.

"Just after midnight."

"Is that your Pa?"

Thad was incredulous. "The ranch hands too. And Ma and Becca!"

"There's my folks too! Why would they do such a thing?"

"I'd say it is because they love us," Thad said wryly. "Guess we better get dressed."

When they came out of their bedroom, they saw that the lights were on in the rest of the house. Food was set out on the dining table, but everyone seemed to be outside. As the couple went out onto the veranda, they were serenaded by music in the form of a violin and a guitar. When the participants saw them emerge, the violin player, who turned out to be Jacob Wells, called out, "Swing your partners!" It was an invitation for a square dance.

"Mrs. Tucker, shall we?" Thad said, offering Belle his arm.

"Why certainly, Mr. Tucker." By now she was definitely wide awake.

However, the shivaree participants had no intention of letting the newlyweds dance with each other and soon they found themselves being passed off to dancer after dancer. Finally, it seemed after a mutual consent, that the weary couple was finally able to share a waltz before the festivities ended with the call to eat. Thad was sure that idea might have come from his pa.

They trouped into the ranch-house to fill their plates with delicious goodies brought by the townspeople. As the darkness of the night sky began to lighten, signifying that sunrise was not far away, Thad stood on the veranda and raised his hand to quiet the rabble-rousers.

"Well, you got us after all," he said. The crowd broke into another round of noise. He raised his hand again. "Seriously, folks, aren't you the least bit tired? But thank you for all the food and for the dance. You can all go home to bed now."

The women came in to retrieve what was left of their food and pack them up while the menfolk brought their buggies up for them. The night was over – literally. Belle and Becca helped Beth to clean up the table. "Well, I think we've pretty well covered breakfast," his mother said. "Let's everyone go back to bed and see if we can get a little sleep."

Thad and Belle retired to their bedroom as did everyone else in the household. They donned their nightclothes once again. Belle pulled back the covers on their bed and let out a shriek.

"What? What's wrong?"

"Bugs! Thad! There are bugs in our bed!"

Thad brought the lamp closer to the bed to get a better look. "Its oats, not bugs. That's from Nate, no doubt." His deduction was confirmed by chuckling coming from his brother's room next door. He apparently heard Belle shriek.

Thad gathered the bottom sheet up and took it out to the veranda, dumping the oats on the ground. He shook the sheet vigorously and went back to their bedroom. Belle helped him to place it back on the bed.

"Thad, this will not work! It feels itchy. The sheet will have to be washed before we can comfortably sleep in it." Belle's voice rose a couple of octives."

"Well, we'll just have to sleep without it then. We'll wash it in the morning - with Nate's help!"

Once again, snuggled into their bed, Thad said softly to his bride, "I love you, Belle Tucker."

"Even when I act like a shrew?"

"Even then," Thad reassured her.

They crawled out of bed close to noon when they heard sounds of life coming from outside their door. When they emerged, Tuck and Beth were at the table drinking a cup of coffee.

"Good morning, you two," Beth said with a smile. "Quite a night last night, wasn't it?"

"Morning. Yes, and thank you Ma, Pa for your parts in the whole thing," Thad said wryly.

"We did give you your wedding night," Tuck replied with a grin.

"Yes, and we are grateful for that."

"Well," Tuck said, stretching. "Chore time."

"Anyone hungry?" Beth asked.

"Not me," Belle responded. "Just coffee is all I need. Lots and lots of coffee!"

Beth laughed. "There's a fresh pot on the stove. Thad, want something to eat?"

"No, just coffee for me too, thanks. Where's Nate?" he asked, looking around."

"Still sleeping," Tuck grinned, nodding toward Nate's bedroom.

"Not for long!" Thad growled good-naturedly. He filled a tin cup with water and went to his brother's room. He tried the door and found that it was not locked. Entering the room, he tossed the cup of water on the sleeping form of his mischievous brother.

Nate woke suddenly sputtering and yelling until he saw it was Thad, then he started laughing.

"Little brother, you have started something now. Just wait until you get married. You better plan to leave the country!" Thad said laughing. "Time to get up and do chores."

"You got my bed all wet!" Nate whined.

"It'll dry. At least you aren't itching."

The brothers laughed again and clasped each other in a hug that if anyone were watching, they would have seen the love that the two felt for each other.

"Rise and shine, oh, and thank you for offering to help."

"Help what?"

"Wash our bedding. You aren't going to make an innocent woman do the laundry herself on the day after her wedding, are you?"

106

Nate sputtered more while he pulled on his jeans. "She can't be too innocent if she married you!"

"Shall I get another cup of water?"

"Nope,   no,   I'm   fine."

CHAPTER THIRTY-FIVE
The Mine

Within one week's time, the machinery needed to run the mine arrived along with an overseer and a crew of workers. Most of them were Chinese with a few Greek immigrants. They set up the tents where they would live temporarily until a bunkhouse was built. Tuck and Thad insisted on this, not wanting the workers to have to live in tents in the elements like they had observed at other sites.

As the machinery began to arrive, the townspeople saw them and soon it was widely known that a coal mine was on Deer Creek Ranch property.

George Cummins was the name of the overseer. Thad and Tuck rode out to the mine site to greet him. "Welcome, Mr. Cummins," Thad held out his hand. "I'm Thad Tucker and this is my pa, Adam Tucker."

"Gentlemen," he acknowledged, shaking their hands. "Well, there are the workings." He pointed to the machinery in the heavy wagons.

"How many miners do you have?" Tuck asked.

"We'll start with twelve. If we need more down the road, I'll send for them. We'll see first how much it will produce. As you can see, I've started them on building their bunkhouse."

"Did you obtain the stoves for warmth, Mr. Cummins?" Tuck asked.

"Yes, per your request."

"Good, good," Tuck replied.

"I've opened an account at Garrison's Mercantile in Mustang Ridge for food supplies. Use that for food. Any other items needed will have to come through one of us," Thad informed him.

"Understood, Mr. Tucker," he replied. "If I need any supplies in addition to food, how will I get a hold of you?"

"You can come out to Deer Creek Ranch. You go through town and take the west road which will come right to the ranch. It's about ten miles from town. Our office is on the north side of the ranch-house. But one of us will check in with you on a regular basis, so you probably won't have to come to the ranch."

"Okay, thanks. I think it sounds like you have everything well covered."

"I know we discussed this before you came, but I just want to address it again. There is not to be any work done in the mine on Sundays. The men are welcome to attend church in Mustang Ridge but if they don't care to, that's up to them," Thad reiterated. "They can spend the Lord's Day any way they wish; just not in the mine."

"Having worked with these fellows before, I don't think the Chinese will be coming into the town's church, but perhaps the Greek miners will. Many of the Chinese are Buddhists and don't speak much English. However, I will plan to come myself and will make sure they know they are welcome there."

"Do you have any additional questions?" Tuck asked.

"Not that I can think of now."

"Good. I hope our business association will be pleasant and profitable for both sides. Oh, one other thing," Thad said. "We installed a steam whistle next to the mine. If there is a problem inside the mine, just blow it. It will be heard at my ranch as well as the town. We'll be here to help as soon as possible."

CHAPTER THIRTY-SIX
Work Begins on New Home

Now that the coal mine was up and running, Thad was finally able to begin work on the ranch-house at Whitehorse Lake. The year had been fraught with one crisis after the other, delaying the building of the house and thereby setting their wedding back. *At last, I can now start building our home.*

Thad pulled the old wagon out of the barn at Deer Creek Ranch; the wagon on which his family traveled to Wyoming Territory via wagon train. This big sturdy wagon allowed him to haul the lumber from the Deer Creek Lumber Mill north of town. The mill utilized the power of the water from Deer Creek, turning the wheel which ran the saw. He had put in his order for the boards long ago, before everything began happening.

As he began to unload the lumber from the wagon, friends and several of the ranch hands, surprised him by coming to help him. A large enough crew came to help that by the end of the day, they had completed the barn. The church women came out around noon with dinner for the hard-working men.

"Sure nice of all of you to help me with the building."

"Well, it's not that your ma and I want you to move out of Deer Creek, but we think a young newly married couple needs their own home," Tuck responded with a grin.

Thad felt his face heat up when the ranch hands let loose with loud guffaws. Tuck came to his rescue, "Son, suppose you tell us what needs to be done first and we can get started."

By the end of the day, not only the barn but the connecting stables had been raised and the frame for the bunkhouse erected. All in all, Thad believed it was a good start, but how he wished the house was completed now and he and Belle could move in. He was also anxious to move out of Deer Creek Ranch. As much as he loved his family, he wished for his and Belle's own home.

The next day most of the same men came to finish the work on the bunkhouse and begin on the ranch-house. A few men came from town to work and Tuck joined them along with Hank, Nash, and Wade. Cookie provided nourishment for the workers since the women wouldn't be providing the noon meal like they had the day before.

Thad was thankful for good weather. Even though it was well into October, it was surprisingly warm. Now that the barn had been completed, a few of the hands were engaged in hauling grain and hay from Deer Creek Ranch for the livestock here. He knew the ranch-house would take much longer to build than the barn and stables. He figured if they could get the frame and a few rooms done, it would at least be enclosed by the time the winter snows came. Seasoned ranchers were predicting a bad one for this year. *If I can get the basics done in the house, then Belle and I can move in.*

# # #

"How's the house coming?" Belle asked her husband as they were getting ready for bed one night.

"The floors are done; the walls and doors are all in place, and the cistern has been dug. I just need to get the pump for the kitchen. Men are out there now drilling for a well for our drinking water and for the livestock."

"It's really coming along then, isn't it?"

"Yes, I think next week we can begin moving our things out there."

"Oh good. I can hardly wait. Has Sam got our furniture in yet?"

"He said it would come in on the freight wagons early next week."

"Oh, I'm so excited!"

"Me too," he agreed. "It feels like snow is on its way, so I'm glad it's all enclosed now."

"Yes, it won't be long before we see snow. I hate to think of the cold coming."

Thad hugged his wife closer as if to ward off the cold of the coming winter.

111

CHAPTER THIRTY-SEVEN
Welcome to Whitehorse Ranch!

"Thad! What are you doing? Don't drop me!" Belle squealed as he picked her up and carried her through the front door of their new home.

"I'm carrying my bride across the threshold. The real one this time. Welcome to Whitehorse Ranch, Belle."

Thad had enlisted the aid of both his mother and Belle's mother to lend a woman's touch to the interior once the building part of the ranch-house was finished. He instructed Belle not to come out there until he gave the word. He'd planned it to surprise her. So, while she was working at Doc's office in town, he and the two mothers decorated and worked to make the house into a lovely home.

"Oh, Thad it's beautiful," she said as he sat her down in the middle of the living area. "How on earth did you do all this?"

"I confess, I got help from both our mothers."

"Well, that does make a little more sense," Belle laughed.

"Do you like it then?"

"I do, Thad. Very much."

He proceeded to show her all the special intricacies of their new home; the little nooks and crannies that he built in just for her. Belle was thrilled with her husband's attempts to please her. The fact that their mothers also prepared their first meal in their house was extra special to the couple. They were able to do nothing but enjoy each other that first evening.

# # #

Life at Whitehorse Ranch was a busy one. It was almost November, the weather turned colder than usual, and Belle finished making her soap. The first year Beth lived at Deer Creek Ranch, Sarah and Martha Garrison came to make soap with her. They continued this endeavor every year in the fall. Beth kept the equipment at her ranch so the ladies went there again to complete their task, this time with Belle Tucker. Belle had been saving ashes since they moved into their new home by Whitehorse Lake. She'd been giving them to Beth to put in the leaching barrel. Belle also saved fat drippings, grease, and bones for the process. The ladies grew lavender to use in the making of the soap.

Belle left her employment at Doc Phillip's office so that she could get her home ready for the winter. The cold and snow would be too much for a daily ride into town.

Since Belle wasn't able to harvest her own garden products, before her wedding she went to her mother's home and helped her, then went to help her mother-in-law. At each place, Belle received a large portion to supply her own pantry for the coming winter. Many of the wedding gifts to the couple also included products from gardens.

Thad worked with his horses now that he and Belle were firmly planted in their new home. The area ranchers provided the biggest market for his horses since there existed a need for good cutting horses, as well as his thoroughbreds. Cutting horses were special horses that could separate cattle from the herd. Not every horse could be used to do this job. He owned several head of two- and three-year-old quarter horses which he and his men were training for this.

Thad had moved a few of the Deer Creek ranch hands into the Whitehorse Ranch bunkhouse. He brought Nash from Deer Creek, making him the foreman, and Doby, Butch, Kid, and Casey to work with him. Slim would serve as their cook. When they weren't working with the horses, they would bring in logs to be cut and chopped for firewood for the winter for both the ranch-house and the bunkhouse.

One day he and Nash along with Doby and Casey were working in the corral with the cutting horses. Thad walked his horse quietly through the cattle herd in the large corral, maneuvering a single cow away from the others. He signaled to his horse that this was the cow by dropping the reins. Working on completely loose reins, his horse took control of the cow that Thad had picked. When the cow attempted to return to the herd, his horse planted himself in the cow's path. He outmaneuvered the cow into giving up. Then Thad took up the reins once again, signaling to his horse to quit.

Thad was more than pleased to see the progress of this. "Boys, I think he is ready. Let's put him in the pen with the other cutting horses."

While Thad unsaddled this horse, Nash began the same process with the next horse. He stopped to watch, leaning against the corral fence next to Doby. He always thought it a thrill to watch a good cutting horse in action. It was a beautiful sight. There were times when the horses were not good cutters. The maneuvers they performed could be hard on a horse's hips, so they had to have good strong bones. In other words, good breeding.

"Looks good, boss," Doby commented.

Thad nodded. "This work is slower than molasses in January though. Tomorrow we'll get the rest of the men to help us with them."

Nash's horse successfully stopped the cow from going where it wanted. He turned to look at his boss and Thad raised his gloved hand in the air and jerked his thumb toward the corral with the other cutting horses in it.

"Doby, you're up," Thad instructed the ranch hand. He watched while Doby's horse passed the muster also. They had been working with these

113

particular horses for several weeks. Nash and Doby joined Thad outside the corral. Thad told Nash what he shared with Doby about getting the rest of the men to work with them.

The next day, all of the ranch hands worked with Thad in getting the horses ready. He believed he'd been lax in their training due to the fact that he spent so much time building the ranch. The horses needed to be worked with on a continuous basis. He would soon have twenty trained cutting horses ready to be sold.

"What now, Boss?" Nash queried.

"We take them to town to the livery corral. I'll post a sign in town that we will bring them in next Tuesday. I'll take a few of the riding horses in also."

"They're all good horses," Nash said. "They should sell well."

"Better hope so," Thad laughed. "This is how you men will get paid."

###

"Yesiree, Thad. These are sure fine cuttin' horses," said Brad Bendix on Tuesday. Bendix owned the Double B Ranch northeast of Mustang Ridge and was in the market for good cutting horses. Bendix operated entirely with cattle so he bought horses when he needed them. He'd done business with Thad in the past, so he knew the good quality of Thad's stock.

"I'll take ten of them," Bendix said. "And a couple of the thoroughbreds too."

"Thanks, Brad. Pick out the ones you want. I'll get the papers drawn up."

Orlo Weaver, a cantankerous old rancher several miles from Mustang Ridge, was not so persuaded to buy horses today or any other day. He used cost as an excuse.

"Pa says we're in for a rough winter, Orlo. Time to move your cattle to shelter."

"Got too many to get into shelter," Weaver grumbled.

"Orlo, I've seen your ranch. You have several deep coulees in that east pasture. Why don't you move your cattle over there?" Bendix asked. "You might lose stock even then, but most will be saved. I think all us ranchers will lose stock this winter, so it seems to me you would want to save as many as you can."

"You just mind your own business, Bendix, and I'll mind my own cattle." Weaver turned and stomped away from the livery corral.

"Hey there, fellas. Boy is it ever cold. What was Weaver growling about this time?" asked Dane Clark when he approached the corral. Clark operated the Windy Ridge Ranch. He had a large ranch and he generally purchased his horse stock from Thad.

"Oh, he apparently thought I was charging too much for my horses," answered Thad.

"Seems reasonable to me," Clark said, looking at the sale bill posted with the prices on the corral gate. "His hard luck if he doesn't want to buy them."

"Thad always has good stock and his cutting horses are well trained," Clark said to those around him. "How many cutters do you have left?" he asked Thad.

"Ten," Thad replied.

"Good, I'll take them all. Better add four thoroughbreds," Clark stated. "Thad, how about we go to Sally's and have a cup of coffee. Then we can take care of the paperwork out of this cold. That wind is starting to get to my bones. Brad, you come along too, I'm buying."

The ranchers instructed their hands to drive their strings of horses back to their ranches. Then they joined Thad in Sally's. Thad produced bills of sale for the cutting horses and thoroughbred horses and the ranchers made payment to him. Once he knew which ones the two ranchers picked, he was able to give them the proper papers. The three ranchers enjoyed a warming cup of coffee and talked about - you guessed it – the weather.

"Gonna be a bad one this year," Clark stated while they discussed the coming winter.

"Yup, I can feel it in my bones already," agreed Bendix.

"Thanks for the sales, fellas," Thad said. "I appreciate your business."

Thad took the money to the bank. He also picked up enough cash to pay the wages to his ranch hands. He ruminated on the ranchers' dire predictions as he and his men rode back to the ranch. How could he protect his horses and cattle? Tuck had many coulees on Deer Creek Ranch and though Thad had several, there weren't as many, or as big. He decided he would bring the horses up to the corrals and they would have the large lean-to on the barn for shelter. He would put his cattle in the coulees. Although he didn't run as many head of cattle as Tuck did, he still had a good number.

"Boys, it's payday," Thad called as he stepped inside the bunkhouse. Amidst the cheer that rose, he paid each of them their wages. It had been a profitable day for him and for his men.

115

CHAPTER THIRTY-EIGHT
Winter Comes Harshly

"Just listen to that wind howling!" Belle exclaimed as she pulled her shawl tighter around her shoulders.

Thad built up the fire in the living room fireplace. "I'm sure glad the men worked hard to get so much wood for our fireplaces. And our own coal for the stoves. We'd definitely be in a rough place without the wood and coal to keep us warm."

Belle worked on a quilt by the light of the kerosene lamp, but it wasn't enough for her to see clearly the small stitches, so she put it down.

"I don't remember it being this cold before Christmas in the past. Snow, yes, but not so cold. That usually comes after Christmas," he said, a note of concern in his voice.

"Will the livestock be okay in this cold?" she asked while pulling her knitting out of the sewing box. It would be easier on her eyes in the low light.

"We'll no doubt lose cattle and horses. That's why I brought in most of my horses and put them in the corrals. Pa said he could feel it in his bones that we would have a rough winter. That's when I moved them into the corrals. It seems all the ranchers are feeling it in their bones," Thad said, grimly.

In the evenings, Thad liked to do wood sculpting or whittling when they were seated around the fireplace. But tonight, the weariness was too much for him, so he just sat in his chair and rested.

"But what about Tuck's cattle?" Belle inquired.

"Pa moved them to the pasture with the coulees in it. That will give the cattle shelter from these strong winds. He hauled hay to them."

"Won't be long before Thanksgiving is here and right behind it will be Christmas. Thad, do you suppose we could have everyone here for Thanksgiving? I know your mother will want to have Christmas at Deer Creek so if we have Thanksgiving, do you think that would be nice?"

"I don't see why not. We can ask Ma about it Sunday at church. What are you knitting?" he asked her.

"A shawl for my mother for Christmas," she answered him. "I'm going to make one for your mother too."

"Nice," he murmured as the warmth from the fireplace began to lull him into slumber.

Belle noticed this and quietly allowed him his small nap while she knitted.

"Thad." He felt a hand on his shoulder, shaking him. "Thad, wake up. Let's go to bed. It's late."

116

Thad woke from a deep slumber. He felt so groggy. "How long have I been asleep?" he asked.

"A couple of hours," Belle said. "But you looked so uncomfortable, I just had to wake you so that you can get to bed and stretch out."

"Okay," he said rising slowly to his feet. "Just let me stoke up the fires in the fireplace and the stove. Then I'll be in with more coal for our bedroom stove."

Thad worked extra hard the next few days. He and the hands continued to chop wood for the fireplaces and haul coal from the mine for the stoves on the ranch. The cold weather had already started the last of October. Soon after their September wedding, construction on their ranch-house began. He was thankful for all the community's help in building their home. But there was no time to sit back and rest on their laurels. No, this was going to be a wicked winter. Possibly his bones were feeling it as well.

First and foremost was the need for fuel. Most of that would be wood. But now that they had a coal mine operating on their ranch, they could take advantage of that. Not too many homes were heated by coal, but Thad and Tuck were pledged to see that into fruition by starting with their own homes. They installed pot-bellied stoves to aid in heating in both the ranch-houses and the bunkhouses. The coal burned hot and provided a lasting and comfortable warmth in the rooms that a fireplace did not. The ranch hands voiced their approval for the centrally located stove. Even Belle appreciated the coal heat.

"Good night, my sleepy husband," Belle said once they were snuggled in bed, and enjoying the warmth emanating from the stove, and the bed warmer which warmed the bedding.

"Good night, Belle..." Thad once again had fallen into slumber, but at least he was in the right place for it.

117

CHAPTER THIRTY-NINE
Belle

Sunday came once again and they experienced a cold ride into town. Even the church seemed cold. Belle heard Tuck and Thad talking to Reverend Prescott about bringing a supply of coal to the church so there'd be more heat in the big stove. She was so thankful for their coal mine. She liked the heat a coal fire produced. It spread satisfying warmth throughout a room, more so than a wood fire.

Beth and Belle talked before church about having a Thanksgiving dinner at Whitehorse Ranch and she thought it was a grand idea. So, Belle began to invite people that very day. She asked her family, Thad's family, the Garrisons, Reverend Prescott and family, and the Cutters. Once she had that all settled in her mind, it was time for the service to start and she could sit back and really listen to the message.

Reverend Prescott's words filled her heart with hope.

"Christ fulfills our need to be right with God. God wants us to love Him with all our heart," he admonished them. "Are you trying to enter Heaven by your own accomplishments? If you struggle to make yourself right with God, it won't work. You're still in need of God's grace to follow Him."

Belle pondered Reverend Prescott's words while she and Thad drove back to their ranch-house following church. She prayed that if there were those in church that morning who hadn't yet, that they would accept God's gift of grace and know what a wonderful God we have.

As she and Thad rode back to the ranch, the cold temperature seemed to seep into her bones. She was so thankful to have a warm home to live. *So many things to be thankful for and at the top of that list is my wonderful husband.*

Belle thought about the things for which she was thankful, which made her think of what to have on the menu for Thanksgiving. She'd have Thad butcher one of the turkeys for the meal. Bread and potatoes would also be on the list, as others were bringing desserts and vegetables. She put Thad in charge of table space for everyone. This was the nice thing about having such a large living room.

When they got home, Thad stoked the fires and Belle began dinner preparations. It had been a nice Sunday morning service. They had been fed from God's Word, now it was time to feed the family from the bounty of their table.

CHAPTER FORTY
Thanksgiving 1883

"Folks, before we sit down, please hold hands and bow your heads while I ask the blessing," Thad said. "Father in Heaven, today we join together in giving thanks to You for all that You have done for us. We thank You for sending Your Son, Jesus, to die for our sins. We thank You for our family members and for our friends here with us today. We thank You for the town of Mustang Ridge and how it has grown, with all the new businesses since my family came here in '76. And thank You for how our families grew and the blessings You have bestowed on us each year. We thank You for our ranches and businesses. You have blessed us beyond what we ever thought possible. In Jesus Name, Amen."

The living room at their ranch-house was converted into a banquet hall of sorts by adding tables made of boards and placed on sawhorses. Thad and his men had constructed benches for seating at the tables. Twenty people were present to celebrate Thanksgiving Day as well as an impromptu housewarming for Thad and Belle. The guests included Tuck and Beth and Nate, Becca and Peter, Jacob and Sarah Wells and Ben, Matt and Mattie Cutter and Little Tuck and Louisa, Reverend and Esther Prescott and Daniel and Davy, and George and Martha Garrison and Rachel. Even Thad's ranch hands came in for a time to fill their plates.

Belle and Thad supplied two turkeys, butchered fresh from their own flock. The Garrisons brought a large smoked ham as well as a couple of Martha's delicious pies. Beth brought a baked bean dish in a large cast iron roaster pan and sourdough bread and Becca made fresh butter. The rest of the guests brought other side dishes and desserts.

With all those people in the house, Thad found that he didn't need a very big fire going in the fireplace. The stove warmed them very well.

"Ma, do you remember our first Thanksgiving at Deer Creek Ranch?" Becca asked while family and guests filled their plates with food from the delicious-smelling assortment on the serving table.

"I most certainly do," Beth said, clasping her husband's hand close to her.

Thad remembered that first Thanksgiving too. Thanksgiving Day in 1876 had also been a day for the stagecoach to stop at the Deer Creek Ranch Station. Therefore, Beth had requested an extra-long stop there so the passengers could share their family dinner. He thought that day had been the first time he observed a growing relationship between his mother and the sheriff. Thad recalled the confusion as his mother asked everyone to hold hands around the table while she offered the prayer. There must have been a spark when Ma and Pa touched hands because she had been tongue-tied and unable to offer the prayer, so the sheriff came to her rescue and asked the blessing in her place. Thad was thankful for God bringing Tuck into their lives. *Yup, sure was a spark between them at that point.*

"I remember that Thanksgiving as well," Matt Cutter recalled. "I was driving the stagecoach at the time. I remember how the passengers enjoyed the time. They felt like they had spent time with their own families."

Beth smiled and said, "Thank you, Matt. I appreciate you mentioning it."

"What's to mention?" Matt declared. "Deer Creek Ranch Stagecoach Station was my favorite stop along the route. Why else would I decide to stay around Mustang Ridge when I left the Overland Company? You Tuckers made it home for me. I was just returning home."

There was much embracing and tears after that. Mattie also in the midst of it all, contributing her joy that she agreed with her husband.

Mattie made some Pfeffernusse cookies for the occasion. Several of the women commented on the flavor in addition to the texture.

"They're like little hard buttons," remarked Sarah. "What did you say they are called?"

"Pfeffernusse, its German for Pepper Nuts. I got the recipe from a German lady who came out on the same wagon train as I did," Mattie explained. Mattie was a young widow who traveled by wagon train to join her brother, Pete Ballard, who ran the livery. "This lady made up a huge batch before she left on the wagon train. They keep for a long time in tin canisters. I thought Thanksgiving would be a good time to share them since I was thankful for her friendship on the train."

"What a good idea, Mattie," Beth said. "For you who don't know, Mattie came out by herself on the wagon train. She hired a young man to drive her wagon for her."

"Amazing," Peter commented. "I'm learning since moving here from Ohio, that Mustang Ridge is comprised of hearty people."

"Yes, indeed," Tuck said joining the conversation.

"Thad. How is the coal mine working out?" asked Sam. He had a bin behind the mercantile from which he sold coal on a small scale to his customers.

"I believe it's going well. As you can see from the stove here, the warmth provided far exceeds that of wood and it lasts longer," Thad replied. "I'm happy with that."

"Yes, it does feel pretty warm in here. You'd never know it was so cold outside," Matt commented.

"Was it a very cold trip for you?" Beth asked him.

"Yes, but we're going to split our trip home into two segments. Tomorrow we'll spend the day with Mattie's brother, Pete. I hope the snow holds off until we can get home," Matt said. "If not, we'll stay longer with Pete. That long a trip in the cold is hard on the little ones. We've got reliable ranch hands, so I trust them if we can't get home."

"I've heard talk we can expect record snowfalls this winter," Reverend Prescott said. "Any truth to that rumor?"

"Oh, it's going to be a bad one for sure," Jacob declared. "There was an abundance of acorns this year and the squirrels were frantically gathering them this fall before the snows come."

"What's that mean?" asked Becca, not sure if Jacob was serious or not.

"Bitter cold and deep snows," Jacob explained.

"Everybody knows that one – squirrels gathering nuts in a flurry, will cause snow to gather in a hurry. I believe that's how the saying goes," Tuck said.

"And the Wooly Bear caterpillar had a narrow orange band and they are fat and wooly this year," shared Matt. "The narrow orange band means heavy snow; a fat and fuzzy caterpillar means bitter cold."

"I didn't know there were so many different ways to tell if there was going to be bad weather for the winter," Belle commented.

"Oh, and there're even more signs; like thick onion skins and leaves falling from the trees late in the year," remarked Beth.

"There's another way too," Sam added. Everyone watched as he rose from the table and went to his coat by the door. He removed a small book and brought it back with him to the table and held it up for all to see.

"What is it?" Nate asked.

"It's called The Old Farmer's Almanac. I ordered a number of them for the mercantile and kept one for myself," Sam replied. He flipped through the pages of the book. "Here's what it says for our winter:

"Prepare for bitter cold temperatures and increased snowfall. Winters in the High Plains will become progressively worse through the next three or four years."

"Doesn't sound good to me," Belle added.

"How much are those books?" Thad asked.

"Six cents," responded Sam. "The 1884 edition should be coming out in January. If you want, I can order one for you then."

"I think you can put Deer Creek Ranch & Sons down for a copy, maybe two," Tuck said, looking at his son. Thad nodded his agreement.

CHAPTER FORTY-ONE
Winter

It was their first Christmas together as husband and wife. It seemed to Thad that Belle went all out to celebrate. They celebrated not only the birth of their Savior, but their first Christmas. He took Belle up to the foothills of the Mustang Mountains to pick out their tree. It was the same place that the new family of Tuck and Beth had gone to get their first tree. Thad believed in setting family traditions. He recalled that first Christmas and the trek to pick out a tree. All five of them had ridden their horses to the foothills where the pine trees began.

They had taken a pack horse along to carry the tree. Thad had even spied a deer and shot it. While field dressing the deer, a pack of howling wolves neared their tree-gathering party. However, they were able to elude the pack and make it back to the safety of the ranch. *I can do without the pack of howling wolves today though.*

Belle even insisted they pick out a tree for the hands in the bunkhouse. They had less floor space, so needed a smaller one. The ranch hands were pleased that they had been included in this thoughtful way.

When they returned to the ranch-house with their tree, Thad set it up in the living room and Belle began immediately to decorate it. She even put him to work stringing popcorn and dried cranberries. They both worked on the stringing at night when all the chores and dishes were done and they could spend time together quietly making decorations.

"What are your plans for tomorrow?" she asked.

"Oh, you know. Ranch stuff, work with the horses if the weather permits."

"It does seem to be getting colder, doesn't it? And the sky is so dreary-looking," she observed. "Do you think we're in for a big snowstorm?"

"I wouldn't be surprised. It's bound to come." Thad put down his popcorn string and went to the sofa where Belle was sitting. "There's one good thing about a snow storm, and that's being snow-bound with just you and me."

Belle put down her string and snuggled into his arm. "I think I see what you mean, Mr. Tucker."

"Well, I'm mighty tired. I think we should go to bed." He faked a big yawn, stretching with gusto.

Once they were settled into their bed with the stove pouring forth comfortable heat, Thad once again found himself and Belle wrapped in a loving embrace in their warm bed.

The next day loomed even drearier than the day before. "I can almost feel the snow in the air," she said. "Just like your Pa can smell the rain."

Thad had brought in more wood for the fireplace and coal for the heating stoves. "I agree. That's why I'm bringing in several days of fuel. There's always the possibility of such an enormous blizzard that we can't see to get to the barn. I remember once when a storm stranded the stagecoach at the station. We needed to use a rope to get to the barn to take care of the animals. By the way, I asked Slim to take care of your chickens and turkeys. He's going to gather the eggs. If we get snowed in, he'll take care of them and use the eggs to cook for the men."

"Sounds good," she agreed. "Look, it's starting to snow now. Such big flakes. I'm glad I gathered pine cones before the snow came."

"Why'd you gather pine cones?" he asked, puzzled.

"They're to hang on our Christmas tree. You didn't think the popcorn and dried cranberry strings were all we were going to do, did you?"

"No, I guess not. Anyway, I better get out there and finish getting ready to hunker in. I want to get a couple of ropes ready to run from here to the barn and the bunkhouse. Hopefully, we won't need them, but it's good to be prepared."

Belle did her part by holding the door open for Thad to bring in more wood to put in the wood box and coal in the coal bin. When the fuel had been brought in, she went to the kitchen to do her baking. She wanted to try her hand at making those German cookies that Mattie made at Thanksgiving time.

When Thad came back to the ranch-house, he was covered with snow. He stomped his boots and brushed it off his coat and took a deep breath. "I smell something with cinnamon in it," he announced as he sat the basket of eggs down by the door. He removed his coat and hung it over a chair that he placed close to the fireplace.

She handed him a mug and said, "Here, come and sit down. I made those German cookies, and here's a hot chocolate for you." His face lit up as he took one of the button-like cookies and smelled the delicious aroma of cinnamon. She knew just what he liked.

"So, it's getting worse, isn't it?" Worry framed her pretty face as she asked him.

Thad nodded grimly. "'Fraid so. I gave the hands last minute instructions. We strung the ropes while we could still see. We added to the supplies of both coal and wood for the bunkhouse and here for us. Now I guess we just wait it out."

"This really tastes good, Belle. Warmed me up from the inside. Thank you." He grabbed her around the waist as she passed his chair. He pulled her

123

down onto his lap and was lovingly kissing her when they were interrupted by a knock on the door.

"What...?" Thad helped Belle up from his lap and rising, he went to see who was at the door. "Must be one of the hands."

Sure enough. A snow-covered Slim was at the door. "Boss, sorry to bother you, but I was checking our supplies and we won't have enough coffee to last more than a day. Don't know how I didn't notice that before this."

"Well, we can't let you men run out of coffee!" exclaimed Thad with a grin. "Belle, do we have an extra bag of coffee beans in the pantry?"

"I'm sure we do. I'll get it."

While she went to get the coffee, Slim spoke in a low voice to Thad. "It's really bad out there, Boss. I needed to use the rope already to get here."

Thad shook his head. "That is bad. Sure hope the livestock that are still out on the pastures will be okay. The cows are heartier than the horses. That's why I brought most of the horses up to the corrals."

When Belle brought back a sack of coffee beans to Slim, he said, "Thanks, Mrs. Tucker. I'd best be getting back to the bunkhouse. Oh, by the way, the men liked how you strung popcorn and dried cranberries to decorate for Christmas. They asked if I'd pop some corn for them to do."

Belle smiled. "I'm glad. Slim, I made those Pfeffernusse cookies that we had at Thanksgiving for the men They go well with coffee. You could try dunking them in your coffee to soften them." She handed him a tin. "Take care now."

"Thanks, Mrs. Tucker."

After Slim left the house with his goodies, Thad commented to Belle, "That was nice of you to give the men your Pfeffernusse cookies. Slim probably doesn't make anything like that."

Belle laughed. "I'm sure he doesn't." She went to the window and looked out onto the mass of white, an anxious look on her face. She saw her husband watching her. "I know there is nothing we can do about the weather. God's in control of that."

Thad said, "There's something we can do though. Come here." They snuggled together on the sofa and bowing their heads, laid their concerns at the throne of God. When they finished, Belle realized her fear of the storm had been lifted and she was able to see the power God showed in the strength of the storm. She saw His creation also in the beauty of the swirling snow

The snowstorm lasted for four straight days. Thad could only hope the ranch hands were able to care for the livestock in the barn and stables. Fortunately, he had built the bunkhouse connecting to the barn. As for Thad himself, he tried to show no concern but he also realized his wife could see

124

right through him. She knew what was in his heart as well as she knew her own. They may have been married only a few short months, but already they thought as one.

On the fourth day, they woke to sunshine pouring into their bedroom. "Thad! It's the sun. Does that mean the storm is over?"

He peered out their bedroom window onto the whitened landscape for as far as the eye could see. "Yes, it appears so, Belle. Come see," he invited her.

"Oh, how beautiful!" she breathed at the wonder. "Only God could paint such an extraordinary picture."

Thad left his wife's side to add more fuel to the fire. Then he pulled on his clothes and headed out to the living room to get the fires going in the stoves and fireplace. When Belle finally emerged from their room, the heat from them was filling the room and the cook stove was ready to begin breakfast. She put on the blue and white enamel coffee pot, a wedding present from Thad's folks, and started the bacon cooking in the big cast iron pan.

Aware that the front door had opened, she turned to look. Thad had opened it and stood back. Nothing but a wall of snow greeted him. "Well," he said closing the door again. "Breakfast first, then I'll have to begin shoveling. Good thing I brought the shovel inside when it first started snowing."

Thad approached his wife from behind and put his arms around her, nuzzling her neck with his beard. "I love you, Mrs. Tucker."

"And I love you, Mr. Tucker. But you need to let me get on with making breakfast or you might go hungry," she responded with a twinkle in her eye.

"Okay. Do I have time to shave?"

"If you get started right away."

He responded by giving her a big kiss, then turning, he headed down the hallway, saying, "Later, my dear."

#

The winter already proved to be a long one with many hardships related to ranching. A few head of cattle were lost, but the majority of Thad's horses were safe in the corrals and barn. He had built the barn so that if necessary, it could be opened for the horses to access and be out of the harsh elements of winter.

Thad had not been able to get out most of the winter to check on Deer Creek Ranch and his parents. He hoped they had fared well throughout the winter storms. The family hadn't been able to get together for Christmas. It was a good thing they had been able to enjoy a large celebration on Thanksgiving.

When the January thaws came and the snow drifts began to diminish in size, Thad said to Belle, "It might be a good thing to try and make our way into town for more supplies, Belle."

"That will be wonderful," she exclaimed. "We definitely need more coffee beans and bacon. And I'm so tired of being stuck inside all the time. It will be good to get out of the house."

"Does that mean you are tired of my company so soon?"

"Never!"

"Well, best get ready to ride then. Dress warm. I'll go hitch up the team to the wagon. The buggy probably wouldn't make it through the mud and snow." Thad left her to prepare herself while he went to see to the hitching up of the wagon. He stopped in at the bunkhouse to tell Slim what they were doing and to see about replenishing his needs for the feeding of the ranch hands.

" If you don't mind, I will saddle up my horse and ride along," Slim said. "Then if you run into trouble, I'll be able to help you."

"Good idea."

The three of them were soon ready to head to town. Thad had thrown a couple of shovels into the back of the wagon in case they were needed. He drove the wagon up to the ranch-house and helped his wife on board, covering her with a heavy blanket. "Slim's riding along with us to get supplies too. That way if we get stuck or something, he can help get us out."

"Great idea. Good morning, Slim. How did the bunkhouse fare these last few days?"

"Morning, Mrs. Tucker. Pretty well. Those coal stoves are lifesavers. Glad we have them. Played lots of poker, drank lots of coffee, and ate up all your little cookies. The men appreciated you thinking of them. Made a nice Christmas. Thank you."

"You're welcome, Slim."

The mercantile proved to be a meeting place for folks after the worst of the winter storms passed. Thad was pleased to see Ma and Pa there along with Nate and Becca.'

Ma rushed up to hug him and Belle. "Oh, it's so good to see you two! It has been a long winter. I really missed Christmas this year. But now that the snow's melting, do you think we can have a small celebration soon?" Ma asked.

Tuck and Thad looked at one another and shrugged, "Sure. Why not?" So, plans were made for a time to meet at Deer Creek Ranch for a belated Christmas. Beth told Belle to be sure to invite her parents and brother and she would tell Sam that he and Martha were also invited.

"We'll have our Christmas yet," his ma exclaimed. "We can celebrate the birth of Jesus at any time of the year."

They said goodbye and after purchasing and loading their supplies, they left to drop in on Belle's folks. Slim went back to Whitehorse Ranch saying, "I'll help unload when you get back."

# # #

Once again Deer Creek was home to a large Christmas celebration even though it wasn't on the traditional Christmas Day. The winter snows held off, allowing the guests to travel to the ranch and Thad was warmed once again by the gathering of his family and loved ones. A magnificent fare of food was available to all who came. He always loved to see his mother engaged in being the perfect hostess. He believed that was why she was such a good operator for the stage line during those days. Once everyone had enjoyed their fill of the delicious food and dishes were washed, presents were exchanged. Soon it was time to say their goodbyes and Thad and Belle drove their wagon back to their ranch-house.

"Wasn't it a wonderful Christmas?" she inquired of her young husband. "It was so good to finally get out and spend time with our families once again."

"Yes, but if that almanac is to be believed, we aren't done with winter by a long shot." He didn't want to discourage Belle, but realistically they were in for a long hard winter yet. They'd only just begun.

The days at their ranch following their Christmas celebration were spent preparing for more winter to come. Thad and the ranch hands cared for the livestock and added to their fuel supplies. Feed for the livestock was distributed to the coulees, as long as they could get out there.

Belle directed Thad to take the Christmas tree out and stick it in a snowbank now that their Christmas had passed. "That way the birds can enjoy the popcorn and berries," she explained.

Thad noticed that before long, the ranch hands had done the same thing with their tree from the bunkhouse. He chuckled to himself. What an influence his Belle has been on everyone at the ranch.

More winter came, which was expected, and spring returned once more in the Wyoming Territory.

CHAPTER FORTY-TWO

Spring 1884

"Belle, can you come out and show us where you want to have a garden?" Thad asked once the frost had left the ground in early May. "I'll have a couple of the men plow it for you once we know where and how big."

"Be right out, Thad. I just want to grab my shawl first."

Armed with Belle's instructions about where she wanted her first garden, he and a couple of the hands soon plowed the ground. Excited about the coming planting season, she said, "I want to set aside an area for Slim to grow vegetables for his bunkhouse cooking. Can you ask him if he wants it closer to the bunkhouse or here?"

Thad was pleased that she included the ranch hands in things as simple as a plot of ground to grow food for them too. He knew his men appreciated her thoughtfulness toward them.

After the garden plots were plowed, Thad hitched a horse to a chained log and dragged it over the plowed ground several times to break up the clumps of sod. Belle approached her new garden with a basket of seeds and potato eyes to begin her planting. It was a daunting task for Belle since she had not planted a garden by herself before. She'd shared in the work with her mother in the Wells family garden, however, and went about this one in the same way.

When the garden had all been planted and the stakes were in place signifying where the rows were located, she began erecting frames for the pole beans. That evening while she and Thad shared their supper at the table, he observed how tired his wife appeared. "Belle, you look exhausted. I think you should take it easy with the garden for a little while."

"Don't worry, Thad. I'm all done with the planting. I just need to wait until things start growing. Then comes the weeding."

The next morning, Belle's back was hurting her and when she rose to go start their breakfast, she found that not only was she experiencing back pain, but she also felt nauseated. She told Thad she must have pulled a muscle which made her sick. She promised Thad she would lie down after breakfast. He worried she'd overdone with the garden preparation.

This continued on in such a manner for several days until Belle sat her husband down one evening to discuss what was wrong with her. "Thad, it isn't so much the work in the garden, though that may have been the problem the first day. I think I might be expecting."

"You mean, we are going to have a baby? That's so wonderful, Belle." He was thrilled. The two of them were about to start their family. He hugged her tightly.

"Don't get too excited until we know for sure. It's quite early yet. I want to go in to see Doc Phillips tomorrow. Maybe he can confirm it as well as help me to alleviate this back pain."

Thad took his wife into Mustang Ridge the next morning to see the doctor. Even though he knew Belle was perfectly capable of driving herself in the buggy, he wanted to be with her when she saw the doctor. As it turned out, he was glad he had gone. He waited in the outside office while Belle and the doctor were in the exam room. When he finished, Doc Phillips came out and asked Thad to join Belle in his office.

"Thad, my boy, you and Belle are going to be parents next January. As far as the back pain goes; it may be nothing or it may be the sign of a hard delivery coming," the doctor said. "Belle, I want you to take it easy for a couple of weeks. I know it started after you worked in the garden so to be on the safe side, no hoeing, or run the risk that you might lose the baby. Come see me in a couple of weeks so we can monitor this closely."

"Sure, Doc. The men and I can help Belle with the weeding in the garden. We'll plan to see you in two weeks then."

Once they were in the buggy, Thad asked, "Do you want to stop at your folks and share our news with them before we leave town?"

"Oh yes. That would be wonderful," she cried with delight.

When the two of them stopped at the Wells home, Sarah came to the front door and flew to Belle. "You're pregnant, aren't you?"

"How on earth did you know?" asked Belle.

"I was just thinking about you and this thought just popped into my head. The next thing I know, here you are. I'm right, aren't I?"

"Yes, Mama. You should have a grandchild by next January."

"Oh, that's wonderful news," exclaimed her mother, hugging each of them. "Jacob, we're going to have our first grandchild!"

Jacob had just walked in after a day working at his blacksmith shop. He barely had his hat hung up when he was bombarded with the announcement. Ben, hearing the commotion of excited female voices coming from the parlor, came out of the kitchen and asked, "What's going on?"

Thad looked to Belle and inclined his head toward Ben. Belle nodded.

"Ben, you are going to be an uncle by next January."

"All right! Glad to hear it!"

"Are you feeling okay, Belle?" her mother inquired.

"I'm doing well, Mama. Doc said I would have to take it easy. I've been tiring so quickly and my back hurts a lot. I barely got my garden planted. But otherwise, I feel good."

"Oh, honey. I'll be glad to help you in any way I can."

"I told her the men and I will take care of the garden. She won't have to concern herself about that. But when it's time to put up the vegetables, I for one would appreciate your help with that," Thad said. "I don't know the first thing about that process."

"I'd be happy to. But if you two need anything else in the way of help, you'll let me know, won't you, dear?"

"Yes, Mama. It's good to know that you will be there for us."

"Well, we need to be heading back to the ranch," Thad said. "We've got a wagon load of supplies to see to."

So, amidst loving hugs from both her parents, Belle and Thad took their leave and made their way to their ranch where he unloaded the wagon with Slim and Hank helping.

In a few days, the opportunity came for Thad and Belle to share their good news with his parents. The two of them traveled to Whitehorse Ranch to visit and were told of the pending birth of a grandchild.

"Did you see Pa's reaction?" Thad asked Belle after his folks had gone back home. "He was near busting his buttons."

Belle smiled. She had seen. "Your mother is planning already what she will make with her knitting needles."

Two weeks went by and the couple returned to the doctor as he had advised. Doc checked Belle thoroughly and asked, "Have you been feeling any better, Belle? Do you still have the backaches?"

"Yes, Dr. Phillips. I spend a lot of time on the sofa or in my rocking chair. I don't even fix meals. Buts still my back hurts."

"Belle, I think you should continue this rest. Spend even more time laying down. I don't like that your blood pressure is still high," Doc said. "This will stress the baby and we don't want that."

"Thanks, Doc. When should she come back?"

"Continue these precautions and come back in a month. If you experience more problems, come back earlier."

So, Belle's pregnancy continued in much the same way except for more time spent laying down. Her garden grew that summer, largely due to the hard work of Slim, and two or three of the ranch hands. Thad made sure that one or two of the men were able to work the garden each day. Observing Belle as she fixed her gaze out the window, he wanted to make sure she had no reason to take up a hoe.

130

Thad Tucker: Wyoming Rancher/Karen Carr

When the weather was nice, she would spend her hours perched in her rocking chair on the covered veranda. While she viewed closely the work being done there, she accomplished a great deal of hand sewing. There seemed to be no end to the holes in Thad's socks and the darning kept her busy. Her favorite hand project was making baby clothes and sewing many flannel diapers. Her large bag beside her chair contained her sewing projects in addition to her knitting

"Thad, could I walk through the garden at least?" she asked one day. "I'm sure I see some green beans that are ready to pick."

"Okay, but just to look," her husband agreed. "But no picking beans." He went along and picked the beans that she pointed out. Belle held her apron out to make a basket for them.

"Our very own green beans for supper," she exclaimed. "At least I can sit at the table and cut them."

"Just tell me how to cook them," Thad said.

131

CHAPTER FORTY-THREE
Belle

"God has so blessed me, not only to be married to such a wonderful man as Thad, but to now be expecting his child," Belle told her mother one day when she came for a visit. "God is so good."

Belle sucked in a breath since her baby gave her a good kick. "He is reminding me that he is here too."

"He?" asked her mother.

"Yes, I said he. I think I'm right in this, that my baby is a boy. With the way I am consistently being kicked, this baby has to be a boy."

Belle was thankful that some of the hands were happy to work in the garden. She knew it was probably hard for a cowboy to take up a hoe, so she really appreciated them. She was quite aware of her own limitations and wanted to follow what Doc Phillips had ordered for her to do. She knew she'd have to spend a lot of time lying down too and now as time went on, it seemed to help her aching back. Belle saw Thad's worried looks cast her way so she tried not to show any discomfort. She didn't want him to worry but she knew he did. *Father, help me through this long pregnancy ahead. I pray for my baby that he will be healthy and help Thad not to worry so.*

A lot of Belle's time was spent knitting and sewing diapers for when the baby would be born. During the warmer weather, she sat out on the veranda to do her work. It gave her a time of fresh air that Doc said was okay. As her confinement continued, Belle became more and more antsy to be up and about.

Her moods seemed to be getting worse as time wore on too. She cried for no reason. Belle knew she worried Thad, though she tried to explain to him how mood changes are normal for a pregnant woman. She was sure he must've been at loose ends about knowing what to do with her because she certainly felt that way herself. Both Beth and Sarah came out to the ranch to help, giving Thad the opportunity to leave the house. You would think when they came, he would run out as fast as his legs could carry him, but he wanted to be with Belle as much as possible.

Belle looked forward to those times with her two mothers since it gave her a change of pace. However, when winter arrived, they weren't able to get out to the ranch as often. During those times, Thad cared for and supported his wife. She shared with them her concern that she caused Thad a lot of undue worry. They promised to pray for them both.

In the middle of all this, Thad and Belle celebrated their first anniversary in September of that year. Thad held his wife close to him as they sat in front of the fire. The nights were starting to get a little chilly, so a fire was a welcome comfort.

"This is a wonderful time for us, Belle. We've been married for one year, you are pregnant with our first child, and through the efforts of the men, the garden produce has been harvested and your mother has put up the vegetables. I'd say we are due for some hugging and kissing."

Belle returned Thad's embrace. *He really is a wonderful husband. I truly thank God for him every day.*

CHAPTER FORTY-FOUR
Lil' Buddy

One day in early January of 1885, after Thad had completed the chores in the barn and stable, he came to the ranch-house to tell Belle of his plans to ride out to the north pasture and check the livestock. Sarah was staying with her for the day, so he felt comfortable in leaving the ranch.

Thad allowed his horse to go at a trot up the valley road. His main reason for going there was to check on the horses that were located in that area. He was proud of his horses and thankful that they were growing as well as they had been. God had been good to Whitehorse Ranch and he appreciated it.

Cresting a ridge out in the middle of nowhere, his horse started whining, shying away from a stand of trees. "Easy, Rowdy," he cautioned the horse. He saw something move and slowly released his rifle from its sheath. Could be a mountain lion or even a bear. He didn't want to take any chances, so he had his weapon at the ready.

Thad was totally surprised when a tiny brown and white form slunk on the ground toward him and his horse. He dismounted and tied Rowdy's reins to a small tree. Walking closer, he saw that it was a mangy dog, well, a puppy really. The pup weakly raised its head to Thad's hand.

"You poor thing," Thad said, holding his hand out. "You are weak from hunger, aren't you, boy?" Thad reached into his pocket and pulled out a bag with his pemmican. He offered a piece to the starving puppy and he readily wolfed it down.

"You probably should have chewed it a bit more, little guy."

Thad retrieved his canteen from his saddle and poured some into the palm of his hand. The grungy canine slurped up the moisture and Thad poured more for him.

A few more pieces of pemmican and more handfuls of water, then Thad lifted the pup to the front of his saddle and mounted behind him. "Okay, little buddy, let's get you back to the ranch and get some more food in you."

When Thad arrived at the ranch, he rode into the barn. While he rubbed Rowdy down, the pup ate and drank more. Slowly Thad gave him a bath with water he warmed on the stable stove. He knew he didn't dare bring the dog into the house as dirty as he was.

"Thad, you were certainly gone a long time," Belle greeted him as he entered. "What have..." She broke off when she saw the puppy following close on his heels.

"I found him when I was coming back from the north pasture," Thad explained. "He was hungry and seemed friendly, so I brought him back and cleaned him in the barn."

Sarah was intrigued with the dog and called him over to where she was sitting. "What a good boy you are," she said. "It is a he, isn't it?"

"Yes," Thad told her.

"Have you named him yet?" Belle inquired.

"No, I don't know what to call him," he answered. "I'll have to ponder on it some".

CHAPTER FORTY-FIVE
1885 It's a Boy!

Thad had been mulling over what to call his new puppy. It was hard to think of the perfect name for his lil' buddy.

"I've decided on a name for the pup," Thad announced at the breakfast table. "I think Buddy is a good name for him. What do you think?"

"That's a good name, Thad," Belle responded. It was a joy to see how much Thad enjoyed that puppy he found. He obviously doted on Thad too. "I'm glad you came up with a name for him finally. I was afraid we would end up just calling him "Dog,"

Thad was aware that his wife was experiencing discomfort different than before, but she refused to acknowledge it. He watched as she slowly rose from the breakfast table, one hand at her back and the other on her swollen belly. As she began clearing things away, he said, "Belle, I'll take care of the dishes. You go lay down. You look exhausted."

"Thank you, dear. I guess I will lie down on the sofa for a while."

He went ahead and cleared the table, keeping his eye on his wife as he did. He had just finished washing the dishes when he heard the creak of a buckboard pulling up in front of the house. Buddy barked once to warn of a visitor. Going to the window, Thad saw that it was Belle's mother. He turned to tell Belle her mother had arrived and saw that she had risen and was bent over holding her abdomen with her hand. He rushed to her side to help her, forgetting for a moment that company had arrived. But Sarah entered the house without knocking, experiencing a feeling that her daughter needed her. "A mother always knows when her child needs her," she said later.

"Oh, Mama. I'm so glad you're here," Belle gasped. "I think it's time."

"Yes, I can see that," Sarah said, eyeing the wetness that showed on the front of Belle's dress.

Thad grabbed his coat from the peg. "I'll send one of the men for Doc Phillips and be right back."

He returned a few minutes later to report that Butch was dispatched to ride for the doctor and that one of the hands had unhitched Sarah's horse and turned it loose in the corral. "How is she?" he asked his mother-in-law. "Is there anything I can do?"

"Yes, Thad. Help me get her into bed." Once she had Belle out of the wet clothes and in her bed, she sent Thad to get a basin of hot water and clean cloths.

"Will the doctor get here in time?" he asked Sarah out of Belle's hearing.

"Probably, because I think she is in for a long labor," Sarah looked worried and that alarmed Thad. If his mother-in-law was showing apprehension, it made him uneasy. However, he was able to hide his concern from Belle and simply showed her gentleness and love.

As Sarah predicted, Doc Phillips arrived while Belle was still in labor. Weakened by the great racking labor pains, she barely recognized the doctor's presence.

"Belle, can you hear me?" he asked her. But Belle only moaned.

Thad's nerves were on edge as he looked on. "Doc, can't something be done?"

"Son, why don't you go out to the kitchen and put on a fresh pot of coffee. I will need a good strong cup when I'm done here. While you do that, I will examine your wife and see what needs to be done."

Thad complied with the doctor's wishes. He knew what Doc Phillips was thinking. Sure, he might've been in the way, but he wanted Belle to know of his presence. *I guess I could use a strong cup of coffee too.* As he entered the kitchen, he suddenly realized he was hungry as well. Casting a glance at the large pendulum clock in the living room, he saw that it told the time of 1:15. No wonder he felt hungry. He knew Doc Phillips and Sarah would also be hungry, so he began to look around to get an idea on what to prepare. About the only things he knew to cook were bacon, eggs, and flapjacks. So, obtaining the necessary ingredients, he set about making an afternoon breakfast.

The coffee was ready along with the food when Sarah came from the bedroom. She carried a pan out the side door and emptied it. Then she came to the cook stove and refilled the pan with warm water from the reservoir.

"How is it going? Thad asked. "How's Belle?"

"It won't be long now. My, that smells so good, Thad." She grabbed a slice of cooked bacon and stuffed it in her mouth as she went back to the bedroom with the water.

Thad poured himself a cup of coffee and filled a plate for himself. He sat at the table and relieved his hunger by eating. Suddenly, he heard the distinctive cry of an infant. He pushed back his chair and hurried to the bedroom door, only to be barred from entering by Sarah coming out carrying a bundle.

"Thad, meet your brand-new son," she had the baby wrapped tightly in a soft blanket. "Would you like to hold him?"

"Yes, I would," he said, gingerly taking the warm bundle in his big hands. "Is he okay? Is Belle okay?"

"He's more than okay, and so is Belle. She's just worn out and will need a lot of rest. You'll be able to see her shortly."

Thad held his son in his arms, noticing his soft fluff of hair and his pink cheeks. The proud father's heart melted when his son clasped his father's finger with his tiny hand. "Jackson Adam," he said. "Belle and I want to name him Jackson Adam Tucker, after both my fathers."

Sarah smiled and patted his arm. Taking back the infant, she turned back into the room to see the doctor nod and beckoned Thad to come in. He slowly neared his wife's bed as Sarah laid the sleeping infant next to his sleeping mother. He took Belle's hand, caressing it gently, but she didn't stir. He looked questioningly at Doc Phillips.

"She had a hard time of it, my boy. She just needs to catch up on her rest. Now, lead me to that coffee. Do I smell bacon too?"

Going back to the kitchen, Thad poured Doc a cup of coffee and filled a plate of bacon and eggs while Doc piled flapjacks on it. He sat with the doctor at the table but out of the corner of his eye, he watched the bedroom door. When Doc finished eating, he said, "Thank you, Thad. I've never tasted such good food and coffee."

"It's about all I know how to make," Thad said.

"Don't apologize, my boy. It was just what was needed. Congratulations. He's a fine healthy boy. Now, what have you decided to name him?" Doc prepared to write the name on the birth certificate.

"Jackson Adam Tucker."

"Fine name, fine name." He wrote it on the certificate and inserted the date and time of birth. He also wrote it in his book, and then handed the certificate to Thad. "Find a safe place to keep it."

Thad nodded.

"Now I'll go relieve Sarah so she can eat." Sarah came out soon after the doctor entered the bedroom. She came to the kitchen and after washing her hands, took a seat at the table.

"You look exhausted too, Sarah," Thad observed, handing her a steaming cup of coffee. "Want a plate of bacon and eggs and flapjacks?"

She nodded, wrapping her hands around the cup and blowing on the dark liquid. "Thank you, Thad. Yes, it has been quite a morning. Belle worked so hard to deliver little Jackson."

"Sarah, tell me. How did you know to come when you did?" Thad asked her. He had been curious since she had shown up at their door just as Belle doubled over from her first pain.

"I was reading my Bible and praying. God just wouldn't let me pray about anything other than Belle. So, I told Jacob that God was directing me to go right away to her. He hitched up my horse while I packed an overnight bag, and here I am."

"Yes, you are, and I for one am grateful to both you and God."

Later, Jacob and Ben came to see how Belle was. Since his wife had not returned, he assumed that the baby had come. Earlier in the day, one of the ranch hands was sent to Deer Creek Ranch with the announcement of the baby's birth. So, about the same time, Tuck, Beth, Nate, and Becca all arrived in their two-seater. Thad experienced more joy at seeing their family's excitement over their new son.

"What are you naming him?" his mother asked.

"Jackson Adam Tucker, after both my fathers," he replied. He was aware of the pleasure his announcement made to his parents, especially his pa.

CHAPTER FORTY-SIX
Belle Weary of Bedrest

Sarah brought Belle out to the living room three days after the birth of Jackson, "It's time to get up from bed and do some moving – but slowly," she cautioned her daughter.

"Oh, I will, Mama. I'm just so glad to be up out of that bed. I have so many things to do. I can't be lingering in bed when my son needs to be cared for and I have knitting and sewing to do, and…"

"Now hold on there!" Thad said with a grin. "Did you not hear what your Mama said? Slowly. And I heard Doc Phillips tell both you and your Mama not to let you overdo."

Belle patted Thad's hand and smiled at him. "I will, husband. But you may have to remind me."

"You can count on that! How long should she stay sitting here, Sarah?"

"Since this is the first time she is up, just a few more minutes. She can increase it each time. I think in a couple more days she'll be able to take over care of Jackson and I'll go back home."

"Oh, Mama. You've been an absolute angel to come and help me."

"Yes, Sarah, we're so glad you were able to come and with such impeccable timing too."

"How are things going in Mustang Ridge?" Belle asked her mother. "Anymore on the railroad coming through?"

"Yes, it appears that the crews will start laying track soon. They plan to begin at Cheyenne and work their way north. It'll be nice to have rail service to Mustang Ridge. I know Sam's looking forward to it. Shipping by rail won't be as expensive for him and things will come sooner." Sarah paused and Thad could see that she had another thought on her mind.

"What is it, Sarah? You see a problem?"

"I'm concerned about the workers who will be hired by the railroad. I've heard stories about how the railroad hires Chinese laborers and treats them atrociously."

"I know," Thad agreed. "I've heard that too. It's the same with the miners which is why we kept ownership of our mine. There's not much we can do about the railroad except treat the workers well while they are in and around Mustang Ridge."

"I agree," said Sarah, and Belle nodded. "We should plan a special celebration when they come through."

"Like what?" asked her daughter.

"I don't know. Perhaps a special picnic with all sorts of good food for them. Maybe a dance or a musical program. You know; to let them know we think of them as people and not workhorses."

"Well, I'm sure the church ladies will come up with a great idea," said Thad. "They'll have the rest of the winter to prepare."

"I think I'll go back to my room now. I hear little Jackson fussing, so it's probably time to feed him."

"No doubt he needs changing too," said his grandmother, smiling.

Thad helped his wife to stand and walked her back to their bedroom. He was so proud of her. And now the two of them had grown to three. *Thank you, Father, for my new son and for my wonderful wife.*

CHAPTER FORTY-SEVEN
Trouble at the Mine

When the warm weather returned to the area, so did the mining crew. George Cummins contacted Tuck concerning their return to work once the winter cold was over. Tuck and Thad went out to check over the barracks that had been built for the miners. Nash went along, driving the wagon with a load of wood for their cooking needs. They helped Nash unload the wood. When they finished the job and Nash prepared to head back to the ranch, Cummins arrived with the miners and the cook in two wagons. Tuck and Thad greeted him and the workers. The ranchers were pleased with how humanely the miners were being treated.

"How was your winter?" Cummins asked. "Did you lose many cattle?"

"A few, but it could've been worse," Tuck replied.

"What do you think about the coal, Mr. Cummins?" Thad inquired. "Will it continue for very much longer?"

"I didn't see any end to it when we left last fall. To my way of thinking, it should yield quite a bit more."

"Good to hear," Thad said. "Do you need anything?"

"No, we're good. Picked up our supplies in town when we came through there. I see you hauled in more wood for the cooking stove. Thanks."

# # #

Several weeks later, Thad and his men were working in the corral with the horses. They started early as soon as breakfast was over. Suddenly, they heard the chilling sound of the mine's whistle and they stopped what they were doing.

"Trouble at the mine," called Nash.

"Mount up boys," Thad directed. "Butch, you and Slim stay here and keep an eye on things. Doby, hitch up the wagon and bring that."

Belle was on the veranda and heard the alarm. "Go, Thad. Take care of the miners. I'll pray for everyone and safety for you and the hands. If anyone is hurt, bring them back here if you can."

Thad nodded and swung his horse around to ride out with his ranch hands. He prayed while he rode that everyone would be safe. He thanked God for his wife and her heart of service.

When Thad and his men arrived at the mine, they saw that several men from town also came to help. They too had heard the whistle. He was glad to see Doc was there, too.

"Cummins," Thad called. "What happened?" He noticed the over-seer had black smudges on his face. Looking around, he saw that most of the miners did as well.

"Had a cave-in," Cummins panted. "Everyone got out except for two of the Greek miners."

"Tell us what to do," Thad said.

Cummins directed the ranchers and townspeople as to what needed to be done. Poles were taken into the mine to help shore up the shaft. Once the shaft was stabilized, other miners began digging out the debris inside. They could not communicate in English, but they did know that fellow miners were in trouble.

It took all day, but just before dusk, a cheer rose and the two trapped miners were brought out on litters. Doc examined them while Thad told him they could be brought to his ranch to be cared for by Belle. Doc set the broken bones and told Thad he'd meet them at the ranch.

One of the miners was still unconscious and had a broken leg as well as the head injury. The other miner had a broken arm and leg. Doc said they would be okay in the wagon ride to Thad's ranch.

"Just go slow," he cautioned Doby.

The miner with the head injury, Demetri Kostas, had regained consciousness by the time they got to the ranch. He also had a broken leg. The second miner, Stavros Papadakis, had a broken leg and arm. Of course, the miners had numerous cuts and bruises as well. Thad moved a single bed into the guest room and the two miners shared a hospital room of sorts. Thad had constructed simple bedframes for the other bedrooms. He was glad that he had done that. After all, Belle had been Doc's nurse for several years and knew just what the physician would order.

After a few weeks of healing, the miners were able to return to the mine barracks. They were given light-duty work, things they could do sitting down. So, a much worse disaster was averted, and the mining proceeded as before, though with even more safety.

143

CHAPTER FORTY-EIGHT
Belle

Belle spent considerable time holding her baby boy. She almost hated to lay him down in his crib. But she found that in order to keep up with her household chores, it was necessary for that to happen. *He is so beautiful. Thank You, Father for giving us this wonderful gift.*

Jackson was such a good baby. He slept most of the night through and was happy to lay on a quilt on the floor while Belle did her work. She discovered that Thad returned to the house numerous times during the day at first. Just to see how the two of them were coming along.

Most of the time, Thad took Buddy with him, but on occasions when the dog stayed in the house, he would lay on the quilt with Jackson. Belle appreciated how well-behaved Buddy was when he laid with baby Jackson. *I think Thad will have to share Buddy's affections with Jackson.*

They had many visitors that summer and fall. Dotting grandparents, Aunt Becca, and many of Belle's friends from Mustang Ridge came to give their good wishes and to admire little Jackson.

The Thanksgiving gathering at Whitehorse Ranch later that year, was an even more thankful time for family as they shared their son with relatives.

Christmas was an exciting time for the new parents because of Jackson's wide-eyed glee at the tree and presents. By this time, he was an active eleven-month-old, moving around the room at a fast crawl. He no longer stayed on the quilt while Belle worked. She was happy to see that he would go there and lay down when he was tired. Especially if Buddy would lay with him.

144

CHAPTER FORTY-NINE
Becca and Peter 1886

The year of 1886 was already warming up in the spring. It looked like the summer was going to be a real scorcher. Thad recalled that was what Sam said the Old Farmer's Almanac predicted. *Guess I'll have to find my copy and read it better.*

Thad and Belle were really thankful they'd built their home next to Whitehorse Lake. It was a blessing to go there and cool off during the hot days. In addition, Thad built a small lean-to with scrap lumber so Belle could be out of the sun with little Jackson. However, it'd been hard to keep the boy out of the sun. He so enjoyed sitting and splashing in the water, especially when he could splash his father. Thad allowed the ranch hands to enjoy the cooling water also, but only when Belle wasn't there. The reason being, the men would be in their red-flannel long johns. That would not be appropriate in front of Belle. He made sure they had time to cool off each of the blistering hot summer days. That took care of their baths too although they preferred to call it swimming.

Thad laughed when he saw Buddy enjoying the lake too. Jackson and Buddy splashed each other when they were in the water. Jackson' giggles showed how much he enjoyed playing with Buddy.

Tuck and family had the creek behind their ranch-house and had been using that to cool off. The ranch hands used it further downstream. Tuck liked Thad's idea of the shelter and built one for his family also.

All in all, the Tucker families and their ranch hands were able to survive the hot summer. They almost looked forward to winter. But then Sam was quick to remind them that winter would be so harsh they would soon be wishing for the heat of the summer past.

Jackson grew and was the apple of his Mama and Papa's eyes. He inherited his father's thick blond hair and his blue eyes, but Thad believed he saw Belle in his little face. Jackson continued to amaze them all with his antics, especially 'Gumpa Tuck.' He would come over to their home with any kind of excuse, but Thad was on to him. He was proud that Tuck enjoyed his grandson so much.

Tuck left a lot of the day-to-day ranching to his foreman, Wade. That made it easier for him to travel to Whitehorse Ranch. Sometimes he even took little Jackson to the lake to splash and he himself would enter the lake in his long johns.

# # #

Thad and Belle were pleasantly surprised when Becca came out to their ranch one evening.

"What are you up to, Becca?" Belle asked her best friend. "I can tell by your face, you're all het up."

"Peter asked me to marry him!" The two women squealed with excitement as they hugged each other.

"Did you say yes?" Thad asked, managing to get a word in edgewise.

"Oh, Thad. Of course, she said yes," Belle said. Turning back to Becca, she asked, "Have you set a date yet?"

"Yes, we want it to be after all this heat has ended," Becca replied. "I want to have your mother make my dress. Of course, I want you to be my bridesmaid." Once again, the two women squealed and hugged each other.

"Congratulations, Becca. I like Peter. You have chosen to marry a fine young man," Thad said.

"Thank you, Thad. That means a lot to me."

Thad, always the voice of reason, asked, "Will Peter's family be able to come for the wedding?"

"Oh yes. And his brother, Steven will be his best man."

"I just had a thought," Thad said. "We have these extra rooms. There would be room for Peter and his brother in one room and another room for his folks. That way they would save money on a hotel."

"That's a wonderful idea, dear. What do you say, Becca?"

"I'll see what Peter says, but I think they'd be open to it. Thanks, you two." Becca paused and seemed to be trying to say more, but evidently, she was afraid to voice it.

"What is it, Becca?" Thad asked.

"Thad, since I was a little girl, I've dreamed of you walking me down the aisle on my wedding day. But... now that Pa...uh...Tuck... is in my life, I feel different. But I want you both."

Thad laughed. "You do what seems best to you. My feelings won't be hurt. I understand."

Becca hugged her brother.

Belle said, "I have an idea." They looked at her questioningly.

"Becca, you have always believed that Thad stood at your side, protecting you through the harsh realities of traveling by wagon train and coming to Mustang Ridge, right?"

Becca nodded, waiting for Belle to go on.

"And the last ten years, you've learned to love and rely on Tuck in a different way, as a father. He also has been at your side. So, since you have

146

two sides, I suggest you have one of them on each side as you walk down the aisle to meet your intended; Tuck on one side and Thad on the other."

"What a marvelous idea!" Becca exclaimed. "Thad, what do you think?"

"I like it. Good idea, Belle."

So, the plans were made for the wedding to be in late August before the fall round-up began. Becca knew that Thad and Tuck would be extra busy at that time. She and Peter hoped it would be cooler by then.

Thad admitted to himself that he was happy with the new plan for both he and Pa to give Becca away. Deep down, he'd felt a little hurt that she might consider not having him to do it. He'd always thought that he'd be the one to give her away. But Belle's idea eased those hurt feelings. *My sweet Belle.*

# # #

Independence Day celebrations were not deterred by the hot weather. Plans were underway to make it a fun day in spite of the heat.

Thad arranged different events such as saddle bronc riding, calf roping, and barrel racing. Each participant needed to pay a twenty-cent fee to enter the contest. Thad provided the horses for the bronc riding since he had several quarter horses that were not yet broken. There was a large grassy field on the south side of town and the flat area made a great place for the community to come. Tuck and some of the men built a stand for spectators for seating.

The ladies of Mustang Ridge planned entertainment with a brass band and fiddle player, while everyone enjoyed a picnic lunch they had brought from home. A few of the men, led by Sam Garrison, were setting up games and races for the younger crowd such as sack races, egg relays, kick-the-can, and other exciting activities. For the older participants, they held a horse race, foot race, and a tug-of-war event. There were also several games of horseshoes going on at various times of the day.

The women participated in a best jelly and jam contest. A panel of three consisting of business people in Mustang Ridge - Sam Garrison, Mabel Patton, and Doc Phillips, judged the best tasting jam and jelly. Thad's mother won the best jam contest and Belle won the best jelly contest.

The evening wrapped up with a whole beef roast, donated by Tuck. A large pit had been dug near the field arena in which the beef was placed on hickory slabs over a bed of hot coals. It was allowed to slowly cook the whole day. The town ladies provided side dishes and pies.

Thad enjoyed the day thoroughly. He didn't remember ever having celebrated Independence Day in such a manner. His brother, Nate, won the horse race hands down. Even Peter, who had spent the holiday in Mustang Ridge, also took part in the horse race. Thad had been pleased to furnish his future brother-in-law with one of his best thoroughbred horses. Although not placing, he expressed his pleasure at being involved in the town's celebration. The men's tug-of-war team which Thad and Pa were part of was the winning team.

As his family sat on quilts eating the roasted beef that night, Thad voiced his thoughts aloud. "This has been a great day," he said.

"Yes, Thad. It's been a wonderful day. The races and contests were fun. Not only to be a participant, but to be a spectator," his mother said.

CHAPTER FIFTY
Belle

The celebration had been a wonderful time for the town. Even though the summer heat had been so oppressive all day, the townspeople still celebrated in fine fashion. It was good to be reminded of what America had gone through to gain independence from the English. There have been other wars since. Sadly, the War Between the States was a devastating one. Hopefully, they will never have something like that again. Then Belle thought about the Indians who were continually being pushed out of their homeland. This saddened her most of all. They had been friends with some wonderful Shoshone Indians and they are not unintelligent, pagan tribes as some politicians would have them believe.

Belle was so pleased that she won best jelly at the celebration, and it was her first batch of jelly all on her own too. She could tell Thad was proud of her accomplishment. Her mother taught her well how to prepare food.

Mustang Ridge really went all out for the celebration. It was geared for young and old alike. There were games for the children, and most exciting - the small parade led by the band and the flag of the country leading the way. Many patriotic songs were sung then and again later before the evening beef feed. The heat just couldn't beat the people down.

Later, after the sun started to set and the air started to cool, everyone took part in a dance held out under the stars. The men had laid down large planks for the dance floor. It seemed that most towns had a dance whenever there was any reason to gather for celebration. Jackson, though only one and a half years old, he still seemed to know something special was going on, and enjoyed himself immensely. Thad and Belle danced together with him until he grew so sleepy that Mama said she would take him home and they could pick him up on their way. They followed soon after since they were getting tired too. All in all, it was a grand celebration.

"Thad, I am so happy," Belle told her husband on the way home.

"Because it's Independence Day?" he asked.

"No, it's everything. We have a fine home and a wonderful son and we have each other."

From his hug and warm kiss, Belle guessed he agreed with her.

It was an excellent thing indeed to see how everyone came together to celebrate even in the heat. If it hadn't been so late when they got back to the ranch-house, Belle would have been happy to take a dip in the lake. *Another time when I'm not so exhausted.*

CHAPTER FIFTY-ONE
1886 Becca's Wedding

The July heat had passed, bringing with it the cooler days of August. Plans for Becca and Peter's wedding were underway. Peter and his family happily jumped at Thad's offer of their home to stay during the days leading up to and after their wedding.

Peter's parents, Chester and Sylvia Rhodes, and his younger brother, Steven, accompanied him on the stage to Mustang Ridge. Thad picked them up when the stage came in and took them in his two-seater out to Whitehorse Ranch. He decided right off that he liked Peter's parents. They had good qualities that drew his ma and pa to them right away too. Chester spent a lot of time with Tuck and showed a keen interest in the running of the two ranches. He accompanied Tuck on a tour of the ranch, equally at home on a horse as in a buggy. Sylvia was no slouch in helping with household chores. She even helped Belle in the garden while she picked produce for their meals. For city folk, they had no problem being at home on the rural plains.

Belle and Mrs. Rhodes traveled to Deer Creek Ranch to meet with Sarah Wells who was there to fit Becca's wedding dress. Thad suspected Ma would regale Mrs. Rhodes with her stories of life at a stagecoach station. In the meantime, Thad was entrusted with the care of his young son, Jackson. He found that he had to watch him every second or he would get into the most awful of fixes. The flour bin was one of his messiest troubles. Thad was more than happy to see the buggy returning at the end of the day.

"Mama!" Jackson called to her. He toddled off to be kissed and hugged by her as if she had been gone a week rather than just for the day

"How did you and Jackson do today, dear?" she asked Thad.

"It was okay," he responded.

"Really?" she asked, coming close to him. "Then why do you have all this flour on the side of your face? And on your jeans? And on the chairs? Jackson, what did you do?"

The little culprit hung his head. Thad felt sorry for him. "He was practicing scooping snow. He heard Pa and me talking about how we expected a lot of snow this winter and that we'd need lots of help to shovel it."

Belle and Mrs. Rhodes laughed. Mrs. Rhodes took Jackson by the hand and the two of them went to sit on the sofa while she read a story to him. Belle softly brushed the flour from her husband's cheek, replacing it with a tender kiss. "Miss me?" she whispered close to his ear.

"Always," he answered softly, taking her in his arms and kissing her.

"How are the plans for the wedding coming?" he asked later.

"We're all ready," she said. "We just need to decorate the church but that won't take long. We'll do that after church Sunday. Then it'll be fresh for the ceremony in the afternoon. How about you? Are you ready to walk your little sister down the aisle?"

"Of course, I am. More to the point though, how are Ma and Pa doing?"

"Well, your ma gets tears in her eyes every once in a while. I think Tuck is a little nervous. But I think that's all normal."

Thad nodded. Truth be known, he was a mite nervous himself. He sure hoped he didn't mess up and make a bad memory for Becca.

# # #

Thad and Tuck stood waiting for the bride to come out so they could walk her down the aisle. It was a fine day; the weather had cooled a mite but the summer blue skies still prevailed.

"Perfect day for a wedding, huh?" Thad asked trying to break the heavy tension he could feel emanating from Tuck.

"What? Oh, yeah. Nice day." *Poor Pa. He can't even think straight. Guess Becca and I will have to walk him down the aisle.*

Smiling at the thought of them walking Tuck down the aisle, he saw the door to the changing room open and his little sister walked out – a vision of loveliness. Thad found himself tongue-tied. He stepped forward and offered his arm to her, then glanced at the statue that was Tuck. He nodded for Tuck to move but he just stood there staring at Becca.

Thad whispered to Becca, "Take his arm. He's not himself today. By the way, you look beautiful."

Becca squeezed Thad's arm and reached over to take Tuck's arm. "Come, Papa. It's time to walk me down the aisle."

That seemed to wake Tuck up. He shook his head to clear it. And down the aisle she went, Tuck on one side, Thad on the other.

The ceremony was beautiful. Thad was surprised that it was over so soon. Following the pronouncement of their marriage, Mr. and Mrs. Peter Rhodes went to open their presents while the guests enjoyed refreshments prepared by the ladies.

Afterward, the happy couple boarded the stage to travel to Cheyenne where they would take the train to St. Louis. Thad and his family, along with the Rhodes saw them off. Becca gave hugs to everyone including Jackson, who didn't want to let her go, or maybe he just wanted to ride in the stagecoach.

"Me go too," he said to her. He became tearful when Thad removed him from Becca's arms and said, "Not this time, Jackson. They need to go by themselves. You can come home with me and Mama. I'll let you drive the buggy. How does that sound?" Apparently, it sounded good because he promptly switched his attention to their buggy.

Thad thought about Becca and Peter's wedding trip, a gift from Peter's parents. They would stay at a glorious hotel in St. Louis and be entertained by an evening at the opera house. *No cowboy shivaree for them.*

Thad wondered what the future held for his sister and her new husband. They'd not shared their plans with anyone yet. Maybe they would live in Mustang Ridge if Becca remained on as the school teacher for the following year.

"Looks like rain coming our way," Belle observed. Off in the southwestern sky, she saw dark clouds forming.

"Hope so. We can sure use the moisture. I noticed the meadows are turning a little yellow," he agreed while he watched the sky. *Father, let it bring moisture for our land.*

That night as the three of them prepared to go to bed, Thad could hear the wind picking up and thunder rumbling in the distance. While it got closer and the lightning began its bright show, Jackson became a little unnerved. So, Thad grabbed a book and took the frightened little boy to the sofa and by the light of the kerosene lamp, he read to him until he fell asleep in his papa's arms.

152

CHAPTER FIFTY-TWO
Fall Round-up

Twice each year, the two ranchers got together to round up the cattle. In the spring, the Deer Creek Ranch hands cut their calves out from the rest of their herd and then branded them. In the fall, they separated the calves from their mothers and drove some of the cattle to the railroad to ship to market.

Tuck appeared deep in thought as he rode his horse, pushing the cattle toward the chute. *I wonder what he his thinking about.*

"So, Pa, what's got your mind in a haze?" he asked him.

"Just thinking about the coming winter. I think we're going to have another bad one."

"I agree."

"We'll have to check the signs," Tuck said, looking sideways to see Thad's reaction. "Like the Woolly Bear and the squirrels."

"Huh?"

"If the orange band on the Woolly Bear caterpillar is narrow, there will be a lot of snow. If he is fat and fuzzy, it'll be bitterly cold. Then there's the squirrels." Tuck was warming to his subject.

"I know, I know. You were all talking about it last year." Thad glanced at his pa. "You don't really believe all those tales, do you? Aren't they just myths?"

"The Shoshone swear by them. They say the Great Spirit gives them signs in His Creation so they can live accordingly. They believe it; it makes sense to me."

'Okay, if you say so."

"The fur on the back of the cow's necks will be thick too," Tuck added, grinning before spurring his horse on ahead.

Thad laughed. *I guess he could be right.* He secretly consulted the Old Farmer's Almanac he had purchased from Sam. There it was - the weather prediction for the winter of '86-'87.

Bitterly cold and extensive snowstorms.

He wondered how any prediction that was based on "sun, moon, stars, and planets," as it said on the front, could possibly foretell winter with any degree of accuracy. *I should think the Indians' way would be better.* He decided he would try to be aware of the signs of which Tuck had spoken. Perhaps his pa was right about the signs after all.

The fall roundup was in full swing back at his ranch. Thad's crew ran his calves through the branding area while he sat astride his horse and tallied the numbers. They separated them from their mothers and put them in a pen.

153

After the calves were weaned from their mothers, they were returned to the herd. Thad hoped they would survive the winter in good shape. He and the hands culled out some of the best cattle to take when they joined up with Tuck's drive to Fort Laramie.

Since the ranchers anticipated a bad winter, Thad had considered driving cattle to Fort Laramie in the fall rather than in the spring. In this way, they wouldn't have so many to care for over the winter months. He spoke to his pa about it and he agreed. So, they set about preparing for the drive to take place following the fall round-up. They'd contacted the buying agent at the fort and he would take a good number of cattle. The rest would be loaded onto a rail near the fort to be shipped east to Kansa City. The rail was new there, but Thad looked forward to the day when the rail came through Mustang Ridge. Word was that they should be done laying rail in 1887.

Thad had not bred all of his mares since the Wyoming winter wouldn't be kind to colts on the open Plains. When the colts were weaned and branded with the Whitehorse Ranch brand, they were ready to spend the winter in the corrals out of the wind.

One evening, Thad sat on the veranda and watched the colts in the pen with Buddy sprawled next to his chair. Thad's arm automatically went down to pet the pup. Buddy was growing and Thad was glad he had found the little guy when he did. Buddy was near starvation at the time.

Thad had a good crop of new horses and this pleased him. Come spring, he would also have several cutting horses ready for market. He and the men had been working them and had several ready for the horse auctions. He was also pleased that one of the big auctions now came to Mustang Ridge every spring. They would be ready for them with newly trained cutting horses after winter was done flinging its bitter cold and heavy snows across the territory.

Belle kept busy putting up vegetables from the garden. The garden produced abundantly due to the fact that water was hauled from the lake to keep it from drying out. Belle's cooking with the vegetables from her garden always inspired Thad. She put up the harvested garden produce in jars and also dried some of the vegetables for soups. It promised good eating in the winter.

Thad sighed and rose to go inside since the sun dipped lower in the western sky. He knew by the aromas coming from inside that supper was ready without Belle telling him. He found her standing at the hot stove and he came up behind her, kissing her on the back of her neck.

"Is it ready?"

"Almost."

"Something I can do to help?" he inquired.

"Sure. Dish up the green beans into the bowl on the table while I mash the potatoes."

"This one?" he asked holding up the blue dish.

"Yes. Can you bring me the bigger one for the potatoes?" she asked, vigorously mashing the potatoes with the green-handled masher.

Thad dumped the green beans into the smaller dish and set it on the table. "Jackson. Come to the table. Supper is ready."

Jackson toddled to the table and lifted his hands up to his papa. He liked to eat and didn't seem to be fussy about what he ate. He had his four front teeth now, so he worked on chewing his food with gusto. Belle ground Jackson's meat so he could eat it.

Once they were all seated around the table, Jackson on Thad's lap, and grace had been offered, they began to eat. He enjoyed this time with his family. Granted, Jackson usually put more food on his papa than in his mouth, but he really tried. His son's eagerness to eat pleased him.

"How are you coming with putting up the food?" he asked Belle, noticing as he did, that Buddy was patiently waiting for Jackson to spill any of his food.

"Almost done. Should finish tomorrow. I want to can a few of those hens if you will butcher them for me," she said. "I'll can them when you do."

"When do you want me to do it?" he asked.

"Tomorrow, if you have time."

Thad nodded. His wife was such a hard worker, yet was considerate of his time.

"By the way," she said. "I noticed that the corn husks have been extra thick this year. Isn't that one of the signs of a bad winter that Tuck talks about?"

"Probably," he answered. He supposed he should look for a caterpillar. They didn't have any trees with acorns, so no squirrels to check on. He'd have to go look at the cattle's necks. Certainly not at a time when any of the men were around to see him though. No sense in giving them more to razz him about. He still wasn't sure about the validity of these so-called signs.

"Thad," his wife said as they sat eating their supper, "I have good news." He looked up from giving Jackson a piece of biscuit as he himself chewed a mouthful. About to take another bite, he nearly choked when she said, "I'm pregnant."

He swallowed the lump in his throat, which it turned out was a chunk of food he had forgotten to chew. He reached over, taking her hand in his, not aware he had just smeared Jackson's mashed potatoes all over her hand.

155

"That's wonderful news, dear. Are you feeling well?" He remembered clearly her pregnancy with Jackson.

"Yes, I think it'll be a girl this time because I'm not even sick. Doc Phillips said it looks like it will be a normal pregnancy." She wiped the mashed potatoes off of her hand.

"Thank the Lord for that," Thad replied, wiping more mashed potatoes from his pant leg and continued to feed Jackson while gazing lovingly at his dear wife.

CHAPTER FIFTY-THREE
Cattle Drive

Cattle from both ranches were gathered all together at Deer Creek Ranch for the drive south to Fort Laramie. The well-supplied chuck wagon with Cookie at the reins stood at the ready. Ranch hands were in full drive mode, their bedrolls and saddlebags packed on their horses. A remuda of replacement horses was made available. As the three Tucker men joined their ranch hands making ready to leave, Beth and Belle, holding Jackson, exited the ranch-house to say their goodbyes and wish their men a safe trip. Although Nate was only sixteen-years-old, the same age as Thad had been when his family came west on the wagon train, he had proved himself to be a good cowhand. A skeleton crew was left at each ranch to supervise the day-to-day needs.

Thad hated to be away from his family for such a long time. Jackson was only one year old and he would miss the little fella as well as his lovely wife. He hoped she would be well while they were gone. Before they left on the cattle drive, Thad had talked to both his mother and Belle's mother about checking in on her while he was gone.

The beginning of a cattle drive was an exciting time what with the shouting and whistles of the cowpunchers and the cattle bawling. Yes, Thad knew he would enjoy this drive, perhaps the last one they'd have if the railroad came through like they said it would. There's excitement when sitting astride a good cutting horse and heading the cattle where he wanted them to go.

They could move the cattle up to twelve miles a day. Of course, it wouldn't be that much every day. There were many factors to take into consideration, weather being a big one. On the second day of the drive, that became evident. During the night, the cattle were in their bed ground and the cowboys on watch were softly singing to them. That's when Thad felt a sudden change in the air. The wind picked up and the temperature dropped considerably. He and his pa felt it at the same time and rushed to wake those sleeping cowpunchers.

"Boss, them cows sure are nervous," Pete told Thad. "Worse than a cat in a room full of rocking chairs."

Wade directed the men to mount up and surround the cattle herd to calm them. Thunder railed and lightning flashed, the frightened cattle became more and more skittish. The men sang songs hoping to calm the cattle but to no avail. The storm was too devastating. Lightning flashed and crackled as it started up small fires in the dry brush, only to be put out by the driving rain.

Thad was completely soaked even though he wore his slicker. A sudden cracking of lightning striking a nearby tree sounded like a gunshot.

"STAMPEDE!" yelled one of the hands while the cattle took off in a westerly direction while the men tried in vain to turn them back on the southward path. It was a tense night with the driving rain and lightning slashing through the black sky. There seemed to be no end to the storm.

"It's a gully washer for sure," remarked Wade.

By morning, the storm had passed and the cattle had been calmed. The weary hands took turns eating and resting, while others plowed their horses through mud up to their hocks. Cookie kept the coffee pot going almost the whole day, so the rain-soaked and exhausted cowpunchers could warm up from the inside. The men were totally tuckered out by the end of the day as they rounded up the cattle that had strayed during the storm. The sun came out full-force and many of the men had their clothing drying on the sides of the chuck wagon.

The next day, the hands were rested up and were back to their jolly selves. Thad took one of the night-time shifts, singing to the cattle as they were lowing in the night. He really missed Belle and wondered how she was doing in her pregnancy. Would she suffer the same as she had with Jackson? He hoped not, and continued to pray for her good health.

When he returned to the campfire, he was shocked to see a few of the men were gambling and passing a whiskey bottle with Nate in the center. He and Tuck had asked them not to involve Nate in their gambling and drinking activities. They had hired on a few extra hands just for the drive, so Thad believed this came from them. He trusted their hands. In fact, they had been asked not to bring drink at all while on the trail. The men looked up as Thad stopped.

One of the new hands, Gil, looked up as Thad entered the camp area. He saw the look on his boss's face but instead of admitting to his error, he made excuses. "Kid needed to learn what life is all about," he said.

"For your information the *kid* already knows what life is all about, and it's not about gambling and drinking." Thad had a hard time controlling his anger, but he knew God would expect it of him. *Help me to handle this well, Lord.* He knew he would not continue to employ Gil after this drive was over. "Is there anymore liquor around? If there is, dump it - now!"

Doby said, "Sorry, boss. We were just...I know better. I'm so sorry," he hung his head.

At that point, Wade and Tuck rode in and after being apprised of the situation, Wade ordered those men involved to cover the watch the rest of the night. Tuck took Nate away from the fire where they sat down to talk. Thad

had no idea what Tuck said to him, but he was glad Pa had been there to talk with Nate. There were no more such incidents for the rest of the drive.

#

The cattle drive finally came to an end and the ranchers returned to Mustang Ridge with their money to put in the bank. Thad hurried out to his ranch, anxious to see his wife and son. It seemed to him he'd been gone an awfully long time.

"Belle, are you here?" he called when he entered the ranch-house. Belle came running out of their bedroom with Jackson toddling behind her. Thad swept her up in his arms and kissed her passionately. He felt a tug on his trouser leg and looked down.

"Papa, me too," he demanded, holding up both arms. Thad put his wife down so he could take up his son. Buddy leaped about, vying for some of Thad's attention also.

"I'm so glad to be home," he said. "I missed you both so much."

"Thad, I'm overjoyed at seeing you and I love you very much, but you need to take a bath. You smell like cows." Belle wrinkled up her nose.

#

Several weeks later, Nash and the men returned from spending time in town. Thad was at the horse corral when he saw his foreman striding toward him. He could tell by the look on Nash's face that he had something serious on his mind.

"Howdy, Nash."

He took his hat off and wiped the sweat from his brow with his bandana. "Boss, I've got some bad news. You know that drover name of Gil that caused trouble on the cattle drive?"

When Thad nodded, Nash continued. "He's in Mustang Ridge and he's drunk. Telling everybody he saw that you are a... well, I won't say what he called you. Claims your bad reference has cost him jobs. He's madder than an old wet hen. Says he's going to make you pay."

"That's not good. Especially since I never made a reference, good or bad about him. Did you or the hands have any confrontation with him?"

"No, I told them to stay away from him. I stopped into talk to the sheriff, so he'd be aware of what it is all about."

"Good. Okay, guess we will try and stay away from town for a while then. Maybe he'll move on," Thad said. "Maybe it will all clear up."

"I don't think so, boss. The men said there was signs of someone butchering cattle up on our north meadow."

"Do you have any proof that it is Gil?"

159

"No, but it's too much of a coincidence to have Gil mouthing off in town and your butchered cattle."

"True. Did you tell this to the sheriff too?"

"Yes, he said not to do anything, that he and his deputies would look into it; see if they could catch him in the act."

"Sounds good to me. Make sure the hands know that too. And thanks, Nash."

Thad told Belle about the problem. He wanted her to be aware of any possible danger. "Keep Buddy close by until this is resolved," he warned her. Buddy was full-grown now and an excellent watch dog,

Nothing more was heard of Gil for a while, although his cohorts were captured. Thad hated to be away from the ranch-house, but a rancher couldn't always hang out at his ranch-house. He left his rifle by the front door, up high so Jackson couldn't reach it. Belle knew how to handle fire arms. Thad just hoped she wouldn't have to draw upon that knowledge.

"Don't worry, Thad. God will protect us."

"I know that, Belle. But there is no sense in being careless about your and Jackson's safety."

"I won't, Thad. I promise to be careful."

Several days later, Belle was in the bedroom putting clothes away. She had left Jackson sleeping on the sofa with Buddy curled up next to him. As she put the last of the clothes away in the chest, her heart leapt to her throat when she heard Jackson's blood-chilling shriek and Buddy's frantic barking. Running down the hallway, she heard a man swearing and yelling.

"Get that animal off me!"

Belle ran to the door and took down the rifle. Quickly opening the door, she fired into the air, knowing it would bring whoever had stayed behind in the bunkhouse. She turned and with the weapon aimed at Gil, she said, "Buddy, that's good. Down boy."

Immediately, Buddy released the man's leg and stopped growling. Jackson stopped his screaming and watched his mother as she held the "persuader" on Gil. "Jackson, did the man hurt you?"

Jackson shook his head. Now that his mother was in control of the situation, he began to play with his blocks. *Crisis averted for him anyway,* she thought.

Slim and Butch came running into the ranch-house with their revolvers drawn. One glance and they both knew what was going on.

"You okay, Miss. Belle?" Slim asked.

"Yes, Slim. Just take him away. I can't bear to look at him."

160

"Yes, ma'am," Butch said. They tied Gil's hands behind him and marched him out the door just as Thad and the other men arrived. Slim explained to Thad what had happened while Butch and a couple other hands got ready to take Gil into town to the sheriff.

"Men, take this scoundrel into town. I don't want to ever see him again."

"Yes, sir."

When Thad entered the house, he saw Belle sitting in her chair rocking Jackson. He could tell her nerves were on edge.

"Belle," he said quietly, kneeling next to the rocking chair and pulling her into the security of his arms.

"Oh, Thad he was going to take our baby!"

"But he didn't, did he? You stopped him. That evil man didn't stand a chance with you protecting our son."

Belle smiled weakly. "Well, I had a lot of help from Buddy. That dog would have eaten him up and spit him out if I hadn't stopped him."

"Kind of glad I brought him home that day."

The following week, Gil and his two partners were sentenced to the Wyoming Territorial prison at Laramie. Gil got a longer sentence for the kidnapping charge. *Thank you, Father, for watching over everyone involved.*

CHAPTER FIFTY-FOUR
Cold and Snow in 1886-87

It was reported that temperatures reached a -47 degrees in January that year. It was hard for the family to keep warm, but Thad was more than thankful for the coal his home and the bunkhouse had available to them. And as he thought about the coal, he was glad that his pa had ordered the closing of the coal mine for the winter again. That had been a wise decision on his part.

During this horrific cold, Thad was concerned about his son, Jackson. The little tyke had a habit of taking off his clothing while he played. Many times, he would see him walking around the house in just his under-drawers; sometimes with nothing on at all. Belle finally sewed up his long-johns and made an opening in the back so that he couldn't get out of them. However, it didn't stop him from taking off his trousers, shirt, and sweater. Thad wondered why he did that. Surely, he must have felt the cold.

Thad was also concerned about his livestock. How were they handling the severe cold? The barn kept the poultry and milk cow safe from the elements. The family's horses were kept in the barn as well as the personal horses belonging to the ranch hands. The family didn't go out much and he made the decision to forego church for a few Sundays because of the safety of his family. They made do with the food supplies they had in the pantry and the fresh eggs and milk. When Slim ran out of supplies, he would restock from the ranch-house. Just being outdoors for even a short period of time made breathing extremely hard. The cold wind was penetrating, painful with each breath.

They got through the hard winter, but as spring neared and the snow began to melt, Thad feared what it would reveal underneath. *Father, help me to trust in You, but please don't let it be too bad.*

The spring of '87 brought ranchers out of their burrows now that the large amounts of snow had melted. They began to ride the range, looking to see how many cattle had survived the treacherous winter weather. Many ranchers were hit hard but Thad and Tuck had the foresight to make the fall cattle drive and keep the rest in sheltered areas during the winter. They didn't know what the result would be until the snow had melted and they could search for them.

Cattle numbers in the Wyoming Territory dwindled that winter. Many ranchers went out of business after the severe losses. Deer Creek Ranch and Whitehorse Ranch, though hit hard, managed to keep their heads above water since the severity of the winters finally began to level off.

162

While the community reeled from the extreme winter elements, plans were underway to complete laying rail for the train to Edgewood, just south of Deadwood. The 300-mile length of train track was an exciting event for the town of Mustang Ridge and for the area ranchers. No longer would Sam Garrison need to hire freight wagons to haul in merchandise for his store. The ranchers could load their livestock on the train going north or south, depending on where they were shipping them. Deer Creek and Whitehorse Ranches usually shipped their cattle to Fort Laramie or wherever military presences were located and a need for beef existed. They had a standing contract with Fort Laramie.

As the track-laying crews came through Mustang Ridge, the good ladies of the community were true to their word to let the foreign crews know they were welcome. They put on a feed for the crews, at no charge, and also a little show of local entertainment. Thad was pleased to see his sister, Becca, sing a solo as part of the program. Music was a big part of the entertainment, along with rope tricks, since they had been told that only a few of the Chinese crew could speak English.

As they moved on past their town and continued north, the good folks of Mustang Ridge cheered and wished them well. Thad hoped they would be treated well once they reached Deadwood. By now, that town's lawless reputation had become widely known. Deadwood had been founded illegally on what was supposed to be Lakota land granted to them by the US government. But once gold had been discovered in the Black Hills, miners and settlers moved in. Other settlements came into being, which were usually lawless, but Deadwood proved to be even more notorious than most. Saloons and brothels were booming, and gunfights and murder took place with alarming frequency. In fact, Wild Bill Hickok was shot in the back in a gambling house on August 5, 1876, the year Thad and his family began running the Deer Creek Stagecoach station. Thad remembered meeting Hickok, since he traveled the stage quite a number of times while he and his family operated the station. He felt sadness when he heard the news of his murder. As Nash would say, "Deadwood's got a monstrous bad name for meanery and shecoonery of all sorts."

The only time Thad had been to Deadwood, was to ride north past it taking cattle to Fort Baxter. He didn't do it often, however, since he didn't have a contract with them. The two times he had taken cattle there, he was contacted by them and they requested cattle be brought to them. Yes, Deadwood was a good place to stay away from as long as there was no law there.

# # #

"It's coming!" Belle called to Thad as she returned from a trip into town. "The Grand Island and Wyoming Central Railroad will stop in Mustang Ridge next Friday," She was greatly excited by the news she had obtained at a church ladies meeting.

"Well, that is long-awaited news," Thad said. He was glad to hear the news of the railroad, but he had been worrying about his pregnant wife the whole time she was gone. Belle was only three weeks away from when Doc Phillips said she would deliver. Thad feared the buggy ride to town and back might not be good for her. But then Belle was of strong stock and this second pregnancy was a good one compared to her first one.

Thad enjoyed the time with Jackson while she had been gone. The two-year-old was wise beyond his years and thoroughly enjoyed riding with his papa. His usual demand on days Thad would take him to ride the range was, "Faster, Papa. Faster." Thad would pack a lunch for the two of them, and letting the foreman know where he was going, would take off with his son proudly sitting the saddle in front of him.

Belle continued talking about the railroad and Thad brought his attention back to his wife. "The President of the railroad will be riding the train in his private car. Can you imagine? Living in a train car like it was a small house! And traveling along on the train!"

"Kind of like on a wagon train, huh?" he said laughing.

"No, not at all," she said firmly.

"What are the church ladies planning to do to welcome the train?" Thad asked her, knowing that the women were busy making plans.

"Oh, banners and a band and a special meal for the railroad president and..." Belle's excitement ran out as she ran out of breath.

Thad laughed and holding out his arms said, "Come here, you. Give me a hug."

Belle did, as well as she could, given her size now that she was almost nine months pregnant.

"I missed you today," he whispered in her ear. "We both did."

"Where is Jackson?" she asked suddenly wondering about the youngster's where-a-bouts.

"Napping. Guess I wore him out. Riding a horse is hard work."

She settled back into his arms on the sofa. They had this quiet moment alone without interruptions just to enjoy each other's presence. Thad loved Belle more each day and thanked God for putting her in his life.

CHAPTER FIFTY-FIVE
Ellen

One of the most heartwarming events of 1887 for Thad and Belle was the birth of their second child in June. They named their new daughter Ellen Rebecca Tucker after her Aunt Becca. She proved to be a happy and robust little girl according to Doc Phillips. Her brother, Jackson, loved her and spent a lot of time just sitting and watching her sleep.

On one occasion, Thad entered the baby's room to find Jackson sitting next to her crib just staring at her. "Hey little man, what are you doing?" he asked his son.

"Wooking," Jackson answered. "Wook, her gots my finner!"

"She must know that you're her big brother," Thad told him. "She's tired though, and needs to rest, so we should leave her alone so she can go to sleep."

"Read her, Papa, like you do me."

"Okay, you find your sleepy-time book and we'll read to her." Of course, Thad surmised that his reading Ellen to sleep would also end with a sleeping Jackson. And that was exactly what happened. Thad laid Jackson in his bed and pulled a cover over him. Then pulling the door almost shut, he went to the living room where his wife sat finally resting herself.

"I heard," she said, looking up. "Both of them are asleep?"

Thad nodded and sat beside her. He knew he should get out to the corrals, but quiet times with his wife were getting further apart, so he took advantage of it. Belle rested her head in the crook of Thad's arm. He leaned against her, smelling the fresh soap in her hair. And before they knew it, they too were fast asleep.

#

Later that same year, Thad and his family rode in the two-seater to town. They needed a few supplies and there would be room to stow them behind the seats. So, with Jackson seated next to him and Belle with Ellen in her arms, they set out for town.

A crowd was gathered when they arrived at Sam's mercantile. It didn't take Jackson long to spy his grandparents. "Gammy. Gumpa," he called, his little voice managing to override the conversations taking place. Everyone turned and laughed while Thad's mother rushed up to them and hugged Jackson. Tuck followed close on her heels. He boosted Jackson up in the air while Beth latched on to Ellen.

"What's going on, Pa?" Thad asked, indicating the crowd with a nod in their direction.

"Sam just got word that the stage is ending. No more stages now that the railroad goes through Mustang Ridge."

"Well, we knew it would come," Thad responded. "It was just a matter of time."

"Yes, but it's sad in a way," his mother lamented, entering the conversation. "If it hadn't have been for the stage, we never would've come to Mustang Ridge. I wouldn't have met Tuck, and you two," she indicated Thad and Belle, "might never have married.

Thad said, "She's right." Belle agreed.

Tuck also nodded in agreement. "True, but as they say, 'time stands still for no one.'"

"Who says that?" Thad asked, giving his father a hard time.

"Oh, never mind."

"You're right though," Thad said. "It's something to ponder."

"We should all ride on the stage, just to commemorate the last of an era," Beth suggested.

"I think I'll have to pass. But the rest of you could," Belle shared.

"Why don't you want to go?" Thad questioned his wife. He was aware that she had not been feeling good the last few days. She had gone to see the doctor before they met the rest of the family.

"I don't think I'd be very comfortable. I don't want to borrow trouble."

Beth peered over at her daughter-in-law, noticing for the first time that Belle was looking at baby items Sam had on display; too small for Ellen. "Are you, uh…expecting?"

Thad began to shake his head no, but as he turned to look at Belle, he stopped. She was nodding her head. "Yes," she said. "I'm about two months along." She looked to Thad. "I'm sorry, dear. I just found out."

"Oh my! That will make Ellen and this new baby really close together," Beth commented.

"Well, like I said before; something to ponder," said the dazed father-to-be.

CHAPTER FIFTY-SIX
Second Hard Winter
Lucinda

The holidays, Thanksgiving and Christmas passed and the winter of 1888 settled into Niobrara County with promises of an exact replica of the previous winter. Thad and Tuck again made arrangements for their livestock to winter in the coulees on their ranches and feed was brought to them as needed. Thad moved as many of his horses into the corrals around the barn as he could. These hard winters were beginning to get old. The summers were hot and dry in comparison and many streams dried up. Deer Creek and Whitehorse Lake being fed by mountain streams kept the two ranches in water, for which they were thankful.

As far as his ranch-house was concerned, coal and wood supplies were increased greatly as well as those for the bunkhouse. Slim and Belle had once again harvested from the garden. They would have plenty of food if they were forced to hole up at the ranch for the duration of the coming winter. One good thing about raising cattle was you had a ready supply of meat for the tables of both the bunkhouse and the ranch-house.

Thad cherished the winter days in their ranch. By now, Ellen was walking, how-be-it ever so slowly and with lots of falls. Buddy tried to keep up with the children, but Thad would find him lolling on the big rug in the living room, sleeping the sleep of the exhausted. Jackson wore himself out too, trying to keep up with his sister. He proclaimed himself to be her special caretaker. Which could have been a Godsend for Belle, however, Jackson's care seemed to turn into tattling on his baby sister with things like:

"Elwy being bad, Elwy crying, Elwy stink, and Mama, come quick! Elwie make a mess."

Then there were times when he projected his desires onto his sister with, "Mama, Elwie wants a cookie."

Thad enjoyed romping with the two of them on the floor. Ellen didn't want to be left out when Jackson and Thad wrestled, so he always included her. He saw his wife shake her head with a smile as she patched yet another of Ellen's torn outfits.

#

February 1888 arrived and so did the new baby girl, named Lucinda Sarah after Belle's mother, Sarah. Belle's pregnancy had been a good one as well as the labor and delivery. Apparently, Belle had gone through the hard one with Jackson, and then the girls came easier.

Jackson barely knew how to contain his joy at having two little sisters. Lucinda was too long a name for him to say, so he called her Lucy, though it

167

came out more like 'Wucy.' The rest of the family took his lead and called her Lucy also.

Ellen and Lucy shared a bedroom now and Jackson had his own bedroom. If they could just get him to stay out of the girls' room! As he had with Ellen, he spent a lot of time watching little Lucy sleep. However, as Ellen grew older, she'd wake when she heard Jackson in the room and end up waking Lucy. So, Belle had to make sure she closed the door to keep Jackson out. Buddy laid in front of the girls' room. He seemed to know that Jackson wasn't supposed to go into their room, so he was doing his part.

Jackson adored his 'Gumpa' Tuck and begged to go see him. When warmer weather came, Thad took him over to Deer Creek Ranch. Many times, Tuck would ask if Jackson could spend the night, making a happy Jackson.

Ellen also spent time with her two sets of grandparents. She was doted on by both grandmothers. Then when Lucy was older, she also spent time with them and was the apple of Grandpa Jacob's eye.

# # #

April 1, 1888 was Resurrection Sunday and it seemed that all of Mustang Ridge came out to the small white church on the south edge of town for the service. Thad proudly walked down the aisle to an empty pew with his family. He carried Ellen while Belle carried Lucy. Jackson walked next to his papa holding his other hand. Evidence of Belle's handiwork at the treadle sewing machine was in the children's clothing; the girl's matching dresses and Jackson's little suit. Thad had given her the sewing machine last Christmas and she used it whenever she was able to purchase the materials for their outfits. She even made shirts for Thad and dresses for herself. Her mother's expertise at sewing was evidently handed down to Belle.

CHAPTER FIFTY-SEVEN
Another Hard Winter
Tuck Is a Delegate to Cheyenne

December 1888 through to March 1889 proved to be the worst winter yet. Bitterly cold with continuous snow storms, there was no respite from the harsh winds, cold, and snow. With all the cattle herds that were wiped out, it seemed to spell the end of the cattle industry in Wyoming Territory. Thad and Tuck's herds were hit hard, but once again the precautions they had taken were a saving grace.

As the two Tucker ranchers salvaged what was left of their herds in the spring, they talked about the wisdom of turning more ground into hay with which to feed their livestock in the winter. They would begin this spring early April. Between them, they purchased an end gate seeder that was placed on the back of a farm wagon. They seeded oats along with a mixture of timothy and alfalfa. The oats would be ready for harvest in late summer and the straw from the oats would be used for bedding for the cold winter ahead. The timothy/alfalfa mix would come up the following year and be cut for hay using a cradle-scythe. With the spring seeding underway, Thad was confident that they would be able to survive this next winter.

Once again, the topic of statehood was being discussed across the Wyoming Territory. North and South Dakota were admitted to the Union in November, so the Wyoming Territory residents were ready to try again. A delegation of men was dispatched to Cheyenne to represent Niobrara County and Tuck was asked to be one of them. While he was away, Thad kept watch over Deer Creek Ranch, though he believed Wade, the foreman there could handle it well.

"How goes the statehood question?" Thad asked Tuck when he returned home in-between meetings.

"Oh, there's the usual arguments against the Territory's suffrage policy. They don't want to approve women's right to vote. Got something new though that isn't helping the cause any."

"What's that?"

"You heard about the hanging of the man and woman not far from the Sweetwater River in July?" Tuck continued. "They were homesteaders and the six men who hanged them were cattlemen who wanted their land."

"Yeah, I heard there was a lot of controversy about what the true story really was," Thad said. "They claimed she was a prostitute named Cattle Kate."

169

"No, Cattle Kate is somebody different. I believe the cattlemen wanted the land this couple had legally filed on, so they murdered them by hanging, and then spread these false stories."

"Think the hanging will be a roadblock to statehood?"

Tuck rubbed his chin. "Well, the women here are probably a little worried. Here they are, living in the only territory or state that allows women to vote. And now a woman has been hanged from a tree in the territory. It's troubling, that's for sure."

The Wyoming delegates told Congress they would go on as a territory for 100 more years rather than take away their women's right to vote. The Federal government acquiesced to demands from the territory and on March 27, 1890. President Benjamin Harrison signed the statehood bill, making Wyoming the 44th state. There was much celebrating on that March day when the telegram came announcing the decision. At last, Wyoming became a state and could take her rightful place along with the other states of the Union.

CHAPTER FIFTY-EIGHT
1890

After Wyoming became a state, many things began to move along for the residents. An exciting invention had taken place several years before that was just now making its way into Wyoming. In '76, a man named Bell obtained a patent to produce the first American telephone, but it wasn't until '90 that service began in some cities. Sam had one installed in the mercantile. The lines only went to Cheyenne as a limited service. It was an exciting event for Mustang Ridge. Several customers cheered while Sam called the freight office in Cheyenne to place an order to be sent by rail.

The warm season turned out to be the same as past summers; hot and dry. And as before, the two ranches survived because of the mountain-fed Deer Creek and Whitehorse Lake. The oats that had been seeded in the spring proved to be a good crop of feed grain for the horses. The straw was used for bedding for the upcoming winter once more. The ranchers had already been using the cradle-scythe which they were able to use in cutting both the oats and hay. This mower would be used again the following year to cut the hay. Belle's garden provided an abundance of fresh vegetables for their home and the bunkhouse. Again, water from the lake lent its moisture for growth, and to provide cooling to the Tucker children.

The year 1890 went on its merry way, stopping for no one, no new babies or pregnancies as time sped on in the lives of the Tucker family. By now, Jackson was five-years-old and a bright star in the eyes of his parents and both sets of grandparents. Belle began to teach him a few things at home. She asked Becca if she had some books she could look at to help her in this process.

Becca and Peter had made their home in Mustang Ridge and Becca continued on as the school teacher. Peter convinced his bosses that he could handle the Education Superintendent duties from there just as well as in Cheyenne. After all, his work took him on the road a lot and he didn't spend much time in Cheyenne anyway. Now that Sam had a telephone at the mercantile, if an urgent situation occurred, they could communicate that way.

Becca and Peter came out to see Belle and Thad one day. Buddy announced their arrival with just the one bark. Belle thought they came to bring the books she had spoken to her about. But it seemed there was more to it.

"Won't you stay for supper?" Belle invited. "We have plenty."

Becca looked at her husband and Peter nodded. While Becca played with her nieces and nephew, Belle prepared the meal faster without children

171

underfoot. She called them to the table and they held hands while Thad asked the blessing.

"Okay, Becca," Belle said as she passed the meat. "What's going on?"

Thad looked up at his wife, then to his sister. He was clueless; unaware of any undercurrents like Belle had been. He watched his sister as Becca held Peter's hand and began.

"I have turned in my resignation to the school," she explained. "And Peter has also resigned his position."

"Whatever for?" Belle asked her friend. "What will you do?"

"We're entering the missionary field," she said. "We'll go up to the Wind River Indian Reservation and work with the Shoshone Indians there."

Thad had remained quiet up until this point. His mind stuck on the fact that his sister and Peter were going to be missionaries to the Shoshone Indians. It certainly would not be an easy life for them. He wondered what Ma would say about all this. For that matter, what would Tuck have to say? He had become quite protective of his adopted children.

"We received a letter from Grey Wolf presenting the problem they are having with qualified teachers and asked what we could do to help out with notifying the proper officials."

Peter laughed. "I don't think Grey Wolf expected us to be the answer, but we spent quite a while seeking God's direction, and now we believe He's leading us to do this."

"I knew that he and his family had gone to Wind River Reservation," Thad commented, finally entering the conversation. "Wait, Grey Wolf can write? He could barely speak English."

"Yes, times have changed, brother." Becca patted her brother on the arm.

Thad rose and shook Peter's hand. "I know this couldn't have been an easy decision, Peter, Becca." He held his arms out to Becca and hugged her. "I've heard stories of illegal practices on the part of the Indian agents. It sounds like the Black Hills Treaty mess all over again."

"Yes, I'm afraid so," Peter agreed. "We are going in as teachers, but I hope to one day be named agent to that area. The Eastern Shoshone Indians are desperately in need of fair and honest representation, as well as good teachers."

"Well, you certainly have your work cut out for you," Belle stated. "When will you go?"

"Soon."

"Does Ma know yet?" Thad asked. Although he knew she figured that Becca and Peter would not stay long in Mustang Ridge, he was pretty sure she

172

wasn't expecting them to go out from Mustang Ridge as missionaries to the Indians.

"No, we're going to Deer Creek Ranch tomorrow and let them know."

#

The day soon came when Becca and Peter made ready to leave for the reservation, far too soon, as far as Belle and Thad were concerned. Belle for her dear friend, and Thad for his beloved sister, and her husband whom he had come to call his friend. Becca and Peter loaded their two wagons with all their possessions and headed for the Wind River Indian Reservation. Thad could see the excitement in his sister's eyes as she sat on top of one of the covered wagons with the reins in her hands. He recalled how his sister had sat on their wagon back in '76 when they first came out on the Oregon Trail. Only this time, she was driving the team. Never would he have dreamed that she would one day be doing this. He swallowed a large lump in his throat. And there may have been a tiny bit of moisture in his eye, though he would never admit to it.

Thad thought his ma was handling it pretty well; maybe better than he was. But then, glancing around the circle of family and friends gathered near the wagons in front of the church, he didn't think there'd been a dry eye anywhere. *Sure enough, Lord. It's a real tear squeezer.* Jackson, of course, didn't understand what was going on and wanted to ride on the wagon with Aunt Becca. So, his tears were soon added to the rest. Goodbyes were said, hugs were given, and vows to write were exchanged. And soon the young missionary couple was gone.

Thad read an article in the newspaper which made his heart hurt for his sister and her husband. The paper called it the Wounded Knee Massacre, although some called it The Battle at Wounded Knee.

> *December 28, 1890, a detachment of the U.S. 7th Cavalry*
> *intercepted Spotted Elk's band of Miniconjou Lakota and*
> *38 Hunkpapa Lakota near Porcupine Butte and escorted them five*
> *miles west to Wounded Knee Creek, where they made camp. The*
> *remainder of the 7th Cavalry Regiment arrived and surrounded the*
> *encampment. The next day, December 29th, the troops entered the*
> *encampment to disarm the Indians. No one knows for sure how it*
> *began, but in less than an hour's time, 150 to 300 unarmed Lakota*
> *men, women, and children had been massacred.*
>
> *Following a three-day blizzard, civilians were hired to bury the*
> *dead Lakota. They found the deceased frozen. They were gathered up*

and placed in a mass grave on a hill overlooking the encampment. It was reported that four infants were found alive, wrapped in their deceased mothers' shawls.

The whole thing saddened Thad terribly. It seemed to him that the Indians were constantly being driven from lands promised to them because the whites found their land to be desirable for themselves. His heart ached for them. How thankful he was that Becca and Peter were not at that reservation. *Father, please keep them safe at Wind River.*

CHAPTER FIFTY-NINE
Molly Beth

Molly Beth Tucker joined her parents and siblings in 1891. Belle's pregnancy had been another good one, leading her to believe she would always have an easy time of it if she only had girls. Molly shared her Grandmother Beth's name.

Jackson barely had time to play by himself, since he watched over his three sisters. Thad wondered if he'd been like that when Becca and Nate were born because he surely did look out for them as they grew up and even now that they were adults. Though he couldn't do anything about Becca anymore, he could lift her up in prayer, which he did often. After all, the Father in Heaven could protect her far better than he could, so he happily left her in God's hands.

Thad was such a proud papa and he dearly loved his son and three girls, but he had to admit, he had been hoping Molly would be a boy. Still, he thanked his Heavenly Father for the safe birth of yet another sweet little girl and that Belle's pregnancies with the three girls had been uneventful.

# # #

During this year, a newspaper owned by Tom and Emma Pike, started operating in Mustang Ridge. The town folk were excited to be able to read a paper that didn't have to come by train from Cheyenne. Of course, the Wyoming Tribune Eagle from Cheyenne didn't have news that pertained to Mustang Ridge, but it did provide world and national news. So, when the weekly Mustang Ridge Patriot opened its doors, the residents backed the Pikes wholeheartedly by purchasing the ten-cent paper. Emma worked at her husband's side, setting the type and other duties at a newspaper. The couple had no children. As Tom often said, "The paper is our baby."

Emma and Mabel Patten became good friends. The paper often ran ads for Mabel's Mountain Hideaway. Mabel even wrote a column on cooking for them to run in the paper. The column became so popular with the ladies in town the paper often sold out leaving disappointed readers. Tom and Emma decided to increase the price to twelve cents and print more copies. It proved to be a wise decision. Tom then began to scour the town in search of a new idea for a column.

Just before Christmas, Emma and Tom ran a Christmas cooking contest with three categories. The best cookie, pie, and cake, all related to Christmas, would win. The ladies were buzzing with excitement over the news, searching through their hidden cookbooks for those elusive family recipes for the perfect winner.

The contest took place a week before Christmas and was held at the schoolhouse. The finished products were presented to a panel of judges for tasting. When the judging was over, the baked goods were sold by auction and the proceeds went to the school. Mustang Ridge actively supported such an endeavor.

Tom was always looking for new items to interest the readers. He wrote in the paper about how astrology was taking off in London and how high society American women began to imitate it in secret. He noted that the popular Old Farmer's Almanac had a section on it, and wondered if the folks in Mustang Ridge would be interested in seeing it in their paper. Therefore, Tom asked that readers respond with a yes or no using the small form included in the paper. Readers could deposit their votes in a box at the Patriot. The result was a resounding NO!

Several customers wrote on their ballots that this was a Bible-believing town and there was no place for such nonsense here in Mustang Ridge. Several people said they would stop buying the paper if such a thing were to be printed. Needless to say, Tom decided there was not a need for astrology in his paper. He later apologized for his error in judgment and thanked the residents for giving their honest opinions.

CHAPTER SIXTY

Independence Day 1893

It was a grand day to celebrate the birth of a great nation. Mustang Ridge went all out this year. In the past they had a band, a small parade, a horse race, and fireworks. But this year, they made plans to celebrate in an even grander fashion. A committee was formed to ensure everything that could be done would be done. Tuck was a member on that committee along with his good friend, Sam Garrison. The Patriot had many articles telling everyone of the events to take place.

As a result of all the planning, the parade was even greater than before. The participants dressed in costumes relating to America's freedom. Prizes were given for the best costume. Area ranchers entered some of their best horses. Cowboys, adept at rope tricks, rode their horses doing their tricks along the parade route with children and adults alike cheering them on. Many children were involved in the parade as well. Dressed in costumes, riding horses, walking, and singing along the way.

Following the parade, a program was held in front of the church at the end of the route. Reverend Peters, the new minister, began the program with a word of prayer.

The Mayor's wife, Martha Garrison rose to address the audience. "Thank you all for coming to the Mustang Ridge Independence Day Celebration. I want to thank everyone for attending this year and helping to make our parade and celebration something to remember. Now we will have fourteen-year-old Louisa Cutter, daughter of Matt and Mattie Cutter come up and read a poem that Katharine Lee Bates wrote this year. This poem is being shared across the country."

AMERICA (Original poem)
O beautiful for halcyon skies,
For amber waves of grain,
For purple mountain majesties
Above the enameled plain!
America! America!
God shed His grace on thee,
Till souls wax fair as earth and air
And music-hearted sea!

O beautiful for pilgrim feet
Whose stern, impassioned stress
A thoroughfare for freedom beat

177

Across the wilderness!
America! America!
God shed His grace on thee
Till paths be wrought through wilds of thought
By pilgrim foot and knee!

O beautiful for glory-tale
Of liberating strife,
When once or twice, for man's avail,
Men lavished precious life!
America! America!
God shed His grace on thee
Till selfish gain no longer stain,
The banner of the free!

O beautiful for patriot dream
That sees beyond the years
Thine alabaster cities gleam
Undimmed by human tears!
America! America!
God shed His grace on thee
Till nobler men keep once again
Thy whiter jubilee!

"Wasn't that a marvelous poem? And thank you, Louisa Cutter for reading it to us. Katharine Lee Bates was inspired to write this poem near Pikes Peak, Colorado, when she was teaching at Colorado College. She said,

> *One day some of the other teachers and I decided to go on a trip to 14,000-foot Pikes Peak. We hired a prairie wagon. Near the top we had to leave the wagon and go the rest of the way on mules. I was very tired. But when I saw the view, I felt great joy. All the wonder of America seemed displayed there, with the sea-like expanse.*"

Martha now turned to the box which held ribbons and the cash prizes for the parade winners. She called the names of the children first and gave them the ribbons as well as the monetary prizes. Then she moved on to the adults following the same procedure. The grand prize went to Jacob and Sarah Wells for their portrayal of George and Martha Washington riding in a buggy. Colorful ribbons adorned the buggy and Sarah had created white wigs for the two of them to wear. They really looked authentic.

178

"Mattie Cutter will now sing The Battle Hymn of the Republic," Martha announced.

Mine eyes have seen the glory of the coming of the Lord;
He is trampling out the vintage where the grapes of wrath are
stored;
He hath loosed the fateful lightning of His terrible swift
sword: His truth is marching on.

(Chorus)
Glory, Glory, hallelujah!
Glory, glory, hallelujah!
Glory, glory, hallelujah!
His truth is marching on.

I have seen Him in the watch-fires of a hundred
circling camps,
They have builded Him an altar in the evening dews and
damps;
I can read His righteous sentence by the dim and flaring
lamps:
His day is marching on.

In the beauty of the lilies Christ was born across the sea,
With a glory in His bosom that transfigures you and me.
As He died to make men holy, let us die to make men free,
While God is marching on.

As Mattie's sweet voice ended the stirring song, applause and cheering erupted. Martha calmed the ecstatic crowd and asked Reverend Peters to close in prayer. As the program concluded, everyone went to get their picnic baskets for dinner. The downtown boardwalks were full of booths either selling food and homemade articles or chances to play a game. Many different games were played during the afternoon hours.

The Cutter family was invited to eat their picnic lunch with the two Tucker families after the program.

"Louisa, dear, that was a fine job of reading the poem," Beth said. "and Mattie, your beautiful voice really did credit to a beautiful song."

"Thank you, Beth," Mattie said.

When evening arrived with the supper hour, another beef roast was provided to everyone in the same fashion as previous years. Then the fireworks, and oh, how magnificent they were this year. Amid the "oohs" and "aahs," many proclaimed them to be even better this year, and no doubt they were.

CHAPTER SIXTY-ONE
New Partner 1893

Thad's little brother, Nate, was twenty-four now. Tuck and Thad had officially made him part owner of the Deer Creek Ranch association. This allowed Thad to devote more of his efforts to his own ranch, since he recently acquired more land. They also agreed to put Nate solely in charge of the coal mining business. Throughout his teen years and early twenties, Nate acted as a partner anyway and was vested in the business through time and resourcefulness. They believed he now needed to be a part of the operation on paper as well.

Thad knew that Pa's relationship with Nate had grown stronger over the years. Theirs had been a special one because of the friendship when Pa had been sheriff. It didn't hurt Thad's feelings because they all had a special relationship with the man who had adopted them as his own. Since Thad owned Whitehorse Ranch, he opted to take a lesser percentage of Deer Creek Ranch, leaving more for Nate. Nate, although still a little mischievous at times, had grown into a responsible young man and they were pleased to make this change a legal one.

They were in lawyer Leonard Cox's office in Mustang Ridge getting the necessary paperwork signed. Tuck thought they needed to have a celebratory meal at Sally's. Beth was there, as well as Thad's growing family. Growing, because Belle now neared the end of her pregnancy with her fifth child. She had wanted to come to town at this time thinking it might be the last time she'd be able to do that before the baby would be born.

Once the papers were signed and Nate was legally an owner of Deer Creek Ranch, the family made their way to Sally's for dinner. When they entered, Sally looked up, wide-eyed. "As I live and breathe! It's the Tucker family, just about all of them."

Thad laughed. He supposed it was rather daunting to have a family of that size come in for a meal. "Nine for dinner, Sally," he said. "We're celebrating."

"Make that ten for dinner, Sally."

Thad turned to see Nate enter the diner behind him with Rachel Garrison's arm linked with his. Thad had noted as of late that his brother was spending a lot of time with Sam and Martha's adopted daughter. The Garrisons had taken her in at age five years when her family died on a wagon train.

"Hello, Rachel," Beth said. "Please, do join us. Has Nate told you what this day is all about?"

"Yes, he did, Mrs. Tucker. I hope you don't mind my joining in the celebration."

"Of course, we don't mind. You are important to Nate, so you are important to us," Beth said.

As Thad watched the interchanges between his family members while they were seated at the table, he contemplated what the future might hold for them. He looked to his wife, plump with baby and beautiful. Would this baby be another girl?

His gaze moved to his parents. Although still vital and active, they were looking older. They each had small amounts of gray hair showing now.

With a father's pride, he looked upon the faces of his four children. Jackson, shoveling food into his mouth like he hadn't eaten for a week; Ellen, seated next to her beloved brother, hanging on his every word; Lucy, his sweet little girl, the very image of his beautiful wife with her dark curls; Molly, headstrong and with a mind of her own.

Thad's look then fell on Nate seated next to Rachel, her long blond hair hanging in ringlets. Would they be announcing an engagement in the near future? Thad suspected so. Now that Nate had the ranch interest, perhaps he would soon be asking Sam for his daughter's hand in marriage. As Thad considered the possibility of Nate marrying Rachel, he recalled the promise he had made to Nate when he and Belle were married. The night of the shivaree when he said to Nate, "Just you wait until you get married. You'd best plan on leaving the country!"

"A toast," Tuck commented as he rose with his glass of water, "to the newest owner of Deer Creek Ranch, my son, Nate."

Glasses clinked with many well wishes offered to the newest partner. Even the little ones participated with the help of their parents and grandparents.

"While we are toasting, Rachel and I would like to announce that we are engaged to be married."

So, not only had Nate been seeing Rachel for some time, but it seemed he had proposed to Rachel Garrison and she'd said yes. They would be marrying within two months' time.

Thad was pretty happy that Nate would be getting married and Rachel was such a nice girl. So, there would be plans underway for a wedding soon. Belle loved weddings and it had been her hope that the newlyweds would be as happy as she and Thad had been.

CHAPTER SIXTY-TWO
Belle

It was a joy for Belle to watch Thad with his son and three girls. He's a wonderful father and everyone could see how much he loved those children. They followed him all over. Their Papa was a hero in their eyes.

A letter arrived from Becca the other day. Belle was so glad they had mail service to Mustang Ridge. It had been so hard the last year since she'd missed her best friend so much. Becca's love for the Shoshone Indians was evident between the lines. Belle was sure she and Peter were a blessing to the Indians since they taught English and other subjects. But still, she missed her so much. The Wounded Knee massacre was always on her mind. She prayed that nothing like that would ever happen at the Wind River Reservation, or anywhere else ever again.

Becca wrote about a little five-year-old Shoshone girl who was now an orphan. Her family died from smallpox, and she had no other relatives. Her name was Rosebud and Becca called her Rose. Becca wrote:

> *She is a beautiful little girl with brown eyes and long brown braids. Rose came with her mother to the reservation when she was just an infant. Her mother was white but had been stolen from a white family in Texas by a band of Comanche and raised by them. Quanah was her Comanche name. She was taken by an Indian brave as his squaw, and she gave birth to Rosebud. Rose's father was killed in a battle and she and her mother made the trip north with the band. Then they escaped and came to Wind River Reservation. Quanah died of chicken pox, leaving Rose an orphan. She is a very smart little girl too. I think one day she will be a teacher since she is always helping me with the classes even at age five.*

> *Did I tell you that Rose is living with us, since she has no home now that her parents and family are gone? In fact, Peter and I have made inquiries to see about adopting her. Are you surprised? It came as a shock to me too, but as the idea grows, I know it's what God wants us to do.*

> *And what about you, dear friend? Are your babies keeping you busy? Mama sent me a letter and she told me you were expecting. I hope you had a good pregnancy. Write and tell me about the new baby when it comes. I pray that you'll have another good pregnancy.*

Speaking of babies, Peter and I are expecting in early '94. I'm feeling good. We're so happy as we look forward to increasing our family to four.

It seems that there is an opening for the Indian Agent and Peter has thrown his hat into the ring, so to speak. The old one (Indian Agent, not Peter's hat) was let go since he wasn't representing the Indians but lining his own pockets instead. Why does there have to be such evil in this world? Oh, I know the answer to that. Just lamenting, I guess.

Time to head to bed now. Rose has fallen asleep and I need to put her to bed. I will post this tomorrow.

Love,

Becca

Belle asked Thad if he wanted to read Becca's letter and he took it from her, asking how she was doing. She told him to read it and he'd see. *My childhood friend, a mother to an Indian girl.* Of course, she was! Her heart was so full of love, it was inevitable. Belle was thrilled for her and Peter that they were also expecting a baby as well as adopting Rose.

CHAPTER SIXTY-THREE
Nate and Rachel 1893

Thad was excited for Nate and Rachel's wedding. Sam and Martha Garrison's daughter was a lovely girl. He had been callin' on Rachel for some time now. Thad was to be his best man and when he gave Thad the ring before the wedding, Nate admonished him not to lose it. "Do you really expect me to lose it?" Thad asked. "I think you're more likely to lose it than me, Nate."

Nate and Thad watched from their position at the altar while Sam proudly walked his daughter down the aisle. Thad and his family had enjoyed a close friendship with the Garrisons over the years, and they'd now be even closer.

Now that Nate was a partner in Deer Creek Ranch, he would take his bride back there to live. With Thad and Becca both living elsewhere, Tuck and Nate had been doing some renovations to the ranch-house. They added to Nate's bedroom from the outside, providing an outside entrance for them. They turned Thad's former bedroom into a sitting room with an opening to the addition so they could have privacy and yet share the kitchen.

Following the wedding reception, Nate and Rachel boarded the north-bound train to spend a few days at Yellowstone National Park. Back in '72, President Grant had signed papers making it the country's first national park. The newlyweds were looking forward to time away at such a scenic area in a cabin they had reserved there.

Thad was greatly disappointed that he wouldn't be able to give his brother and his bride a shivaree like Nate had done for him and Belle. The night Nate led a shivaree for him and Belle, Thad made a promise to Nate that he would reciprocate, so he had to think of something. He volunteered to load Nate and Rachel's luggage onto the train's baggage car. A perfect opportunity availed itself and Thad took complete advantage of it. Opening his brother's luggage, he tied his clothes all in knots. He then placed a cowbell inside and closed it. Satisfied that he'd done all he could to cause even the tiniest bit of irritation to his little brother, he rejoined the group for the send-off.

So now both of Thad's siblings were married. He hoped Becca and Peter and Nate and Rachel would be as happy as he and Belle had been.

#
Twins 1894

When Rachel told Belle that she and Nate were expecting later in the year, Belle was ecstatic for the young couple. They would have their babies around the same time. So nice to have cousins near the same age.

Belle got together several pieces of clothing that could be used for either boy or girl that she wouldn't need with her baby. With Thad's help she loaded all the clothing and the crib into the back of the buggy. They had two because the girls had been close together, so she could give one to Nate and Rachel. Thad went along, He said it was to help her unload the crib. However, she knew her husband pretty well by now,

Thad knew there would be a lot of female squealing, along with hugging going on. After all there was a lot of it when Rachel came to Whitehorse Ranch to tell them about the baby expected. But Nate was his little brother and he loved him dearly. He felt like he wanted to be there for him. Maybe he could give Nate some advice.

When Belle and Thad arrived at Deer Creek Ranch, he helped unload the crib and they went inside using Nate and Rachel's entrance on the side of the ranch-house. Nate came to the door to help them with the baby things. Rachel was not to be seen.

"Where is Rachel?" she asked Beth.

"She's in bed. She's been pretty sick," Nate explained.

"Oh, no!" Belle said. "Do you think I could go see her?"

Nate led them to their bedroom. The door was ajar, so he rapped softly and said, "Rachel, dear, are you up for company? Belle is here to see you."

"Oh, Belle. Just the person I want to see," she called in a panicky voice. Nate and Thad went back to the sitting room to wait.

Belle couldn't believe how much Rachel's appearance had changed in just a few days. The young woman was a sickly shade of white and was wrapped up to her neck in the bedcovers. Belle could see that she was chilled.

"Rachel, what is wrong?" Belle went to her bedside and touched her arm.

"The nausea and vomiting of pregnancy. I haven't been able to keep anything down."

"Oh dear. What have you tried eating?" Belle asked.

"Roast beef with potatoes and gravy a few days ago. Then fried chicken the other day. Since then, I've just had chicken broth. I'm hungry but nothing stays down."

"When I was pregnant with my babies, I handled my nausea by consuming only cold food. When they are warm, you are able to smell them better and it

186

causes the nausea," Belle. "Maybe try to eat some dry crackers if you have any."

"I'm so thirsty," Rachel said.

"You're probably not getting enough fluids and you are drying out," Belle explained. "Try some herbal tea, like mint. You can use that until your baby is born."

"Oh Belle. What would I do without your help?"

"You'd probably get by, just as I did. But it is always good to have someone else to lean on. My years as a nurse with Doc Phillips helped me. "I'll go talk to Beth about what you should have."

"I don't want to bother her."

"Nonsense, she would feel hurt if you didn't ask her."

Rachel eventually revived from her time of sickness and her pregnancy continued on with no further problems. Belle went out to visit her every so often and took the time to include Beth in the visits also. If Tuck was around, she visited him as well.

The day came as Belle's own pregnancy neared an end when she received the exciting news that Rachel had delivered twin boys! She and Nate named them Jon and Tony. The babies were doing well and Rachel, after and exhausting delivery, was also doing fine. Belle heard that Beth was beside herself. Her mother-in-law was an enormous help to Rachel in caring for the new babies.

Belle was excited for Rachel, but wanted more than anything for this baby to be born. If truth be known, Belle was tired of having babies. Oh, not of the babies themselves but of the long nine months preceding their birth.

CHAPTER SIXTY-FOUR
At Last 1894

At last! Thad was blessed with another baby boy. Benjamin Jacob Tucker entered the world in the spring of '94. Thad had begun to think there'd be no more babies since there were nearly four years between Ben and Molly. But God had answered his prayer for another boy and also his prayer that Belle would have a good pregnancy. And because her pregnancy had been another good one, he thought that it would be another girl. It even surprised Doc Phillips that Ben was not a girl. *Thank you, Father. I have been greatly blessed.*

Ben was a happy baby and even though he had three sisters and a brother to watch him sleep, he was able to get the job done.

Belle and Thad received a short letter from Becca two weeks after Ben was born.

> *I got your letter about Ben's birth. Congratulations, my friend. And Thad, I know you're pleased to have another boy. Praise God. My prayers continue for you and your family.*
>
> *I suppose you're wondering about our newest family member. Adam Steven Rhodes was born just three days after your own Ben. Adam is named after Pa and Peter's brother Steven. He is a healthy baby and doing well, as am I. Isn't it nice that we will have sons to raise that were born almost the same day? There's so much we can share as they grow up into young men.*
>
> *The adoption of Rose went through but not without problems. I thought we might not be able to keep fostering her, let alone adopt her. The tribal leaders weren't willing at first to let us adopt her, but neither were they ready to take her themselves. You see, she is part Comanche and part white. The Comanche and the Shoshone have been bitter enemies. Therefore, none of the Shoshone at the reservation wanted to take her. Finally, they ruled in our favor and we are now the parents of two children. Praise God for His goodness.*
>
> *Love,*
> *Becca*

Thad poured over drawings of what he could do to make more rooms for his growing family. Now Jackson and Ellen each had their own room and Lucy and Molly shared one. For now, Ben would have his crib in his parent's room but that would have to change down the road. Perhaps it would be okay to have the boys in one room together. Nine years separated Jackson and Ben, but he knew Jackson had loved his sisters to the point of distraction, so maybe he would like having Ben share his room.

Thad put the papers away, satisfied that no new construction would be needed at this time. He pulled out his Bible and began reading. When he finished, he sat back and thought a while, then bowed his head in prayer, asking for clarification of what he had just read.

Belle exited their bedroom, having put little Ben down to sleep after his feeding. "What has such a pensive look on your face, dear?"

Thad read from 1 Samuel to her and upon finishing, looked at her and explained what he thought. "What do you think?" he asked her.

"I think we need to pray about it. It might be that God is directing us to do something like what Hannah did in 1 Samuel, Thad. We need to talk with Reverend Peters if God directs us."

CHAPTER SIXTY-FIVE
Dedication

Nine-year-old Jackson watched with pride as their family entered the church. Jackson appeared to be just as proud as his papa. He knew a special event would be taking place because Papa explained it to him. He helped direct his sisters into the family pew to be seated.

Thad and Belle were anxiously awaiting the service today because they were to dedicate their children to the Lord. Not a widely done event, especially in western states. However, Belle and Thad believed it was something they should do given different verses in Scripture they'd been reading. In 1 Samuel 1:11, Hannah was a woman unable to bear a child. She prayed for a child and promised to dedicate him to the Lord if He'd give her a son. And in Luke 2:22, Joseph and Mary took baby Jesus to the temple for a dedication, a common practice under the Jewish law. Although Thad had not made any such promise to God if He would give him another boy, he did, however, feel the need to make a formal dedication of all of his and Belle's children to God.

Reverend Peters asked the Tucker family to approach the platform. "These children, Jackson, Ellen, Lucinda, Molly, and Benjamin and their parents Thad and Belle Tucker are being presented to you, the congregation, today that you may witness the vows Thad and Belle are making to raise them in the Christian faith," he said.

"There are several Scripture references whereby we can see that this is nothing new. One such passage is Deuteronomy 6:4-7:

> *Hear, O Israel: The LORD our God, the LORD is one. You shall love the LORD your God with all your heart and with all your soul and with all your might. And these words that I command you today shall be on your heart. You shall teach them diligently to your children, and shall talk of them when you sit in your house, and when you walk by the way, and when you lie down, and when you rise.*

"Today, Thad and Belle believe they are obeying God's command by making their vow before this congregation to raise their children in the faith. We, as their friends, family, and congregation can help them in this endeavor through prayer for their family. Let us pray."

CHAPTER SIXTY-SIX

Frontier Days in Cheyenne-1897

It was a big year for Cheyenne, Wyoming. The mayor wanted to bring more business to his city so he devised a plan. They would have a Frontier Day on September 23rd. Since Cheyenne sat along the rail line, he believed having this "western celebration" would bring in a lot of business. He even arranged for excursion trains to come through and stop there.

Thad and Tuck made plans to take their families to see it. Thad provided a string of his best cutting horses for the ranch hands to use in the events. They drove them down with the covered wagon while the women and children traveled by train and met them there. They stayed the night before in tents and the large covered wagon. Thad's children were excited to make camp just as their grandparents had done many years ago on the Oregon Trail. The women were anxious to see the stores in the town and the men to watch the cowboys participate in the arena.

As the train pulled into Cheyenne, twelve-year-old Jackson could hardly contain his enthusiasm. Everywhere he looked, cowboys in western hats and wide sombreros rode their horses, their spurs jingling as they walked the boardwalks of downtown. The cowboy's saddles were of the finest quality leather and were decorated with polished silver. He'd been excited to ride on the train, but the town of Cheyenne far outweighed the train ride for him.

Thad and Tuck met them at the train station. Beth and Belle were fondly greeting their menfolk with hugs and kisses because it had been about four days since they had seen the men. The ranch hands picked up the luggage while Thad carried three-year-old Ben, and six-year-old Molly walked beside her grandpa holding his hand. Ellen and Lucy walked with Jackson. The men led the way to the Tucker campsite.

When they approached, they saw the big covered wagon pulled up close to a stream with a tarp extending from the side to protect them from the hot sun. A camp stove had been set up under it, as well as a long table and benches. Several tents surrounded this area and would be used by the men of the family as well as the ranch hands. They planned for the women to sleep in the wagon, maybe even one or two of the smaller children. Jackson, of course, wanted to sleep in a tent with either Papa or Grandpa.

"What do you think about all this?" Thad asked his family while they were seated around the table.

"Papa, can I ride in the arena with the cowboys?" Jackson asked.

"No, you have to be a contestant and you're too young for that," his father replied. "Maybe when you are older."

Knowing that Jackson wanted to ride with the cowboys gave Thad a moment of pride. This held a promise to him of a future ranching partnership with his eldest son. He imagined their names on the ranch sign, "Whitehorse Ranch, Thad and Jackson Tucker Proprietors." But for now, he would enjoy the enthusiastic youth of his children.

"Ladies, what do you think about the camp? Any changes you need?" Thad inquired of his mother and wife.

"You men have covered everything as far as I can see," Belle replied. "All the comforts that we require."

"I think so too, but perhaps gather a little more firewood. This will be used up just in our first meal." Beth pointed to the pile of wood next to the camp stove. The men complied with her wishes and soon a large stack of wood that would more than suffice stood by the wagon.

# # #

The day of the festivities arrived and the Tucker families were up early to get ready for the big day. Jackson could barely sleep the night before due to his anticipation of what the day would hold. His siblings slept well, however, and were raring to go.

Beth and Belle were busy cooking breakfast not only for their family but for the ranch hands as well. The mouthwatering smells of bacon cooking wafted throughout their camp. No one could sleep after catching a whiff of the delicious bacon cooking. Flapjacks with sorghum and fresh coffee completed the menu. They all gathered around while Tuck asked the blessing over the food and also asked for God's protection over those participating in the contests.

Several of the hands entered various competitions and Belle had sewed scarves with the same colors for them to wear so they would feel they were part of a team. They proudly accepted the scarves she presented to them.

Tuck and Thad directed their families to a bleacher with six rows. They had reserved seats ahead of time for their family. Other spectators who didn't have bleacher seats sat astride their horses while the women folk sat in wagons with parasols to protect them from the sun.

The day began with a cannon salute by the 17th Field Artillery from nearby Fort Russell. Train whistles, church bells, banging of pots, and spectator's hand guns added to the uproar. The Tuckers watched and cheered as their own ranch hands took part in bull riding, bucking broncs, horse racing, calf roping, barrel racing, and steer roping.

192

CHAPTER SIXTY-SEVEN
Belle

What a thrilling time for the family to be spectators at the Cheyenne Frontier Day celebration. It was a show testing the skills of cowboys. Their children were mesmerized by the events. Jackson was so excited, he wouldn't sit down. Guess he feared he'd miss out on some of the action.

A thrilling stagecoach hold-up was enacted right in front of them. This brought to mind events at Deer Creek Stage station prompting Lucy to ask, "Grandma, did this happen with your stage?"

"No, but it was under Indian attack once. And one time, we were held up in the stage station itself by bad men with guns."

Lucy's eyes grew big as saucers. Belle guessed that Beth would be called upon to explain her statement at a later time. Probably that night around the campfire.

Several of their own cowboys did well in the competitions, taking home cash awards. Belle learned that this was a common occurrence for cowboys since it supplemented their ranch wages.

Toward the end of the day, an alarming event occurred when wild horses broke free and stampeded toward the flimsy, wooden bleachers. They scrambled for safety when the horses smashed the bleachers into a splintered heap. They were all safe. Even though no one was injured, it ended the day with a bit more excitement than they had anticipated.

The town held a barbecue afterward, but the family opted to go back to the camp and have their own meal. Besides, the children were getting tired and needed to unwind before bedtime. The ranch hands were on their own, so they went to participate in the town's meal as well as the street dance that followed.

Their family had a great time relating to the children stories about their travel on the wagon train. Thad told his children about hunting on the wagon train and learning how to make pemmican from the Indians at Fort Laramie. Belle told about how they cooked during their travels, gathering dried buffalo chips for the fires, and searching for wild berries. Beth regaled them with stories of her episode with and Indian brave who wanted to trade his pony for Becca. She then related stories of being an operator of a stagecoach station, including when the robbers held her hostage in the station. Tuck divulged stories about his days as sheriff and how he met the Shoshone Indian, Grey Wolf, and his family.

The children were exhausted by the time the evening meal was done and the singing around the campfire put them to sleep before the second song was finished.

193

All in all, the Tucker family had a wonderful time. Thad asked if they wanted to take the train back home again. Jackson wanted to ride in the wagon, so they decided he could. After all, at age twelve he was the same age as Belle had been when they came out on the wagon train.

Lucy announced that she also wanted to ride with the men, but she wanted to ride a horse. At nine-years-old, Lucy had become an excellent horsewoman and spent her play-time pretending to be a rancher. Belle knew Thad would have to consider his decision. *I don't think he is willing to let the girls grow up too soon. My dear husband, I'm afraid life will give you a surprise or two.*

#

The next morning, they boarded the train bound for home. Jackson and Lucy stayed with Thad. Belle wasn't surprised that Lucy had won him over. Even at nine, she had a way of making her father see what she wanted him to see. Belle knew there would be an ample amount of family and ranch hands to watch over her and Jackson, so she wasn't concerned. Ellen, Molly, and Ben, slept most of the way home on the train. She and Beth took the time to rest also. When they weren't sleeping, the children were excitedly talking about the celebration they had just taken part in. She was quite pleased with how well they had all behaved, even little Ben.

CHAPTER SIXTY-EIGHT
Belle

In '98, Belle took her Mama by train to Cheyenne. She presented her with this trip as a birthday present. Belle remembered the stores there from last year when they went for Cheyenne Frontier Day and knew she would love to shop there. Sarah wanted to get new material for her dressmaking and maybe even a new sewing machine. Beth offered to watch the younger children while they were gone. Jackson stayed with Thad while the rest spent their time with Grandma Beth.

Sarah bought several yards of pretty material and other things to use in her sewing. And she found a great deal on a treadle sewing machine as well. They also went to the Cheyenne Opera House to see a show. The programs were perfumed and made of blue and silver silk. It was so elegant. Sarah had made the two of them dresses with matching wide-brimmed hats to wear on the occasion. To be able to take her dear Mama to such a wonderful place made her glad. Sarah had worked so hard all her life and it made Belle happy to share this time with her. The hotel they stayed in for two nights was elegant and provided a relaxing time for both of them.

The two women especially liked the two bathtubs where they could both soak without worrying about taking time away from the other. It was so luxurious to sit and soak with lots of silky bubbles after a day on their feet shopping. They even enjoyed the train ride. It was much more comfortable than a stagecoach would have been.

All too soon, their time in Cheyenne had drawn to a close and they had to board the train for the ride home. They'd made several purchases which had to be stored in the baggage car.

Thad stood waiting at the Mustang Ridge depot for the train to pull in. *What a fine-looking man, waiting for us to disembark.*

Belle could tell he was happy to see her. She may have imagined it, but she thought his eyes looked a little wet. Hers certainly were. Mama spied Papa hurrying over to the depot and she took off to engage in a little welcome of her own.

While Sarah and Belle were in Cheyenne, Thad's beloved Buddy passed away. Thad found him lying in the barn one morning, as though he were peacefully sleeping. Thad mourned Buddy, though he wouldn't say so. But Belle knew her husband. Buddy had been his faithful companion for twelve years. He had led a long and happy life. His loyalty to Thad was wonderful, even though he loved their children too.

Belle recalled how Buddy had come to Jackson's aide when that horrible man had attacked. Belle didn't know if Thad would be looking for another puppy. He said maybe, sometime later, but he had enough to keep himself busy for now.

CHAPTER SIXTY-NINE
1900 It's a New Century!

The Tuckers of Niobrara County began the twentieth century with good health and prosperity. Both Deer Creek Ranch and Whitehorse Ranch were doing well financially.

Garrison's mercantile was the scene of many discussions regarding new inventions, news-worthy events – both worldwide and locally. New discoveries pointed the way for improvement in the lives of the citizens of Mustang Ridge and surrounding areas.

One discovery that Dr. Ward found quite useful was the creation of Aspirin. In 1899, Felix Hoffman, a German Chemist who worked for Bayer created Aspirin for pain relief. However, it took Joshua's patients a while to confidently try the new medication. Nate thought it might have been useful to him if they'd had it available when he had his surgery.

"That laudanum left me in a haze," he commented.

Thad poked his brother in the ribs. "You were in a haze anyway," he joked.

Tea bags were introduced in 1904 by the tea and coffee importer Thomas Sullivan from New York. Belle found these to be an essential addition to her pantry. She liked that she could use her dried herbs and fill the little gauze tea bags. Seeing that they made lovely gifts, Belle bought several for her three daughters and told Sam that he should carry more of them in his store. Belle was Sam's best form of advertising when she came to get additional bags.

Also, in April 1898, Spain declared war on the United States after rejecting America's ultimatum to withdraw from Cuba. Dr. Tucker Cutter left to go to Cuba to offer his medical services. Mustang Ridge citizenry had differing opinions regarding his bold action. Some thought he was butting his nose into business that was between Spain and Cuba. Others commended him for standing up for the Cubans and the poor treatment they received at the hands of the Spaniards. His father, Matt Cutter, defended him by arguing that Tucker's mission was a humanitarian one. He treated both sides.

Crayola crayons were made available to customers in 1903. The crayons sold for a nickel a box with the colors black, brown, blue, red, purple, orange, yellow, and green.

Sam set up a hands-on display in the back of his store for the children to draw pictures with the colorful sticks. He obtained a roll of paper from the newspaper for them to color. Thad was so enamored with the crayons when he saw the display in the mercantile that he purchased several boxes for his future grandchildren. Belle laughed at his reasoning.

"We'll eventually have some," he told her. "With all the children we had, some are bound to give us grandchildren." In fact, you could often see Thad drawing at the table in the back as he talked with other ranchers about the weather, prices, etc. His claim was that he was supervising the little ones while their parents shopped.

That same year, the Wright brothers had the first powered flight. The mercantile carried toy aero planes like the ones flown at Kitty Hawk. Jackson's interest in the news of their aeronautical feat left him dreaming of flight himself. Sam provided him with a magazine regarding the plane and future predictions about planes and he also purchased one of the toys.

Something that Belle found useful was when Kellogg's corn and wheat flakes were introduced in 1906. She thought it was nice for a change not to cook bacon and eggs. The whole-grain replacement for meat would save time over the hot stove, and provide excellent nutrition when there wasn't time to cook over a fire.

Thad wasn't so sure about it. He still enjoyed a stick-to-your-ribs kind of breakfast, although if he had to fix his own breakfast, it certainly worked for him. One thing Thad was sure about though, was when Gillette introduced the safety razor, he definitely wanted one. Once again, Sam displayed the razors in his mercantile. Sam even talked George into demonstrating the use of one. Belle surprised Thad with one for his birthday as soon as they were available.

CHAPTER SEVENTY
1908 *Tuck's New Auto*

One day in 1908, Tuck was expecting his new purchase to come in on the train. Thad knew if it indeed came, that Pa would bring it out to Whitehorse Ranch so he and his family could see it. Tuck had been reading earlier that year about a horseless carriage invented by a man named Henry Ford. Production for his Ford Model T would start during the year. After discussing it with his partners and his wife, Tuck placed an order directly to the factory.

Thad hoped it would be all that Pa thought it would be, but he was skeptical. Then too, if everyone bought one, what would that do to his horse sales? But Pa believed it would be useful as a family conveyance.

"I'm concerned about your mother. She's having trouble riding the bumpy wagon or buggy into town," Tuck argued. Thad couldn't recall his mother ever complaining about it.

"This would alleviate some of the discomfort. Lookee what it says here," he showed the newspaper article to Thad and Nate. "It can go 40 to 45 miles per hour. We'd get to town in no time."

"But Pa, the road would still be bumpy. It's noisy and dirty and..." Thad trailed off. Pa had set his mind to this, so might as well give in to his whim. "If you think so, Pa. Might as well give it a try. But $800 is an awful lot of money."

"I know it is, but I think it'll be worth the cost," Tuck said. "Besides, I saw a guy in Cheyenne last year who had designed and built his own. He'd been driving it around Cheyenne for two years. Heard a lot about it when I was down there.

"Okay. Guess you've made up your mind. I just worry that these autos will replace horses and then where'll I be?"

"Thad, ranchers will always need good cutting horses for their cattle operations, not to mention your excellent thoroughbred horses. They can't do that with an auto."

Thad was in the stables using a curry comb on one of the horses. He laid aside the comb and walked outside when he heard a loud sound. *Must be that confounded horseless carriage Pa bought. Sure is loud.*

While Thad went outside, Tuck squeezed the big black bulb which honked the horn with an 'ahooga, ahooga.' The horses in the corral became spooked and raced around the enclosure, whinnying with fright.

The ranch hands raced to calm them, fearing they would hurt themselves as they slammed against the corral fence. The chickens flew around their fenced-in pen squawking, feathers flying. Thad hurried to the auto where his pa and ma were seated. "Shut it off!" Thad called but knew Pa couldn't hear him. He drew his hand across his throat in a signal to stop and pointed to the corral of spooked horses.

Tuck finally got the idea and shut it off. "Well, I guess that is one problem we have to deal with. Horses don't seem to care for the noise. Or chickens either."

"They probably think it's going to replace them," Thad commented. He took a closer look at his parents. Each one wore goggles and a long coat, even though it was a hot day. "Do you have to wear a special costume to ride in it?"

"If you're going to be out in the country, you should. It gets pretty dusty and you need to protect your eyes," Tuck explained.

"Uh-huh," Thad replied dubiously.

"Want to go for a ride?" Ma invited. "You can have my riding costume while I go in and see Belle and the children."

"I suppose," Thad replied, reluctantly taking the cloak and goggles.

Tuck went to the front of the auto and inserted the crank. "This is how you start it," he demonstrated. He turned the crank and jumped back while it grabbed hold and the engine started.

They drove out of the ranch area away from the rearing horses and frightened chickens. Thad agreed with Tuck that it was exhilarating. As he became used to the jolts and bumps, not to mention the loudness, Tuck asked if he'd like to try driving. Thad nodded and Tuck braked to a stop.

"I'll just leave it running while we change places," he said. He explained how to use the floor pedals and how to use the stick on the floor to change gears.

As he drove back to the ranch-house, he saw Belle and Jackson waiting, apparently for their turn. Tuck laughed and got out of the car handing his cloak and goggles to Belle. He pulled out an extra pair of goggles for Jackson.

"Don't have a coat for you, young man, but the goggles should help."

"What do you think, Belle? Thad asked his wife as they motored down the valley road.

"I think we should get one too," she responded.

"Really?" He was sure she'd not want one of their own.

"Yes, just think of how that will help me. I can drive into town and it won't take so much time out of my day."

"Oh, you think you can drive it, do you?" Thad returned with a smile.

"Of course!" Belle declared emphatically. "If your mother can, so can I."

"Jackson, what do you think about it?" Thad asked his son. Jackson was now twenty-three.

"It's great!" Jackson exclaimed. "Are you going to get one too, Pa?"

"I guess I'll have to," Thad replied. "Want to give it a try?"

Well, of course, Jackson did, and he drove back to the ranch which upset the horses all over again. Jackson switched the car off as soon as he coasted to a stop.

"You'll have to get the horses used to the sound of the engine," Jackson suggested.

"Me! Why me? Why not you?" Thad asked.

"I won't be here," Jackson replied.

"Where are you going?" Belle asked.

"To North Platte, Pa," Jackson answered. "I've wanted to tell you for some time now, but I haven't been able to broach the subject until today. I'm going to work on engines to be used in the new aero planes invented by the Wright brothers."

Thad felt his hopes for a father and son partnership drop with a crash. However, he tried not to show his disappointment to his son. "I heard about them. They made their first flight three years ago. So, I guess this means you don't want to be involved in the family ranch any longer?" Belle had been quiet in the backseat. He turned to look at her, noticing she applied her hanky to her tear-filled eyes.

"I'm sorry, Pa, Ma. I know you always wanted that but I want to do other things. I hope to one day become a pilot myself, and by working on the engines at the North Platte airfield, I can get my foot in the door."

Thad didn't say anything for a while. This really wasn't what he wanted to hear, but he and Belle had encouraged their children to follow their hearts and the Lord's leading in what they wanted to do with their lives. His thoughts returned to the days when Jackson grew excited to ride on his pa's horse with him while he rode the range. Thad had been so proud of Jackson then and looked ahead fondly to a time when they would ride the range together. Now that Jackson was twenty-three-years-old, he thought that his son was staying on at the ranch. Even so, Thad would always be proud of his son, no matter what he did. Instead of flying across the hills on horseback, Jackson wanted to fly above the ground in an aero plane.

Finally, Thad said, "I guess if it's what you want to do, I can't say anything to change your mind. At least I have one more son who can ranch with me when he is old enough," he said contemplating fourteen-year-old Ben.

"What about Lucy?" Jackson asked, thinking of his sister who was now twenty. "She wants to be a rancher."

"What? Lucy? Why didn't I know about this?" Thad demanded. He looked at Belle.

"Pa, she's been telling you. You just don't listen to her because she's a girl."

"Belle, did you know this?" Thad asked.

"Yes, dear. She's dreamed of running her own ranch someday since she was nine. Hopefully Whitehorse Ranch."

"Well, I'll be!"

CHAPTER SEVENTY-ONE
Thad Talks to Lucy

As Thad walked out onto the veranda of the ranch-house, Lucy came up from the horse stables. She sat down there to rest with a glass of lemonade before returning to her work. Thad wanted to talk to her about what he had learned from Jackson earlier in the day. His little Lucy wanted to be a rancher. He just didn't know how to broach the subject with her.

"Lucy, if you have the time, I'd like to talk to you about something."

"Sure, Papa. What is it?"

"I...uh...I heard today that you want to have your own ranch. Is that true?"

"Yes, Papa. It is."

"Are you sure this is something you want to do?"

"Yes, Papa. Why? Don't you think I can do it?"

"Well, uh...no...I mean yes, I think you can do anything you put your mind to."

"There, you see? Good talk, Papa," she said rising, and giving Thad a peck on his cheek, she returned to the stables.

Not sure what had just transpired, Thad just sat there. Had he given his approval? He guessed he had. He heard a quiet chuckle coming from inside the screened door to the house. He looked around and saw his wife with a grin on her face.

"Yes, Thad. Good talk."

"Come out here, you."

Belle came out to the veranda next to her husband of twenty-five years. He pulled her down to his lap and kissed her with passion.

"Mr. Tucker! What if the ranch hands see us?"

"I think they have seen us before," he responded. "Mrs. Tucker, what do you think I should do about Lucy?"

"Well, I think you will just have to talk to the Father about that," she answered him.

And that's just what he did later that night. He and his Heavenly Father had a great conversation and when he finished, Thad believed he could make a decision based on the will of God. The next morning, he saddled his horse and rode out to Deer Creek Ranch. He needed to have a talk with Pa.

"So, she wants to run her own ranch, huh?" Tuck said. "I know she's just as good a horsewoman as any of the ranch hands. Guess it shouldn't be a surprise that she wants to be a rancher. So, what is your problem again?"

"Well, you know I always dreamed of having Jackson join me in running the ranch. Now that's not going to happen."

"Why not?"

"Oh, guess you didn't know. Jackson is leaving soon for North Platte. He is going to work on aero plane engines in hopes of eventually becoming a pilot."

"Guess you do have some changes going on, don't you?" his pa chuckled. "Have you talked to Lucy yet?"

"Yes, but I was having a hard time with just the right words and apparently I gave my approval without realizing it."

Tuck laughed heartily. Sheepishly, Thad looked at his pa. He was seventy-seven now. That meant his ma was seventy-two. He felt a jolt in his chest. The thought that his parents might not be around forever surfaced. He had not really thought so much about it before, but now he was seeing them in a different light. Tuck was completely gray now and his mother's hair turned gray around the front. They both moved a little slower and each had added wrinkles. *Where did the time go? And where have I been while my parents grew older?*

Beth came over and sat down with her son and husband. "Thad, why is Lucy being a rancher a problem for you? Don't you think she can do it?"

"Well, of course, I do, Ma. It's just that women don't usually run ranches. Not around Mustang Ridge anyway."

"Then it's about time they did," she said firmly. "Here's what you two should do. Give her a small portion of both the ranches so she can prove herself to you, perhaps over a year's time. Nothing big - just enough for her to show what she can do once she has been given the chance."

Thad's jaw dropped. Both Tuck and Thad turned to look at Beth. He had not considered that. Yet, thinking about it now… well, why not? If it didn't work out for her, then she could back out and save face.

"Pa, if I did that, what part of the ranch would you suggest?"

"Let's go in and take a look at the map."

Just then Nate rode up to the ranch-house and dismounted. As Nate, now thirty-three, tied the reins to the rail, Tuck said, "Nate, come on into the office,"

Nate did as requested and followed his pa and brother into the ranch office. "What's going on?" he asked.

"This involves you too, Nate, since you're managing owner of Deer Creek Ranch." Tuck explained Thad's dilemma with Lucy. He pointed to the boundary line between the two ranches. "There is a fairly decent line shack right here. It's nicer than most line shacks. We could fix it up for her and build a barn for some of the horses with an addition for a small bunkhouse. Wouldn't take much to do. Nate, you have a say in this. What do you think?"

"I think it's a good idea. That way, if she finds she's not cut out to be a rancher, there won't be a loss for us. And we'd get a few extra buildings out of the deal," Nate said laughing. "But I think you underestimate our little Lucy. I think she'll make a go of it both now and in the future."

Tuck and Beth both agreed. "I say, give her the chance," Tuck suggested.

Thad nodded. He guessed it would work. "I'll talk to Lucy and see if she wants to do this."

"Oh, before you leave, Thad, I need to talk to you and Pa about the mine," Nate said.

"What about it?" Thad asked.

"It petered out. No more coal from it," Nate responded. "George Cummins stopped me in town and told me he's pulling up stakes. He will have the miners tear down the buildings and haul the lumber over here to Deer Creek Ranch. Not sure what you want to do with it, but we can store it in the barn."

"Sounds good, but we can probably draw on some of the lumber to fix up the line camp for Lucy," Tuck said. "That way we won't have to spend so much in building materials."

"That's a good idea," Thad agreed.

#

Upon entering the stables, Thad found Lucy cinching up the saddle on her horse. "Lucy, are you going somewhere?"

"Just going for a ride, Papa," she answered him.

"Mind if we ride together? There's something I want to show you."

"Okay, Papa," she readily agreed. "What do you want to show me?"

"Wait until we get there."

They both finished saddling their horses and rode out of the ranch yard, heading northwest. Thad wanted to show her the area he and Tuck had talked about and see what she thought of the idea. As they rode out of the ranch yard, Thad took the time to enjoy the comradery that he and his daughter had together. He wondered if she would agree to this plan or not.

Coming to the line shack, he stopped. They continued to sit on their horses while he searched for the right words to talk to his daughter.

"Papa, what's going on? Why are we here?"

"Let's go inside," he said.

They dismounted and tied their horses to the rail and entered the dusty line shack. The interior of the one-room building consisted of a bunk, a rickety table, and two chairs. An iron cook stove provided heat for the little room as well as a cooking area. *This isn't bad. Just needs a good cleaning and with the addition, should provide a good house for Lucy.* Thad dusted off the chairs and took a seat. Lucy sat too.

"So, here's the deal. We fix up this line shack, add on to it. Then we build a barn with a bunkhouse attached. Also a corral. We already know that the well works since it has been in used. This would be your ranch for the period of one year. You'll be given a small start-up fee in an account at the bank, which I will open up if you agree to this. This will be a loan to you. If your books are balanced and you show a profit, including the paying back of the loan at the end of the year, I will make you a partner at Whitehorse Ranch. What do you say?"

"I'm speechless, Papa. This is a great opportunity. Thank you for allowing me a chance to prove myself. I appreciate your belief in me," Lucy gushed, hugging her father and kissing his cheek. "You won't be disappointed in me, I promise."

"I'd never be disappointed in you, Lucy dear. No matter how this may turn out."

"Papa, what about Jackson and Ben?"

"Jackson doesn't want to ranch. He wants to work on aero plane engines and eventually become a pilot. He'll soon be leaving home for North Platte. Ben is only fourteen but when he is older, he will become a partner in the ranch along with you, if this works out."

Thad pulled some papers from his saddlebags and showed Lucy how their contract would work. She enthusiastically signed her name along with his at the bottom of the contract.

"I'll get four men out here to build the structures we've discussed and pay for them myself. We are dismantling the bunkhouse at the mine, so we'll use that lumber. That will save us all money. Then when it is ready, they will be your ranch hands and you'll be responsible for their pay."

206

CHAPTER SEVENTY-TWO
Lucy

Thad pulled the wagon loaded down with Lucy's belongings up to the line shack-turned-ranch-house. It was April and they were moving her into the renovated line shack. Four ranch hands had already taken up residence in the bunkhouse. Casey from Whitehorse Ranch and Curly from Deer Creek Ranch, as well as two new hires, Joe and Stub. As Thad stopped the wagon, they emerged to help unload. Lucy could barely contain her excitement.

Papa admitted that it looked nice inside. He and the men had built a fireplace in the main room, a bedroom had been added, and on the outside, a small porch with a planter of red geraniums was positioned next to a wicker rocker.

Mama and Lucy had been out earlier in the week to add curtains to the windows and rugs to the floors. Lucy brought bedding to put on her bed and Mama had furnished kitchen utensils she didn't use much anymore. A kerosene lamp graced the living area next to her easy chair, as well as her bedroom. Lucy brought the furniture from her bedroom at Whitehorse Ranch.

"Looks downright homey, Lucy," Papa remarked. "You and your mother have done wonders with it."

"Yes," Lucy agreed. "And the hands have built a really good barn and they have a nice bunkhouse too." She threw her arms around him. "Thank you, Papa, for giving me my chance."

"Well, now that the men have the furniture and crates inside, why don't you tell them where they should put them?'

Lucy directed them where to take the things and thanked them when they left to go to the bunkhouse. Mama and Papa had supplied her and the bunkhouse with enough food for a couple of weeks, giving her a chance to earn some money until she could take over. The money he had set up at the bank should help her to start buying the livestock. Papa hoped Lucy would be okay. She had the ranch hands there to help. He had given them instructions about that earlier. She noticed that he had also installed a bar across the door. *I will certainly feel safe.*

Mama hated to leave Lucy there and Papa was just as bad. She could see her parents had a harder time with this than she did. "Okay, you two. You can go home now. I'll be okay. You don't have to worry about me. I am an excellent horsewoman as you know. My ability with a rifle is also excellent. I know how to handle myself around the livestock, as soon as I get some, so off you go." Lucy laughingly shooed them out the door. "I've got work to do."

The next morning, Lucy made a list of the things that she needed to purchase right off.

> Goat and cattle from Grandpa
> > Chickens from Mama
> > Milk pail, egg basket, chicken water pan, seeds, hoe, shovel from Sam
> > Rent bull
> > Horses from Papa.

Not to mention purchasing food and planting the garden.

When she finished breakfast, Lucy went to the barn and saddled her horse. Silk was an Arabian horse and she was like a friend. Her silky brown coat earned her the name Lucy bestowed on her. The ranch hands came to the barn when they saw Lucy and asked for instructions.

"Casey, I want you to hitch up the wagon to haul a goat back from Deer Creek Ranch. The rest of you come on your horses. I will need your help in driving cattle back."

"Yes, Miss Lucy," they chorused.

"I'll just throw together a cage to put the goat in on the way back," Casey said. He drove the wagon and they all rode to Grandpa's ranch. When they got there, Lucy found him in the ranch office along with Uncle Nate.

"Well, girl, what brings you around this early in the day?" Grandpa asked.

"I need to talk business with the two of you." She saw the look the two of them gave each other and wasn't too sure what that meant. She knew Grandpa to be aware of her deal with Papa because the site had been his idea.

"Well, this is the place to do it," he said rising to close the door. "Have a seat."

"I want to purchase livestock from you," she said watching their reactions. None.

"Okay," Grandpa said. He wasn't revealing any emotion. She guessed this might be part of her education; how to speak up for what she wanted.

"First, I'd like to buy one of your goats."

"Just one?" he asked. He might have been disappointed that she didn't want more. Her grandparents were thinning their goat herd. They were probably getting tired of milking and caring for them.

"Yes, for now anyway-- for milking. I suppose I will need her kid too."

"Done. And what else?"

"Six cows."

"Do you need a bull too?" he asked while he began writing out a bill of sale.

"No, I plan to rent one when the time comes."

"Rent!" Uncle Nate exclaimed loudly. "Never heard of such a thing."

"That's because you have a large operation. Mine is small."

"I see you brought your hands along to herd them back."

"Yes, do you think the goat and kid will go into the wagon?" she asked. "I've got a cage we can put them."

"Yeah," Uncle Nate said. "We'll help you get them in the wagon."

Grandpa handed Lucy the bill of sale and she filled out the check for him. Lucy had just bought the first of her livestock for her ranch.

Once Daisy and her kid were in the cage in the back of the wagon, Casey drove it back to her ranch. Joe, Stub, Curly and Lucy rode out with Grandpa and Uncle Nate to the cattle herd. Grandpa showed her men where they could pick the cattle. Lucy noticed a bull in with the herd.

"Have the cows been with the bull, Grandpa?"

"Yes," he replied.

"How long?"

Grandpa looked to Uncle Nate who shrugged and said, "Long enough."

Lucy was pleased. She wouldn't need to rent a bull. Once they had them separated, they began to drive them back to her ranch. *My ranch. I need to come up with a name for it.*

When they returned with the small herd of cattle, they put them in the corral. Casey already had the goat and her kid bedded down inside the barn.

"I will need a small chicken coop built tomorrow," Lucy told the hands. "One that will hold about ten chickens. You can use the leftover lumber from the barn. I'll get some chicken wire too."

Daisy, the goat, needed milking and though Lucy hadn't bought the milk pail yet, Daisy couldn't wait. So, she used a crock and filled it with milk. "There you go, Daisy. Feel better?"

The sun dipped lower in the western sky and Lucy was exhausted, but after supper, she sat down with a glass of fresh milk to go over her list. She could cross off the cattle and goat. She wouldn't have to deal with renting a bull from Papa just yet. Tomorrow she'd go into town and buy her supplies from Sam, then swing by Whitehorse Ranch and buy chickens from Mama. As soon as she decided what to call her ranch and designed a brand, she could get the men working on branding them.

Lucy spent time trying to come up with a name and a brand until she had one side of a sheet of paper completely filled. Papa had his initials for his brand, **TT**. She had decided at last that she would have hers be **LT**. Simple, but maybe it would look different to her in the morning. For now, she was hitting the hay.

After giving the men instructions to build the chicken coop, Lucy headed to town with the wagon. Her first stop was to the blacksmith. Grandpa Wells was more than happy to fashion an iron with her new brand. While he was doing that, she went to the mercantile.

As Sam filled her order for the things on her list, plus a few personal items, he asked, "How's it going, Lucy? Heard you have a ranch all your own now."

"Hard to say yet, Sam. I'm just getting started, but I'm eager to make it work. I want to be a partner with Papa."

"What about Jackson and Ben?" Sam asked.

"Well, Jackson's leaving soon for North Platte. He wants to work with aero planes and become a pilot. Ben's too young yet, but when he's old enough, Papa said we will take him on as a partner."

"Sounds like a good plan. I didn't know that about Jackson. Things sure do change around here. Well, here's your bill. Do you want it on credit?"

"No, Sam. I'll pay it now." She didn't want to start credit unless she had to. It was too early to be starting something like that. She paid in cash since she'd just come from the bank.

After Sam helped her load her purchases into the wagon, she drove out of town, heading toward Whitehorse Ranch.

Mama came out of the house when Lucy pulled into the yard. Then Papa came from the stables. "What's wrong?" Mama asked.

"Is everything okay?" Papa asked.

Lucy groaned. Such faith they had in her. "Everything's fine. I stopped by on the way back from town because I need chickens, Mama. I know you'd said your flock was getting too big and I could help with that," she said grinning.

"How many do you want?" Mama asked with undisguised eagerness. She really did want to thin her chicken flock.

"Can you spare eight young hens, a rooster, and two old ones for butchering?

"That won't be a problem at all."

"I'll get a crate and help catch them," Papa said. He fashioned a chicken catcher out of heavy gauge wire which he bent into a hook at the end. He reached toward the chicken's leg and hooked it before the unsuspecting fowl knew she was caught.

The chickens and rooster were caught and loaded in the wagon in their crate. As Lucy paid her in cash for the chickens, Mama asked if she could stay for dinner, but Lucy told her she had to get back since there was work waiting.

"Maybe Sunday dinner after church then?" she asked. Lucy nodded. "See you then."

Mama whispered to Lucy so Papa wouldn't over-hear, "How's it really going?"

"It's all going fine, Mama. I bought cattle and a goat from Grandpa yesterday. The boys have built a chicken pen and I milked my goat last night. Got to get home so I can milk Daisy again. Or she will be upset with me."

Mama laughed, as well as Papa who overheard them. Everyone knows how ornery and upset a goat can get. They hugged goodbye, saying, "See you Sunday," and Lucy drove back to the **LT Ranch**. *Yes!!*

CHAPTER SEVENTY-THREE
Ellen

Ellen's dream had always been to be a newspaper reporter. She almost made a pest of herself at the Mustang Patriot. Every once in a while, she'd go into the paper's office to ask the editor if he could use her as a reporter. Tom Pike always told her that he and his wife took care of any reporting and he wasn't ready to take on any more help. Time and time again, Ellen tried to convince Tom her writing could enhance the paper with her stories, news items, anything, but he sent her on her way every time.

Then the day came when Ellen made a decision and ordered a small table-top printing press through the mercantile. It wasn't as high a quality as the large press at the *Patriot*, in fact, it was even advertised as a toy, but it would suit her needs perfectly.

When Sam notified her that her item had arrived, Ellen took the two-seater into town and pulled it around back of the store. She'd also ordered a roll of paper on which to print her newspaper. Sam and George helped to load the wooden crate onto the back of her wagon and she went back home. There she enlisted the help of the ranch hands to haul it into the ranch-house. They took it into her room and set it on the table. Ellen was ready to print her page.

Ellen sat on her bed and read the operating instructions and wrote out what needed to be printed. Next, she took the rubber type and began setting up the columns of the page on the tin-plated sheet metal. Once that was completed, she added the ink to the inking roller. Laying a blank paper on top of the columns of rubber type, she ran the inking roller over the top. It took a few tries for her to achieve the desired outcome. Ellen held it up and examined her finished product closely.

"Eureka!"

She heard Mama come to the door. "Ellen, is everything okay?"

"Mama, come in. I want to show you something."

Mama entered and looked at the page Ellen showed her. "What on earth? Are you making a newspaper?"

"Yes, Mama. For now, I'm Tom's competition. Perhaps when he sees what I'm doing with my own little paper, he will hire me so he won't lose business."

"You are... I don't know what to say. Just quite the businesswoman," Mama said. "How will you sell it and for how much?"

"Sam said I could sell it out in front of the mercantile. I'll sell it for two cents," Ellen replied. "What do you think about the name?"

Mama read, "Tucker's Tidbits. Well, I guess you leave no doubt as to who is printing it. Go show your papa."

Papa's pride in his daughter's initiative was evident while he read the printed page. "This is great, Ellen. How many are you going to print?"

"As many as I can, Papa. It takes a while to print them, so as many as I can print before tomorrow. I want to sell them when the *Patriot* is not for sale."

"Sounds like you have thought it out. but have you considered how this may hurt Tom's business?"

"Yes, Papa. I prayed about it for quite a while before I ordered it. I don't want to continue to run my own paper. It's just to show Tom that he really needs to hire me."

"Well, I wish you well, Ellen. Just remember to follow God's will in whatever you do."

"Yes, Papa. I will."

"And always get permission from folks before printing their information," he added.

"Yes,   Papa."

TUCKER'S TIDBITS
Ellen Tucker, Editor

This is to introduce a new paper to the town of Mustang Ridge. Tucker's Tidbits is edited and published by Ellen Tucker, daughter of Thad and Belle Tucker of Mustang Ridge. Ms. Tucker has always wanted to be in the newspaper business and is taking this opportunity to follow her dream.

Tucker's Tidbits will be sold every Wednesday for two cents. Advertising is welcome. Tucker will also take submissions to be printed. She is open to those who may also have a dream of writing for a newspaper.

Local resident Adam Tucker received his new horseless carriage last week. He ordered the Ford Model T direct from the factory and took possession Mr. Tucker reports satisfaction with his new purchase. "The horses don't like it much though," Tucker stated.

Jackson Tucker has accepted a position at the North Platte Regional Airport. He leaves next week. Jackson will be working on engines and hopes to one day be able to pilot aero planes. Good luck, Jackson

Windy Ridge Ranch is offering cattle for sale. Contact Dan Clark
Whitehorse Ranch Horse Sale:

Cutting horse sale next Tuesday. Horses will be brought to the livery stable corral for the sale. Contact Thad Tucker for more information.

Free puppies. Contact Nick Bendix at Double B Ranch.

Mustang Ridge Community Church service time: 10:30 a.m.
Sermon Topic: Listening for God's Voice.

Garrison's Mercantile Specials

Bring this coupon into the store and receive 50% off the original price of any item purchased.

#

The next day Ellen stood out in front of Sam's selling the one-page newspapers. Everyone that came by bought one of her two-cent papers. Many went into Sam's to redeem his coupon. She heard several conversations about Jackson leaving for North Platte next week. People were surprised that he'd not be ranching. Many ranchers read the ad about Papa selling more cutting horses and made plans to be there.

Ellen was pleased that her little paper was so popular and that people found her news useful. Tom Pike stood at the outskirts of the crowd watching. This was working even better than she'd hoped. The papers sold out in less than an hour. She could have sold more copies if she'd had time to print them. As it was, at two-cents a copy, she had sixty-cents to show for her work. She might even be able to pay for the $5.00 printing press.

This went on for four weeks. Ellen printed up even more of the one-page *Tucker's Tidbits*. And each week she sold more. Perhaps it was the fact that anyone could place an advertisement in her small paper for no fee. She was trying to make a point to Tom Pike, you see, not a profit. By the end of the fourth week, Tom conceded that she'd indeed made her point. He hired Ellen to start immediately. As long as she got rid of that little printing press, that is. She agreed and promptly donated it to the school. They were happy to get it.

Ellen's newspaper career was running along smoothly. Since her duties grew to include not only writing, but type-setting as well, she discovered the need to move to town. Sam Garrison fixed up a room over the mercantile and rented it to her. Sam has been a good friend to the Tucker family ever since he and Grandpa Tuck met. He was a little younger than Grandpa, maybe by about ten years. But Ellen guessed friendship doesn't keep a record of age.

CHAPTER SEVENTY-FOUR
Thad's New Auto

Thad and Belle recently became owners of a 1908 Ford Model T, just like Tuck and Beth's auto. Belle was so excited when it arrived on the train and it rolled off at the depot. Thad had promised her she could drive it home. It surprised her that he would let her be the first to drive their new Ford. But then he wasn't as eager to get an auto as Tuck had been.

Once they had received the auto at the depot, Thad taught her how to start and drive it. Thad taught Belle how to start their new auto using the crank in front. It seemed there were a lot of steps in starting it. He pointed out the three pedals on the floor; the brake, the reverse pedal, and the clutch. He showed her how to use them. Then he instructed her about what had to be turned, pushed, and switched to even begin to start it. Belle had to pull the handbrake back. Next, she had to make sure the throttle and spark advance on the sides of the steering column were situated midway. Then she had to turn on the fuel switch located in front of the engine. Once all that was done, she had to prime the engine in front of the car. With her left hand on the choke and her right hand on the crank, she had to turn it three times, always using her right hand. Thad said she needed to adjust the spark advance until the engine ran smoother or it would die.

Next came the actual driving of the car. *Land sakes alive but that is hard*! Those floor pedals kept her feet quite busy, and her hands were just as busy. *It's like whisking an angel food cake and threading a needle all at the same time*. But she persevered, and even though the ride back to the ranch took twice as long, Thad seemed quite pleased with her progress.

Belle wore the riding costume like Tuck and Beth had, the long coat and the goggles. *I must say, when it's hot outside, it's not very comfortable.* Maybe next time she'd just wear an old dress. She did see the need for the goggles though, and used them.

Driving home was exhilarating. Thad sat beside her watching her closely. She wasn't sure if he feared she would wreck the auto or another reason. She turned and smiled at him to show her confidence in her own ability to drive. She knew then why he was watching her so. When she smiled, he leaned over and kissed her on the cheek.

"My love for you is growing," he said. "When I see you driving with such joy and abandon, I am overcome with thankfulness to God for bringing us together."

What a wonderful husband! Here they were, in their forties and the romance in their marriage grew with each passing year. *Thank you, Father, for this wonderful man.*

Belle brought the auto to a stop and turned to embrace her husband. "Dearest, Thad. My love for you grows too." She kissed him and fondly ran her fingers through his hair.

Thad worked with his wife on starting the auto by herself until he was satisfied that she could do it without breaking her wrist. She was glad Thad had driven his pa's auto so he knew what to do with theirs. It was no easy task to turn that crank. Belle ended up with a bruise but that was much better than a broken wrist. She was told that happened frequently.

Now that Belle had been driving the auto by herself for a few weeks, she decided to drive out to Lucy's ranch for a visit. She hadn't seen her except at church for some time. Oh, Lucy would come out to the ranch when she wanted to purchase some of her father's horses. But it hadn't been a time for mother and daughter, and Belle wanted, no needed, to spend some time with her. All three of Belle's daughters had lives of their own now, all living away from home. The house was so quiet without her girls there. She missed them so much.

The thought occurred to Belle as she drove up to the one-time-line shack, that Lucy didn't know her folks had purchased an auto. She probably thought it was her grandpa come to visit. Her daughter came out to the auto, eyes wide. Belle knew she would be surprised to learn that her father had actually purchased one.

"Mama! Why are you driving Grandpa's auto?"

"No, dear. This is our own auto. It came in on the train a few weeks ago. See, it's dark green. Grandpa's auto is black. Are you surprised to see me driving it?"

"I sure am. Come on inside, Mama."

Once they were inside and seated on her sofa, Lucy offered her some coffee. "It's fresh," she said. "I just made it."

"That would be nice, dear. Thank you."

Lucy handed her mother a cup of coffee and as she sat down, Belle saw the smile leave her face. "Okay, Mama. Did you come out to see if I really am making it? To run a check on me for Papa?"

To put it mildly, her daughter's words hurt Belle deeply. Here she'd come out to see her daughter whom she missed so much and this was her response. Belle put the still-full cup of coffee down on the table and with tears in her

218

eyes said, "I can see this was a mistake. I must go now." *Quickly, or I will begin bawling like a new-born calf.*

Belle went to the front of her auto and began to crank to start it. The tears overflowed from her eyes and dropped down to her arm as she bent over, leaving wet stains on her sleeves. Then she felt her daughter's hands on her shoulders, turning her around, holding her mother close to her.

"Mama. Oh, Mama, I'm so sorry. That was so awful of me to say to you. I'm sorry I hurt you. Come back to the house. Please?"

Belle wiped her eyes with her sleeve and followed. They sat on the sofa once again only this time, Lucy laid her head against her mother's chest, as she had done when a little girl. This, this was what Belle had been seeking. She caressed Lucy's head, brushing her dark curls back behind her ears. She looked with love into Lucy's eyes, the same as her own, the face so much like hers.

"Yes, I did come to see how you are doing, but no differently than I would any of my children. You see, I was missing my girls something awful. The house seems so empty. Ben is still there, of course, but it's just not the same as you girls."

"No, I don't imagine it is," she agreed, smiling. "Please forgive me, Mama. I'm a terrible daughter to question your reasons for being here."

"You're forgiven, dear. Now, we won't speak of this occurrence anymore. It's forgotten and forgiven. Show me your ranch while I take you for a ride in my auto."

The work Lucy had accomplished impressed her mother and she told her so. "You won't have any problem convincing your father to make you a partner."

"Do you think so, Mama? I hope you're right."

Giving her wonderful daughter a kiss and hug goodbye, Belle was soon back on the trail to their ranch. Thad was happy to see that she had safely returned. Had he been worried that she would have trouble with the auto? Possibly, but it was nice to be back safely held in her husband's embrace. Belle never did recount to Thad what had transpired between Lucy and herself. It was between mother and daughter.

CHAPTER SEVENTY-FIVE
Lucy

Lucy's ranch was growing. She now had all the livestock that was on her list. Well, except for the bull, that is. But she wouldn't need to rent him until the future calves were old enough to be weaned. She would have a year to prove herself to Papa. She saw that her cow's bellies were growing larger with their calves, proving that the bull had taken. She knew that sometimes you didn't know if the bull got to the whole herd or not, but apparently, he got to all six of her cows.

The garden was all planted and vegetables had started to emerge. She even planted extra so the ranch hands would have fresh garden produce. She learned that from Mama. Her Mama always planted an extra plot so that Slim could have it for cooking. Lucy's four ranch hands took turns cooking for themselves, so they would be able to use the vegetables. Daisy produced enough milk for her to share with the men, and the chickens were prolific in their egg-laying so the men could use them too.

Papa and Grandpa had arranged to give Lucy the ranch on land next to Deer Creek. That would be good for watering the garden when the hot dry days of summer came. And she could swim in it to cool off. But first she'd need to get herself something to swim in. Lucy went into Garrison's Mercantile and ordered a swimming costume. The top was dark blue flannel with puffed sleeves and a sailor collar with white trim. The top was worn over knee-length bloomers trimmed with white. It came with long black stockings, fancy lace-up slippers, and even a fancy cap to match. George and Sam were intrigued by her purchase. Lucy thought they wanted to see what it would look like on her. But they would have to be happy with seeing it out of the package, not on Lucy. She remembered that Mama had one like it when she was growing up.

While Lucy was in the mercantile, she saw a flier announcing the Cattlemen's Association meeting in a week. She decided she'd need to go to that even though it would no doubt create uproar – having a woman in their midst. She also knew that they talked about things of importance for area ranchers. Papa and Grandpa belonged but didn't always attend unless there was some important issue to discuss.

"George, do you know of anyone who has a dog?" Lucy asked. "I'd like to get one to keep me company out at my ranch."

"Matter of fact, I do. The Double B Ranch had a notice for some pups in your sister's little paper." George searched through the papers. "Here it is.

This was a week ago, so he might not have any left. You could always check with him."

"Thanks, George. I'll ride out there now."

# # #

As Lucy rode her horse into the yard of the Double B Ranch, she saw the men were at the corral. Dismounting, she led her horse over to where they were standing. She recognized Nick Bendix, the new owner now that his father Brad, had passed away. He stepped forward to greet her. He was a tall man and he wore his cowboy garb well. In his leather vest, blue denim shirt and jean, and black cowboy hat, he exemplified the quintessential rancher. His brown hair showing below his hat and his deep brown eyes were so much a part of the man he was, Lucy was very nearly tongue-tied.

"Hello. How can I help you," he asked as he came near?

"Mr. Bendix, I'm Lucy Tucker. I came about the ad you had in town about pups. Do you still have them?"

"Yes, they're in the barn," he said and led the way. "There're only three left. How many did you want?"

"Just one." She could hear their playful yips when they neared the pen where the pups were held. "Oh, they're so adorable."

"They're four weeks old and were weaned last week," he said. "Forced to wean them early since the mother died in an accident. Do you know which one you would like? They are all males."

"What kind are they? I know the ad didn't say, but what was the mother?"

"She was shepherd, though not a purebred."

Two of the pups where brown and white with the shepherd look. One little guy was black and white and he seemed to gravitate Lucy's way. He reminded her of Papa's dog, Buddy. They connected--just like that. "I'll take this little guy," she said picking him up and hugging him. "How much?"

"They're giveaways. No charge," he said as he walked her back to her horse. "So, I heard about your deal you made with your Pa about ranching. Good luck to you. I hope you succeed."

"Why thank you, and thanks for this little guy." She tucked him into one of her saddle bags with his head sticking out. He seemed to enjoy riding that way as he didn't try to get out.

As Lucy left the Double B Ranch, she turned in the saddle and observed that Nick Bendix was still looking her way with his hat in his hand. She lifted her hand in a wave, and he did the same.

CHAPTER SEVENTY-SIX
Molly 1908

Doc Phillips, who'd been Beth's doctor as well as Belle's, had long since passed away. He had birthed all of Thad's and Belle's children. He pulled Nate through an emergency appendectomy as well as numerous childhood ailments throughout the years. She'd stood at his side through many of the town's illnesses and scrapes as his nurse. Doc had been replaced by another doctor who was now also gone. He married a mail-order bride and they left for California soon afterward. Now a new doctor had taken over the practice in Mustang Ridge.

Dr. Joshua Ward from Ohio, newly out of medical school, came to Mustang Ridge after answering and advertisement in the Patriot. He fell in love with the town as well as the people. He took the position and stayed. As he adjusted to western life in general and Mustang Ridge more specifically, the residents found that they loved him as well.

After his first year as the town physician, Dr. Ward saw the need to hire a nurse. He went to the town newspaper and placed a notice, saying he would train the qualified applicant if necessary. When Molly applied, it pleased her that he hired her on the spot. Then began Molly's training to become his nurse.

As her training neared its end, little did Dr. Ward know that his protégée began to see him in a different light. Molly had become smitten with the good doctor. She confided to her mother one day of her infatuation with her mentor. Belle hardly knew what to tell her.

The next day, she came back to Belle with her plight. "He doesn't seem to notice me, Mama. What can I do?"

"Are you learning from his teaching?"

"Oh, yes. I am. He's such a good teacher, and I'm so happy in doing this type of work."

Belle thought for a moment. Needing divine help, she silently sent a prayer up to God, then said, "How long before you'll be finished with your training?"

"I guess I'm done, but I'm always learning from him. He's such a good teacher."

Uh-huh. Belle looked closely at her daughter. Her cheeks showed a rosy hue just talking about her doctor. *My, she really has it bad.*

"Perhaps we could start by inviting him to Sunday dinner at our home," Belle suggested. She knew Dr. Ward attended church where the Tucker family did, so she thought it would work for him to come to the ranch after church.

"Oh, Mama. I could never ask him," Molly wailed.

"I didn't mean you, dear. I'll stop in the office sometime this week and invite him to our home. As a thank you for taking on the education of our daughter."

"Okay. I guess that would work."

# # #

Wednesday morning, Belle asked Thad to accompany her in the auto to town. She did have some things she needed to purchase at the mercantile as well as stopping to see the doctor. "I thought we could take Molly to dinner at Sally's," she suggested to Thad.

While they were in the store, Molly came in also. She was on her dinner break from the office so they asked her to join them at Sally's for dinner. As they headed to Sally's, Belle said, "You two go ahead. I'll join you in a few minutes."

Belle noticed Thad glance at her with a strange questioning look. Molly nodded and pretty much ignored her mother's statement, going ahead with her father into Sally's. Belle made a bee-line directly to the doctor's office. When she opened the door, the bell above the door jingled, announcing the arrival of a patient, *or as in my case, a busy-body.*

"Good afternoon, how can I hel…? Oh, Mrs. Tucker. Molly's gone on her dinner break."

"Oh, Dr. Ward, it's you I wanted to talk to anyway. I just wanted to ask you out to Whitehorse Ranch for dinner this Sunday after church. You've been a great help to our Molly with her training, so Mr. Tucker and I want to thank you by inviting you to dinner."

"No need to thank me," he protested.

"Regardless, we want to. Will you be able to come?" Belle asked, not letting him off that easy.

He nodded. "I'd be happy to."

"Okay, then. See you Sunday after church." She vacated the premises, strangely out of breath, and quickly made her way to Sally's where she rejoined her daughter and husband. Poor Thad. He really seemed at a loss when she explained she'd by chance seen Dr. Ward and invited him to their home for Sunday dinner. Belle saw him look from her to Molly's reddened face and back to her again. But he said nothing – not then anyway. She knew the subject would be discussed on the way home once they were alone.

Belle's supposition had been correct. They did discuss it. Or rather, Thad did. He'd figured out what she'd been up to by the time their dinner was

223

finished. He wasn't pleased with Belle's interference into their daughter's personal life.

"But Thad. Molly wanted me to ask him. She okayed it so it wasn't interference."

Thad grunted. Belle noticed her husband did that a lot these days instead of a verbal reply. *I've yet to understand just what the grunt means.*

CHAPTER SEVENTY-SEVEN
Lucy and the Cattlemen's Meeting

The day of the Cattlemen's Meeting, Lucy rose early, fixed herself some breakfast, and fed the goats and chickens. The ranch hands took care of the cattle and the horses. Shep was fed too. She was so happy with that little guy. He was pretty much a house dog, and he slept with her at night. His soft, warm body was a great comfort to her alone in the house. She took him in her saddlebag when she was out on the range. He grew fast, so he soon was too big, and she had to leave him at home. Lucy told the ranch hands about her pup so if they heard him when she was gone, they should not be concerned.

After dressing in her buckskin riding outfit, she saddled Silk and left for town. She went early so she could stop at the mercantile first to see if her order was in yet. It had arrived, and she said she'd be back after the meeting to pick up the package. That done, she headed to the Mustang Hotel where the Cattlemen's meeting was to take place. There were many members heading into it. When she entered the door and looked for an open seat, she saw the looks directed her way. The din of conversation quieted somewhat. *Oh, this should be fun. I hope they don't throw me out.* The place appeared to be full and she didn't see either Papa or Grandpa in attendance.

As Lucy walked down the center aisle, she heard her name called. She turned to her right to see who it was. "Miss Tucker, here's an open seat if you wouldn't mind sitting by me." It was Nick Bendix, standing and pointing to the one empty spot on the bench next to him.

"Thank you, Mr. Bendix. I wouldn't mind at all," Lucy said as she lowered herself to the bench. He sat back down. *He certainly is a gentleman.* The din of conversation once again filled the assembly hall. "You can call me Lucy," she offered.

"And I'm Nick." He responded. "How is the little guy? Have you named him yet?"

"He's great. Yes, I named him Shep. We're getting along just wonderful."

When the meeting concluded, Nick asked if Lucy would care to accompany him to Sally's for dinner. She agreed, and they walked across the street to the diner. Nick was a nice-looking young man, tall, with brown eyes. His brown hair was still lighter than Lucy's dark brown curls. She had inherited her mother's curls as well as her hair coloring.

Lucy enjoyed the time she spent with Nick, and he asked if he might meet her again. She agreed. All in all, it turned out to be a pleasant day. She'd been able to pick up her package containing her swimming costume, had been able to attend the meeting where she was the only female without making too great

225

a stir, and had a pleasant dinner with a handsome cowboy, with a promise of more to come.

CHAPTER SEVENTY-EIGHT
Lucy

As the year went on, Lucy continued to see Nick. They met at Sally's sometimes. Several times he came out to her ranch. She was impressed by that. Since his ranch is on the other side of Mustang Ridge, it was quite a long ride for him. They went riding on their horses when he came. She usually had some baked product which she would take on their rides. Sometimes they had picnics. Her ranch hands didn't know about their rides since they would meet somewhere away from the ranch. Lucy was afraid they would report it to Papa. She wasn't ready to let her parents know just yet. She was still trying to prove her ranching skills to Papa.

Lucy and Nick talked about their faith quite a bit. She'd seen him at church, but he didn't ask to sit with her. She was glad because she believed it was too early in their relationship to sit together in church. Maybe later.

Jackson had moved to North Platte now, and Ellen had moved into town to be close to the newspaper office. Lucy realized how hard this must be for her parents. Lucy wasn't home, but she fully intended to move back in the spring and become part owner of Whitehorse Ranch. So at least she and Ben would be there. She wondered about Ben though. He seemed to be so moody lately, spending a lot of time riding his horse up on the ridge. When Lucy asked him why he went there so often, he said he went there to think and pray. She thought he must have had a lot of important things on his mind, because he had been going up there a lot lately. *I wonder…no… he wouldn't do that, would he? Leave the ranch?*

When Thanksgiving was a few weeks away, Lucy asked Nick if he would like to come to her family's big gathering. He said he would meet her there. She anticipated that day with a little trepidation since she and Nick would publicly announce their relationship. *It will surprise my parents, I'm sure.*

CHAPTER SEVENTY-NINE
Ellen

Ellen had been considering a feature article about Grandpa Tuck, and when she approached Tom with the idea, he was all for it. She knew Grandpa would not want it to be about him, so she planned to get input from others also. She told Grandpa the article was a history of Mustang Ridge, and she was talking to those who had been here the longest. In a sense, it was a history of the town as well since Grandpa had been a big part of its growth. Ellen planned to talk to the town's businessmen also. She told everyone else that the article was about Grandpa's life, and she needed input from his friends, but that it was a surprise for him.

Ellen began her article by going out to see Grandpa and Grandma. Actually, both of them were a big part of the town's history. So, she talked to both of them, mainly to get Grandma's side of when the two of them met. She told them this would take more than one session, and that she had to head back to the paper. They were both happy to talk about their town.

Next Ellen sat down to talk with Sam Garrison. He really sang Grandpa's praises. Sam and Grandpa have always been such good friends. Martha Garrison also spoke highly about him.

Grandpa Wells was also a good one to get input from. Ellen talked with various other people who had known Adam Tucker over the years. This article was growing. She talked to Tom about a special edition to make room for the whole of the article and he readily agreed.

# # #

Running around the countryside doing interviews for her article on Grandpa left her hungry. Ellen came back into town and headed to Sally's for dinner. Coming around the corner, she ran right into a man who was standing in front of Sally's.

"I'm so sorry," he said. "I didn't mean to block the way."

"Oh, no. It's entirely my fault. I'm hungry and all I could think about was getting some dinner at Sally's."

"Just where I was going. Perhaps we could share a table?"

"Well…uh…I don't know you," Ellen objected. Although he was a nice-looking man, she had never seen him before.

"Well, I know the both of you, and I can vouch for his good character if need be," said a voice behind them.

"Reverend Peters," she said. It was apparent that they knew each other.

"Stephen, I thought you had a meeting."

228

"Yes, but it ended early, so I thought I'd see if we could still have dinner together. Miss Tucker, may I introduce my cousin Liam Peters. Liam, meet Miss Ellen Tucker. Now, how about the three of us go in and get a table?"

Ellen nodded and they did. Throughout the meal, she learned that Liam lived in Cheyenne where he was a lawyer. They had a good visit, and Ellen enjoyed getting to know him. After they said their goodbyes to Reverend Peters, Liam asked if he might walk her back to the paper. On the way, he asked if she would meet him for dinner tomorrow also, and she consented.

#

Throughout the week that Liam was in Mustang Ridge, he and Ellen arranged to meet nearly every day. After he returned to Cheyenne, they often exchanged letters. He was planning to return to visit his cousin in one month's time, and Ellen was looking forward to seeing him again

In the meantime, she'd completed her article on Grandpa, and Tom made plans for a special edition of the paper to be printed. Ellen hadn't mentioned this soon-to-be-printed paper since she wanted everyone to be surprised. She knew that Papa and Grandpa had been getting the paper ever since she began writing there, so she would wait until she heard from them.

Meanwhile, Ellen became quite excited as the time drew near for Liam's arrival. She'd told him she would meet him at the train.

CHAPTER EIGHTY
News

Thad hurried home from Mustang Ridge where he'd purchased the weekly newspaper. "Belle, come here. I've got the newspaper!"

Belle came hurrying into the living room from their bedroom. "My goodness, Thad, it's just the paper. Why all the drama?"

"Have a seat, and I'll read it to you. Then you'll see. It's a feature article written by Ellen."

"Oh, that's wonderful," she said sitting next to Thad on the sofa. "What's it about?"

"Listen and I'll read it to you."

Adam Tucker, as written by Ellen Tucker

This story has its beginning back in 1869 when Adam Tucker moved to the village of Mustang Ridge. His parents, who owned and operated a cattle ranch called Deer Creek Ranch, were getting on in years, so he left his position as foreman to a rancher in the Territory of Montana to be closer to them. He took the position of sheriff.

During his first years as sheriff, he was married to Mary Yeager. However, both Mary and their baby boy died in childbirth. A faithful son, he was close by when first his mother, then his father passed away. Sheriff Tucker, or Tuck, as his   friends called him, closed up the ranch buildings and continued on as sheriff of the area.

When the Overland Stage Company announced they were looking into establishing a   route from Deadwood to Cheyenne, Sam Garrison became a superintendent for the Overland Stage, a Division Director. Tuck, also an agent for the company, offered Deer Creek Ranch as a stagecoach station. Then they began the search for an operator. Beth Eastman answered the advertisement and she and her three children, Thad, Becca, and Nate came to the ranch to run it as a stage stop in 1876.

Tuck, in his capacity as sheriff and assistant agent for the stage line, provided help to the young widow and her family and became fast friends with young Nate Eastman. Nate was the same age as Tuck's baby boy would have been. He brought Nate a puppy which he named Bandit and brought a nanny goat and her two kids to Becca Eastman.

Tuck was involved in many dangerous escapades in his role of sheriff. However, most people who knew him respected the law

230

because of their respect for him. Many people were happy to call him their friend. One such person was a Shoshone Indian named Grey Wolf. They became good friends, visiting and helping each other. Tuck even helped Grey Wolf build his hogan for his family up in the mountains.

Tuck resigned his position as sheriff and became a full-time rancher.

Beth and Tuck were married later that year and Tuck adopted her three children, giving   them his last name. The next year Tuck lost another child when Beth suffered a miscarriage early in her pregnancy.

Another of Tuck's good friends is Matt Cutter who was the driver of the stage until wounded in a Sioux Indian attack and had to retire from driving. Mr. Cutter had many stories to tell about Tuck. He said Tuck and Beth stood up with him and Mattie McLeod when they were married. "Tuck was instrumental in freeing me when I was arrested and taken to Fort Laramie for trial. The charge was desertion because I ran away from the Army in the War Between the States when I was nine. I owe him my life for his help."

Sam Garrison said, "He's my best friend. We've always worked together for the good of Mustang Ridge." Everyone knows that hardly an event is ever planned in either of their homes that the other one isn't invited. Birthdays, Christmases, and others will find them both in attendance. Martha Garrison commented, "He was always partial to my fried chicken and pies. We would   have him to our house once a week for a meal after Mary died. We felt he needed a good home-cooked meal every once in a while, for the good of the town, you know"

Pete Ballard, livery owner said, "Tuck was instrumental along with Sam in getting the church built and later on, they got the school house built. A good community man."

Jacob and Sarah Wells shared, "We met Beth on the wagon train and came to Mustang Ridge when she did." Jacob opened a blacksmith shop and Sarah became a dressmaker. They were also guests at Dear Creek Ranch and Sarah stood up with Beth when she married Tuck. Eventually, Thad married their daughter, Isabelle.

Tuck later shared his ranch with Thad Tucker and formed a partnership with him. "Pa had the cattle, I had the horses. He helped me get my start in ranching." Later when Thad built up his own ranch, Whitehorse Ranch, Nate became a partner with them.

231

Nate Tucker is now the manager of the ranch. "Pa became a good friend to me when I was six years old. It sure made me one happy boy when he and Ma got married and then he adopted us. Thanks for all you've done for us, Pa."

Becca Tucker Rhodes was a school teacher here and when she married Peter Rhodes, they went to teach English at the Wind River Reservation. "Papa is a great man. He exemplifies what being a Christian is all about. He knows how to show love and compassion to all."

Beth Tucker said, "I love Tuck with all my heart. He is kind and gentle and shows it to everyone. My life with him has been filled with love. Shortly after we were married, my heart was full when he adopted all three of my children giving them the name of Tucker."

A list of his accomplishments for the town follows:
Built the school and church with Sam Garrison
Helped with the stage route, offering his ranch
Brought the law to the area
Donated beef to town roasts for Independence Day
Organized town events
Deacon of the church
Took part in area barn raisings
A lifetime of faithful Christian living
Went on numerous cattle drives with area ranchers
Helped friends in many ways
A wonderful and loving father, a loving grandfather, a loyal friend

In closing, Adam Tucker has made Mustang Ridge what it is today; a thriving, loving, and God-fearing community. Mustang Ridge and surrounding ranchers say, "Thank you, Tuck, for all that you have done."

"Oh my! What an article," Belle exclaimed when Thad finished reading.

"I know," Thad replied. "I'm really proud of Ellen. Wonder if Pa has read it yet."

# # #

The next day Thad and Belle drove the auto to Deer Creek Ranch. Thad carried with him the extra copy of the paper he purchased yesterday. He didn't know if Pa would get one or not, so he was prepared.

On the way to his parent's ranch, Thad asked, "How do you like the auto by now, Belle?

"I like it very much, I'm so glad you bought it. This is the first time I've seen you drive for a long time though. Don't you like to drive it?"

"Oh, yes. I do, but it's your auto."

"No, it's our auto, dear. Please don't feel you can't drive it because you think it is mine. It belongs to both of us."

Thad gently squeezed her hand and smiled.

When they pulled up to his parent's home, he grabbed the extra copy of the newspaper and the two of them went up to the porch. He knocked on the door and opened it, saying, "Anybody home?"

His mother came to hug them and Thad saw his father still at the breakfast table. "You sure are out and about early," Tuck commented. "Join me for a cup of coffee?"

Both Thad and Belle nodded while Beth went to get the coffee pot and a couple of extra cups.

"So, what brings you out here so early?" his mother asked.

Thad handed her the paper. "Just came to give you the paper. Ellen has a pretty good article in it this time." He and his mother exchanged knowing looks.

"Here. Tuck, dear. You read it first. I need to clear off the breakfast dishes." She handed him the paper and went about her work, yet keeping an eye on her husband as he read the paper.

Rachel carried dirty dishes in from the sitting room. "Oh, hello Thad, Belle. I didn't know you were here."

"They came to give us the paper," Beth supplied.

"Where's Nate?" Thad asked.

"He's in the office," Rachel said.

"I'll just go have a word with him," Thad said, heading that way.

"What is this? This isn't about Mustang Ridge. It's about me!" Tuck was confused. "She told me it was about Mustang Ridge."

"Just keep reading, Pa. You'll understand," Thad said coming from the office with Nate.

When Tuck had finished reading the article, he had tears in his eyes. "I don't know what to say. Did all those people really say all those things about me?"

"They did, Pa. Ellen interviewed everyone she could think of who has known you," Thad said. "What'd you think of her article?"

"Well, what can I think?" Tuck replied with a grin. "Always knew there was something special about that granddaughter of mine!"

CHAPTER EIGHTY-ONE
1908 Thanksgiving

Once again Whitehorse Ranch hosted a large Thanksgiving celebration. The ranch-house was full to overflowing with all the friends of the family, relatives, and new additions through birth and marriage.

As they waited for the women to tell them the food was ready, Thad's gaze swept the room, acknowledging to himself everyone who had come today.

In addition to his parents, his brother Nate was there with his wife Rachel, but his sister Becca was missing. Molly, Ellen, Lucy, Ben, and Jackson were all there. Also joining the family were Jacob and Sarah Wells, Matt and Mattie Cutter, and Sam and Martha Garrison.

"Matt, what do you hear from Little Tuck?" Thad inquired. He knew that their son, Dr. Tucker Cutter, had gone to Cuba to offer his medical services during the Spanish American War in 1898. When he was born, they had named him Tucker after Pa, who had been a good friend of Matt's.

"Well, no one calls him little Tuck anymore," Matt said with a chuckle. "He's taller than you are, Thad." Anyway, there were so many deaths on both the American side and the Spanish. But not due to war; it was from the diseases. Typhoid and yellow fever, you know."

"Yes, and that is where he met and married Ramona. She was a nurse in the hospital there. When the war ended, they left Cuba and moved back to America."

"Oh, he's back here now?" Belle asked. "Where is he living?"

"He and Ramona live in New Mexico where Tucker established a medical clinic," Matt replied. "They have two small children now."

"And what of Louisa?" asked Beth. "We know she married Daniel Prescott, but now that the Reverend had moved to California to start a new church there, we don't hear about her."

"Daniel has joined his father as pastor of the church there. He and Louisa have one child," Mattie answered.

"I hate that we don't see you folks much anymore," Belle said.

"I know," Mattie replied. "But it made more sense to travel only five miles to church as opposed to the thirty miles to Mustang Ridge. I'm just glad they built a church in our tiny town."

Thad noticed that Lucy kept lingering next to the front window. He wondered what that was about. Was she looking for someone? Just as Belle appeared about to announced that dinner was ready, he saw Lucy stop pacing and hurry to the door. He held up his hand to Belle, and inclined his head toward Lucy at the front door. Belle nodded in understanding.

Lucy opened the door as a young man entered. Thad didn't think he knew the young man, though he looked a bit familiar. After Lucy helped him with his coat, she brought him to her parents. "Mama, Papa, this is Nick Bendix. His Pa was Brad Bendix. I invited Nick to join us today."

"Welcome, Nick. Pleased to meet you. I've heard good things about how well you're doing with the Double B Ranch." Thad reached out and shook Nick's hand. Belle did as well.

"Thank you, sir. I hope this is okay," he said looking around the large living room. "It looks like you have a full house already."

"Not a problem. We are usually this full at Thanksgiving time," Thad replied. "Anyway, the more we have, the more we can give thanks to the Lord," Thad replied.

"Food's ready," Belle announced.

"Everyone. Thank you all for coming. Before I ask the blessing, just a little introduction. Not everyone knows all the people here." He proceeded to make introductions all around.

"Let's all hold hands and pray. Father in Heaven, how thankful we are that so many of our friends and family have been able to come today. But we are reminded of those who could not be here today. Belle's brother, Ben and his family are in Omaha, and my sister, Becca and family, are at Wind River..."

"No, we're not. We're here!" shouted a voice from the open front door. Beth and Belle both let out a squeal and rushed to Becca for hugs. After greeting his sister with a brotherly hug and shaking hands with Peter, Thad said, "Let's continue our prayer. Father, thank You for bringing my sister and her family here today. Bless all these loved ones under this roof. In Jesus Name, Amen."

Everyone was excited to see Becca and her family. She and Peter shared about their work at Wind River Reservation. Rose also told them about her work with her parents. Fourteen-year-old Adam entertained them with his stories of life on the reservation. Becca told Thad that Adam wanted to be a writer and a teacher. He saw a need for school books and wanted to write them.

It was a fantastic day for everyone. The weather for the day was very mild and there had been no snow yet. This enabled Becca and family to travel down for the holiday. Thad was glad to see his sister and Peter. "Glad you could come down, Peter. Good to see you again."

Thad continued to look over his guests, happily chatting and laughing. His eye fell on his father-in-law, Jacob Wells. Because Jacob had a gray color to his face, Thad wondered if Belle's father was sick. Maybe he was coming down with something.

CHAPTER EIGHTY-TWO
Saying Goodbye

In January of 1909, Jacob Wells passed away. Dr. Ward said it was his heart. Belle was devastated since she and her father were so close. Thad too had a close relationship with him and was saddened by his passing. Perhaps his heart had been bothering him at Thanksgiving time. Following his funeral service, Thad spoke to Belle about her mother.

"Belle, what do you think about asking your mother to come live with us so she won't be alone. That way, you would be near her if she needs you."

Belle nodded, tears spilling over. "Yes," she finally said. "I think that would be a good idea. Although she tries to keep it from me, I'm aware that her eyesight is failing. I'd be more comfortable if she were with us."

"We have extra room now that Ellen's living in town, and Jackson's gone. She could have Ellen's room," Thad said.

Belle agreed. "I'll talk to her in the next day or so. I want to go check on her anyway."

#

Thad and Belle moved several of Sarah's more personal items to their ranch. Sarah had been overjoyed at Belle's invitation to live with them. Her mother's reaction revealed that she had been afraid to live alone.

Sarah made the decision to rent out her house for now and perhaps to sell later on. Belle's heart constricted when she realized her mother's eyesight was even worse than what she'd first thought. Thad was glad he'd suggested she live with them. He knew Belle was thinking about this vibrant woman and the changes ahead for her.

Once Sarah became acclimated to her new home, she was able to do simple chores by memory. Dr. Ward told both her and Belle one day, "Sarah, you know your eyesight has diminished greatly. Before long, you'll only be able to see shadows."

Belle caught her breath but not before her mother heard her. "Don't worry, dear. I still have my hearing. God has blessed my life richly. He gave me my dear husband, wonderful children and grandchildren. Don't you worry about me losing the rest of my sight. I'm just thankful you and Thad have asked me to live with you. It gives me great comfort to be here with you. I feel safe and secure. Now Ben won't have to worry about me either."

Ben Wells was a lawyer living in Omaha, Nebraska. He'd married a girl from there and they had two children. He didn't get home very often but wrote his mother on a regular basis. Now his letters would need to be read aloud to Sarah.

237

CHAPTER EIGHTY-THREE
1909 Molly and Joshua

One year after Belle had invited Dr. Joshua Ward to Whitehorse Ranch for Sunday dinner, he asked Molly to marry him. Molly, of course, said yes. Plans began to take shape as the wedding date came closer. Belle's mother, still the sought-after dressmaker, began designing her first granddaughter's wedding dress with Belle's help.

Joshua's parents lived in Ohio, so they would have a bit of a trip to come out. Belle thought it a little ironic that she and her family had come from Ohio to Mustang Ridge. Now her daughter's new husband also came from there.

While he rode the range, Thad spent his time thinking about his youngest daughter getting married. *Is she ready for marriage?*

"She's only nineteen years old," Thad told Belle later. He felt chagrined when she reminded him that was how old Belle had been when he married her. He prayed that Molly's marriage would be as happy a one as he and Belle's had been.

It would be the second time Thad had walked a bride down the aisle. His sister, Becca, was the first. He hoped to be able to do it two more times with Ellen and Lucy, though there didn't seem to be any thoughts of matrimony on their part. Lucy was working hard at proving her ranch, although she had invited Nick Bendix to Thanksgiving. Ellen seemed to be too wrapped up in the newspaper.

Ellen was now a reporter at the Mustang Patriot, having convinced Tom Pike she was worthy of his hire. Lucy was doing well with her ranch. Thad saw no reason why she wouldn't soon be a partner.

He hoped to bring Ben into the partnership, too. Ben was now fifteen and though they hadn't spoken of the partnership, Thad was confident he'd soon have one of his boys on board as a partner.

Joshua had built a house just up the street from the Garrisons the first year he lived in Mustang Ridge. Afraid it would look too much like a bachelor's home, he asked Belle to accompany Molly to see what changes they could make to give it a feminine touch.

Between the two of them, they added curtains to the kitchen and parlor. They left Joshua's office alone, observing that it already had that lived-in look. Molly wanted to leave some things the way Joshua was used to. She asked him to come one day while they worked. She made dinner for the three of them and explained what she wanted to do. He concurred with her diagnosis of his home, and they were able to convert it into their own home.

It was Molly and Joshua's wedding day and a beautiful December wedding. Molly, who always loved Christmas decorations, wanted to use them in her wedding décor.

Joshua's parents were concerned that the Wyoming snows would cause a problem getting here. To be on the safe side, Joshua's parents had come out two weeks early and stayed in his house. That way they would be there if winter did cause a delay in their trip.

The church was decorated for the Christmas holiday. Molly's dress, white with forest-green velvet collar and cuffs, made her look like a sweet fairy princess. Sarah constructed a fur muff with matching green trim for her to carry the bridal bouquet. When Thad walked his precious daughter down the aisle, he saw the love in Joshua's eyes as they neared the altar. *Please guide her through her marriage, Lord. May they both put You first.*

After the wedding was over, Joshua and Molly left for a wedding trip to Denver by train. The next day, Joshua's parents left on the train, going back to Ohio. It had been a wonderful wedding with no bad snows to delay either the wedding ceremony or the trip. Thad and Belle returned to their home after saying goodbye to Molly's in-laws. Belle breathed a sigh as they entered the ranch-house. A sigh that nearly turned into a sob.

Thad heard and took his wife in his arms. "Belle, dear. We raised a fine young lady and now she is going to be starting her life with her new husband just as we did. I love you for what you have taught our Molly. And they will be making their home here in Mustang Ridge, so we are blessed." Then he kissed her.

"Oh, you know me so well," she responded, returning his kiss.

Her verbal response triggered a memory of his mother saying the very same thing to him shortly after they had come to Deer Creek Stagecoach Station. Beth had been worried about the lie she was perpetuating so she could run the stage station. He shook the thought away and turned his attention back to his wife.

Just as he had known his mother's heart, Thad loved his wife and knew her heart as well. "Come; sit, while I lay a fire in the fireplace."

They sat snuggled together, watching the fire until the shadows started to announce that evening had come and it was time to see to supper. Neither was very hungry, exhaustion taking away their appetites.

"How about some popcorn?" Thad asked. She nodded and he went to get the long-handled basket and they popped it over the open fire.

Just as they were about to eat, Ben came home. "Mmm. Popcorn. Got enough for me?" Ben asked. Thad nodded and the three of them ended the day with popcorn and hot chocolate which Belle made.

"A fine day," Thad commented and they all agreed.

Ben watched his parents as they sat closely together. He had grown up seeing the love shared by them. It gave him a feeling that all was well with the world.

#

One year had passed since Thad had installed Lucy in her own little ranch. She had proved herself doubly. She increased the cattle herd, selling them to happy buyers. She proved to be equally astute at the financial end also. She paid off the loan Thad had made to her at the bank and gained quite a sizable profit. Thad was so proud of her.

Lucy brought her books to her father's ranch office and sat quietly while he perused them. When he finished, she handed him a check for repayment of the loan.

"Lucy," he said rising from his desk. "You have excelled in ranching. Welcome to Whitehorse Ranch."

"Thanks, Papa."

"When will you move back home?"

"As soon as the hands move my livestock over here."

"It will be good having you back here," Thad said giving her a hug. He noticed that Shep seemed to want in on the hugging too. "But there is one more condition,"

Lucy's face fell. "What is it?" she asked.

"That you bring Shep too," he said laughing.

"Deal."

CHAPTER EIGHTY-FOUR
First Grandchild

Molly and Joshua announced early in 1910 that they were expecting their first child. By Christmas, Thad and Belle would be first-time grandparents. Thad was overcome with joy at the prospect of welcoming his first grandchild into the world. Belle, on the other hand, said it would take some getting used to for her. One day, he noticed Belle in front of the dresser mirror in their bedroom, looking at her hair.

"What are you doing?"

"Looking for gray hair."

"Belle, gray hair doesn't make a grandparent," he told her.

"Oh, is that so?" she asked, smiling.

"Yes, pretty sure."

"So, what does make a grandparent?"

"Love, Belle. Simple as that."

Even though Thad had been joyful at the prospect of becoming a grandfather, he found as time went on, there wasn't any way to slow it down, so he embraced his grandfather status. As Molly's pregnancy advanced, Thad was reminded of Belle during her pregnancies. Though Molly's hair was blond like Thad's, she resembled Belle in her face.

Now that his children grew older, their resemblance to Belle became clearer, the girls anyway. Jackson looked a lot like Thad, which was one reason why it hurt him that he didn't want to ranch with his father. Ben, however, was the splitting image of Thad. Maybe his second son and he would be able to partner in Whitehorse Ranch. Well, along with Lucy, that is.

Molly had an uncomplicated pregnancy. Belle went to help Joshua with the delivery when the time came. The birth of Molly's son had been a smooth delivery for which Joshua was grateful. He admitted later to Thad how nervous he'd been that he'd forget something. He was so thankful to have Belle there to help him. Thad had a good laugh over that but promised Joshua he'd never breathe a word to Molly.

The proud parents named their son Samuel Thaddeus Ward after Joshua's father and Molly's father. Thad held little Samuel as much as Molly would let him. He offered to care for him so that Molly would be free to do other things, any excuse to hold the sweet little boy.

Molly, oblivious that she had brought about such thoughts in her father's mind, and that she was unaware of her husband's fear during the delivery, held her newborn baby close. Her mother helped her even after the baby

241

came. She was happy to have Belle's help but wanted to be able to get up and care for her baby herself, to do her housework and to care for her husband as well.

Belle felt slightly useless and so after two days, returned to her own home and husband in her Model T. But first, she stopped at the mercantile.

"George, I need more gas for my auto," Belle said. George and Sam had installed a pump at the side of the store to provide gas for the auto carriages.

"Come around to the pump and I'll fill it up. I guess you can see why it's called that," Sam informed her while George filled her gas tank which was located under the front seat. Belle asked George to also fill the portable gas can to keep on the ranch. They kept it there because they lived out so far from Mustang Ridge.

The gasoline was shipped in on the train from Southern Wyoming Refinery in the south of the state. Before the mercantile opened their filling station, the Tuckers had taken delivery of their gas from that which was shipped in by rail.

When Molly was ready to go back to her position as Joshua's office nurse, he set up a crib in the back room so Samuel would have a place to sleep. As he grew older, he wouldn't stay in the crib, so Joshua made a play area for him so he wouldn't get into trouble.

The next year, 1911 gave Belle another chance to be of more help to her daughter. Molly gave birth to a little girl named Sarah Isabelle Ward. With a busy one-year-old boy constantly needing attention, Belle was needed in the way that she had wanted to be needed with Samuel.

Even before Molly delivered, Belle was able to help out by caring for Samuel. Sometimes Belle spent the night with the Wards to take care of him so his mother could get some rest. It was on one of those nights that Joshua woke her up to tell her that Molly was in labor. By morning, Belle was a grandmother for the second time. She was so busy with those two little ones that when she was finally able to leave and go back home, she was utterly exhausted. She fell into Thad's arms as soon as she walked in the door to their ranch-house and after telling him about his new granddaughter, she promptly fell asleep.

CHAPTER EIGHTY-FIVE
Lucy and Nick

In April of 1912, Thad found himself once again walking a daughter down the aisle. Her husband-to-be, Nick Bendix, waited at the altar for his bride. Lucy was beautiful. She had chosen to wear her mother's wedding dress, the one her grandmother had made for Belle. Thad remembered fondly how beautiful Belle had been when she walked down the aisle on her father's arm. Now, here he was, walking a daughter down the aisle again.

Lucy had made him proud when she passed the year's test by keeping the books well and showing a profit on her little ranch. She was back at Whitehorse Ranch as a partner with her father. Up until now that is.

Thad wasn't too sure what they would do about Lucy's third of the partnership. Eighteen-year-old Ben had been working even more as a partner of the ranch but soon Thad wanted to make it permanent and legal. Maybe another year. Thad was fifty-three now, but he didn't feel as though he were slowing down any.

Once again Thad drew comfort from the sight of all his family members gathered here to see his daughter married. Both of his siblings were here since Becca had arrived on the train yesterday. His eyes rested on his mother and father sitting amongst their children and grandchildren.

Lucy had fallen in love with Nick, son of Brad Bendix of the Double B Ranch. Brad had passed away a few years ago and Nick had taken over the running of the Double B. His mother, Beulah, didn't want to stay on the ranch and moved to Cheyenne to be with her daughter. Thad thought Nick had done an excellent job of running the ranch. He would be proud to have him for a son-in-law.

The congregation's applause for the newlyweds brought Thad's attention back to the front of the church. Refreshments were served while the bride and groom opened their gifts. Belle was holding her grandson while Molly helped with the gifts. Two-year-old Sam was sleeping peacefully in Belle's arms when Thad took a seat next to her.

"You make a beautiful grandma," he told her softly.

Belle smiled at him. "You make a pretty spectacular grandpa yourself."

Nick had opted to take his bride to Cheyenne once the wedding festivities were over. They would visit the opera house there and shop in the stores. As their train pulled away from the Mustang Ridge station, family and friends waved and wished them well.

Sam woke up with all the noise and began crying. Molly came and reclaimed her son from Belle's arms. "Probably needs a change as well as a feeding," she said. Fortunately, their home was only a block away so she went home to take care of him. Belle followed her along with Ellen. Thad went back to the church to gather their things. *Time to head for home. Funny how a wedding can make a person so tired.*

Shep remained at the Tucker ranch, at first while Lucy and Nick were on their wedding trip. As time went on, Shep just became a permanent fixture. Thad and Shep had become as inseparable as he and Buddy had been. Thad hadn't wanted to replace Buddy, but Shep seemed to work his way into his heart. Lucy would miss the little guy, but Nick had two dogs, Shep's siblings, so that was plenty.

CHAPTER EIGHTY-SIX
Ellen's Headline News

Early on the morning of April 18,1912, Ellen awoke to the sound of Josiah, her press operator, knocking on her apartment above the newspaper.

"What is it, Josiah?"

"Urgent telegram, Miss Tucker."

After she made a telephone call to get more facts, Ellen sat down in her office chair with a thud. What she had just learned was horrific. How was she going to report this? There were no words. But Ellen was a newspaper woman and it was her job to report news. Her press operator had already put the weekly paper to bed, but maybe it wasn't too late to add a short news story. She didn't have much information yet, so this might work.

"Josiah, can we add a new headline with a short story?"

"I guess so, if it's important."

"Oh, it's important all right." They busied themselves with setting the type for the new headline and a short column on the front page. They booted the "this week in history" story about the assassination of President Lincoln back in 1865. By 3:00 in the morning, they had it ready to go to press.

"This is the most horrendous story we've ever had in the paper," Josiah said. "These headlines will certainly sell copy, but I wish we didn't have to report such a thing."

Ellen nodded and patted his shoulder. Since they were getting a late start in printing, she told Josiah that she would stay and help. No way could she sleep anyway.

Ellen held up the first copy fresh off the press. Josiah continued to print while she took it to her office and sat down to read it. Even though she had composed the article, its chilling headline leaped out at her.

TITANIC SUNK
GREAT LOSS OF LIFE

R.M.S Titanic sank in the early morning of April 15, 1912 in the North Atlantic Ocean, four days into the ship's maiden voyage from Southampton to New York City. The Titanic was struck by an iceberg off the coast of Newfoundland and sank to the bottom of the Atlantic, taking the lives of over 1,500 people.

When Ellen took the stack of papers to the mercantile later, she thought it unusual that so many people had shopping to do. She found out later that word of mouth sent customers to the mercantile to purchase their own paper. She knew their conversations would be about the tragic sinking of the Titanic and the great loss of lives.

As Ellen thought about the news story and the response of the citizens of Mustang Ridge, she sincerely hoped she would never have to report such horrific news ever again.

CHAPTER EIGHTY-SEVEN
1912 Death Comes to Deer Creek Ranch

"Rider coming, Boss," Nash said. "Coming pretty fast too."

Thad, Nash, and Hank were working in the corral with the cutting horses. Thad looked up when Nash made his announcement. He saw a plume of dust rising from a rider as he rode into the yard.

"It's Wade," Nash announced. "Wonder what's up."

The Deer Creek Ranch foreman dismounted and removing his hat, approached Thad. "Sir, I'm sorry, but I have bad news. Your pa passed away in his sleep last night. Your brother sent me to get Doc and to stop and tell you."

Thad sucked in his breath at the awful news. His chest thudded behind his ribs. "Thanks, Wade. I'm on my way. I need to change and tell my wife, then I'll come," Thad said. "Nash, could you bring the auto around for me, please? And make sure it is filled with gas."

"Sure thing, Boss," Nash said. "Sorry, Boss."

Thad hurried into the ranch-house where he was met by Belle. "What's going on?" she asked, having heard the horse racing into the yard.

"It's Pa. He's dead." Thad turned and sobbed into Belle's shoulder while she held him close.

"Oh, no! Oh, my darling, what happened?" she asked patting his back, her own tears falling now.

"He died in his sleep."

"I'm so sorry. Are you going there now?"

"Yes. I need to change my clothes. Do you want to come too?"

"Yes, I do."

"Nash is getting the auto ready. I'll be out in a bit."

Thad and Belle entered the ranch-house at Deer Creek. He went straight to his mother who had risen from the sofa when they came in. He took her in his arms, holding her tight.

"Ma, I'm so sorry."

Tears streamed down Beth's cheeks. "He wasn't feeling good when he went to bed. I could tell he wasn't having a comfortable night. When I got up to make coffee this morning, I kissed him and told him to try to get some more sleep while I made breakfast."

Belle hugged her mother-in-law. "I'm so sorry, Beth."

"I shouldn't have left him alone. I figured he would finally get a little sleep, so I didn't bother him. If only I had checked on him…," Beth wailed.

"Ma, it's not your fault," Thad said wiping his teary eyes. He patted her back while she sobbed into his shoulder.

" What am I going to do without him?" Beth cried. "I miss him already. We spent the last thirty-six years together."

Thad just continued to pat her back. He could have told her she had her three children and their spouses. He could have reminded her about her nine grandchildren and now her great-grandchildren. But it was early days yet. The wound was too fresh to remind her of such things. Too fresh for him also.

Nate had been outside doing chores and now he entered the ranch-house. Belle went to him and hugged him. "I'm so sorry, Nate."

Nate nodded. "Thanks, Belle." He and Thad hugged and he went to sit next to his mother while Thad sat on her other side. Belle went into the kitchen where Rachel was preparing dinner. "Can I help you, Rachel?"

"I don't know if anyone will want to eat or not, but it gives me something to do. I'm just making some sandwiches for dinner." Rachel did seem to be at a loss as to what she should do.

"Here, let me help. It'll give me something to do too," Belle said with a weak smile. "Has Becca been notified?"

Rachel's eyes went wide. "No. I never thought of it. Maybe you and I can ride into town and send Becca a telegram."

"Thad, Rachel and I are going to take the auto into town to send a telegram to Becca," Belle told him quietly.

"There's some sandwiches made if you get hungry," Rachel offered. She kissed Nate goodbye as he helped her with her cloak. "Tony and Jon are in the barn. See if they'd like something to eat."

Thad rose and came with Belle to the door. "I'll start the auto for you. Can you stop and ask Reverend Peters to come out? We will need to make arrangements."

Belle nodded and kissed her husband. "I'm sorry, my love."

Belle drove the auto with Rachel quietly riding beside her. As they neared town, Belle asked, "What should we say in the telegram?"

Rachel started and looked at Belle. "I don't know. Probably less is better."

They discussed various wording until they reached the telegraph office. Once inside, they stood at the counter and began to write the awful words they would wire to Becca.

> *Your Pa passed away in his sleep last night. Arrangements pending.*
> *Rachel and Belle*

Belle pushed the paper over the counter to Mark Gordon, the telegraph operator. "Can you let us know if an answer comes, Mark? I don't know how easy it'll be to reach them on the reservation."

"There's a telegraph office in the Indian Agency." Mark said. "Isn't that where Peter's office is?"

"Yes," Belle said. "That's good. Maybe we will stop back after we've been to see Reverend Peters. Just in case she answers right away."

They started for the door when Mark called, "Ladies, I'm sorry for your loss."

"Thank you, Mark." Belle responded.

As the two of them walked outside, Rachel said, "I should stop in at the mercantile and tell my father."

"He still works there? I thought George took over," Belle said.

"You know my father. He just can't give it up totally." Rachel added. "He and Tuck were such good friends. It'll be a painful loss to him as well."

When they entered the mercantile, George was at the counter, "Hello, ladies..." His voice trailed off, noticing their red eyes. "Something is wrong. What has happened?"

"Oh, George. You're right. We bring bad news. Is my father here?"

"Back in the office, resting."

"This news will hit him hard, George. Tuck passed away last night. Maybe we should take him home to Mama."

They went back to see Sam Garrison. He smiled wistfully when they came in. "It's Tuck, isn't it?" he said. "My good friend has gone home to be with the Lord."

"Yes, but how on earth did you know?" Rachel asked, going to her father and embracing him.

"I've been sitting here in my chair reading my Bible. I don't know how to explain it. It just came to me that Tuck had passed on. Then I saw your red eyes and knew."

"Papa, can we give you a ride home so you can tell Mama?" Rachel asked him.

"Yes, that would be a good idea."

So, they all got in Belle's auto and she drove them to the Garrison's house. Rachel went inside with her father while he told her mother. In the meantime, Belle said she'd go see Reverend Peters and let him know he was needed at Deer Creek Ranch. Then she'd come back to get Rachel. When Belle pulled up to the Garrison's home again, Rachel came out and climbed into the auto.

"How did it go with your mother?" she asked.

249

"Pretty good, really. Mama was sad, of course, but she knew Tuck believed so she knows he's in Heaven right now."

"Oh, I almost forgot. We were going to stop back at the telegraph office," Belle stated. Belle left the auto running while they went in to see if Becca had responded yet. When they entered the office once again, Mark said, "Glad you ladies stopped back. I just received a wire from Becca." He handed it to Belle. She read it out loud.

> *Received wire. All 4 will arrive tomorrow morning on the 10:00 train.*
> *Becca.*

"Good thing we stopped back. Thank you, Mark. I guess we're ready to head back to the ranch now, Rachel."

# # #

"Beth, Becca returned our telegram while we were still in town. They'll all be arriving on the 10:00 train tomorrow morning," Belle told her taking her hand in her own. Belle and Rachel had returned to the ranch and saw when they got there that Reverend Peters had arrived before them. Beth, Thad, and Nate were seated at the table with Peters. The Reverend had his Bible open and was writing on a sheet of paper. Belle assumed he was planning the service.

"Thank you, dear. I'm glad they can come. We're planning the service now. Tuck left a document stating that he wanted Psalm 23 read and for Reverend Peters to preach from it. He also wanted his favorite hymn sung, 'Amazing Grace.' We're going to have more than just a graveside service. Tuck wanted to have a message preached, one of hope, for those who don't know the Lord. He'll be buried at the church cemetery, next to his parents," Beth continued. "As you know, we never did start a family one here."

Reverend Peters took his leave after spending a few hours with the family and preparing the service with them.

# # #

That night, Thad and Belle sat on their sofa in their living room after a light supper. Neither of them really had much of an appetite. Belle had done her chicken chores when they returned and Thad helped her. He was at a loss as to what to do with himself.

"Your mother's outlook seemed to change quite a bit in the time Rachel and I were gone," she said.

"Yes, she went in their bedroom to see Tuck one last time and to pray before they moved him to town. When she came out, she had everything under control."

250

"Your mother is a remarkable woman, Thad."

"Yes, I know. Her strength has always been unique. Ever since we ran away from Boston, she has displayed that quality. I guess she needed to be strong for us. When Tuck became part of our family, she drew on his strength. Now I guess she'll have to rely on her strength once again."

"No, Thad. She'll rely on the strength of the Lord. She would be the first to tell you that she is weak and God is strong."

"You're right, Belle. How could I forget that? God has been such an important part of our family's lives. And it's a blessing to know that Pa is in heaven right now."

CHAPTER EIGHTY-EIGHT
Tuck is Laid to Rest

The church was overflowing when Reverend Peters rose to begin the service. The organist played hymns of joy, not sorrow, according to Tuck's wishes. Beth sat in the front pew with Becca, Nate, and Thad next to her. Their spouses and children, and grandchildren sat in the two pews behind them. Thad noticed that Matt and Mattie Cutter were also present. He nodded slightly to Matt.

Reverend Peters rose and began reading:

"Adam Tucker was born in 1849 and went to be with his Lord early in the morning two days ago at the age of 81. Tuck, as he was known to his friends and family, was the sheriff for many years here in Mustang Ridge. In 1876 he married Beth   Eastman and then adopted her three children. He gave up the law to become a full-time cattle rancher on Dear Creek Ranch. This ranch had been his parent's ranch until their death at which time Tuck leased it to the Overland Stage Line. Tuck's parents were the last of his family. But he is survived by a large adopted family and many, many friends. Tuck is preceded in death by his parents Douglas and Katherine, his first wife, Mary and their infant son, Jonathan. He leaves behind his wife, Beth Tucker; his son, Thad and wife Belle Tucker; daughter, Becca and husband Peter Rhodes; son Nate and wife Rachel Tucker; nine grandchildren, Jackson Tucker, Ellen Tucker, Lucy Tucker Bendix and Nick Bendix, Molly Tucker Ward and Dr. Joshua Ward, Ben Tucker, Rose Rhodes, Steven Rhodes, Tony Tucker, and Jon Tucker. And two great-grandchildren, Sam Ward and Sarah Ward.

Reverend Peters sat down as the soloist stood to sing 'Amazing Grace.'

Following the song, the minister rose to give the message. "It was Tuck's wish that I read Psalm 23 today. Please join me in reciting Psalms 23. I know you all know it."

> *The LORD is my shepherd; I shall not want.*
> *He maketh me to lie down in green pastures: he leadeth me beside the still waters.*
> *He restoreth my soul: he leadeth me in the paths of righteousness for his name's sake.*
> *Yea, though I walk through the valley of the shadow of death, I will fear no evil: for thou art with me; thy rod and thy staff they comfort me.*

Thou preparest a table before me in the presence of mine enemies: thou anointest my head with oil; my cup runneth over.
Surely goodness and mercy shall follow me all the days of my life: and I will dwell in the house of the LORD forever.

"Tuck wanted all his friends to know that those who believe in Jesus' finished work on the cross will be saved. Tuck's prayer has always been that all of you would trust Jesus as his Savior, realizing that you're a sinner and confess that sin. Believe that He laid down His life for you. You will then be welcomed into His Kingdom because His death on the cross paid for your sins."

The ladies of the church had prepared cake and coffee to serve following the burial in the church cemetery. There were many friends who stayed to talk to the family. Many told wonderful stories of how Tuck had helped them over and above his job as sheriff. Matt Cutter was one such person. It was quite evident that Adam Tucker was well-loved in the community. He would be greatly missed by his many friends.

Following the service, the family went back to Deer Creek Ranch. They had plenty of food supplied to them by friends from town and church. They nibbled on sandwiches and desserts.

Tuck's lawyer, Leonard Cox, arrived with the will. Beth called them together in the living room, so they could hear the will.

Mustang Ridge, Wyoming, Niobrara County, 1909

In the name of God, Amen, I ADAM TUCKER in the County of Niobrara and State of Wyoming, being of sound mind, memory and understanding, Praise be to God, do make this my last will and testament in manner and form following:

1st I give and bequeath to my beloved wife BETH TUCKER with my son NATE TUCKER all of my real estate for their sole benefit after my death. During her natural life and widowhood BETH TUCKER is to be allowed to remain at Deer Creek Ranch, it being the same tract or parcel of land on which I now reside containing 1030 acres more or less, and at her (BETH) death the same land shall be divided between my two sons THAD TUCKER & NATE TUCKER each share to be allotted as follows: NATE's portion west of the tract, containing eight hundred thirty acres and THAD's portion east of the tract containing two hundred acres.

2nd I give and bequeath to my daughter BECCA RHODES, my favorite horse, Thunder, and saddle, along with the silver statue of

253

a horse which she always liked. In addition, a monetary sum of $1000.00 is to be given her.

3rd I give & bequeath to my beloved wife BETH all of my household & kitchen furniture, domestic foods, and 10% of the livestock raised on the ranch. I also give to my beloved wife BETH, the herd of goats to do with what she wants.

4th I give & bequeath to my son NATE 70% the cattle and horses on the ranch.

5th I give & bequeath to my son THAD 20% of the cattle and horses on the ranch.

6th And at the death of my wife all property donated her shall revert to my sons THAD and NATE to be divided 80% to Nate and 20% to Thad.

7th And all other articles (not enumerated in my will) of property shall be equally divided between my two sons THAD & NATE.

And I do nominate, constitute and appoint my sons THAD and NATE TUCKER my executors of this my last will and testament & declare this to be my last will and testament.

In witness whereof I the said ADAM TUCKER have hereunto set my hand this the 15th day of January 1909, in the presence of these witnesses

LEONARD COX, ATTORNE
NAOMI BEHRENDS, Secretary
THOMAS THATCHER, Banker

#

After the reading of Tuck's will, his family members were quiet. It seemed to make his death more of a reality than even the funeral service. Lawyer Cox asked if there were any questions. Everyone quietly shook their heads no.

"Well, then. I think I will head back to town. Again, folks, I'm sorry for your loss."

Nate seemed to snap out of his daze and accompanied the lawyer to the door. He opened the door for him and followed him out onto the veranda.

"Thank you, Leonard. We really do appreciate your help. I'm sorry we're not being very vocal at this time. It's just that Pa was such a great man in this family. I guess we aren't ready to see him gone from here."

"I understand, Nate, believe me. Tuck and I were friends as well. If you have any questions later, feel free to ask." He shook Nate's hand before getting into his auto and driving away.

#

Goodbyes were said to Becca, Peter, Rose, and Adam who were taking the train back to Wind River Reservation. Thunder was also taking the trip. Becca saddled him and rode him into Mustang Ridge, removed his saddle and stowed it in the baggage car. The horse was loaded into one of the stock cars. Becca was pleased to have Pa's horse, though saddened at the reason for receiving him. Thunder was a beautiful buckskin, and the black saddle looked wonderful on him. She told Thad, "It's like having a piece of Pa to take back with me and when Thunder is no longer with us, I'll have Pa's beautiful black leather saddle with the silver trim to remember him." The silver horse statue would have its home on their mantle.

It had been a rough few days for the Tucker family. They had said their goodbyes to a great man and now they would be returning to their daily lives. Thad said his goodbyes also to his sister and his friend, Peter.

Thad told Belle, "Now I have lost a pa for the second time in my life, both of them beloved."

Belle nodded. She held her husband tight – wishing that in so doing, she might ease his pain.

"I'm thankful Nate and family live with Ma now. It will make it easier for her to continue on. She and Tuck spent the last thirty-six years enjoying being married to each other. Their love definitely lasted."

"It certainly did," Belle agreed.

255

CHAPTER EIGHTY-NINE
Thad and Nash

Thad asked five of the ranch hands to come with him out to the northeast meadow. He wanted to move the herd of horses to the next pasture. When they arrived at the meadow, Thad said, "Doby, Kid, and Butch, you men stay by the gate and Nash, Casey, and I will herd them your way so you can turn them to go through the next gate."

When he and his two ranch hands reached the far end of the meadow, Thad turned back to Nash and noticed with alarm that the foreman was slipping from his saddle. He spurred his horse to Nash and quickly dismounted in time to catch him as he fell. He lowered Nash to the ground, noticing as he did that his face was deathly pale.

"Nash! What's wrong?"

Nash clutched the front of Thad's shirt in his fist. "I want what Tuck had. I want what you have," Nash rasped. "I want to know Jesus."

Then Thad understood what was happening. Nash knew he was dying and that he needed to be saved. He was asking Thad to show him the way. *Help me Lord Jesus to help this man find You.*

"Sure, Nash." Thad knew that time was of the essence, so he quickly asked, "Do you confess that you are a sinner?"

"Yesss." Nash's reply came out almost like a hiss.

"Do you believe that Jesus is the only way to Heaven?"

Nash nodded.

"Then all you need to do is tell Jesus that you know you are a sinner and ask him to be your Savior. Can you do that, Nash?"

"Jesus." Slowly Thad's beloved foreman weakly repeated Thad's words. "I know... I'm a sinner. I want you... my Savior."

"There, Nash. Now you are a child of Go..." Thad's words trailed off as Nash's head lolled to one side and he took a last shuddering breath, then he was still. Thad held Nash in his arms, more for his own comfort than anything else because he knew Nash was gone. With tears streaming down his face, Thad became aware that Casey was standing nearby with tears running also. His eyes were as big as saucers.

Thad lowered Nash's body to the ground and stood, wiping his eyes with his bandana. "Casey," he said when he could speak again. "Go signal the men to come here."

Casey complied. Thad watched while he mounted his horse and rode a ways, then took off his ten-gallon hat and frantically waved for the men to come here. Thad was thankful that Casey hadn't used his gun as a signal, as that would have started the herd to stampede. Before long, the other three men came riding up to where Thad stood over Nash's body.

"Boss, what happened?" Butch asked. "Is he...?"

"Yes," Thad replied. "We need to make something so we can carry him back to the ranch. A couple of you go find some strong tree limbs. We can use my rope and blanket to form a travois."

A mournful procession filed slowly into the ranch yard. Nash had been a well-liked foreman - a friend to all the men. He had started out working as a cow-hand for Tuck, and then when Thad married and established his own ranch, Nash came on board as Thad's foreman. Thad would miss him. But he was thankful for the confidence that Nash had knowing Jesus was his Savior before he died.

"We need to get the buckboard hitched up so we can take him into Doc's," Thad said.

A few of the men went to take care of that, while Thad went into the ranch-house to tell Belle what had happened.

"Are you going into town too?" she asked.

"Yes. I want to go see Reverend Peters about a service for him," he said.

When he turned to leave, Belle said, "Thad, it was good you were there to lead him to the Lord. God was unspeakably merciful to give you that moment with Nash."

Thad nodded again. With sorrow, he went out to get back on his horse and went with the slow-moving wagon into town. All the ranch hands accompanied the wagon, Thad leading the way on his horse and the men mounted and riding at the side. He told his men to take Nash's body to Doc's office while he went to see Reverend Peters. The two of them made arrangements for a graveside service for Nash, since he had no family, in fact, no one even knew his last name. That was the way with ranch hands; they only went by their first names. Sometimes, only a nickname. They set the time for the service the next day.

"You should know that before he died, he told me he wanted what Tuck and I had, that he wanted to know Jesus. So, I led him to Jesus." Thad found that he had tears in his eyes again.

Reverend Peters clasped his shoulder saying, "Praise God! Tuck's service has had an answer."

Then Thad rode out of town and headed toward Deer Creek Ranch to notify others that were as close to Nash as family. As he anticipated, there was much sorrow from both the ranch hands as well as his family. He noticed tears in his mother's eyes. She had known Nash as long as she and Tuck had been married.

"The graveside service will be tomorrow at 1:00," he said.

"We'll all be there, including all the hands," she said. "The ranch will be okay without anyone here for that time, just as it was during Tuck's service. And thank you, Thad, for leading him to the Lord. Thank goodness you were there."

The day of Nash's service the sun shone and the weather was warm but not hot. Thad was surprised to see that so many attended. Nash didn't have a family, except for those at the two ranches, but he had many friends around Mustang Ridge. Thad looked around as the Reverend spoke.

All twelve ranch hands were there. Ma, Nate, Rachel, Tony and Jon; Belle and Sarah; Lucy and Nick; Molly and Joshua; Ellen; and many friends from town. Even the Garrisons were there.

After the service was over and those who attended went their way, Thad noticed that Wade stood talking to the Reverend a short distance from the grave. He watched as Peters placed his hand on Wade's shoulder and they both bowed their heads. Tears came to Thad's eyes once again as he watched Wade walk away, turn towards him with a fisted hand thump against his heart and a smile on his face, raising his hand heaven-ward. Thad nodded with a smile. *Thank You, Lord.*

"I saw that, Thad! Praise God. And I know Tuck is greeting Nash right now," Belle joyfully exclaimed.

"Yes, Pa and Ma and I prayed for Nash and Wade from the day they came to work for us thirty-six years ago. Wade will tell Ma, I'm sure. He looked pretty happy," Thad said.

"And why wouldn't he? He and Nash were good friends. Now he knows he will see not only his friend one day, but your pa as well," Belle said. "For a person to know that one day they will see their Savior as well as their friends and loved ones in Heaven, well, what more can you ask?"

"What indeed?" Thad replied. "What indeed?"

CHAPTER NINETY
Reminiscing

Several days later following Tuck's funeral, Thad and Belle sat on their veranda with Sarah. Tuck's death had brought back memories of Sarah's husband, Jacob. Thad remembered how Jacob had been a help to him as a sixteen-year-old boy on the wagon train. He recalled hunting with Jacob and the other wagon train members.

"Mama, I'm so glad you and Papa decided to leave the wagon train and come to Mustang Ridge with Thad and his family," Belle contributed.

Thad took his wife's hand. "I am too. We've been fortunate to have a lot of family that stayed in the area. Your brother Ben is in Omaha with his family and Becca and family are still in Wind River Indian Reservation. But they are not really that far away. Now with railroad service, it makes them seem closer. Molly lives right here in town, and Lucy is just over at the Double B Ranch."

"Do you suppose they'll change the name of the ranch?" Belle asked. "Since Brad Bendix passed away, it seems funny to call it Double B."

"I don't know," Thad answered her. "Probably not. They may feel it was his legacy."

"Does Lucy still have an interest in Whitehorse Ranch?" Sarah inquired.

"Yes, I'm not sure what to do about it. Something keeps telling me to hold off on any decision. Ben is old enough now, but I get the sense he's not all that interested."

"Really, Thad? I didn't get that," Belle said.

"Well, maybe it's just me trying to keep Lucy in the partnership."

"I know how you have always wanted one of your sons to ranch with you," Belle patted her husband on the arm. "Let God lead them where to go."

"You and Belle have certainly done well by your children and it's wonderful that you have your first grandson. Sam is such a cute little boy and little Sarah is precious," Sarah commented, changing the subject after hearing the sad note in her son-in-law's voice.

"Yes, he is that," Thad agreed. "I suppose Lucy will be next to give us grandchildren."

"She'll have to get off her horse then," Belle laughed.

"I understand that Ellen has been keeping company with a young man," Sarah said.

"What?" both Belle and Thad exclaimed.

"Oh, you didn't know?"

"No," Belle said looking at Thad. "Who?"

259

"I don't know his name, but Martha Garrison was talking about what a nice young man he is. She said he's a cousin of Reverend Peters."

"Wonder why Ellen hasn't said anything. And how long this has been going on," Belle mused. "I know she is so busy running the paper. I do think she makes a good editor."

Thad agreed and commented, "I am also thankful that Molly lives in Mustang Ridge. Joshua is well respected by the town-people."

"Do you think Beth will stay at Deer Creek Ranch?" Sarah asked.

"Yes," Thad replied. "She has Nate and Rachel there as well as Tony and Jon. I expect she will live out her days there as Tuck's will stated. Deer Creek Ranch provides a bit of safety and security for her, I think."

"Yes," Belle added. "I feel the same way about Whitehorse Ranch. It has the same meaning for me as Deer Creek has for Beth. We both have special memories associated with our ranches." Belle took her husband's hand and held it tightly.

"Well, I think I'll head to bed and leave you two alone. Goodnight," Sarah said, grinning.

"Goodnight, Mama. Do you want me to walk with you?"

"No dear," Sarah said patting her daughter's hand. "I can find my way okay. You stay here with your husband."

"Goodnight, Sarah," Thad said.

"Well, husband. What do you want to do?"

"Is there any of your wonderful pie left?"

"Yes, dear. I'll get you a piece. Keep my spot warm."

While Belle went to get the pie, Thad's thoughts turned to his family, of his and Belle's children. He wanted so much for all of them. Thad recalled times as they grew up and became adults, their chosen careers, and their spouses. Of course, Thad's mind moved on to his precious grandchildren whom he dearly loved. *Father in Heaven, You have given Belle and me so much. I'm so thankful for our home and our wonderful family. Please continue to bless us in the future. Jackson and Ben have not married yet and I pray that if You have someone for them, that they might follow Your leading. Amen*

RECIPES

Peppernuts (or Pfeffernusse Cookies) a traditional German cookie
2 sticks unsalted butter, room temperature
1 1/2 cups dark brown sugar, lightly packed
2 large eggs
2 tsp anise
1/4 tsp salt
1 tsp cinnamon
1 tsp ground ginger
1/2 tsp white pepper
1/2 tsp clove or cardamom (clove is more traditional)
3 1/2 cups all-purpose flour
In the bowl cream together, the butter and brown sugar until light and
fluffy. About 3 minutes.
Add the eggs, anise extract, salt, baking soda, cinnamon, ginger, white
pepper, and clove or cardamom into the bowl and mix until everything
is incorporated.
Add the flour into the dough and mix just until it is incorporated. You
do not want to mix for a long time, just until the flour is incorporated
in.
Chill the dough in the refrigerator for at least 30 minutes and up to 3
days.
Preheat the oven to 350F. Divide dough into 8 pieces. Press 1 piece of
dough into a ball and roll it out between your hands and a clean work
surface to form a thin rope, about 1/4" thick. Use a sharp knife to cut
out tiny nut size pieces of dough. Place on a baking sheet. You can fit
quite a few on one baking sheet but you will need to bake these in
several batches to get them all baked. It typically works out to be
cutting out the next sheet pan of cookies while the one before it bakes.
Bake at 350F for 15-17 minutes, until a dark golden brown. The
cookies will be slightly soft when they first come out of the oven but
will become very crispy as the cool. Store the completely cooled
cookies in an airtight container at room temperature for up to 1 month.

RECIPE NOTES
This dough can be made up to 3 days in advance and stored in the refrigerator until you are ready to bake.
These cookies keep a very long time, up to 1 month, and the flavor keeps developing. Make them far in advance of holiday party or for gift giving!
If the dough is too sticky to roll out, let it chill for longer and add a little bit
of flour to your work surface while rolling them out.

ACKNOWLGEMENTS

The Archway – Kearney, Nebraska
Fort Kearny Park – Kearney, Nebraska
Pioneer Village – Minden, Nebraska
Chimney Rock National Park – Bayard, Nebraska

Song Lyrics found Online – Public Domain
When We Get Home by Luella B. Henry -1888
Oh, Perfect Love by Dorothy F. Gurney- 1883
Come My Soul by John Newton - 1725
What Wondrous Love is This Unknown Author -1811
Battle Hymn of the Republic - Julia Ward Howe, 1861

Original Poem of America – Katharine Lee Bates – 1893 – Public Domain

Scripture References from King James Bible – Public Domain

From the Author
After retiring from my position as mental health secretary in a local hospital clinic, I have devoted my time between four grandchildren, writing, and travel. My writing career began with children's picture books, written while I still worked full time. Once retired, I became intrigued with the historical Christian fiction genre, which took me down a path of research and travel. I grew up on westerns and wanted to write my own. I also wanted to show how the pioneer spirit encompassed a strong belief in the God Who sustained them.

I enjoy book signing events where I can talk with other authors, as well as readers who are eager to hear of my writing process for a historical novel. I love it when my grandchildren come to help me at those events. When I'm not writing, I enjoy reading mysteries and spending time with my family.

Visit Karen
Website: https://karenmcarr.vpweb.com

Twitter: https://twitter.com/@carrkm12

Facebook: https://www.facebook.com/karencarrauthor/

Amazon: https://www.amazon.com/-/e/B004AN327G

Also Available From Karen Carr
Children's Picture Books
Littlest Penguin – Guardian Angel Publishing
My Hot Air Balloon – Mirror Publishing
The Many Hats of Jeremiah Porter –Shapato Pub/CreateSpace.
What's That Strange Noise? –co-authored by 6-yr- old granddaughter
Guardian Angel Publishing
A Daisy for Sarah – Guardian Angel – in the publishing process
Mystery
Mystery at Burr Oak: A Dog Named Wang – Mirror Pub
Anthologies
Christmas Story Collection-"The Christmas House" - Little Cab Press
Needle in a Haystack – "Mama's Sewing Machine"- Shapato Publishing
Threads – An Anthology of Short Stories & Poems

Save Haven Series
#1 A Safe Haven for Beth
#2 Thad Tucker, Wyoming Rancher

Made in the USA
Middletown, DE
22 March 2019